THE FALSE DOOR

BRETT KING
THE FALSE DOOR

THOMAS & MERCER

The characters and events portrayed in this book are fictitious. Any similarity to real persons, living or dead, is coincidental and not intended by the author.

Published by Thomas & Mercer, Seattle
www.apub.com

ISBN-13: 9781477833445
ISBN-10: 1477833447

Cover design by Inkd

For my cherished parents, Dee and Don King,
who have inspired me with lessons of love and laughter,
along with the value of hard work, patience, and
perseverance.

PROLOGUE

The more hidden the venom, the more dangerous it is.
—Marguerite de Valois, Queen of France

The Return

Nearly five years ago
Washington, DC
New Year's Eve

Edgar Wurm had spent his entire life in shadows, escaping the notice of the world. For decades as a cryptanalyst, he had solved classified puzzles for the United States government, helping it track threats to national security.

Now the government was hunting him.

Wurm had never liked cemeteries—he had seen enough reminders of death in his day—but this was the first time he had visited a graveyard at night. *First and last time*, he told himself.

Taking a ragged breath, he brought the service pistol in close to his body. He had stolen the weapon, a Kimber 1911, from the people who had detained him. He was thankful to have it now. Flicking off the thumb safety, he pulled back the slide far enough to confirm that the chamber was loaded. After making the press check, he hurried toward the private mausoleum. Cut from white granite, it resembled a small Greek temple with twin Doric pillars flanking the doorway. Before entering, he glanced back. Anxiety tightened his throat as he scanned the moonlit cemetery. Were they out there? Had they followed him?

Wurm had crawled out of hiding on this raw winter night. It was a risk, but he had to know the truth. He had to find out before they tracked him here.

Going back two generations, the Wurm family had paid top dollar to place their dead in Mount Olivet Cemetery. Some were reduced to ash and stuffed inside urns while others rotted in caskets housed inside marble crypts. Except for two children, he would be the last of his kind to be entombed here. Emblazoned with the Wurm coat of arms, a stained-glass window offered the only symbol of light and beauty inside the gloomy mausoleum. In one measured step after another, he crept over to examine a freestanding crypt in the center of the room. It was a big chunk of polished Belgian marble topped with a stone lid.

He brought out a small flashlight and studied the cover. His name was sandblasted onto the flat surface, right above his birth and death dates. Wurm stared at the lid, unblinking, like he was hypnotized. It was a curious and terrible thing to see your name engraved with a death date on a crypt. The experience unnerved him more than he had imagined.

A cryptanalyst puzzled by his crypt. Stupid humor, to be sure, but it brought an unexpected belch of gallows mirth.

He holstered the pistol then suspended his hand above the lid. Dropping his fingers, he scraped his nails along the black marble shell. They had the birth year right, but the second date was part of an orchestrated cover-up. A ruse designed to trick the handful of mourners who attended his funeral earlier in the day. They had gathered at this cemetery, all thinking that he would never return. He was content to let the world believe that lie.

At age fifty-five, Wurm had been declared dead almost a week ago, right after Christmas. Officers from the Central Intelligence Agency had arrived shortly after it had happened. They had flown his body back to the United States. Big surprise when he had revived. He had overpowered two guards before escaping from the low-security facility where they were holding his body for examination. Still, they had held to the story that he was dead. The cover-up worked for Wurm. A faked death was the best way to stay alive in the shadows.

Maybe he should have died last week in Europe. Turns out, the Radix had other plans for his body.

He drummed his fingers on the lid. He wanted a look at the casket inside this crypt. The CIA had taken steps to entomb someone in his place. Who was inside his casket?

Wurm had to know.

Weighted with anticipation, he pressed his palms flat against the lid's edge. Bunching his muscles, he pushed on it. His face, gray and weathered, brightened to a sweat-drenched scarlet. Cords bulged in his neck as the grinding sound of stone against stone told of his progress. The crypt wasn't easy to open, even for a man of his size. Teeth gritted, he gave a final heave and quietly eased the lid to the stone floor.

He brushed stringy hair from his face. Shining the flashlight into the crypt, he found a bronze casket inside the dead black space. In the suffocating hush of the mausoleum, he raised the hinged lid. The quilted velvet lining was as white as bleached bones and surrounded a matching pillow and mattress.

Wurm blinked.

The casket was empty.

He hadn't expected that.

Glancing down, he discovered a funeral program inside the casket. The folded card showed a flower-choked meadow on the cover, a tranquil scene no one in his or her right mind would associate with him. The inside featured a quotation from Machiavelli— he liked that—along with a dreadful picture of Wurm after the madness came. His black eyebrows and mustache contrasted with his slate-gray hair and beard. Along with craggy wrinkles, it all gave him the look of a Civil War veteran. Since escaping the CIA compound, he had trimmed the beard and cut his hair. Beneath the picture, the program announced in flowing script:

In Loving Celebration of
Edgar Wurm
A man who shared of himself
Without thought for himself

He snorted.

What perfect rubbish.

Eighteen months ago, Wurm had been diagnosed with mild schizophrenia. He never regarded himself as crazy, just a slave to obsession. A parade of doctors had pretended to understand his paranoia and eccentricities, but all had failed. He might have been lost in his mind for a time, but he was lucid now. He was sure of it, not like the old days when obsession took him hostage and ruined his career. Because he knew secrets that the United States government feared would leak out with his mental condition, arrangements had been made for his psychiatric care. The government had sequestered him in a secret ward of a hospital. He had spent the time conquering his illness and reading and painting.

And thinking.

Wurm was always thinking.

He looked again at the funeral program. Turning it over, he found a handwritten note on the back. Someone had scrawled four words in black ink.

You can't hide forever

A chill tickled his neck. It was a warning. A threat. They knew he would come here. He had walked right into their trap.

A sound echoed off the granite wall.

Wurm squinted, looking outside the mausoleum's doorway. Cursing under his breath, he stuffed the flashlight and the program inside his wrinkled coat. He reached for his shoulder holster and brought out the Kimber.

He slipped outside the mausoleum, fresh air streaming into his nostrils. No sign of anyone out here. The moon appeared as a watery circle in iron-gray clouds. In the distance, the Washington Monument glowed like a phantom obelisk. New Year's Eve had arrived along the East Coast, and fireworks painted the far night sky with explosions of color.

That sound again.

A woman in her early twenties darted past a darkened tree. It was a relief when he recognized Cori Cassidy, a little thing with short blonde hair and more than her share of spunk and brilliance. A woman doomed, at times, with a terrible curiosity. She had traveled to Europe with him the night before his alleged death.

Wurm lingered behind an oak tree. Why in the world was she in this graveyard at midnight?

He spied a second figure on the cemetery grass. A CIA officer? Wurm's stomach muscles clenched. The man pointed a handgun at the woman.

"Stop right there," the man barked.

Cori screamed as she stumbled back against a tree. Wurm aimed the Kimber at the stranger. He relaxed his guard when the dark-haired man holstered the weapon.

"John," she choked, "why are you here?"

"Long story," he said, walking to her. "What about you?"

Wurm recognized the man. In another era, John Brynstone would have made an unflinching gunslinger with his lean rugged looks, onyx-black hair, and mesmerizing ice-blue eyes. Thirty years old, he stood a robust six feet two inches, only a little shorter than Wurm. He worked for the Special Collection Service, the elite intelligence organization that combined stealthy CIA operations with National Security Agency technology. Brynstone was their star agent.

Wurm wasn't a man who craved friendship. But right now, Cori Cassidy and John Brynstone were the closest people he had to friends in the world. On impulse, he decided to reveal himself. He hungered to see looks of surprise brighten their faces.

He took a step forward, his size-fourteen shoe smashing fresh snow under leather. Then he stopped, his breath visible in the frosty air. Brynstone was a hard man to figure. How would he deal with news of Wurm's return?

He debated it for a moment.

Wurm decided against showing himself. He walked off into the night, leaving footprints that curled past the oak tree and disappeared at the wet road.

Now was not the time.

The Recovery

Alone in a Mercedes sedan, Edgar Wurm brought binoculars to his eyes. In the middle of a brisk September night, Metropolitan police constables drove a Vauxhall Astra SUV along a lonely road not far from Victoria Street. Wurm spied two members of the police service inside the black vehicle, each wearing fluorescent yellow jackets, riot gloves, and navy-blue custodian helmets. Their mission? To transport an ancient relic from New Scotland Yard headquarters to a high-tech storage facility on the outskirts of London. The Met provided serious protection for the Scintilla, a little patch of vellum that dated from two thousand years ago.

The Scintilla was priceless. Scotland Yard knew it.

Their London Stolen Arts Database listed more than fifty thousand items of stolen property including paintings, gold textiles, furniture, coins, and manuscripts. Some were invaluable. Others were insignificant. Their database of art, antiquities, and cultural property made no mention of the Scintilla. In fact, the Art and Antiques Unit at Scotland Yard denied its existence among their vast holdings. Wurm knew the truth, thanks to an inside source. After two years under secure protection, the Scintilla was on the move.

The mysterious vellum contained a formula that could unlock the power of the Radix, a legendary root rumored to hold the power to either heal or destroy. When combined with ingredients listed on the Scintilla, the Radix could create the White Chrism, a consecrated ointment so powerful that it was called the "perfect medicine."

That wasn't all.

According to legend, the Scintilla also contained a more menacing secret. A second formula scrawled on the vellum was said to unleash the root's darker power. Known as the Black Chrism, it offered the threat of an unholy death.

The Radix, when joined with the secrets of the Scintilla, could deliver good *or* evil. But tragically, the vellum had been torn in half centuries before and remained hidden for ages. Two years ago, Wurm had discovered the Scintilla, but only the top half. The Art and Antiques Unit at New Scotland Yard had confiscated it after his alleged death.

Now was the time to correct that injustice.

His team was in place. He leaned forward, his arms braced on top of the steering wheel as the police vehicle rolled past his Mercedes. The explosive was positioned near the SUV's wheelbase. The charge was set. No more waiting.

Wurm touched his throat mic. "Do it now."

His men put the plan into action. A blinding light cut into the night as the blast erupted from beneath the vehicle, flipping it. In a screeching chorus of metal scraping concrete, the SUV rocketed onto the pavement.

"Go," Wurm ordered over the mic. "Make it fast."

Two Audi SUVs squealed onto the scene from opposite directions. Climbing out, Wurm's men scrambled to the overturned Astra and dragged the bewildered and bloodied Metropolitan police constables onto the street. Like their fellow officers in the

United Kingdom, they did not carry firearms. Three of Wurm's security operators restrained the men and marched them at gunpoint behind the gray Audi, taking the constables out of view—a good move, since Wurm couldn't afford to be seen. He ordered four additional operatives to search the Astra and a few minutes later, a burly Samoan named Tupa reemerged from the overturned vehicle.

Wurm pulled his shoulder-length hair into a ponytail, then slid on gloves. He lowered the driver-side window.

Dressed in black, Tupa hurried across the street carrying a small metal box. Coming up beside the car, the big man handed it through the window.

"This it, sir?"

Wurm opened the box, then inspected an innocent scrap of calfskin. A thin smile crossed his lips. He had craved this moment for two years. The Scintilla—or at least one half of it—was back in the hands of its rightful owner. He closed the lid.

"Took you long enough," Wurm grumbled to Tupa. "Now, clear the scene."

Wurm brimmed with giddy excitement as he stole another look inside the box. "You have no idea what I've gone through to possess you," he told the aged vellum. "Once again, your secrets belong to me. Now I must find your missing brother."

Sirens wailed in the distance, their abrasive cries drawing closer. Wurm and his men sped away in separate vehicles, escaping into the night.

The Quest

Five months ago
New York City

You can't hide forever, read the note someone had scrawled on Edgar Wurm's funeral program.

But he had. Wurm had spent much of the last four and a half years hiding in Asia and Europe—always on the move, always looking over his shoulder. Now he was back in the States. Another risk, but a necessary one.

A record-breaking late-February storm had dumped more than a foot of snow on Manhattan overnight. A pristine white blanket draped Central Park, drawing people in bundled clothing to celebrate a reprieve from work and school. No one had noticed an isolated figure scaling a snow-draped boulder along the park's southwest corner. Wurm wanted it that way.

Beneath his walking hat, his long gray hair reached to the shoulders of his wool twill coat. Fresh from his climb, he loosened his scarf and surveyed the view from Umpire Rock. It conjured fond memories of a winter long ago when he had lived in the city.

At the time, Wurm had been obsessed with a mysterious medieval document known as the Voynich manuscript. Known as the world's most mysterious book, it was written in a bizarre and undeciphered script. After three decades of painstaking work, he had succeeded in breaking one section of Voynich code. It had offered clues and insights about the Radix, the great prize of alchemy. Wurm needed to understand how the Radix had changed him. To find answers, he needed help.

He cast his gaze down at the Heckscher Ballfields, where John Brynstone and his small daughter rolled a ball of snow across center field. Beside them, Brynstone's black cat peered from a crimson sled and poked an apprehensive paw in the snow. Testing it, she jumped high in the air then landed, disappearing in a spray of white, then scrambled back onto the sled. The sound of laughter from the man and the little girl in the pink coat drifted up to Umpire Rock.

Brynstone hoisted a smooth round head onto the snowman's shoulders. He was around thirty-four, but he looked years younger. Except for the girl's blonde hair, daughter and father shared an uncanny resemblance, right down to their blue eyes. Shayna Brynstone had turned five last autumn. Wurm had never met the child, but he had researched her. Like him, she had a secret all her own.

John Brynstone looked happy.

Wurm was about to change that.

More than two years ago, he had stolen a scrap of aged vellum from the Metropolitan Police Service at New Scotland Yard. When the time was right, he would tell Brynstone about his discovery. When he did, Wurm knew it would force Brynstone to confront the biggest decision of his life—and perhaps his greatest mistake.

But first, he needed Brynstone's help.

Wurm clambered down the rock. As a young man, he had traveled to Switzerland and scaled the north face of the Eiger in the Bernese Oberland. Famous for its German nickname, *Mordwand*, or "death wall," the Eiger's north face made Umpire Rock seem like a pebble.

He jumped to the ground, snow crunching beneath his boots.

The Bombay cat snapped her head around, watching Wurm approach. He'd met Banshee once before, during her inaugural year as a kitten. This cat was a curious thing with her midnight-rich coat and solitary green eye, like something in an Edgar Allan Poe tale.

Brynstone noticed the cat's reaction and turned on instinct. His eyes widened when he saw Wurm's face, but beyond that he concealed any hint of surprise. *The man must be one hell of a poker player.*

"Dr. Brynstone."

"Dr. Wurm? That really you?"

"So you are surprised. I couldn't tell for a moment there. You can trust your eyes, John. It's me."

The little girl curled around her father's leg. "Daddy, who is that?"

Brynstone looked down at her. "Just a man, sweetie."

Wurm hunched down, then knelt close to the child. "Don't you believe your father," he said. "I'm much more than just a man."

She scrunched up her nose. "You have frost on your beard."

"Do I?" Taking both hands, Wurm ruffled his gray beard, showering the black cat with tiny diamonds of snow. Shayna giggled as Banshee darted away.

Rising to his full height, Wurm unraveled the patterned scarf from around his neck. He handed it to the child.

"Give this to your wintry friend. He looks cold."

Shayna smiled, revealing two missing front teeth that gave her the look of an adorable little vampire. She grabbed the scarf, carrying it like some sacred offering as she presented it to the snowman. Winding it beneath his head, she then hurried back, pointing. "Doesn't Frosty look awesome?"

"Just missing one thing," Brynstone said, smiling.

"Arms," she squealed. "You're right, Daddy."

"What an obedient child," Wurm said, watching her rush toward a fallen branch. "Government people have the most obedient children."

"Don't work for them anymore."

"You quit the Special Collection Service? What a shame."

"Not really. A lot has changed."

"So I understand. Sorry to hear about your and Kaylyn's divorce."

"Never thought I'd see you again," Brynstone said. "Cori Cassidy told me you died in Europe."

"Forgive the morbid conceit, John, but did you attend my memorial service? I've often wondered who cared to pay their respects."

"Cori and I showed. Later that night, we saw each other again at your family mausoleum."

"Why in heaven's name were the both of you traipsing around a cemetery on New Year's Eve?"

"Wasn't planned. We didn't arrive together, but we went inside the mausoleum and discovered that someone had removed the lid from your crypt. Your casket was empty. I had wondered if your body had been stolen. Or maybe—"

"Yes, I have much to explain about that whole affair."

"I found footprints in the snow that night. Maybe size fourteen, if I remember."

"It wasn't Bigfoot." Wurm grinned. "I'm afraid that was me."

"I wondered."

Wurm glanced at Shayna. "The details of that night are best suited for another conversation at another time. You have my dedicated promise."

"Don't get me wrong. I'm glad you're alive, but why are you here, Edgar? Why now after all this time?"

"We were part of a quest, once. A quest for something big."

"The Radix."

"Century after century, a legion of adventurers and scholars searched for it. They were a rare breed who dared look into the face of history, great men and women united throughout time. A brotherhood of blood and dust who used brutal force to answer the call if their quest demanded it. Like me and you, John."

Brynstone held his gaze on Wurm, but said nothing.

"So many have failed," Wurm continued. "Five hundred years had passed without anyone coming close to discovering it. Then we came along and five years ago, we teamed up to find the Radix."

"Seems like an eternity," Brynstone answered. "Face it. The Radix is gone forever."

"The Radix changed your life, John."

"No. An assassin did that."

Wurm knew the story. Brynstone's life had turned upside down when an elite killer named Erich Metzger had targeted Brynstone's family. INTERPOL had described Metzger as "the most feared assassin on the planet." His artistry at commissioned homicide had earned him the nickname the Poet. He was a phantomlike figure who frustrated law-enforcement agencies all over the world. Time after time, he managed to elude the best.

Even Brynstone.

"What's inside your heart, John? I know the answer. You want to find Metzger. You want to kill him."

He remained silent.

"Perhaps, I can help." Wurm reached into a leather bag. He brought out a curved piece of metal about a foot in length, tapering down to a wide flaring strip. "See this relic? It belonged to a Roman cavalry soldier two thousand years ago."

Wurm slid it behind his neck like some kind of metal neck brace.

"To protect against an assault to the neck," Brynstone said.

"Precisely." Wurm pulled it away from his neck and studied the object with reverence. "It attached to a Roman helmet at the base of the skull."

"Since when do you have a thing for old cavalry helmets?"

"Since I discovered this."

He turned the neck guard over, revealing leather padding that lined the inner shell. He peeled back the leather. A series of peculiar symbols were engraved on the inner surface.

"A code," Brynstone said. "I'm betting you deciphered it."

"I'm working on it," Wurm said, smiling. "Long ago, someone called the Keeper engraved a message on this helmet. He knew answers to questions that you and I are only beginning to ask. Centuries back, someone separated the helmet and scattered the pieces, each to its own hiding place."

"And you want me to help track them down." Brynstone glanced back at Shayna. "Sorry, Edgar. Not interested."

"Listen to me. I need someone with remarkable skills, someone who possesses cunning and strength, someone who is a quick thinker. Someone capable of finding the rest of this relic."

"Call Indiana Jones."

"I'm serious, John. I need your help to retrieve the helmet pieces."

"Why do you want it anyway? What's in it for you?"

A sly grin slid across Wurm's face. "I believe, John, that the reunited helmet pieces will lead us to the missing Scintilla."

"The formula for the Black Chrism? That's what you want?"

"Knowing what it can do, who wouldn't want it? I believe the helmet can also shed insight into the power and mysteries of the White Chrism."

Brynstone looked down at the snowy ground. "I don't know, Edgar."

"Unfortunately, I'm not alone in my interest," Wurm continued. "A competitor wants the helmet pieces as much as I do. He works for an international crime organization called the Shadow Chapter. Ever hear of them?"

"What's this have to do with me?"

"My competitor? The man I'm talking about? He groomed Erich Metzger in his early days. He is close to the assassin. Very close."

"What are you getting at, Edgar? I help you find the pieces of that helmet and you help me track Metzger?"

"Team up with me again, John." Wurm smiled as he looked down at the neck guard. "We both need answers."

"I don't need answers."

"From what I understand, you took a desperate chance when your daughter was a year old. You saved her life."

Brynstone made certain Shayna wasn't listening. The chill air had cast her nose in scarlet. The child seemed uninterested in the temperature and their conversation.

"Erich Metzger put me in a bad situation."

"That's his job," Wurm said. "Because of our teamwork, you created a special medicine using the Radix."

"She's alive because of the White Chrism," Brynstone answered.

Wurm narrowed his eyes. "The chrism saved your daughter's life in ways we don't comprehend." He held up the Roman neck guard. "Shayna is no longer a normal child. If we find the helmet pieces, we can gain insight into how the chrism changed her."

As Brynstone listened, Banshee rubbed against his leg.

"What is the most precious thing in your life, John?"

Shayna jabbed forked branches on opposite sides of the snowman's round abdomen. She pushed her mitten-cloaked hand into the snowman's face, shaping a round mouth.

Wurm frowned. "A terrible man tried to destroy that little girl. You want him as much as I want this helmet. If we work together, then we both get what we want."

"I'll think about it."

"The Shadow Chapter is searching for the helmet. They are a formidable opponent with substantial resources, both in finance and manpower. If they find the formula for the Black Chrism, there'll be no stopping them." Wurm placed his hand on Brynstone's shoulder. "Help me find the pieces of this helmet. I'll help you find Metzger. At the same time, we'll figure out what the chrism did to your daughter."

PART I

The Lazarus Cross

Present Day

The more perfect a thing is, the more susceptible to good and bad treatment it is.

—Dante Alighieri

Chapter 1

Paris, France
Early August, 9:05 p.m.

"Dig," the pale woman sneered, looking down from the edge of the grave. "And make it fast."

John Brynstone wiped sweat from his tanned face. Blood coated his forehead and the stench of mud filled his nostrils. Standing in the grave, he craned his neck and glared up at Nessa Griffin. Was it his imagination or did moonlight glint off the woman's glass eye?

"You're in over your head, Griffin," he growled.

"No one can stop me. My brother found that out."

"You made a big mistake killing him."

"I do what is necessary, Dr. Brynstone." She traced her hand along the arched headstone. "We have that in common."

"Difference is, I'm not a psychopath."

Four men flanked her, all armed. She had more men posted around the cemetery. Griffin had brought along a French woman named Véronique, a scared and helpless-looking hostage.

An hour before, Brynstone had arrived at the largest graveyard in Paris. Located on the city's far eastern edge, Père Lachaise Cemetery sprawled over more than a hundred acres of rolling hills and forested lanes. Deep in its earth, a host of scientists, artists, philosophers, and composers rotted into nothingness. Among its cold citizens, Père Lachaise boasted such celebrated figures as

Oscar Wilde, Gertrude Stein, Frédéric Chopin, Marcel Proust, and Édith Piaf. Even Jim Morrison of The Doors was interred there beneath graffiti-spattered marble.

In daylight, Père Lachaise glowed with poetic mystery. In the dark of night, it was haunted with eerie shadows.

"We're running out of time, Dr. Brynstone." Griffin flicked hair from her bony face. "Perhaps an assistant will inspire you to work faster."

She reached behind Véronique and shoved her. Arms cutting through the air, the French woman gasped a choked scream as she dropped into the grave. She landed on her knees at Brynstone's feet and muttered a profanity.

He dropped the shovel and reached to help her.

"Who are you?" he asked in a low voice.

"Chief historian for the cemetery." Véronique's lip quivered as she wiped blood from her chin. Mud stained her white blouse. "They abducted me from my home and killed two cemetery guards getting in here."

"Lucky it wasn't more," he answered.

Griffin pitched a shovel into the grave, nearly striking the woman's leg.

"I don't want her down here," Brynstone called. "I'll handle this myself."

Griffin shined the flashlight into his eyes. He blocked the glare with his gloved hand. She waved her fingers. In response, the men trained their weapons on the couple.

"Dig. Both of you. Or this grave will become your grave."

<hr />

The night air seemed stagnant with little breeze. Brynstone paused to brush dirt from his black hair. He had arrived here alone and had cleared three feet of dirt from the grave before Nessa Griffin and her men discovered him. Digging at gunpoint, he was several feet deeper now.

"You okay?" he asked under his breath.

"I suppose," Véronique whispered in flawless English. "Griffin believes a Roman artifact lies down here. Do you think we will find it?"

"Our lives depend on it."

Brynstone's shovel slammed into a hard surface.

He looked up. "Hand me a flashlight."

Griffin's men tossed down two LED headlamps. Brynstone caught them and handed one to Véronique. They strapped them around their foreheads.

He crouched and cleared away the surface, excitement flashing in his eyes as the dark lid appeared beneath clods of dirt.

Crafted in hardwood and shaped like an oversized cigar, the casket was thinner than the modern style. Bronze flourishes decorated the lid. From the look of it, he guessed the casket had been manufactured in the early 1800s.

Véronique crowded against the dirt wall, giving him room.

Rusted hinges squealed as he raised the lid, releasing a musty vapor. The interior was inlaid with rich lavender velvet. It was clear that the deceased came from greater wealth than the thousands of paupers buried in the cemetery's mass graves. Dressed in fashion from the late Georgian period, the crumbling skeleton wore a swallowtail coat with a high collar and wide lapel, adorned with fabric buttons. The skull rested in a knotted silk cravat tucked inside a wrinkled waistcoat of grimy white silk. Affixed to a braided chain, a silver-rimmed glass monocle balanced above the darkened eye socket. The coat was open, revealing twisted vertebrae.

In addition to working as a covert operative for the United States Special Collection Service, Brynstone had earned a doctoral degree in the field of paleopathology. More than once, the study of ancient diseases had proven helpful in his former intelligence work.

He couldn't be certain without diagnostic parameters like age of death and lesion morphology, but he guessed that the man in this grave had died of tuberculosis. It was a challenge under the current conditions to assess paleoepidemiology based on skeletal remains. However, looking at the dry bone sample, he noted the sharp angulation in the spine, which was a telltale sign of tuberculous spondylitis. At the time of his death, the man had been afflicted with a humpbacked condition found in cases of advanced Pott's disease. Even down in a grave with guns pointed at his head, Brynstone couldn't suppress his fascination with bones.

Véronique pointed to the decayed body. "He is a later relative of Jeanne d'Arc."

He nodded. Before becoming a folk hero of the Hundred Years' War, Joan of Arc came from the peasant class in eastern France. The man buried in this casket was a descendant of Joan's older brother.

Brynstone crouched beside the body.

"Get down there and search it," Griffin called to her men, Léon and Kane, one French, one Irish.

"Stay up there," Brynstone demanded. "There's no room."

"Do you see the Roman helmet fragment?" Griffin asked.

"Not yet."

"You sure this is the grave we want?" Léon asked. He was a hulking presence with a pinched face.

"We found Brynstone digging here, didn't we?" she said. "Hate to admit it, but the man does his homework. It's the proper grave."

Opening the deceased's rumpled coat, Brynstone slid his fingers inside a pocket. Véronique hovered behind him, watching. He discovered a simple drawing of a young woman holding a rose.

The daughter of the deceased. Brynstone had researched the man, knew all about him. He hadn't gone through all this trouble to find a portrait.

He rolled the skeleton onto its front, snapping a fragile bone in the process. Too bad, but delicate scientific care wasn't an option right now. He searched the man's breeches and ran his hand alongside the bony legs, as if frisking the corpse, but there was no sign of a helmet piece. He slid off a boot, then tunneled his hand into it, but he found only loose dirt. After inspecting the second one, he held it upside down and shook it before tossing aside the boot.

"Stop playing with the dead," Griffin called from above. "Find the helmet."

Ignoring her, he studied the coffin's velvet lining. He yanked, pulling it free from inside the lid. It revealed a wood-grain surface, nothing more. On his knees now, Brynstone examined the interior of the casket near the skull. He moved his fingers along the side lining, finding a small bump. A tingle of excitement ran down his spine. Maybe this would offer a clue about where to find the helmet piece.

He yanked back the lavender velvet. Running his hand along the wooden surface, his finger traced over a hole, a little smaller than the diameter of a pencil. *Interesting.* He thought it over, then glanced back at the boot.

Brynstone brought out a knife. Véronique looked frightened and backed away.

He grabbed the boot. Slashing it, he peeled back the leather skin above the toe, then stripped the insole. Nothing. He carved open the left boot then cut into the heel pad, revealing a hollow heel base.

Now we're getting somewhere.

"What did you find, Dr. Brynstone?"

No chance hiding it from Griffin. He removed a small golden medallion and held it in the light for her to see.

"Pitch it to me," Griffin said.

Brynstone had another idea. Staying down, he snatched the monocle from the skull and examined the medallion. Interlaced Celtic knots encircled an embedded emerald protruding from a cross-shaped end. Was the medallion a sort of skeleton key?

"What do you see?" Véronique asked.

He didn't answer. Pushing aside the corpse, he studied the small hole inside the casket. It had to be a keyhole.

Before Brynstone could insert the medallion into the keyhole, he heard a churning sound overhead. It was August, a time when Parisians slip away on vacation and the city night slowed to a hush. The cemetery had been still and somber until now.

He glanced at the sky.

It sounded like a single-engine light utility helicopter heading toward the cemetery. He guessed it was the French National Police running a security patrol.

"They have a spotlight," Griffin cried. "Stay down there, Brynstone. If you dare signal the chopper, I'll put a bullet through your skull."

———◆———

Griffin and her men scattered as the helicopter buzzed across the far end of the cemetery. Brynstone was trapped down in the grave.

"Will the helicopter spot us down here?" Véronique asked.

"Better not," he said. "I don't want the police involved."

Fortunately, a network of century-old trees provided cover for the seventy thousand monuments crowded together inside the cemetery. Still, the pilot might spot mounds of dirt piled around the d'Arc gravesite.

Ignoring the helicopter, Brynstone slid the medallion's cross-shaped end into the keyhole. It was a perfect fit. He turned the medallion. There was the sound of a dull click.

The coffin jolted.

Brynstone felt movement beneath his feet, and the floor shuddered.

The broken skeleton slid toward the foot of the casket, pulling Brynstone with it. He was sliding backward. His vestibular sense told him he was dropping downward. His eyes darted around, trying to make sense of the collapsing floor, but it was too dark, and everything was happening too quickly. Véronique screamed as she clung to the side of the grave. On instinct, he grabbed the casket's edge. He swung his right foot up and over the side of the coffin. Before he could rise up, the bottom of the casket dropped out from beneath him.

The skeleton plummeted into the darkness below.

Brynstone's left leg dangled beneath the open-bottomed casket. Cold air blasted his face from an unseen cavern below.

There was a cave beneath the grave.

He kicked his free leg to the side, trying to find a foothold. Suspended by only his fingertips and right foot, Brynstone looked like he was doing a one-legged push-up over the chasm. Véronique tugged on his right leg, trying to secure his foot on the side of the casket. Instead, she fumbled and he lost his footing as dirt slid out from beneath his boot. Brynstone clutched the edges of the casket as his right leg dropped into the empty cavity below.

Overhead, the police helicopter swept its spotlight across monuments and the surrounding trees.

Hanging from his hands now, he realized what had happened. Turning the medallion key in the lock had activated a mechanism that released the casket floor. Like a trapdoor, it had detached from three sides and now hung vertically below the grave. Only hinges attached the swaying floor to the casket's front edge.

Moving hand over hand, he made his way along the edge of the casket. Loose dirt rained down into his face. He blinked it away. Biting in concentration, he crunched granules of earth between his teeth. A soft whoosh came from Brynstone's mouth as he spit out dirt.

He couldn't see the floor of the cavern. It had to be deep down there. No sign of the d'Arc skeleton, but he spied a small rock ledge about eight feet beneath the casket. With arms extended on his six-feet-two-inch frame, it was a short drop.

He let go.

Véronique screamed.

He fell into the darkness, but landed on his feet.

"It's okay," he called, catching his breath. "There's a small ledge down here."

The chopper roared closer. The sound surprised the woman, and she lost her footing and toppled into the grave. Brynstone reached for her, but she caught the edge of the casket and swung down. Véronique was a better athlete than he had expected. Grabbing a stalactite for balance, he grabbed her hand then brought her to safe footing. She curled onto the small ledge with him, seeming almost ready to cry.

Looking up, he used the headlamp to study the bottom of the casket. It was anchored on each side with beams embedded in the surrounding rock. From down here, the suspended coffin looked as if it were floating in the black air.

It was hard to hear, but it sounded like the helicopter had buzzed away from the gravesite.

He moved around the ledge toward the head of the casket. The floor hung straight down. He grabbed for it, pushing it up. A metal dowel was suspended from the bottom of the casket, designed to hold the floor in place. Raising his arms, he had a standing reach of over eight feet. He grabbed the dowel, then swung up the floor to reconnect the foot end to the casket frame. He repositioned the dowel, clicking closed the lock. It held the whole thing in place like it had never dropped open.

"God, don't close it," Véronique said in a panicked voice. "We'll be trapped down here."

"See this?" Brynstone said, holding the metal dowel. "It locks and unlocks the casket floor. We're safe."

The cavern was darker with the lid closed. Dust particles drifted in lazy patterns inside the glare of their headlamps.

"Listen," Véronique said. "I hear voices."

Although muffled overhead, the words made their way down through the casket. The helicopter had flown away and he heard Griffin's voice in the stillness.

"What happened to Brynstone?" Griffin demanded. "Where's the bloody skeleton?"

"Tried to watch the grave, but the helicopter was too close," Torn Kane explained. "Brynstone and Véronique crawled out."

"He found a medallion," Griffin spat. "Where is it?"

Brynstone frowned. When the casket floor had swung open beneath him, he dropped to the ledge, denying him the chance to remove the medallion key from the lock. It was still up there.

"Search the coffin," Griffin ordered. "Maybe he dropped the medallion when he escaped. The rest of you, come with me. We need to find him."

Brynstone glanced at Véronique. In the illumination of his headlamp, he saw her crooked smile. She held up the medallion key.

"You have it?" he whispered in disbelief.

"That's why I was worried about you locking us down here."

"Like I said, we can unlock the floor with that mechanism." He took the medallion. "Nice work."

There was a loud thud overhead as one of Griffin's men dropped into the casket. The impact caused a dark cloud of dust to billow around the pair on the ledge below.

Brynstone covered his mouth, suppressing a cough. Moving from beneath the grave, he made a discovery. Carved from limestone, a series of stairs descended about twenty feet down, melting into blackness.

He looked back.

Véronique reclined on a flat rock to shake pebbles from her shoes. Not waiting for her, he moved down the stairs and peered around the corner. He had to see.

He found a second ledge down here. It curved around the rock wall, but it was difficult to see without exploring. He knew something had to be down here. The casket had served as a trapdoor for a reason.

The ledge ran narrow and disappeared deep into the cavern. He heard footfalls behind him.

"You did not wait for me," Véronique called, brushing dust from her hair. She hurried over, excited to see him.

"I was coming back."

"How long should we hide down here?"

"Griffin's men still searching the grave?"

"*Oui.* Nothing is safe as long as they remain up there."

He glanced at the ledge. "Might be another way out. Don't know. I'll check."

She clutched his hand. "I will not stay here alone."

Brynstone studied her. "Let's go."

Chapter 2

He was watching her.

Cori Cassidy was sure of it. She had first noticed the man after stopping to buy water from one of the many street vendors lining the Central Park Reservoir. She had spotted him lurking behind the drooping oak trees as she slowly unrolled dollar bills stuffed in her running shorts. He was super fit and bare-chested like some guy you'd see on the cover of *Runner's World*. She placed him at around thirty. The stranger grabbed his right foot and pulled it behind his butt, doing a standing quad stretch.

Is he one of them?

She couldn't tell and she wasn't hanging around to find out. Cori tried to look casual as she capped her Poland Spring bottle and adjusted her sunglasses. Petite in build, she was dressed in high-cut black running shorts and a plain white T-shirt. Her short, sun-bleached blonde hair was pulled in a barely there ponytail that poked through the back of a pink baseball cap. She had been listening to her favorite "get pumped" running mix, but she pulled the earbuds out of her ears now and tucked them into her bra strap to stay better aware of her surroundings.

She hurried out from beneath the leafy canopy overhanging the bridal path and navigated around a chocolate-colored puddle.

Summer rain had hit the city during the night. The early-August storm had bled muddy ruts in the track hugging the reservoir. Dodging tourists and locals, she weaved around them as she headed for the street. Despite all the people, she felt vulnerable here.

At the park's edge, a dozen Girl Scouts headed her way, drawing attention with their exuberance. Three giggling blue-eyed girls took the lead, their hands interlaced. Two Scouts had straight, shimmering brown hair, and there was a curly blonde between them. Their perky Scout leader offered a warm smile as they passed. Moving alongside the troop, Cori turned and looked for the man. No sign of him.

As she sprinted to the edge of the park, she took another quick glance. The stranger hadn't followed her. At least, not that she could see.

At twenty-seven, she was a graduate student at Columbia University. She had studied at Johns Hopkins before meeting John Brynstone and Edgar Wurm, two men who had changed her life. Her world was turned upside down after Wurm's death. Against her father's wishes, she'd dropped out of graduate school four years ago and had drifted from one soul-draining job to another, before deciding to return to psychology. To her relief, Columbia had taken a chance on her two years ago. She'd completed her master's degree and was hard at work on a doctorate. Starting next month, she would become an extern at the university's Clinic for Anxiety and Related Disorders for Children.

She'd turned her life around, big-time. Still, something kept pulling her back here.

Exiting on Ninety-Second Street and walking along the cobblestone sidewalk that lined the outskirts of Central Park, Cori headed down Fifth Avenue for several blocks before making a left on Eighty-Sixth. A feeling haunted her. She shouldn't be here. It was a bad idea. That's what she was saying to herself, but another part of her mind won the battle today, drawing her to this street. She was in a war with herself, thoughts and emotions colliding inside her head. But none of that made her stop—she had to see for herself.

Around the corner, a doorman in a gray suit watched her suspiciously from the Neue Galerie, and Cori thought he recognized her from other times. The man reached for his cell. Was he calling the police? Frozen on the sidewalk, she thought about running, until an elderly couple approached the doorman. He ditched the phone then opened the door. The couple entered the museum's Café Sabarsky, no doubt to enjoy a Linzer torte with a nice cup of Viennese espresso.

Making it look like she belonged here, Cori headed for a hotdog cart parked near the corner. Ducking beneath the cart's yellow and blue umbrella, she stood behind an overweight guy, his stomach bulging in a gray Tribeca softball shirt, and a woman dressed in a fashionable black jacket with matching skirt.

Cori shifted her head, making a discreet glance at the museum. The man had moved inside. She heaved a sigh of relief. First the runner in the park. Now the doorman. Her paranoia was on hyperdrive today.

Peering around a row of soft drinks perched atop the silver cart, she glanced across East Eighty-Sixth. The Brandonstein Center for Gifted Children occupied a narrow four-story building in the middle of the block. With a distinctive brick façade, the building was wedged between a parking garage and a suite of dental offices. It didn't look like a school. Most people probably didn't know it was one. Pots of shrubs and flowers dotted the balcony. The Brandonstein Center operated year round and was dedicated to working with exceptional kids while charging their parents an exorbitant tuition. Only twelve children were accepted each term. The school had been anxious to recruit Shayna Brynstone. Throughout its twenty-year history, she had been only the third child to receive a full scholarship.

A few months short of her sixth birthday, Shayna emerged from the private school along with a handful of children and adults. Cori couldn't explain it, but she knew the child was special, even though they hadn't spoken since Shayna was a year old. More than anything, Cori wanted to spend time getting to know the little girl, but that wasn't a possibility.

She searched for Shayna's mother in the small crowd. Strange. Kaylyn Brynstone usually waited on the steps outside the school. Where was she today?

"What can I get ya?" the sidewalk vendor asked.

"Bottle of water."

As she handed over cash, her cell rang. It was her brother, Jared. She grabbed the cold drink before answering his call.

"Guess what, Cori? I'm in town. Last-minute business trip."

"I thought you were in Boston."

"Finished early," Jared Cassidy answered. "I'm at the airport."

As her brother talked, Cori glanced halfway down the street and noticed a bald man standing outside a suite of medical offices. He wore eyeglasses and a suit, sporting a European dark-on-dark look. It was the third time she'd spied the man near the private school. He seemed to be watching Shayna.

"Cori?" her brother asked. "Did you hear me?"

"Hmm? Yeah," she said, returning attention to his call.

"Everything okay?"

"Yeah. Great. Kinda busy right now."

She watched the bald man. There was no mistaking it; he was looking at Shay. Was he a creepy child molester scouting his next prey? *No.* He wore an earpiece this time. He also had his cell out now. Was he running surveillance on the child?

"So, I need to ask something," Jared said. "Be honest, sis. Are you watching that little girl again?"

The question shocked her back into the conversation.

"Um, no," she lied.

"Cori, you need to stop it. I'm serious. You're not a stalker or anything, but this is turning into an obsess—"

"It's not an obsession."

"Yeah, it is. You don't go out anymore. You haven't dated anyone in forever. I talked to Troy. He's asked you out three times. He said another guy tried, too. You're turning everyone down."

"I'm a grad student. I don't have a life. I don't have time for a relationship right now."

Cori studied the bald man, trying to memorize his features. Really, he looked no different from any other business guy outside a Fifth Avenue town house. Oval-shaped face with a narrow forehead. Pronounced cheekbones. Rectangular frameless glasses.

On the phone, Jared was saying, "Look, I know you feel responsible in some weird way for that Brynstone girl, but you shouldn't."

"I'm worried about her."

"And I'm worried about you. Listen, I need to grab my bags and make another call. We'll meet at your apartment in an hour or so. Get an early dinner or something."

"'Kay, great," she said, ready to end the call. "See you soon, Jared."

Hanging up, she gulped a drink of water. The condensation-covered bottle almost slipped out of her hands. Steeling her nerves, she made up her mind to confront the guy who was watching Shayna. Cori had to know why he was here. Clenching her fists, she marched toward him. The man didn't see her coming. She tried to work up a tough look. She played the conversation in her head, deciding what to say.

From behind, a hand grabbed her arm. Cori yelped in surprise.

A woman with honey-blonde hair came around to face her. John Brynstone's ex-wife. Shayna's mom fixed her hands on her hips, pressing down on a cotton sundress. Kaylyn Brynstone's eyes blazed with fury.

"What are you doing here?"

Shocked, Cori fumbled over her words. "Central Park. I was jogging. It's just that I was thirsty—"

"You're watching her," Kaylyn said. "I ignored it at first, but I've had enough of you watching my daughter."

"Honestly, I just come this way after the park."

"Last Tuesday, Shayna and I were headed into Norma's for breakfast when I saw you. You followed us."

Cori was flustered. She didn't like getting caught. She had followed them for a few blocks in Midtown West. The night before, she had awakened from a terrible nightmare about Shayna. She had wanted reassurance that the little girl was safe. As much as she hated to admit it, the whole thing did sound stalkerish.

"Tell me something," Kaylyn said, anger flickering in her voice. "You're working with my ex-husband again, aren't you?"

"No. You're totally wrong about that, Kaylyn."

"I'm not wrong. John is out of the country. He sends you to spy on my daughter, doesn't he? Tell the truth, Cori."

"I haven't talked to John in over four years. That's the truth."

"Then why are you watching my daughter? Why are you following us?"

Cori looked down. "Look, it's not easy to explain."

"I know you're training to be a psychologist and all that, so you should understand this. Shayna has been through enough without you stalking her."

"I'm not stalking your daughter, but"—she fixed the woman in her gaze—"other people are."

All at once, Kaylyn's expression went blank.

"What are you saying?"

"There're these guys." Cori glanced down the sidewalk, looking for the bald man, but he was nowhere in sight. She cleared her throat. "I saw one today. Like, just a minute ago. He was watching Shayna."

Kaylyn rolled her eyes. "You're impossible."

"You haven't seen them?"

"You're the only one I've seen watching Shayna."

"I'm serious. This scary bald guy was right down there. I was going to talk to him when you stopped me."

"I see why you and my ex get along so well. You're just like John." Kaylyn narrowed her eyes. "Do me a favor, Cori. Stay away from my daughter."

Kaylyn marched across the street, heading back to the school.

Cori bit her lip, fighting back frustration and resentment. Her younger brother's words started sinking in.

Getting ready to leave, she saw Kaylyn hug her daughter outside the school. Cori's gaze drifted down the street. She noticed a black car parked along the curb on the opposite side of the road. The bald guy. He was back. Only now he was in a sedan, watching from behind the steering wheel. Watching Shayna again.

Buzzing with adrenaline, Cori curled her lip and started walking down the sidewalk. She intended to cross the street and find out who he was and why he was watching the little girl. She had questions and, damn it, she was determined to get answers.

Chapter 3

Paris
9:20 p.m.

John Brynstone had no idea where he was going. He inched along a narrow ledge carved from stone that ran along the cave wall. From the edge, it made a sheer drop into blackness. He stopped to get his bearings. The cavern beneath Père Lachaise Cemetery was no place for people with claustrophobia or a fear of heights. And it was a certain hell for anyone afraid of the dark.

Water dripped from an overhead limestone rock, leaving the narrow ledge wet. Bracing himself with palms flat against the wall, he sidestepped slowly along the ledge. Thirty feet in, he drew in a quick breath then glanced back. Véronique followed close behind. Her eyes were closed. He wondered briefly if she was afraid of heights, but didn't bother to ask. If so, it wasn't slowing her down.

As they made their way through the winding cave, Brynstone reflected on his reason for being here. He had tried not to act surprised when Edgar Wurm greeted him on that snowy February day in Central Park. He still didn't know how the man came back. Right now, he didn't waste time trying to understand it.

In May, Wurm had explored an archive in France. He had discovered a journal belonging to a fourteenth-century woman named Jeanneton de Paris. Numerous entries described her relationship with a Knight Hospitaller named Tyon d'Arc, his last name spelled as "Darc" during the Middle Ages. Both Joan of Arc and the corpse buried in the false-bottom coffin above were said to be descendants of the knight. Some even claimed that Jeanneton served as a namesake for Joan of Arc. The iconic French hero was also named Jeanneton, later known as Jeanne or Jehanne d'Arc. According to a 1333 entry in her journal, Jeanneton de Paris had possessed a piece of a Roman helmet. Brynstone had hoped to find it in the grave.

He knew now it wasn't going to be that easy.

Her journal had mentioned a cavern, but he and Wurm hadn't realized it was hidden beneath the grave. Was it possible the helmet piece was hidden down here?

After another ten feet, the wall curved. As Brynstone shuffled around it, he peered down at the ledge. A word was carved into the surface between his feet.

CAPIO

Véronique placed her hand on his shoulder, moving beside him. "What do you see?"

"Latin word," he answered. "*Capio*. It means *choose*."

"Choose what?"

He looked across the cavern. Two long cords dangled side by side, reaching down into darkness. On the right, a marine rope, thick and braided, lingered against the cave wall. Dull and yellow, the cord on the left was fashioned from human skeletal remains—a cluster of femur, humerus, and tibia bones wired together.

"That's our choice?" she asked. "We climb down a rope or climb down bones?"

"Looks that way."

"Took me two seconds," she announced. "I've made my choice."

"First," he said, "we need to get across this chasm before we can climb down the rope."

The twin lines dangled twenty feet from where Brynstone stood. Even with an approach run, the gap was too far to jump. He looked down at the narrow ledge.

"At one time, it was possible to walk across this chasm. That's my guess from the look of it. A narrow strip of rock had spanned from this side to that one, connecting it all. A natural catwalk. It's long since crumbled and fallen away."

"Unhappy news for us," Véronique sighed, looking down. "One moment, John. What is that down there? Do you see?"

He did. Brynstone crouched for a closer inspection. He discovered a tightwire attached a few feet beneath the rock ledge.

"Who put that there?" she asked, leaning over with hands palming her kneecaps.

"Someone who wanted to get to the other side. After the catwalk collapsed, a tightrope offered a way for the adventurous to cross this chasm."

"Why not a bridge? Even an old rickety one would be far better than a tightrope."

He arched an eyebrow. "Too damned easy."

The two-inch wire spanned the cavern. The tightwire ran all the way to the twin cords, stopping between them. Make it across on that thing and he could grab one line and climb down. Only problem? He'd never been on a tightwire in his life.

"I'll go," Véronique announced. "My father is a funambulist."

"A what?"

"An acrobat who performs on a tightwire. He had me walking a high wire when I was three."

Brynstone smirked. "When it comes to parenting, your dad makes me seem downright responsible."

He studied the wire.

"I'll go first."

"I don't mind," she said.

"Stay there."

Sliding his back against the wall, he dropped his butt on the ledge. He extended his right leg a few feet until it rested on the wire. He spied a guy-wire anchored to the cliff. The tension cable added stability to the tightwire. He bounced his foot on the line.

"Seems secure," she observed.

"The wire has been here for decades. Maybe going back to the 1800s."

"Not to worry," Véronique said. "The French are accomplished in such matters."

"Know all about this, huh?"

"My great-great-great-grandfather was an assistant for Charles Blondin. In 1859, he witnessed the Great Blondin cross Niagara Falls with a man clinging to his back. Five years later, Blondin walked above the roaring falls on a pair of stilts. At the Zoological Gardens in Liverpool, he pushed a lion strapped in a wheelbarrow across a wire."

Brynstone knew that tightwire walking had been around since ancient Egypt. Some critics had condemned it as supernatural, at best, or demonic, at worst. Four hundred years ago, a horse had been trained to perform tricks on a tightrope. Consumed with paranoia, a Lisbon court had the animal arrested. After a high-profile trial, the horse was convicted on charges of witchcraft. The really crazy part? The court ordered the horse to be burned at the stake.

"You're not experienced," Véronique said. "Remove your socks and boots. Cross on bare feet and you can grab the rope between your toes."

He glanced up at her. "Not my style."

"Follow my advice if you care to do what is best for you."

"If I did what was best for me, I wouldn't be here right now."

"You need good balance. To do this, you must be confident."

"Believe me, that's not a problem."

She said something more, but he didn't hear. Brynstone was already on the wire, at least in his mind. He formed a mental picture of himself crossing the yawning cavern, focusing on the vivid image of his body from behind, seeing it in third person like he was watching a movie. He had learned about guided visualization as a child, back when illness had ravaged his body. He had been immobilized, sometimes for months at a time, in a body cast or a wheelchair. Childhood illness had forced him to develop a disciplined mind even as it sapped his body. In later years, he conditioned his body to match his mind.

Brynstone now visualized himself reaching the end of the tightwire. When he arrived at the dark wall ahead, would he choose the braided marine rope three feet to the right of the tightwire or the skeletal cord the same distance on the left?

"Of course, that is my opinion," Véronique continued. "Dr. Brynstone, are you listening?"

"Need to concentrate," he answered.

Brynstone pushed off with his hands, moving away from the ledge as he stepped onto the rope. His body swayed—back and forth, back and forth—as the pull of gravity flirted with the immutable outcome of success or death. Drawing in a full breath, he moved one foot in front of the other, keeping the proper biomechanics as he stretched his arms away from his body. It was better this way with the black chasm below. He couldn't see a thing down there, allowing him to focus on the wire without visual distraction.

He had an uncanny sense of balance, contributing to his skill as an athlete, although he had stayed away from team sports in school. Too much conformity for his taste, a way of thinking that haunted him later as an Army Ranger. He had been recruited out of the military to join the elite American intelligence agency called the United States Special Collection Service, created in 1978 as a covert joint operation between the Central Intelligence Agency and the National Security Agency. As an operative there, he had finally been given freedom to handle jobs his own way.

And the one time he didn't?

It had resulted in the most devastating black op of his career. Not long after, he had quit government work and returned to his first love, dedicating himself to paleopathology. Still, he couldn't help but look for answers to questions that went back to that terrible night years ago. The night his family changed forever.

"Your form is excellent," Véronique called. "You appear to be a quick learner."

Her words came as a faint impression that dissolved the second it hit his ears. Brynstone had a peculiar ability to concentrate on a task, immersing himself in a vacuum of self-determination. It was almost surreal, losing himself in the goal, not so much overcoming the duality of self and object as much as merging them.

Halfway across the rope, something pulled him out of his psychological immersion. Something he hadn't imagined during his guided visualization.

Someone had invited in the demons.

A blast of cold air seemed to shoot up from the darkness, bringing joyless questions to a man given to confidence at the expense of introspection. So much of his life had been turned upside down when he had taken a desperate risk to save his daughter. He still loved Kaylyn, but so much bitterness had divided them and his marriage had been falling apart ever since that fateful night. For the last several years, he realized now, his life had been in a delicate balance.

He had been a man out of time, frozen on a high wire.

No past.

No future.

Other than his daughter, the pride of his life, nothing else drove him but the hunt for one man. One enemy. The world's most elite assassin.

"Dr. Brynstone," Véronique called. "Are you all right?"

He couldn't block her words now. They came with the force of an alarm blast in his ears. The loss of self-consciousness?

Gone.

The steely concentration?

Gone.

That old fear? The one haunting him for the past four and a half years?

It returned. With a vengeance.

He closed his eyes. *Not now.*

Fighting it off, he took a step, guiding one foot in front of the other. His body rocked in an awkward sway. The rope seemed to take on a life all its own.

"Dr. Brynstone. Careful."

Too late.

He couldn't control the rhythm. His boot slid off the line as his body dipped the opposite direction. He overcorrected, trying to maintain his balance on the terrible motion of the tightwire. He came close—but not close enough.

He was going down.

The dark face of the cavern glared as John Brynstone toppled from the wire.

Chapter 4

Viktor Nebola crushed a smoldering cigar beneath his shoe, watching the warehouse doors roll open. At fifty-three, he was agile and well dressed, his regard for Italian designers bordering on a fetish. His outsized menace seemed inconsistent with his quiet demeanor and five-foot-six frame. His ex-wife had joked that he had a Napoleon complex— a rare attempt at teasing from a woman with no sense of humor. Nebola had never figured out why she had dared to mock him, but it proved to be a critical first step in her becoming his ex-wife.

A silver SUV cruised through the open doors toward him, coming to a halt a few feet away, then the doors rumbled to a close behind the vehicle.

Three men climbed out.

At gunpoint, two figures escorted a tall fair-skinned man named Abder Visser, who was cuffed, hands behind his back. He was all disciplined muscle in his tight workout shirt, the cut revealing sculpted grooves in his arms. One of Nebola's men directed Visser into a chair. They handcuffed the guy to a cuff bar attached to the metal table.

Milking the moment, Nebola studied the trampled cigar, then considered Visser.

"You disappoint me. I personally recruited you out of the Korps Commandotroepen. You were one of the best special operators in the Royal Netherlands Army. Hell, you were one of the best men in the Shadow Chapter."

"Still am, sir."

"You betrayed my operation."

"If I may, sir, your operation betrayed me. It took fast thinking for me to rescue the Brazil project."

"You left a trace of our activity." Nebola reached behind his head and brushed a ring of black hair that reached from ear to ear. "You nearly exposed the identity of your leader. Possibly also our organization. Big mistake."

"What will you do to me?" Visser asked.

"Everything I can think of."

Nebola didn't tolerate mistakes, in part because he had made too many in his early life. His old man had abandoned his family while Nebola had been a toddler. His mother had been a drunk. His upbringing had taught him to rely on his gut and never trust anyone. He'd committed mistakes as a teenager, an assortment of minor crimes like car theft and burglary. He had been convicted of manslaughter at age twenty for killing some stranger he had met on a cold March night. After serving fifteen years in prison, he finally got smart. He stopped making mistakes, and he didn't permit it now in himself or in anyone else.

"I've heard stories about the Boston compound," Visser said, looking around. "I know the things you do in this place."

"Then you have reason to be afraid."

"You wouldn't do that to your own people."

"You're no longer one of my people."

The Dutch commando gritted his teeth. "I'm not afraid."

"Give yourself time."

Nebola's assistant Porter Harris grimly marched across the warehouse.

"Thought I made it clear," Nebola growled. "No interruptions from you or anyone else."

In a low voice, Harris said, "Yes, sir, but I wanted to brief you. We're ready to go with the New York operation. Do we have your authorization?"

"Is everyone in place? We can't afford to blow this."

"Affirmative, sir. We're ready."

"Proceed," Nebola answered. "Let me get started on this Dutch scum. After that, I'll be right up to supervise the operation."

Harris headed for the door at the back of the warehouse.

Nebola turned a silver ring around his finger. "You're a mistake, Visser. Mistakes need to disappear."

"What are you gonna do?"

"I won't hurt you."

"You won't?"

"Nah. Now that guy back there?" Nebola gestured with his thumb toward a figure standing alone in the shadows. "That guy you need to worry about."

Visser squinted. "Who is it?"

"Guy I hire for a few jobs. Ever read Dante's *Inferno*?"

He shook his head.

"Dante uses this method when he writes about hell called *contrapasso*. Basically, it's the idea that you punish a sinner in a way that fits his crime." Nebola glanced at the solitary figure. "My friend over there? He's an expert on *contrapasso*."

"Are you talking about the Poet?" Visser swallowed. "The guy who made a kill for you in Thailand? I saw his work. That's him? That's Erich Metzger over there?"

Nebola frowned. "My friend likes a low profile. Right there? You didn't make him happy mentioning his name."

The blonde commando closed his eyes.

"If it helps any, think of it as an honor." Nebola brought out another cigar. "You're about to be killed by the best assassin money can buy."

———————

New York City
3:22 p.m.

Cori Cassidy drew in a breath, preparing herself to confront the bald man. He was sitting behind the wheel of a black sedan, talking on his phone with the window rolled down. She wasn't a confrontational person—not at all—but she was determined to find out about this guy and learn why he was stalking Shayna Brynstone.

It still rankled her that Kaylyn had directed her blame to Cori and not to people like him. Moving to the curb, she took a quick glance at the school. Shayna and her mother stood on the sidewalk, talking to a male teacher. Another five or six children and parents lingered near them. Shayna seemed distracted, staring at a black fire hydrant with a silver top. She pulled away from her mother's hand. Engrossed in conversation, Kaylyn Brynstone didn't notice as the child wandered to a green metal mailbox.

As Cori waited for an oncoming commercial truck to pass, a slender African American man walked along the driver's side of the bald man's sedan. He moved with elegance, like a dancer. As the truck drove past, it blocked her view. Seeing that the street was clear, she crossed it. The black man had already passed by the bald guy and was now cutting back toward the sidewalk in front of the sedan.

Playing a conversation of defiant words in her mind, Cori trained her gaze on the bald man. He wasn't talking on the phone now, but he stared straight ahead, watching Shayna.

Cori was ready to face him. She hurried to the car.

She clamped her hands on the open window, playing it tough. "You guys aren't as smooth as you think. Tell me what you're doing here."

The man didn't answer. Didn't even turn to look. Didn't acknowledge her presence. He didn't pull his gaze from Shayna.

"I said, tell me—" Her mouth gaped open as she took a closer look at the bald man.

Blood dribbled from his ear, then traced a slender line down his neck. The man stared ahead, the seat belt strapping him into place. His shattered earpiece rested on his shoulder. His right hand was slung across his lap, still holding the phone. Blood speckled his frameless glasses and his fingertips. Someone had shot him at close range. Her breath caught in her throat. Blood droplets glistened on the opposite window and the dashboard and the seat.

Her legs buckled and she covered her mouth as the acid taste of vomit rose in her throat. She heard a small tinny voice coming from the phone. The words were faint, but distinct.

"Do you have a visual on Cori Cassidy?"

She raised fingers to her forehead, surprised to hear her name.

"Sparta," the caller said in an urgent voice. "Your earpiece is off-line. Please confirm. Are you maintaining a visual on Cori Cassidy?"

Instinctively, she reached inside the window and snatched the phone from the dead man's bloodied hand. She raised it, but didn't allow it to touch her ear.

"Who is this?" she demanded.

The call ended.

A black van roared around her on the street. Dodging it, she pressed her body against the dead guy's car to avoid being hit by the reckless driver. The van swerved to a stop along the curb in front of the school.

From the sidewalk, a man moved into position behind the van. She recognized him—it was the agile African American man who had walked past the sedan as she crossed the street. Did he shoot the bald guy? He was now leaning against the van, craning his neck around the vehicle to see Shayna.

Shayna Brynstone had moved away from the mailbox. She stood beside her mother, holding her hand. The male teacher made a flirty laugh at something Kaylyn Brynstone had said.

The guy behind the van was shielded from their view. He reached into his suit coat and removed a gun with a suppressor. With one fluid motion, he pivoted, bringing up his foot as he stepped onto the sidewalk. Raised the gun. Set his sight. Took aim.

Cori was suddenly terrified for Shayna.

And she screamed.

Chapter 5

John Brynstone fell from the tightwire into blackness. Arching his leg, he snared the wire with the back of his knee. It saved him. He swung for a second, upside down, with a rush of blood driving toward his head.

An impression of Shayna's face stole its way into his mind. Everything changed in that moment and a new clarity came to him. He knew he couldn't die. Not yet.

Tensing his abdominal muscles, he curled up and grabbed the wire with his right hand, clinging to it as he grabbed its taut surface with his other hand. He wasn't going to try to get back on top of the rope now.

He considered going into a monkey crawl across the rope, but decided to take it hand over hand with a mixed hanging grip. With care and deliberation, he eased his leg from the rope and dropped it beneath him. He flexed his elbows, keeping the rope in line with his ear. Moving his legs in a stepping motion, he avoided a sideward swing.

Véronique shouted instructions, but he didn't listen. He was absorbed. Immersed. Lost in a stubborn determination to make it to the other side. After a few minutes of work, he faced the twin cords that dangled on either side of the tightwire's end.

Choose.

Two cords hanging six feet apart. One a marine rope, the other made of bones.

Choose.

The rope seemed an obvious choice. It was sturdy, even after all this time down here. He thought back to the word engraved on the ledge. *Capio* was a Latin word meaning *choose* or *seize*. But it could also mean to take something in a violent or hostile manner. And the derivative term, *capi*, could mean a state of injury or disease.

Violence. Injury. Disease.

He had chosen.

Hanging on the tightwire with his right hand, Brynstone reached with his left for the skeletal cord. He grabbed a thighbone, then pulled himself to it. The bones rattled an echo, but the cord held his weight. He started climbing down.

"I'm joining you," Véronique said, testing the wire.

Her words finally sunk in.

"Stay there," he demanded. "Let me see where this goes."

Brynstone moved down the cord of bones formed from the countless remains of appendicular skeletons. Most had been lashed together from adult cadavers, but he came across a small tibia that had belonged to a child. He couldn't bring himself to touch it.

From overhead, dust sprinkled onto his face. Blinking, he looked up.

Véronique balanced above him, hovering on the tightwire. He was surprised to see her up there on the rope. She stared straight ahead, not glancing down.

"Damn it, I told you to stay back. This cord might not support both of us."

"Not a problem," she answered. "I'm choosing the other rope."

He saw her feet leave the wire. Before he could make another protest, Véronique reached to her right, seizing the braided marine rope. The minute her weight yanked on it, the rope snapped free.

Bad choice.

She dropped.

———✦———

Straining, Brynstone reached out. He grabbed Véronique's arm as she fell past, her screams resonating in the cavern. Jerking his shoulder, he swung her around in an arc, straining to keep his grip on the cord. The question was, could a cord made of skeletal remains support their combined weight?

Despite a cracking sound near the top, it held. Their bodies swung in the darkness. Moving down his leg, she scrambled for a hold on the cord, clawing at a femur bone.

"I've got it," she choked. "You can let go of my hand."

He released his grip around her wrist.

Close to his foot, she clung to the cord, pressing her body tight to its bony surface.

"I thought the rope would be safe," she said.

"That's what they wanted you to think."

"Who?"

"People who designed this place. Now start climbing down."

She didn't argue.

A rocky L-shaped platform waited below. Véronique touched down first, climbing off the cord. She backed against the wall, showing relief on her face. Now with her weight removed, the cord swung back toward the abyss, taking him with it.

Brynstone climbed down as the cord swayed out.

It was headed back to the platform where Véronique held out her hand. Timing was everything right now.

Taking a breath, he jumped.

Brynstone landed on the platform, his feet slapping dust as he hit. Véronique grabbed his arm. He released the cord and watched it swing back into the cold dark air. An upside-down human skull was affixed to the end of the cord. It seemed to watch them.

"Now what?" she asked.

He pointed. "That way."

She inched along the platform. He glanced down and saw another Latin word carved on the surface.

OCULUS

It was another message.

Eye.

Was he supposed to see something significant? *Look around,* he told himself. *Work it out.*

Sensing movement, he turned. The cord was swinging back and forth, the skull at the bottom moving in then pulling away, all the while watching him.

He held his gaze as the skull approached the ledge. Bending a little, he caught the thing and pulled it toward him, rotating the skull in his hands, the long chain of bones reaching above like some exaggerated spinal cord. Peering inside the skull, he studied the orbit, the cavity that had once housed a right eye. He found a small object secured near the sphenoid bone.

Brynstone smiled. The skull contained a golden key.

Chapter 6

"He's got a gun!" Cori Cassidy screamed.

She pointed at the gunman as he stepped from behind the van, aiming the weapon at Shayna and Kaylyn Brynstone. Hearing Cori's warning, the African American man turned and aimed the firearm at her.

Her breath caught in her throat. She ducked beside the black sedan, moving out of sight. Crouching close to the door, Cori heard people screaming near the school. A bullet glanced off the side mirror above her head. She was down on the hot asphalt now, hands and knees pressed against the pavement. Windshield glass exploded in a volley of gunfire. Hit again, the bald driver's head slumped out the open window. Blood dripped from the dead man's face, splattering her arm. She inched closer to the tire.

The gunfire seemed to stop.

Where was he? Maybe coming around to this side of the car to shoot her? From her crouching position, she looked back. He wasn't there. Cori peered over the sedan's hood, its black surface riddled with bullet holes. It sparkled with shattered glass.

The gunman stood beside the van, his weapon trained on the crowd. "Shut up, people. Everybody slap those hands behind your heads. You hear?"

The passenger door on the van opened. A white man burst onto the sidewalk, wearing a dark suit. He moved to the small crowd, shoving children and adults to the sidewalk. He grabbed Shayna's arm, wrenching it to the side as he dragged her to the van. The little girl tried to drop down and resist as she screamed in terror.

"Let go of my daughter," Kaylyn shouted desperately, chasing after them.

The white guy turned and punched her in the stomach. Despite the pain, she clung to him, trying to pry away her daughter.

"Let go, bitch," he yelled, "before I put a bullet through your head."

The black gunman watched them as he waved his weapon. Cori sprinted toward him. Leading with her elbow, she hit him from behind, colliding into his shoulder. It felt like slamming into a brick wall. He must have squeezed the trigger because a bullet hit the man holding Shay.

Clutching his chest, the man released her. Blood spread across his shirt. He collapsed on his knees, then fell headfirst onto the sidewalk.

Kicking as high as she could, Cori struck the black guy's hand. The handgun spiraled from his grip and landed beneath the van. Anger burned in his eyes as he reached back for Cori, but she was smaller and faster. She scrambled around him, making her way to Shayna and her mom.

A second white guy scrambled out from the driver's seat. He had a handgun, but it didn't have a sound suppressor. Cursing, the black man looked around for his gun.

"I called for backup from the second team," the driver shouted to him. "They're almost here."

From the crowd, a male teacher ran to the driver and tackled him. They both hit the sidewalk.

The school door swung open. A security guard hurried past the crowd. He brought out a gun and aimed in the direction of the van. Kaylyn screamed.

"Get inside the school," Cori demanded.

She jumped over a woman curled on the sidewalk. Reaching for Shayna's wrist, Cori jerked on Kaylyn's arm at the same time and brought them both toward the door.

As the security guy rushed past them, Kaylyn ripped away to grab her daughter's free arm. Gunfire crackled around them. At first, Cori thought the guard had fired his weapon. Instead, the security guy flipped around as bullets tore into his neck and arm. She flinched, trying to block the image from her mind.

Cori made it through the door, pulling Shay with her.

"Let's go."

"Who are they?" Kaylyn shouted, her face red. She stumbled behind them, losing her grip on her daughter's arm.

Cori didn't let go of Shayna's hand. She led her inside the school, knowing Kaylyn would follow. And she did. Cori sprinted down the hallway with Shayna.

She heard a gunshot. On instinct, she looked back.

Ten feet behind Cori, Kaylyn Brynstone hit the wall in the school's foyer. Her eyes widened as a red mist erupted from her back, blasting hair around her head like a golden halo. She shuddered as color drained from her face.

Choking on her fear, Cori didn't hesitate. She turned and headed up the stairs, running as hard as she could with the child keeping up beside her, hand in hand. She had to get Shayna to safety. She prayed the girl hadn't witnessed her mother's shooting.

Another security guard and several staff and teachers hurried toward them, all rushing to the school's entrance. A man said something, but Cori burst past him. Two or three wore white lab coats, looking more like scientists than teachers.

What kind of school was this?

"Where are we going, Cori?" the child cried.

"You know my name?" she huffed.

She had talked to the child only one time. That was back when Shayna was a baby.

"My dad has a picture of you," she explained. "Is Mommy coming?"

"She'll catch up. We've gotta get you to safety first."

"Who are those bad men?"

"Don't know."

They hustled around the corner. The walls were covered with ornate paneling in dark wood. There were marble fireplaces and big potted plants scattered about. It looked like something in a turn-of-the-last-century mansion. In other words, nothing like any school she'd ever seen.

She checked a door. Locked. She tried the next one. Same thing.

A man's voice called from around the hallway.

Gunfire rattled again, a quick *pop pop pop*. They were getting close.

Still running with Shayna, Cori hit full panic mode. She darted around a corner, seeing an office at the end of the hallway. The door was open.

Thank God.

———•••———

Cori and Shayna rushed into the office. A woman dressed in a white lab coat jumped up from behind a desk and met them near the door.

"Stop right there," she said, glaring at Cori. "Who are you?"

"Um, friend of the Brynstone family," she panted.

Staring through glasses, the woman's eyes looked cold and probing. "Your name, please?"

"Cori Cassidy."

The woman checked a clipboard.

"Dr. Resnick?" Shayna asked. "Bad men are outside. They shot at my mommy. They killed Mr. Hansen."

The woman stared at her.

"The security guard? When?"

"Just now," Cori answered.

As Resnick turned to look at the door, Shayna reached up and unclipped a smart card from the researcher's coat. The woman punched numbers into her cell, unaware of the theft.

"Stay here," she ordered.

On her way into the hall, Resnick closed the door, locking it behind her.

Cori stared in amazement. "You stole that woman's card."

"We need it." The girl hurried to the desk. "Dr. Resnick is wrong. We better not stay here." She pulled open a drawer and grabbed keys. "Can you drive a car?"

"A car?" Cori blinked. "Yeah. I can drive."

"Good, 'cause I can't. There's this girl in my class. Dianne Callaghan? Her mom has lived in the city her whole life and she can't drive."

She hurried to a metal security door and swiped Dr. Resnick's card.

Cori stared in disbelief. The kid was unbelievable.

Kind of like her dad.

She glanced at Dr. Resnick's desk. Cori saw folders bulging with paperwork that looked like they contained confidential information on students at the Brandonstein Center. Maybe Shayna's folder was in there. It might answer questions she had about the girl.

"C'mon," Shayna called. The door opened into an adjacent office suite.

Cori ignored the folders and headed for the child. Shayna's small hand pressed against the metal door to prevent it from closing.

Gunfire snapped in the hallway. A muffled sound came next, like a woman screaming. Glass shattered outside. The knob rattled. Gunfire again. Someone shot at the locked door.

Shayna screamed. Cori scrambled to join her, hugging her close.

A man kicked the office door. The sound rifled throughout the room. It burst open. The security door began to close with a soft metallic whoosh.

The door was an inch or two from shutting, and in that gap Cori saw the white gunman's face. It was the driver. He glared and raised his gun.

No. God, no.

Cori reached for Shayna, grabbing the back of her shirt. The child was already headed to the floor. They both dropped.

Bullets sprayed the security door as it closed.

Chapter 7

Rashmi Raja stared at the ribbon of blood trickling from the man's neck. She hadn't broken into this mansion with the intent to hurt anyone. Some nights, though, things never worked out the way she planned.

The mission tonight? Break into the mansion. Steal a relic. Break out. Collect the money. Simple as that. The plan had worked before.

It wasn't working tonight.

Wearing a small backpack, Raja crouched over the security guard and checked his GPS monitor. Four additional guards were scattered around the home. Two blocked her path to the library on the second floor. She had to move fast.

As she pulled her war quoit from the guard's throat, it made a soft wet sound. She had inherited the Sikh throwing weapon, a deadly but invaluable heirloom, from her grandfather. Wiping blood from the flat stainless-steel disk, she carefully folded the razor-sharp teeth inside the outer rim. Glancing down the first-floor hallway, she snapped the war quoit around her wrist like a brace-let.

In her early twenties, she wore black from head to toe with a fitted long-sleeved crewneck T-shirt, skintight leggings for easy mobility, and ankle socks paired with low-top Gucci sneakers. Her long black hair was pulled back in a tight ballerina-like bun and wrapped in the darkest scarf she could find in her wardrobe.

Raja crept inside the thousand-square-foot vaulted room, staying in the shadows. The mansion hinted at the triumph of the Bulgarian *mafiya*. During its reign, a surge of drug smuggling, prostitution, and racketeering had swept over the country after the collapse of the former Soviet government. Few benefited more from *mafiya* corruption than Georgi Paskalev.

He had been an Olympic wrestler when freedom had arrived in the former Eastern Bloc. As a down-and-out athlete, Paskalev had cut a deal with corrupt government officials who created insurance and security groups as a cover for illicit activity. When the Bulgarian government shut down the *mafiya* in the early twenty-first century, Paskalev found himself out of business, but not out of money. He was allowed to keep his mansion on the slopes of Mount Vitosha, a towering range on the outskirts of Sofia. When Paskalev died a few years ago, his son Nikola inherited everything.

Nikola Paskalev was a legitimate businessman with a high-end boutique on Vitosha Boulevard. Wealthy Bulgarians flocked to his store and so did foreigners like Raja's own family. Two years ago, in fact, she had traveled with her mother, Harita Raja, from Chandigarh in northern India to purchase jewelry from Paskalev.

Would the man recognize her tonight?

Not an issue. Raja didn't intend to be seen.

She had planned to take the stairs, but the patrolling guard had changed her strategy. She found another way. A two-story waterfall framed the south wall. Raja sprinted toward it.

Up close now, she saw the wall was an enormous slab of Vratsa marble. Mined from a local quarry, its gray surface was neither polished nor smooth, but marked with rough-hewn pockets. The marble wall reflected the personalities of the corrupt wrestler and his son—imposing and coarse, but with a hint of sophistication.

Looking up, she spied a balcony trimmed with wooden railing. Above it, a horizontal pole was anchored to the wall. Ivy encircled the decorative iron fixture. She needed to search up there.

Glancing at the splashing falls, she noticed water did not touch a margin of wall beneath the balcony. She started climbing.

Halfway up the marble wall, she heard a door close across the room. Snapping her head around, Raja glanced back. Beneath her, Paskalev's guard strolled past the waterfall, heading toward a fireplace. With water roaring close to her ear, she almost hadn't heard him. She remained motionless on the wall, poised like a spider on her web.

Down below, the guard called out a name. He was searching for someone named Stepan. Raja assumed that was the security guard with the slashed throat.

She held her breath, suspended against the wall. Her arm and leg muscles quivered. The guard ran his flashlight beam along the walls. Crossing the water, the shaft of light darted a meter or so beneath her foot. He chattered into his walkie-talkie, then took his time leaving the room. Raja began climbing again. Sooner or later, she knew, the guards would discover Stepan's body.

———◆———

Nikola Paskalev was a proud Bulgarian. Refined tapestries, historical emblems, and ornate crests reflected his patriotic fervor. The upper floor of his mansion displayed even greater elegance than anything downstairs. Priceless artwork and antique furniture adorned every room.

Making her way down the hallway, Raja peeked inside a library graced with custom bookshelves. She covered her mouth in surprise. *He's here.* Reading a newspaper, Paskalev reclined behind a carved mahogany desk. Smoke curled around his wavy brown hair as he tapped cigar ash into a tray.

Back in his prime as an Olympic wrestler, Georgi Paskalev had measured in at six foot two with a girth that put him north of 250 pounds. Watching now, she could tell Nikola Paskalev had another two inches and an additional hundred pounds on his father.

Finding Paskalev here put her in a bad mood. A century before, his great-grandfather had collected relics from the Roman Empire. She spied an oval box on his desk. Maybe it contained a section from a Roman helmet.

Footsteps plodded in the hallway.

Raja suspected a guard, coming to warn about Stepan.

She opened the door to a nearby room and ducked inside. Raja formulated the plan in her head, thinking through alternatives. She had to take out the guard before bursting into the library, an action requiring more force than her ancestral bracelet could provide. Reaching into her leg holster, she brought out a Beretta PX4. Despite India's strict gun laws, she had learned to shoot a firearm by age six.

Raja braced herself against the door, ready to hit the guard. She made a quick look into the hallway. The footsteps had not come from security personnel as she had suspected. Instead, a woman lingered outside the library door.

Paskalev's wife, Raja quickly realized.

As a family friend, Simona Bakalova had married Nikola Paskalev while both were in their early twenties. She was short and squat, her lifeless hair matching her shapeless gray dress. Balling her hands into fists, she stomped into the library.

"Nikola!" she yelled. She rattled a few more words, some of which Raja identified as profanity. She spoke fast, but there was no mistaking her emphasis on the Bulgarian word for *whore*.

Okay. Wow.

Georgi Paskalev had been passionate about collecting antiquities. His son was more interested in collecting mistresses. Judging from Simona's tone, she had discovered her husband's indiscretion. Nikola Paskalev had been cheating with a woman half his age, a former Miss Bulgaria who had competed in the Miss World Pageant. Raja knew all about this cheating prick.

Careful to remain hidden, she moved beside the door. She held steady on the gun, keeping it in a two-handed grip.

Paskalev waved his arms, his face turning red and purple in full bluster, a bull of a man. He slammed his fist against the desk. Simona responded with a dramatic scream.

Raja checked her watch. Bulgaria family drama wasn't on her schedule. It was only a matter of time before a guard discovered Stepan's body. In other words, only a matter of time before all hell broke loose in here.

Like it hadn't already.

The argument escalated. Simona slapped her husband's face. Paskalev erupted in a towering rage. He grabbed his wife's wrists and yanked her across the desk. With the back of his hand, he slapped her cheek. Blood spurted over her lips.

Okay. Enough.

Raja stepped inside the door and raised the Beretta. Time to pit her black angel against Paskalev's bulk.

The phone rang.

Holding Simona's throat, Paskalev glanced at it. He shoved his wife off the desk.

Raja winced as the woman hit the floor, then pulled back, moving into shadows outside the library.

Paskalev answered the call. He said Stepan's name. They had discovered the guard's body.

Terrific.

Nikola Paskalev slammed down the phone. He told his wife about an intruder, urging her to hurry to the safe room.

Dropping back, Raja slipped into a nearby room. Perfect timing because Paskalev hurried past the door, wrenching his wife's arm as she sobbed.

After they passed, she stepped back into the hallway. As they headed for the stairs, she brought out the Beretta. For fun, Raja posed both arms straight out from her body, capturing the big man in her sight. It would be easy to take a kill shot right now, nail the guy in the head. She had not been hired to murder Paskalev.

Still . . .

Chapter 8

John Brynstone was standing in front of a massive door embedded in the cave wall. It was locked. And it was blue.

"Why blue?" Véronique asked.

"Maybe to scare off evil spirits."

"I didn't realize blue had such power."

"Going back to ancient Egypt, people believed the color could ward off evil," Brynstone explained. "Some speculate that's the reason pharaohs often wore blue. After the rise of Christianity, the color became associated with the Virgin Mary and heaven." He studied the door. "They painted it blue for a reason. Maybe something in here needed protection."

Brynstone brought out the golden key that he had discovered inside the skull and lifted it into the light of his headlamp. It had an oval top, cast in the shape of an eye. He slid the key into the lock beneath the doorknob. The door clicked open.

"Allow me." On impulse, Véronique pushed open the blue door on rusty hinges, unconcerned about possible danger waiting on the other side.

A big and dusky parking garage stood adjacent to Shayna's school, seemingly empty. Cori Cassidy patted the frightened girl clinging to her waist. Passing a row of cars, she held out the keychain Shayna had stolen from the school researcher's office. Cori clicked the power-lock button. A silver BMW sedan parked against the back wall of the garage honked in response and its lights flashed.

Running to it, she opened the rear door. The girl scrambled onto the backseat. Cori hurried around and climbed in the driver's side door.

She had to keep her cool and stay in control. Graduate students were used to stress and pressure, but nothing like this. She wasn't alone in this situation. Shayna Brynstone depended on her.

Cori glanced at the keychain in her hand. "Shay, what's that researcher's name? The one who owns this car?"

"Dr. Resnick."

"Know where she lives?"

"Um, nope. Sorry."

Cori opened the glove compartment. She pulled out the registration and saw a Park Avenue address.

"Dr. Resnick married a businessman. She misses him 'cause he's in Japan. She was gonna pick him up from the airplane after school. I don't know where they live."

"That's okay," Cori said, smiling. "I do."

"This thing won't work. The seat belt won't buckle me right."

Cori glanced in the rearview mirror. She pivoted with a stretch to reach Shay's seat belt then decided it was faster just to climb out and buckle the child.

Moving outside, she opened the rear passenger door and reached for the belt. She heard footsteps and saw a man enter the parking garage. He wore a dark suit like the guys who had shot Kaylyn Brynstone, and he looked to be in his late twenties, but his thick black hair was scored with a white streak above his forehead. Turning his head slowly, he scanned the vehicles. Cori panicked when she spied a gun in his hand. If she climbed back in and started the Beemer now, the engine noise would rumble throughout the garage and the guy would hear. Even if she could drive past him, he could fire several shots before she made it to the exit. She didn't think she could make a move like that.

The man dropped down to the floor. It looked like he was searching beneath a car in the next row.

With the door already open, Cori took Shay's chin in her hand. She raised her finger to her lips. "Shh."

The little girl got the message.

"Follow me. Be super quiet."

The child nodded.

Cori eased the car door closed. She slid along the trunk, bringing the girl along as they edged around the BMW. The gunman didn't hear, but he still headed their direction.

Cori and Shayna crawled along the back wall, trying to stay out of sight. The man came closer, his footsteps growing louder on the cement floor. Cori couldn't see him. He huffed like he was disgusted. Or angry.

Crouching behind a yellow car with Shayna, Cori brought out her cell and turned off the ringer. A call would make too much noise, so she decided to text instead. She frowned as she stared at the touch-screen display. No service.

Seriously?

Putting away the phone, Cori dipped her head toward the concrete floor to look beneath a dented Nissan Sentra. Peering around the tires, she saw the man's shoes. He pivoted, like he was noticing someone behind him.

"Any luck?" a voice called.

"Keep it down, okay?" the man with the white streak urged. "Stop waving that gun."

Cori bit hard on her lip. *Great*. Now they were trapped in here with two killers.

"Can't believe this bullshit," the second man said. "They gotta be here somewhere. You see 'em yet?"

"Think I'd be standing here holding my dick if I did?"

"What about the BMW? That one there. See what I mean? Door's open a little."

Cori smothered a breath.

"So what? Somebody forgot to close it."

"In New York City?"

"Big deal. What're you doing?"

"Slashing the tires. Just in case it's their car."

Her shoulders sagged. Taking a chance on the distraction, Cori tugged on Shayna's hand. Crouching, she pulled the child to the next vehicle. As they eased past the step bumper of an older Chevy Blazer, the hitch ball caught the girl's shirt. Two or three stitches ripped apart. Shayna unhooked the fabric and looked up, fear sparkling in her eyes. Taking a deep breath, Cori led Shayna around the back of another vehicle.

"Say we lose that little girl. Know how screwed we'll be?"

"Shut up that talk. We'll find her."

"Yeah? Not so far we ain't."

"Do us both a favor. Be cool and keep looking."

Cori spied a metal door at the far end of the garage. If they could sneak around a couple more cars then maybe they could escape through that door. Or maybe not. Two more cars and they would be at the exit.

White Streak guy was getting closer. He wasn't far away now. If they made a move for the door, he'd hear. Shayna clutched Cori's hand, the child's soft fingers squeezing tight.

One more car to go. An Audi compact.

"We're running out of time," White Streak said.

Cori and Shayna squeezed around the car at the end. The driver had parked the vehicle close to the wall. It was a tighter squeeze than the others, but they made it to the door. Staying low, she ran her arm around the child, hugging her.

"Hey, man, how about that door? You check it?"

"What door?"

"One over there."

They were talking about the door beside the Audi. Could she and the girl sneak out before the men checked? She couldn't risk opening it without them hearing. Cori was in good shape. She could outrun the men, but what about Shayna? No way she could beat their size and speed. If she carried the child, they wouldn't stand a chance.

A new and terrible thought hit her. What if the door was locked?

She pressed Shayna against her chest. She wanted to be brave for the kid. So far, she wasn't succeeding.

"Think they went out that door?"

"Worth a shot," the second man said.

"I'm on it."

Cori nudged Shayna, moving her back from the door toward the black Audi. White Streak was walking again, coming closer. In a near panic, Cori motioned and the child joined her. They had no choice but to crawl under the vehicle. Moving to the ground, they slithered beneath the car, feeling the coarse bite of cement as it scraped their forearms.

As the gunman approached the Audi, his black shoe moved close to Cori's face, only inches away.

Without warning, the door burst open, bringing a splash of sunlight into the dark garage. A man walked in from the street.

Cori bristled with fear. Now there were three.

"How you doin'?" White Streak asked. His voice sounded strained.

"Do I know you?"

The words gave Cori hope. The new guy wasn't one of them. Still, what could he do to help? He wasn't a cop. Plus, White Streak was armed.

Stomach flat on the concrete, Cori twisted her head for a better look. The man from outside walked toward the Audi. He moved toward the driver's side of the vehicle. She heard keys jangle.

Oh, God, no.

They were hiding beneath his car. The man was going to climb in the Audi and drive away, exposing them. The killers would discover her and Shayna on the ground.

The little girl closed her eyes, waiting with apprehension.

"Hey, they're calling us back," White Streak's partner shouted across the parking garage. "We need to roll. Now."

Ignoring him, White Streak opened the door. He took a quick look outside. At the same time, the driver's-side door opened. The guy from the street climbed inside the Audi.

The engine started, making the vehicle's steel belly rumble above them. The deafening roar caused Shay to cover her ears. The driver shifted and the car lurched ahead.

Why is this happening?

Just as quickly, the man slammed on the brakes, jolting the Audi. He wasn't going anywhere.

Wait. What?

She saw now. The gunman had walked away from the door. He was standing in front of the Audi. Cori could see the gloss on his shoes. He stopped, it had seemed, for a stare-down match with the driver. The man in the Audi honked his horn. Beneath the chassis, the sound amplified to an earsplitting blast.

It was too much for Shayna.

The little girl rolled away, moving between frozen tires and out from under the idling car. Cori grabbed to pull her back, but it was too late. Shayna rolled out of reach.

White Streak didn't see her. Bored with the confrontation, he had sprinted to join the other guy.

The driver released the brake and pulled forward. Cori pressed her body flat against the concrete as the Audi whooshed over her body and turned away from the parking spot, leaving her behind as the car squealed past the two men.

She made it to her feet and scrambled to catch Shayna in her arms. Cori's heart lifted with happiness and relief as they hugged. She pulled the girl beside the next closest car, seeking cover until she was certain the men were gone.

Out on the sidewalk, Cori scanned the face of every person she passed. Her white shirt was blackened from crawling under the car. She looked suspicious and she knew it. Her thinking was jumbled and her emotions were coiled.

Shayna seemed dazed. She had to be in shock. Cori had seen Kaylyn get hit and she had seen blood, but was the woman still alive? She wished she knew.

Cori thought about finding a police officer, but wondered how she would explain everything that had happened. She decided to contact John Brynstone first.

At an intersection, they crossed in front of a dark-colored van. Wearing sunglasses, the driver had his window down and his arm hanging out. He watched them as he waited for the light to change. He was riding with a woman dressed in a green blouse. She was talking on her cell. They didn't look like the team who had almost kidnapped Shayna. Not a threat, she decided.

As they reached the sidewalk, Shayna said, "Can you tell me about the bad thing that happened outside my school?"

"I'm not sure myself. We'll go somewhere and talk." Cori knelt, coming eye to eye with the girl. "Shayna, I need to call your dad."

She brightened. "Daddy? He's on a trip. Really far away. I don't think my mommy likes him anymore. That makes me sad because I love my daddy."

"I know your daddy loves you, too. Listen, it's really important I talk to him. Do you know his number?"

Shayna recited it for her.

Years before, Baltimore police had linked Cori to twin homicides. Brynstone had given her good advice at the time. She trusted him and wanted to consult him before calling the police.

Cori dialed John Brynstone's number. It rang until voice mail picked up. Anxiety filled her in that moment, but it was a comfort hearing his voice on the outgoing message. She left a hurried message with her number, not wanting to get into details in public and in front of Shayna.

After making the call, she remembered the phone she had taken from the dead man in the car outside the school, and she relived the sight of his blood-spattered body. It made her break out in a shiver.

Cori checked the phone, looking for the name of the bald guy. Nothing about him. She remembered he had been talking to someone about her, which gave her an idea. Taking a deep breath, she called the last number the man had dialed, but got only a busy signal. She hung up.

If they knew her name, then they knew where she lived. Cori decided it made sense right now to hide out at the Resnick home, to go there and think.

She had to get off the street.

Chapter 9

New York City
3:59 p.m.

It wasn't supposed to play out like this. Stephen Angelilli shuffled in his seat as the CIA helicopter buzzed above the Manhattan skyline. As the lead officer on Operation Red Opera, he was sweating the situation with Shayna Brynstone.

Prior to joining the CIA, Angelilli had spent a decade with the New York Police Department, including five years as a SWAT officer for the Emergency Service Unit. He knew the city well. Glancing out the window, he shouted into his headset mic, "Give me a status update, Midnight."

Patrick Langston, code name Midnight, was Angelilli's man on the ground. He was stationed outside the Brandonstein Center for Gifted Children.

After Midnight gave a briefing, Angelilli asked, "Is Sparta still in his car?"

"Affirmative, Scarecrow. He's been hit."

Jason "Sparta" Drakos was a field operations officer who had been recruited into the CIA after graduating from American University with a degree in foreign affairs. Angelilli liked the kid.

"Details," he demanded.

"We have a visual from inside his car, sir." Midnight paused. "Sparta is dead."

Angelilli cringed.

"What did Sparta report at his last check-in?"

"He said Cori Cassidy was sighted on the corner. After that, all hell broke loose."

"Where is Wonderland?" Angelilli asked, using the operation name for Shayna Brynstone.

"Wonderland has been abducted, sir. The van I told you about? It pulled outside the Brandonstein school. Three unidentifieds involved. All men. We believe two were injured during a firefight. They were loaded into the van and taken away."

"Where are they?"

"Unknown at this time, sir. This thing caught us off guard."

Angelilli fumed. Under his direction, Operation Red Opera ran surveillance on Shayna Brynstone. He had surveilled her every day for the last several years. This operation was a pet project for CIA Director Mark McKibbon. Angelilli knew he better not screw it up.

"I want answers, Midnight. I need to know who abducted Wonderland."

Bedford, Massachusetts
4:01 p.m.

Viktor Nebola climbed out of his oxford-blue Arnage, a favorite because it was one of the Final Series models Bentley had manu-factured before ceasing production. On the sedan's opposite side, Erich Metzger stepped out. He walked with Nebola to the private jet waiting at Hanscom Field. Nebola loosened his tie as he hur-ried up the ramp, a phone pressed to his ear.

"You still at the school?" he demanded.

"Negative, but we tore up the place," Markus Tanzer answered. "The little girl ran inside with a woman."

"A woman?"

"We have now identified her as Cori Cassidy."

"Not with her mother?"

"Actually, sir, Kaylyn Brynstone is dead."

"That damn well complicates things," Nebola said with an annoyed breath, "but not as much as losing Shayna Brynstone."

"I'm telling you, sir, we searched the place upside down. We'll find them."

Inside the jet, Nebola slid into a leather club chair. Metzger took a seat across from him. The assassin wore a cold grin, like nothing gave him greater pleasure than eavesdropping on this conversation.

"I'm on my way," Nebola barked. "Give me an update the minute you hear something."

"You're flying here?" Tanzer sounded surprised.

"As we speak," he barked. "If you wanna hang on to your pathetic little ballsack, you better find Shayna Brynstone before I arrive."

Nebola ended the call.

He studied the assassin. The reptilian smirk lingered on Metzger's face.

"My situation seems to amuse you."

"*Ja,*" Metzger answered, his flat wintry eyes somehow twinkling. "I warned you. Remember what I said? When you face John Brynstone and his family, you're in for more than a fight. You're in for a war."

Chapter 10

The cavern was breathtaking.

Moving past the blue door, Brynstone and Véronique stared at the natural grandeur before them. The arched ceiling had an unmistakable majesty, giving it the look of a cathedral hewn and shaped by nature's hand.

Walking a little farther in, they found something more.

Centered beneath curving rock, a standing cross was cast in gloomy silhouette. The thing was massive, reaching fifteen feet in height. He admired the effort it must have taken to transport and assemble the cross down in this cave.

He took a better look.

Something didn't seem right.

Moving nearer, he saw that the crossbeams hadn't been formed from wood alone. The lines were not smooth or uniform, but bumpy and misshapen. His headlamp beam danced across the irregular contours of the cross. That's when he made the discovery.

The cross was made of human bodies.

Lashed together, the cadavers of more than one hundred men formed the outline of the cross. Thick leather cords gripped each body against the crossbeams. The vacuum-like atmosphere in the chamber had produced a spontaneous mummified state, preserving

the corpses. Their tattered uniforms, now dingy white, were emblazoned with a symbol: a green Maltese cross. He recognized it as the
Order of Saint Lazarus.

Coming closer, Brynstone studied the faces of the dead knights.
The cross gave the look of a sculpture composed from wasted flesh
and pitted skulls, like some kind of surreal and terrible art. The
arms of the Lazar brethren were as thin as broomsticks, their skin
scored with soft-tissue infection. Their hands and feet looked
swollen and ulcerated. Fingers and toes had decayed long ago into
eroded stumps.

Véronique moved alongside him, her shoulder nudging his
arm. "What happened? Why are they like that?"

"Leprosy."

During the Crusades of the eleventh century, a small army of
Templar and Hospitaller Knights had contracted leprosy. They later
banded together to create the Order of Saint Lazarus of Jerusalem.
Lazar Knights had belonged to an order of chivalry dedicated to
the protection of the Christian faith, ranking among the less familiar orders of the Latin Kingdom of Jerusalem.

"Why are they down here?" Véronique asked.

"Because they were outcasts."

As early as the fourth century, Brynstone explained, Europe
played host to hospitals designated for the treatment of leprosy.
For centuries, it had been a disease on the move, affecting everyone from the emperor Constantine to a legion of crusading knights.
Afflicted knights like the ones in this cavern contributed to the
spread of leprosy throughout Europe. Often, stereotypes intermin-
gled with paranoia and led to oppression.

In 1321, lepers had been accused of dipping their poisoned
hands into public fountains and wells to better spread their disease across the Kingdom of France. It counted as an early version of biological warfare, but one based more in rumor than fact.

Still, the stories inspired panic. In response to the prejudice, the spiritual order of Lazarus had been created to comfort and support leper knights. At times, their mission placed them at odds with the church. In an aggressive move, Pope Innocent VIII had suppressed the Lazar Order a century after the end of the Crusades. Like the men in this cave, leper knights were literally driven underground.

In some cases, insanity followed the disease as lepers were isolated and shunned from society. Housing them in caves seemed justified because it was believed that shelter protected them from the moon. A medieval physician named Paracelsus had believed that the phases of the moon could lead to madness. Insanity became associated with moonstruck behavior. Drawing on inspiration from Luna, the Roman goddess of the moon, the disease of madness later became known as *lunacy*.

Leprosy treatments seemed even less enlightened than the ones for lunacy. In lairs such as this one, people tried desperate methods to banish the wasting disease. Some remedies were based on the alleged healing properties of blood. It was an idea dating back to Rome when Constantine the Great attempted to cure his leprosy by bathing in the heart blood of a virgin.

Brynstone walked around the human cross, considering every gnarled face and disease-ridden limb. The leprosy bacillus had ravaged the victims in this cavern, leaving facial disfigurement and bone lesions. The leper knights had been lashed together to form a towering cross, perhaps not of their own free will.

Were they hiding part of the Roman helmet? He had to find out. Brynstone opened his knife.

"What are you doing?" Véronique asked.

"Ruining a treasure. Sometimes, it's the only way to find a greater one."

"You think this cross is a treasure?"

"Don't you?"

He slashed a leather band, then grabbed it and tugged. Four bodies cascaded to the floor. Stepping over them, he moved around the cross, unwinding the thick band as if unwrapping ribbon from a massive present. More bodies dropped, knight after knight hitting the ground. He kept going, pulling on the band and unraveling diseased cadavers as he circled beneath the cross. Two and three at a time plummeted as they accumulated in a growing mound of Lazar brethren.

He jerked on another leather band, stripping men from the crossbeams. He pulled on still another to unwind bodies trapped on the high vertical beam. As leper knights dropped from this height, cadavers and skeletons thudded against stone, their brittle bodies cracking apart as they struck the floor. Giving a final yank, he liberated the remaining bodies. The leather band snapped free from the cross.

"I must tell you," Véronique confessed, "that is the most disturbing thing I have ever seen."

"Spend more time with me," Brynstone said, "and you won't be able to say that."

Reaching under the arm of one knight, he dragged the corpse away from the cross. The man showed signs of tuberculoid leprosy, leaving him with a clawlike hand. Leprosy had corroded his ear and cheek. Another knight's long red hair was preserved, along with his thin moustache and forked goatee. Brynstone inspected the body.

"How can you touch them?" Véronique asked.

"I've touched worse things." He studied the knight. "I'm not certain this man had leprosy. He might have suffered from porphyria."

"A disease?"

"Group of disorders, actually. Rare and genetic. People with porphyria get a buildup of tissue-destructive chemicals called porphyrins in their bodies. Due to an enzyme deficiency, porphyrins are not incorporated into hemoglobin, the oxygen-carrying agent in red blood cells. As a result, porphyrins start to accumulate in the tissues. A blood pigment called heme—"

"You lost me at *porphyrins*."

"Yeah? Well, trust me. It can be a brutal disease."

"But it affects skin? Like leprosy?"

"Not in the same way. Photosensitivity is a problem. Exposure to sunlight can cause blistering, scarring, and discoloration. Even severe disfigurement. You'd want to avoid sunshine." Brynstone looked around. "If this guy had porphyria, living in a cave would be a pretty good idea."

"Can it make you go mad? Would he have been considered a lunatic like the others?"

"Types of porphyria have been linked to everything from depression and mania to hallucinations and paranoia." He thought about something and it must have showed on his face.

"What?" she asked.

"Some people think porphyria gave rise to legends about vampires. That light sensitivity issue I told you about? It factors in. You know that whole deal about vampires disintegrating in daylight? Obviously that's not true for people with porphyria, but sunlight doesn't do them any favors. The rarest type is congenital erythropoietic porphyria. It can cause the gums to recede, making the teeth look larger, especially the maxillary canines. Supposedly, it makes our cuspids look even more like fangs."

She glanced at the redheaded knight. "You really think he had porphyria, not leprosy?"

"Just a guess. Couldn't be certain without testing."

It was a guess, but one he had thought about before coming down here. Brynstone remembered what Wurm had told him before coming to Paris. He had described an entry in the journal from the woman in the fourteenth century. In one section, Jeanneton de Paris mentioned that she had cared for lepers in 1333. She mentioned several by name, including a man named Lost John. Her description of him sounded more like porphyria than leprosy. Was this man Lost John?

While caring for lepers, Jeanneton hinted that she had owned a piece of the Roman helmet. The rest of the story remained murky. However, in her journal, she made it sound like a cross would lead to the helmet piece. Back while searching the coffin above, he was looking for a small cross like on a rosary. Not a massive one like he had found down here.

Brynstone continued to clear the dead, dragging them from the pile of corpses surrounding the cross. Reluctantly, Véronique helped, but she couldn't hide her disgust.

"This better be worth the trouble."

"Can't guarantee anything. Including getting out of here."

"I am astonished this is beneath Père Lachaise. I wonder if the men who founded it knew about the cavern."

"You're the cemetery historian, right?"

She nodded. "Someday I hope to be promoted to *la directrice du crématorium*."

"Maybe the founders designed the cemetery to conceal this cavern. That's my private hypothesis."

"It's possible," she said, thinking it over. "The land has a rich history. In the twelfth century, it was owned by the bishop of Paris and was known as Champ l'Eveque, or the Bishop Field. Two centuries later, a hospital dedicated to Saint Lazarus was built on this land. In 1430, a wealthy merchant named Régnault de Wandonne built a mansion on the property. During the seventeenth century, the Jesuits turned it into a convalescence house. That was all before it became a cemetery."

Véronique explained that in 1804, the founders had been criticized for building a cemetery far from the city and so they hit upon a plan to promote Père Lachaise. They dug up famous people from other cemeteries and transported them here. They unearthed the poet La Fontaine and the celebrated playwright Molière from their initial resting places and buried them in new graves in this cemetery. Little more than a decade later, they disinterred the medieval star-crossed lovers, Abélard and Héloïse, and enshrined their remains in an impressive tomb at Père Lachaise.

This hadn't been a new idea. Reburials of everyone from Copernicus to Descartes had gained attention before the founding of this cemetery. The whole thing had been a publicity stunt, but one that had paid off, bringing recognition and acclaim to Père Lachaise. Before long, requests flooded in as people hungered to be buried alongside the renowned dead, basking in their reflected glory. Even back then, the status of a celebrity had marketing power.

Brynstone believed that the cemetery founders had devised a way to cover up the secret they were looking at now, buried deep beneath the earth. Although not as famous as Molière and the others, the descendant of Joan of Arc was one of the first to be moved from his original burial spot. Brynstone guessed that the cemetery founders had some connection to the Order of Saint Lazarus and knew about this cave chamber. Following their plan, the d'Arc corpse had been buried above the entrance, concealing this cavern from the world.

After clearing the area around the cross, Brynstone grabbed its base. He struggled, but managed to lift the heavy beam inside its deep pivot.

"Help me balance it," he grunted.

Véronique grabbed the cross and helped guide it. The beam came out fast and they nearly dropped the thing. Lowering it to the floor, they stood back and caught their breath. She dusted her hands.

He knelt beside the cross, examining its oak surface and running his gloved hand along the grain. This side contained no secrets.

"Flip it," he said.

They raised the cross on one side, then turned it. Starting at opposite ends, they pored over its surface, exploring every crevice and pit.

Nothing seemed relevant.

"It's a waste of time," she announced.

He arched an eyebrow. "Was there something else you were going to do?"

"I'd like to escape this place, for one."

"Good luck doing that by yourself."

Brynstone glanced at the hundred leper knights. Dragged away now, their bodies formed a mummified ring around the cross. It got him to thinking. In the third century, an Egyptian theologian named Origen had researched Golgotha, a hill outside of Jerusalem where Jesus Christ was allegedly crucified. According to Origen, Golgotha also marked the site of Adam's burial. His claim inspired generations of artists to paint an image of a skull at the base of the cross.

"Later legends claimed," he told Véronique, "that a great treasure could be found beneath the cross of a martyr. Maybe the Lazar brethren followed that tradition."

He dipped his hand into the small crater that had housed the cross and started digging. In the darkness, something scrambled across his wrist. He flicked his fingers and three albino spiders flew into the air.

Véronique made a startled squeak. The creatures scrambled away on spindly white legs.

"Was the helmet piece beneath the cross?"

"Nothing down there but spiders."

Not giving up, he studied the circle of mummified knights. He walked along the ring stacked three bodies high. He paused beside the redhead with the forked goatee. The man he suspected might be Lost John. Kneeling, he lifted the man's arm, rolling him onto his back. This knight was one of a hundred lashed to a fifteen-foot cross, but something made him different.

It wasn't just the porphyria. In a cavern with knights of Saint Lazarus of Jerusalem, this knight belonged to a different order, bearing a white Maltese cross on his black mantle. He was a knight in the Sovereign Military Hospitaller Order of Saint John of Jerusalem. Brynstone didn't know why a Hospitaller was down here in a cave full of Lazar Knights. It was uncommon to have banished knights of different orders in hiding together.

Tyon d'Arc had been a Knight Hospitaller. Was it possible he had entrusted Lost John, a Brother Hospitaller, with the helmet piece?

Brynstone searched the knight. Frisking the corpse, he ran his hand down the withered arm then across the man's chest. His fingers traced over a bumpy metal surface beneath the mantle. He tore back the uniform. Positioned on the knight's chest, a bronze face stared up at Brynstone. It was the facemask from the Roman helmet.

He smiled. It was right there. *As easy as that.*

Crafted in the first century, the mask had once protected a cavalry soldier's face. Stylized and three dimensional, the features lent a human appearance to the mask.

Sculpted lines suggested eyebrows above slit-like eye-holes. Nostril holes had been cut into the metal with the curved impression of a septum connecting the raised nose to a slit for the mouth. Smooth contours around the mouthpiece mimicked the shape of human lips. Centuries of oxidation and corrosion had converted the surface from bronze to copper sulfate, coating the facemask with light green patches and streaks of brick red and black. Brynstone imagined the sight of marching Roman soldiers, all dressed in identical facemasks, their bronze features gleaming in sunlight. In the ancient world, it must have been a menacing spectacle.

He turned the facemask over. Like the neck guard Wurm had shown him in Central Park, a series of bizarre symbols were carved on the inside of the mask.

"*C'est magnifique*," Véronique said, coming over. "May I see it?"

Still kneeling, he handed the facemask to her. "Careful with it."

"That evil woman who shoved me into the grave? She was correct about a Roman artifact after all."

"Maybe she found out from her brother," Brynstone said, rising. "Reece Griffin was a brilliant historian. Years ago, I traveled to Cork, Ireland, to meet with him. It was too late."

"What do you mean?"

"His sister hired a man to murder Reece. Nessa Griffin is dangerous."

"Glad you noticed," a voice called from behind.

Near the open blue door, Nessa Griffin stood with her hands fixed on her hips. Five men moved in behind her. Léon and Kane were armed with FAMAS assault rifles.

"You and my brother are the same, John. Always gettin' in the way." She looked at Véronique. "Give me the mask. Now."

Véronique studied Brynstone.

"Don't," he said in a controlled whisper.

Griffin's men pointed their rifles at her.

Véronique swallowed. Worry colored her expression.

He narrowed his eyes. "Don't do it."

She looked down. Thinking it over, she walked toward them.

Brynstone cursed.

Looking back, she said, "I'm sorry, John."

She opened her hand. Griffin snatched the Roman facemask from Véronique's fingers.

"How'd you find your way down here, Nessa?" he demanded. "The lock beneath the coffin only closes from inside. Unless you have the amulet key."

It didn't make sense. He had pushed the dowel into place, locking the coffin's trapdoor. The only way to open it was with the key.

Griffin gave an icy smile. "Véronique can answer."

The French woman shrugged. "Remember when we used the lever to lock the coffin door from down here? You left me behind for a moment as you walked down the stairs to explore the cavern."

Brynstone smoldered at the betrayal. "While I was gone, you released the dowel for Griffin. You knew she'd figure out to follow us down here. Don't you know what a bad idea it is to work for her?"

Véronique sashayed over to him, innocent but sexy with hands interlaced behind her butt.

"You must admit," she said, reaching in his pocket and removing the eye key. "We had a lovely adventure, John. Perhaps, just perhaps, we will do it again sometime."

Véronique kissed his cheek, leaving a faint trace of moisture on his skin as she turned to join the others.

"I'm afraid this will be the final adventure for Dr. Brynstone," Griffin said. "He loves bones and mummies. The leper knights will keep him company down here for the rest of his short life."

"Take their company over yours any day, Nessa."

She laughed. "When you get to hell, John, say hello to my brother."

As Véronique followed Griffin through the doorway, Brynstone sized up the men. He thought about making a move. Earlier in the night, he had faced off against Léon and Kane and a third man in the cemetery. Both guys were decent fighters, and like before, their numbers and weapons favored them in a big way. He switched to thinking about an escape plan.

Torn Kane closed the door, sealing Brynstone in with the leper knights. The lock clicked into place.

Now alone, Brynstone rushed to the cross. It was his best hope of getting out alive.

Chapter 11

Nikola Paskalev had vacated his office, leaving it a mess. The big man had shoved his wife around the desk, and now the carpet was littered with a spill of papers. Rashmi Raja pushed them aside and discovered the oval box on the floor. She opened it, but found only Cuban cigars. She snapped one in half in frustration.

I should have shot Paskalev after all.

Raja moved around the room, going from bookshelf to bookshelf, exploring every table. Where had he hidden the relic? She dropped to her knees and searched desk drawers. Two were locked. She opened a third and found a necklace box from Paskalev's boutique on Vitosha Boulevard. She popped the lid and marveled at a teardrop-shaped blue diamond haloed by smaller clear diamonds on a delicate gold chain. It wasn't what she had come for, but she pocketed the necklace anyway.

"Welcome to my home."

At the sound of the words, Raja jolted back in shock. She peered over the desk. Paskalev stood in the doorway of his study, grinning.

"I was told an intruder had invaded my house," his voice boomed. "I was taken to the safe room. There, I can watch security cameras." He pointed to a small camera mounted on a branch of a decorative tree. "When I saw that my unexpected guest was nothing more than a girl, I decided to greet you myself."

"You caught me," she admitted, moving to her feet. "Now what?"

He walked into the room, studying her. His tenor shifted from amusement to flirtation. "Others have broken into my home, but never before have I seen such a beautiful intruder."

Paskalev came over and pulled the silk scarf from her head, freeing sleek black hair to spill around her shoulders. He examined the scarf, noting the white Hermès Paris logo.

"You have exceptional taste for a common thief." He looked down at her. "And gorgeous skin." He stepped closer. "Did you come here for my money? Or did you come for me?"

"Your father owned a Roman relic. He stored it in a glass box."

He rumbled with laughter and tossed the scarf at her. "You bypassed security and killed one of my men, all so you could get your hands on that thing?"

"Where is it?"

Paskalev walked to a bookshelf. He pressed on a notch in the wood panel and a recessed drawer popped open. Removing a rectangular glass container, he held it out for her inspection. The box stored a curving piece of aged metal.

"Is this what you wish to steal?" he asked. "My father cherished it, God knows why. In all honesty, I'd forgotten about this thing. I'm told it was part of an old helmet."

"It's a cheek guard," she answered. "At one time, it protected a cavalry soldier's face during battle."

He gave an indifferent look. "It's been in my family longer than I care to remember."

Raja held out her gloved hand. "Give it to me."

Another grin. "I could be compelled to sell if the price were right."

"How much?"

With a wolf's stare, his eyes made close measure of her body.

"I don't want your money."

She walked to him. Reaching up, she traced her fingers along his round cheek and snared his neck, pulling him down to her. A whiff of acrid breath hit her nostrils. *Nauseating.* Finding courage, she kissed the big scary man. His meaty hand closed on her breast.

Raja shoved away from him.

"First," she said with a pout, "the Roman cheek guard."

He studied her before handing over the box.

She rotated it, making certain the helmet piece was authentic. Designed to curve around the cheekbone and down to the chin, the shield featured raised contours that formed a stylized impression of a human ear. At one time, Roman warriors attached a cheek guard like this one to an Imperial Gallic helmet.

A business card was inside the glass container, trapped against the cheek guard. She tilted the box and read the name on the card.

"Math McHardy?"

"He wished to purchase it from my father long ago. You're not the only one interested in Roman helmets, you know."

"Why did he want it?"

"Symbols are engraved on the inside. He thought he could decode them."

"Did he?"

"He never saw it. Mr. McHardy offered a great sum of money, but my father refused. He said the man was psychotic."

"Was he?"

"How should I know?" He smirked. "You have what you want. Now it is my turn."

She placed the glass container in her pack. Glancing at the camera on the tree branch, she said, "Take me somewhere private.

I don't want your depraved men watching with their little cameras."

"Why don't we go—"

"The balcony overlooking the waterfall," she interrupted.

"You'll make love to me on the balcony?"

"I'll do what I must to leave here with the relic. But I do not wish to be seen doing it."

"But what if my wife catches us?"

"You don't seem like a man who wastes much time thinking about his wife."

She headed for the library door.

Paskalev followed.

As they walked the long hallway, his hand glided down her butt, surveying the curve in her black leggings. She didn't flinch. She wouldn't give him the satisfaction. Past the view of cameras, she glanced around to make certain security guards were nowhere around.

Now. She had to act now.

She blasted into a full sprint, running ahead of him.

Footsteps pounded loud as he chased after her. He chortled, the man still thinking this was a game. Rumbling down the hallway, Paskalev was closing in. He was fast for a big man, faster than she had expected. She focused on the decorative iron pole ahead, the one protruding from the wall at the edge of the balcony. The one adorned with curls of ivy.

He was close behind, ready to lunge. She had to time her next move with precision. Years before, she had trained as a gymnast. She never guessed it would help in her new line of work.

Raja jumped and grabbed the iron pole above the balcony. Swinging a full 360 degrees around the horizontal pole, she moved in a graceful arc, coming behind Paskalev on the downswing. At the edge of the balcony, he turned as her feet struck him. Paskalev lost his footing and smashed through the wooden railing. Reaching out, he grabbed her ankle.

That wasn't part of her plan.

As his body broke through the balustrade, Paskalev ripped her from the pole. Falling toward the waterfall, his eyes blazed. He held his grip on her ankle. The falls roared in her ears as the sheet of water blurred past them. Paskalev landed hard, his body smashing into the pool at the base of the waterfall. In reflex, he released her foot. When he hit, she flipped off his chest. Somersaulting in air, she landed outside the pool, nearly twisting her ankle. Raja rolled to absorb the impact of her fall. Water splashed her back. Dripping wet, she turned with fists clenched, ready to fight.

Not necessary.

Nikola Paskalev floated on his back in a pool of bloodred water, staring at the ceiling with glazed eyes. Water splashed around him, leaving droplets on his vacant face. She flipped long wet hair from her forehead then reached for the pack to check on the Roman cheek guard.

Raja heard footsteps. She pivoted, ready to face Paskalev's men, but there were no guards to be seen. Instead, a woman stood beside the door. Simona Paskalev had seen her husband crash into the pool at the waterfall's base. Had she called security?

No.

The woman opened the door and pointed outside. Simona Paskalev's mouth was swollen. A reddish welt had risen near her eye. Without blinking, she said, "Thank you."

Rashmi Raja nodded.

She slipped outside, moving into the night.

Chapter 12

New York City
4:05 p.m.

Filthy habit, Stephen Angelilli thought as he ripped a cigarette from his lips. He dropped it on the sidewalk, crushing the ember beneath his shoe. *Good thing I'm cutting back.*

He stood on Madison Avenue, looking down Eighty-Sixth where Shayna Brynstone had been ambushed outside her school. Angelilli was here with one of his men, a CIA officer named Mason Eisermen, who was ending a call on his cell. Another member of his team, Patrick Langston, escorted an NYPD detective toward Angelilli.

Angelilli glanced across the street, thinking about his wife. She had said this morning that her mother was flying in for a last-minute visit. It was nice of her to give a heads-up, but it felt more like a threat than a warning.

He turned to Eisermen. "I gotta talk to this cop coming up with Midnight. While I'm doing that, get in touch with that data scientist I like. The cute one."

"Linda Lund?"

"Her. Someone took the mobile device Jason Drakos was using. Get her on it."

Eisermen turned away to make the call as Langston walked up with the cop.

"This is Detective Leland Aker."

Angelilli extended his hand. "Detective Aker, pleasure."

After a beat, the cop decided on the handshake. "We have a crime scene at an upscale private school," Aker said. "I expected FBI, not CIA."

"Special case," Angelilli answered. "Need to know."

"Last thing I need is your spooks stepping on our toes."

"It's a delicate situation, detective. I get that."

"Sure is. A woman was murdered at the school and so was—"

"No, she wasn't," Angelilli interrupted.

The cop's eyes widened. "What are you talkin' about? She was shot back there. Right inside the school."

"I'm not talking about where she was shot. I'm telling you Kaylyn Brynstone wasn't murdered."

"We loaded her onto the ambulance. They pronounced her dead en route to Lenox Hill."

"We contacted the hospital. Word going out is that Kaylyn Brynstone is in surgery and is expected to make a full recovery."

Aker squinted. "Look, some guys came in here and killed this woman. As far as we can tell, they kidnapped her daughter."

Angelilli watched a news van squeal a hard left off Madison onto Eighty-Sixth.

"That's your version," he said. "That's not what your people will tell the reporters. Instead, you'll report that the child is now with her grandmother."

Angelilli wanted the men who shot Kaylyn Brynstone to think they had failed to kill her. He wanted the hostiles to think the child was safe with her grandmother in the hope they would go there. It was never an easy call going this direction.

"Sorry." The cop crossed his arms. "Can't do it."

"Look, detective, I was NYPD for ten years. Five with SWAT. I know about the emphasis on honor and integrity."

"Yeah? What truck were you assigned to?"

"ESS-2, Upper Manhattan. After leaving the force, I joined the agency. I'd appreciate your cooperation."

"Glad to hear you wore a shield." Aker licked his lip. "Look, it's one thing to withhold details from the media, but I'd rather not lie in front of cameras. Not unless you have a real good reason."

"I'll give you a good reason," Angelilli answered, bringing out his cell phone. He punched in numbers, said a few words, then handed the phone to the cop. "You're going to do it because the guy on this cell is ordering you to do it."

Aker raised the phone to his ear. "Who is this?" Surprise registered on the detective's face as he heard Isaac Starr's rich baritone on the other end. "Mr. Vice President? That r-really y-you, sir?" the man stammered.

Angelilli left him to talk to Vice President Starr and pulled aside Patrick "Midnight" Langston, a twenty-seven-year-old former lieutenant with the Navy SEALs. He was a good kid with a big smile. Funny, but Angelilli wasn't used to seeing a smiling SEAL.

He whispered to Langston, "Is the team ready, Midnight?"

"Affirmative, sir. We're mobilized to search for Wonderland."

"Get on it," Angelilli ordered. "We need to find her immediately."

Airborne over Connecticut
4:06 p.m.

Viktor Nebola interrupted his chess game to take the call. He glanced at the configuration of pieces on the board, then shifted his attention toward the window of the private jet. A landscape of clouds hovered below, canyon after canyon of feathery nothingness. With the cell pressed to his ear, he listened to the caller.

"You're not gonna like this," Markus Tanzer reported on the phone. The strain was evident in his voice.

"Tell me anyway."

Nebola sensed Erich Metzger's gaze. He was seated across the table with arms folded over his chest. The assassin didn't need to say a word—even in silence, his presence filled the cabin. He never seemed to blink, always maintaining a cold stare.

"Know that CIA agent?" Tanzer asked. "Stephen Angelilli? He's on the scene."

"I thought I made myself clear, Mr. Tanzer—I ordered a clean operation. In other words, no federal authorities."

"Yes, sir. You made it clear."

He traced his tongue along his bottom teeth. "Have you recovered Shayna Brynstone?"

"Afraid not, sir."

"If you don't find that little girl, you'll be in a real shitstorm."

Metzger liked the line. He chuckled.

"We're underway, sir."

"Make it happen, Mr. Tanzer. It's critical that you get this right. Do I need to remind you about your father?"

Long pause. "No, sir." Another pause. "Don't hurt him."

"You understood the deal. You deliver Shayna Brynstone and Martin Tanzer will be released."

"I know, sir, but—"

"I'll tell you what," Nebola interrupted. "I'm sending an updated image of your father in fifteen minutes. Bring me the Brynstone girl and you'll make life a lot less painful for your old man. Now get to work."

Nebola ended the call and tossed the cell on the seat beside him.

Metzger studied him. Nebola had known the assassin for years. He had been one of the first to recognize Metzger's potential, and Nebola had given the man some of his first assignments for the Shadow Chapter. Justified or not, he saw himself as a mentor.

"You see now why I work alone." The assassin raised the queen, twirling the black piece once around before advancing her attack across the board.

Nebola glared at the move. An isolated pawn several moves back had changed the complexion of the game and reminded him of Markus Tanzer. A misplayed pawn could wreck a brilliant strategy.

"You don't work alone," Nebola answered, moving his rook. "You have Franka."

He had introduced his niece to Metzger years ago. Nebola could never determine if they were lovers, but Franka had become Metzger's trusted ally and assistant.

Metzger waved his hand. "I do the heavy lifting. For Franka, it's an arson here, an arson there to conceal evidence. She seldom takes on a hit. The sight of blood troubles her."

Nebola frowned at the board, then motioned for an aide to bring over cigars. "At least she's reliable. She completes her assignments without screwing up everything."

"This is true," Metzger answered. "Because Franka understands the consequences if she disappoints me."

Chapter 13

In the darkness, John Brynstone's boot crunched down on a knight's mummified chest. Bringing out his knife, he stood over the fallen cross. He had a plan, but would it work? He sliced the rope, unbinding the horizontal plank from the vertical one. Straining, he dragged the longer beam to the locked blue door. He had to act fast.

Summoning his strength, Brynstone hugged the beam and slammed it into the door like a battering ram, the impact jarring his body. Backing up, he headed for the door again. This time, there was a loud cracking sound as he broke a hole in the door. Drawing in a breath, he made a third run. He smashed the door, rocking it on aged hinges.

Hands sweaty, he dropped the beam. His intense hatred of Nessa Griffin drove him now. He kicked open the shattered door. He had to stop her.

———◆———

Brynstone stood on the L-shaped platform, his boot covering the word *oculus*. He looked up and saw without surprise that Griffin and her thugs had climbed the cord made from human bones, and then after reaching the tightwire, they had severed the cord. When he had first moved across the wire above, two cords hung side by side, leading down here. Both were gone now, lost to the dark pit below.

He had to find another way out.

Brynstone traced his hand along the smooth rock. He knew a thing or two about climbing, but this would be a tough ascent. The wall was stubborn about offering decent hand- and footholds.

Thinking it over, he returned to the chamber and stepped through the gaping hole where his battering ram had smashed open the door. Highlighted in the glare of his headlamp, the broken knights of the Order of Saint Lazarus littered the floor. The warriors rested together, their heads drooping on the shoulders and chests of their fallen brothers. Despite their sunken eye sockets, it felt like they were watching him. He squinted, impossibilities filling his imagination as he searched for any sign of movement among their dead ranks. His mind was playing tricks on him. He'd studied dead bodies for years and it had never bothered him.

Until now.

Flushed with sweat before, a chill now came over him. Would he be forever trapped down here with these forgotten men? He rubbed his face. If he didn't escape, he'd never see Shayna again. His little girl. For a time, he had become obsessed with protecting his child, but he'd overcome that obsession. Was he now paying for his loss of vigilance?

Brynstone hurried to the long crossbeam near the door. He crooked his shoulder beneath it. Bracing the fifteen-foot beam, he lifted the front end and pushed it out the open door.

It wasn't easy going. The platform curved, making it a challenge to move the long beam. Raising it, he leaned the crossbeam against the wall. Then Brynstone pivoted the beam so it aligned with the tightwire above.

Gripping with his arms and legs, Brynstone shimmied up the fifteen-foot beam. He hadn't done mast climbing since the military. Adrenaline burned inside as he scrambled to the top of the cross.

He found a rough groove in the rock and pulled himself onto the wall. Beneath his boot, the crossbeam teetered then toppled off the platform, dropping into the abyss. There was no going back now. He spied the tightwire not far above, then looked around for a better handhold. Scaling the wall, he made his way up to the high wire.

Beneath it now, he grabbed the wire and swung away from the wall. Brynstone decided against climbing up to walk across it again. Taking it hand over hand again, he moved across the wire with his body swinging below. He made it halfway across when his hands started to ache and go cold. The problem with going hand over hand this far across a cable is that blood drained from your fingers. When that happened, it increased the chance you would lose your grip.

He swung his legs over the tightwire. He could hang by his feet—he had done that once from the bottom of the Golden Gate Bridge to impress a girl—but he decided to crook his legs and hang upside down with the wire trapped behind his knees. Brynstone allowed his arms to drop straight down past his head. He took a breath and closed his eyes. Hanging upside down with his arms stretched out, the blood rushed back down into his hands.

Better.

After a minute hanging upside down in the darkness, he rolled back and grabbed the wire. He resumed the mixed hanging grip, going hand over hand again, making his way to the place where he had started. With a final huff, he snared one leg over the tightwire and reached for the ledge to pull up.

His headlamp spotlighted a boot moving in from the shadows. Not what he wanted to see.

"Nessa Griffin warned us about you," Léon said.

The man stepped on Brynstone's fingers, smashing them against the ledge. Pain sizzled in his hand. With all the energy he could muster, Brynstone reached up with his free hand to grab Léon's ankle. With one hard yank, he stripped the guy off the ledge.

As he dropped, Léon managed to catch the line. Twisting his body, Brynstone grabbed the tightwire, his fingers still bright with pain from the crush of Léon's boot. His body jerked downward and he lost his grip. Swinging upside down from one leg, Brynstone curled and reached up for the tightwire.

Léon had a different idea. Hanging from both hands now, the man took the offense. Swinging in one fluid kick, his boot connected with Brynstone's jaw. His head rocked back and his vision blurred. Léon didn't quit. He kicked Brynstone in the chest. Fighting to stay on the wire, Brynstone wrapped his free leg around his other foot.

"Playtime's over, lads," a gruff voice called from above. Standing on the ledge, Torn Kane pointed a handgun at them.

He fired.

Brynstone winced.

It wasn't meant for him. The bullet ripped through Léon's arm. The man lost his handhold and dropped.

Brynstone caught Léon's wrist.

Cursing in French, the man dangled beneath him. Red spots pulsated in Brynstone's vision as he held on to the guy. Exhausted and hanging upside down, he had to find the strength to pull up the man.

"Léon's not worth saving."

Kane fired the gun a second time. The bullet found its mark in the Frenchman's body. The vibration rattled Brynstone's hand, making it difficult to keep his grip. He looked down. Smoke drifted from Léon's chest and blood coated his face. His mouth gaped open like a dead fish.

Brynstone released his grip on the man's wrist, watching him drop into darkness.

"Now get up here," Kane demanded.

Brynstone curled up and reached for the wire, his right hand still aching. After a struggle, he brought himself to a sitting position, balanced on the wire. The ledge was close.

"You've forgotten, haven't you?" Kane asked. "About the first time we fought."

"Wasn't memorable."

"Don't remember Ireland? You tossed me out a second-story window."

"That was you?" Brynstone growled. "You killed Reece Griffin?"

"Nessa hired me to neutralize her brother. A college professor, he should have been an easy hit. Then you showed up."

Finding a new determination, Brynstone moved across the wire, closing in on the ledge.

"Reece Griffin was a good man."

"His sister had a different opinion."

"His sister is crazy."

"True, but she pays well." Kane grinned. "I remember seeing you in Reece's flat. I had already killed him. You were in my sights. Then that blasted cat blew my cover. Next thing I knew, you sent me out a window. I hit a parked car when I landed, ended up with two broken ribs."

Almost to the ledge, Brynstone said, "Now you want your revenge."

"Precisely," Kane answered. From behind, two men moved into view, flanking him. "This time, I brought a little help."

Brynstone sagged. "You bastards left me down in that cave. Why'd you come back?"

Kane grinned. "Nessa heard from her boss. He thinks you might be useful."

Chapter 14

The researcher from Shayna's school lived in an apartment on the Upper East Side. The problem was, to get into Tina Resnick's building, they had to pass a doorman. *Just what I need. Another doorman.*

Cori watched the guy who worked the door at 1111 Park. He seemed attentive, dressed in a dark green uniform with a gold pinstripe running down his pant legs and another set encircling his wrists. There was no way to sneak past him. She scanned the area around the building's green awning and didn't see many options for hiding, either.

Taking Shay's hand, Cori tried to hail a taxi. Dozens of cabs came speeding along the uptown lanes of Park Avenue, but she couldn't get one to stop. Lighted medallion numbers atop each cab signaled that they were off duty or already carrying passengers.

She glanced down at Shay. Mesmerized by a burst of bright azaleas blossoming along the Park Avenue median, the little girl didn't speak or move a muscle. Just then, a cell started ringing—the one belonging to the dead guy in the black sedan. Cori debated whether she should answer the phone.

You said your brother would call," Shay said. "Is that him?"

"Someone else."

Uncertain what to do, she decided to answer. The caller was a man. He sounded professional but edgy.

"Mind telling me who I'm talking to?" he asked.

Summoning courage, Cori said, "Mind telling me why you people were stalking a little girl?"

She immediately regretted saying anything.

"Who is this?"

Her heart drummed in her chest. Cori punched a button and ended the call.

Looking up, she saw a medallion cab switch lanes. The aging Crown Vic pulled up at the curb. Still shaking from the mystery call, Cori opened the door, but a hand grabbed her from behind and jerked her back. She saw a middle-aged man in a suit with a terse expression on his face.

"You think you need this cab, lady? Trust me, I need it more."

He shoved a briefcase into the taxi's backseat. His suitcase remained on the sidewalk next to Shay, a messenger bag looped over the pull handle. Cori was tempted to kick it.

She tugged on his arm. "Hey, this is our cab."

"Not anymore." Leaning inside the vehicle, he said to the driver, "Wanna pop the trunk here? I need to get to LaGuardia."

Cori glanced down at the man's messenger bag. She slid the dead man's phone into a deep open pocket inside the bag. Shayna shot her a curious look.

The man grabbed the suitcase and messenger bag and placed them inside the trunk. He slammed the yellow lid, then scurried around and jumped inside the taxi. The cab pulled away from the curb and merged into traffic.

Cori looked down at the kid. "Saw that, huh?"

"You gave that mean man your phone? How come?"

"Wasn't my phone."

"Then how come you gave him someone else's phone?"

She gave a weak smile. "Because I'm paranoid."

Cori decided it was time to improvise.

Walking to the corner with Shay, she peered around the side of the Park Avenue apartment building. She spied black gates about three windows down from the side entrance to a medical office. At the gates, a custodial worker was hauling garbage bags out of the apartment building. The man's phone rang and he dropped the bags to take the call.

It sounded intense.

"Listen, Janie, don't talk about a divorce lawyer," he said, kicking one of the black bags. "Don't go there, okay? How many times I gotta say I'm sorry?"

Cori saw her chance when the man paced away from the door. Bringing Shay with her, she stayed close to the building as they passed the stack of garbage bags and slipped through the black gates. They ran to the closest side entrance and moved inside the apartment building.

Bad luck kicked in again when she glanced down the lobby and discovered a second doorman, who seemed like he was manning the phone. If they tried to take the elevator, the guy would notice. They skipped it and headed for a stairwell instead. Running up steep metal steps, they moved upstairs without being seen.

Cori lived in a fifth-floor walk-up on Amsterdam, west of Morningside Park. It was a decent place with hardwood floors and exposed brick, but it was nothing like Tina Resnick's home. The sprawling three-bedroom apartment was ten times nicer than Cori's place.

From what Shay said, the Resnick children were grown. By the look of things, though, grandchildren visited from time to time since Shay had discovered a small collection of toys in a guest bedroom. She busied herself with a Barbie doll dressed as a witch in Halloween colors.

As Shayna played, Cori tried to reach John Brynstone again. No luck. This time, she left a more detailed message, sharing that it was urgent and adding that her call involved Kaylyn and Shayna. That should get his attention. After ending the call, she wandered into a dimly lit study.

Bookshelves lined the east wall behind a mahogany desk. Each volume was color-coded and encased in tooled leather with a gold lining. The books looked amazing, but Cori wondered if anyone ever touched them. Other than a small gold chandelier, the only light came from a lamp positioned beside a computer on a green leather desk mat.

Fueled by curiosity, Cori was hit by an idea. She eased into the desk chair and grabbed the mouse. She was happy to discover that Resnick's home computer wasn't password protected. Cori searched the hard drive and found confidential material from the Brandonstein Center, including information on Shayna.

What she was doing?

She knew it wasn't ethical.

Then again, today wasn't about ethics.

Interesting stuff here. She read one report that outlined the decision to admit Shayna to the Brandonstein Center. John and Kaylyn Brynstone had attended couples counseling with Anne Bliss Niess, a licensed therapist with a practice on Fifth Avenue.

It looked like the Brynstone marriage had been collapsing for years, even before the fateful night when Cori had met Brynstone. During therapy, Dr. Niess had met with Shayna and had recommended testing for a gifted and talented program. A school psychologist named Kristyl Williams Boies had met with Shay and administered assessment instruments, including the Otis-Lennon School Ability Test and the Bracken School Readiness Assessment. Based on the data, Dr. Boies identified Shayna as a kid who would benefit from Brandonstein's G and T program. Kaylyn Brynstone was thrilled. Her husband was more reluctant. John told the psychologist that he wasn't a fan of testing. Cori sensed, somehow, that the truth went beyond that.

She found data comparing Shayna with other Brandonstein students. Something didn't add up. Several kids had scored higher than Shayna, but she alone had received a full scholarship to their G and T program.

Someone had wanted her in that school; someone with connections had made it happen. That was Cori's guess, anyway. Someone had placed Shayna in a controlled setting where researchers could keep the child under scientific observation.

Scanning data from test batteries and behavioral measures, Cori discovered that the school had given Shayna multiple tests, including the Wechsler Intelligence Scales, the Woodcock-Johnson Tests of Achievement, and the Minnesota Multiphasic Personality Inventory. Scientists at Shayna's school had also observed her interaction with other children in play-based behavior.

Shayna seemed to be a healthy, well-adjusted child with high energy and excellent language development. According to the report, she had a vivid and wild imagination, related well to adults, asked a lot of questions, and worried about things kids her age didn't think about. A confirmed perfectionist, Shayna might grow frustrated if she was unable to complete a beloved task that met her high standards. She could be hard on herself, especially when she didn't feel in control of a situation. If she thought it necessary, Shayna was good at controlling her emotions. On the MMPI scale, she showed a spike on the dimension measuring paranoia.

Cori guessed John Brynstone would show a similar score if he had taken the same personality test.

There was another document in Shayna's files, this one bearing the title "Rapid Cellular Regeneration." Cori read how scientists at the Brandonstein Center had documented Shayna's ability to heal more quickly than normal from a variety of cuts, scratches, and bruises. Cori felt a chill burst up her spine. She had witnessed Shayna do the same thing when the girl was barely a year old.

The report took a disturbing turn. During a field trip, Dr. Resnick had staged an "accident" in which another researcher deliberately bumped into Shayna. Tripping, the girl had slammed onto rough pavement, scraping open her palm and forearm as she reached out to catch herself. Resnick had filmed the staged incident and had later made extensive notes about the "conclusive data regarding the subject's rapid healing ability." Resnick had added, "Within minutes, the two incisions on her right hand and arm had vanished."

Cori rolled back in the chair, troubled with the idea. Shoving little girls to test a hypothesis? *What kind of school is this?*

There was more. According to the report, Shayna had developed a gift of some kind that the child had called "the Hollow." Cori searched but couldn't find additional information. *Maybe it's buried here somewhere.* She didn't have time to dig deeper.

Grabbing an empty USB drive from the desk, Cori plugged it into the computer and copied the information on Shayna. She thought John Brynstone should see it.

Her cell rang. Initially startled, she was relieved to find her brother calling and scrambled to answer the phone.

"Jared, thank God. So good to hear you."

"Is something wrong?"

"You could say that. Yes, things are seriously wrong, but I can't get into it now."

"Where are you, Cor? I'm waiting at your apartment."

It caught her off guard.

"You are?"

"I told you I'd meet you. You know the cute girl next door? Ashlee? She buzzed me in. She said a guy was here looking for you."

"Wait a minute. *What?* A guy was there? At my apartment?"

"They talked in the vestibule. She thought he was the police at first, but the guy didn't show a badge or leave a card. Didn't sound like NYPD either, she said."

"What did he look like? Did she say?"

"Don't know. Maybe you should call Ashlee. All I remember is he had a white streak in his hair."

Her throat went dry. "Jared, get away from my apartment. Get out now."

"Calm down. I'm already outside."

"Start walking. Get away. Make sure no one's following you."

"Cori, what's going on? Where are you?"

She gave directions to the Resnick apartment.

"Know what, Cor? I'm worried. Gotta tell you, this phone call isn't helping."

"Just get here as soon as you can."

She ended the call with her brother. She stared at the phone in her lap. Her heart pounded when she thought about White Streak visiting her apartment.

She checked on Shay. The little girl sat cross-legged on the living room carpet with a parade of My Little Pony figures. It brought back memories of Cori's childhood toys.

"You okay?" Cori asked, joining her on the floor.

"I think, yes." She looked up. "I'm playing with my I-Fs."

"Your *what*?"

"My I-Fs." She added, "Imaginary friends."

"You have more than one?"

"Twelve." She moved a pony with a flowing mane of pink near Cori's shoe.

"Twelve? Wow. Do they all have names?"

"My imaginary friends? Well, there's April Rainbreeze and Raven Rainbreeze. They're sisters. Princess Rosalina. Finn and Jake. Isabella. Uni. She's an invisible unicorn."

"Cool."

Shay positioned Twilight Sparkle behind Pinkie Pie, then added a mint-green one, diverting the parade as it wound around Cori.

"The other four I-Fs are friends," the girl continued, "but they argue. Sometimes after a big fight, they don't talk to each other. It's a shame because they like each other."

"What are their names?"

"The Quiet One, the Smart One, the Cute One, and the Funny One."

Cori wrinkled her forehead. "The Beatles?"

"You've heard of them?" Eyes wide, the girl looked up. "You know about the Beatles?"

"Yeah." She made a soft laugh. "Sure, I know them."

"Billy Ellison at my school says nobody but me likes the Beatles."

"You tell Billy Ellison he doesn't know what he's talking about."

"He has a special power."

"Yeah? Billy Ellison does? Like what?"

"He can squirt spit from his eye."

"*What?*"

"I've seen it, Cori. He closes his mouth and plugs his nose. It only works if Billy takes a drink of water first. Plus, it doesn't really squirt, it bubbles up right here." She pointed to the corner of her eye. "Really gross."

"Never listen to a boy who bubbles spit from his eye," she laughed. "Anyway, I think it's great the Beatles are your imaginary friends."

"Mm-hmm. I like how they sound when they talk. They say silly things when they're happy. Especially the Funny One."

"That's how many friends?" she asked, counting to herself. "Eleven? There's one more?"

The smile disappeared. "I don't talk about the last one. I don't say his name. He likes to scare me."

Cori made a concerned face. "I'm sorry."

"The scientists at my school make me talk about him. I hate it."

Burning with curiosity, Cori fought her instinct to ask more questions. "You, uh, don't have to talk about him."

"Thanks."

As they chatted, Shay reconstructed the line of ponies, positioning one after another until the plastic figures encircled Cori. Studying the winding pattern, Cori realized the little girl had built a symbolic fortress around her, as if her play behavior represented a need to protect Cori. Based on her training in child clinical psychology, she wondered if it was Shay's subtle way of demonstrating concern for someone special in response to threat.

Cori noticed a small plastic house on the floor nearby. Stretching across the pony circle, she reached into the toy bin and pulled a small figurine molded in the shape of a child with a dress. She showed it to Shay.

"Can you put this little girl in the house for me?"

Shay nodded and placed it on the second floor of the house. Cori grabbed a female figure with a matching dress and handed it to Shayna.

"Where are you going to put the mommy?"

Shay placed the small plastic woman on the first floor, right beneath the daughter. Cori reached for a male figurine.

"Where are you going to put the daddy?"

Shay placed the man outside the house, away from the mother's sight. Her small fingers adjusted the child on the second floor so that she appeared to look out the window at the man.

"If you wanted to change anything about the people, Shayna, how would you change it? What would you do to make it better?"

Shay removed the woman from the first floor and placed her outside the house. She grabbed the man and moved him to the second floor, so that he faced the little girl. She considered it, then nudged them closer.

"That's how you think it should be? That's how you want it?"

The child nodded. "Is that okay?"

"Yeah."

"Let me tell you something. I feel bad moving the mommy outside, but her and the daddy can't be in the same house 'cause they fight. It's like when the Smart One and the Cute One fight. I can tell they like each other and they were happy one time together, but it's better if they don't be together anymore. It's too bad, but everyone's happier that way."

"Makes sense."

Shay blinked. She realized Cori was looking at the play behavior like one of the scientists at the Brandonstein Center. Something changed in her eyes. She started removing ponies, breaking the symbolic wall around Cori.

"I'm going to play with my ponies now, okay?"

Cori ached a little, afraid the child was pulling back, but she didn't want to push it.

"That's fine, sweetie. Thanks for talking to me."

She smiled. "I like you, Cori."

"I like you, too." She hugged her then stood, giving the kid some time alone.

Chapter 15

"Explain yourself," Torn Kane said as he twisted around in the front passenger seat to face Brynstone. He held up the Roman facemask. "Why do you want this thing?"

It was a good question.

But not good enough to make John Brynstone answer.

He stayed quiet, riding in the backseat of a black Citroën sedan. Outside the window, the Parisian skyline glittered as they raced down a rain-swept boulevard. Some French thug in his late twenties was behind the wheel, not saying a word. Neither did the man with long hair and stubble seated beside Brynstone. His name was Serge—at least that's what they had called him getting into the car—and he acted exhausted and distracted.

Kane, however, wouldn't shut up.

"Nessa decided to throw Véronique in the grave with you, get her to notice things you wouldn't tell us. We figured she could win your confidence. It worked."

Brynstone took a sudden interest in his hands and ankles, all shackled. He didn't know where they were taking him. The long-haired guy next to him looked over. He wasn't as tough as the two up front, but he packed a Walther PPS in his shoulder holster.

Brynstone didn't have a weapon. Back at the cemetery, Nessa Griffin had taken his phone and his Glock.

Dissatisfied with the silence, Kane fidgeted in his seat, staring now at the windshield. He gave directions to the driver, then added, "Understand something, Dr. Brynstone. We are relentless. We *will* find the truth."

Brynstone glanced over. Serge rubbed his eyes.

Perfect time to make a move.

Hunching down in the seat, Brynstone raised his legs. He looped the shackle between his ankles over the driver's head, pulling the man back in his seat as he ripped his hands from the steering wheel. At the same time, Brynstone reached over and shoved Serge, smashing his head into the window.

The car swerved on the slick street.

Caught in his seat belt, Kane reached over and tried to gain control of the vehicle. Brynstone crossed his feet, choking the driver. Unable to reach the steering wheel, the man tried to pull apart Brynstone's legs, but he couldn't free himself. Fighting for air, he rose from the seat and in doing so floored the accelerator, sending the car headlong into the next lane. His face showed up in the rearview mirror, cords straining in his scarlet neck. Opening his mouth, he bit down on Brynstone's ankle. The dazzling pain caused Brynstone to briefly relinquish his hold around the driver's neck. Quickly recovering, Brynstone tightened his abdominal muscles and shifted his legs to the side, slamming the driver into Kane. The man sputtered as Kane grabbed the wheel and tried to navigate the car. Holding his head, Serge shouted something in French, unholstering his Walther. As the car spiraled hard in the middle of the road, Brynstone reached next to him and grabbed the man's wrist. Serge squeezed the trigger before the gun was on target. The first bullet shattered the rear window an inch from Brynstone's neck. The second burst into the driver's head above his ear. Blood spurted across Brynstone's boot and splashed Kane in the face.

From the right, a white supermini slammed into the Citroën.

Brynstone didn't see the vehicle coming. The impact came on Kane's side, flipping the Citroën. The Walther flew from Serge's hand and hurdled over Brynstone's head. He tried to catch the weapon with cuffed hands, but couldn't reach it. Their vehicle was upside down now, sliding across the Paris boulevard as orange sparks showered the window. Confined in his seat belt, he grabbed Serge and jerked him close. Brynstone slammed his head into the man's forehead.

The guy was tougher than he looked.

Serge reached for Brynstone's neck as the car spun in one sickening turn after another. Still hanging upside down, Brynstone reached with cuffed wrists and hit the release button on the seat belt. The belt snapped back like a whip, dropping him onto the ceiling below. Kane was already down here, holding his bloodied head. It was difficult to tell if the blood belonged to him or the suspended driver. From above, Serge dropped down, landing on Brynstone's leg. Even worse? His hand was near the Walther. He grabbed it.

Brynstone jerked his leg from under Serge then kicked out, directing both feet into his face and slamming him backward against the crumpled door. There was a cracking sound—he had shattered the man's nose and the car window at the same time.

The vehicle stopped.

Still in his seat, the driver's face dripped blood down onto the ceiling. Groaning, Kane raised his head and looked back with a glassy expression. His pupils were dilated. *Concussion.*

Outside the vehicle, cars skidded to a stop, jamming traffic. Horns blared all around. Brynstone fished his shackled hands into the jacket of the now-unconscious man beside him. His leg burned with pain, but he ignored it. He reached into Serge's pants pocket as his fingers brushed a metallic surface. He drew out a key and used it to unlock the cuffs around his feet. With more concentration, he unlocked the handcuffs.

Grabbing the Walther, he tucked it inside his waistband.

He reached between the front seats to find the Roman facemask. Kane had lost hold of it while fighting to grab the steering wheel.

Brynstone crawled from the Citroën onto the street. He rolled onto his back, looking up with sweat coating his face.

That's when he noticed that a gawking crowd had gathered in the street. Looked to be about fifteen of them, maybe twenty.

Brynstone sighed. Still groggy, he rolled to his knees and stood.

Lines of crisscrossed vehicles were frozen in the street. It was amazing more cars hadn't plowed into them. A distant siren signaled the approach of French police. Limping, he made his way around the Citroën.

A small man with a thin mustache pointed at the wrecked white supermini. He waved his fist and shouted obscenities.

Ignoring him, Brynstone walked around to the Citroën's passenger-side door. He crouched and peeked inside. Beneath a blanket of shattered glass, Kane held his head, still disoriented.

He wanted to drag Reece Griffin's murderer out into the street. Brynstone tried to open the door.

Jammed.

Spurred by the growing crowd, the little French man became more confrontational. He tapped Brynstone's shoulder, then landed a soft fist on his arm. Emerging from the white supermini, an angry woman joined the man. She stepped in front of the door as Brynstone tried to pry it open.

She spat on his face.

Okay. That cut it.

As mucus dripped from his cheek, Brynstone brought out the PPS and flashed the gun. The woman yelped and backed away. The little man noticed the Walther. Color drained from his face. Losing the momentum of his protest, the man stumbled back before disappearing into the crowd.

Longfellow had said that music was the universal language.

Maybe so, Brynstone thought, *but guns come in a close second.*

He peeked inside the vehicle again. Framed inside the window, Kane made a slow crawl into the backseat. Was he afraid or disoriented? There was no time to answer that question—the blare of sirens drifted over the crowd. Now there was no chance to get to Kane and to avenge Reece Griffin's murder.

Another time.

Brynstone darted into the crowd. Frightened people collapsed on each other to clear a path for him. He hurried down the Rue du something or other, the name spelled in white letters on a blue sign on the rock wall, but he'd already forgotten it.

He cut across the street.

That's when a vehicle squealed its brakes behind him.

Bringing out the Walther, he turned to see a European Ford Cargo, the truck's white surface tattooed with green and blue graffiti. Were these good guys or bad guys? He got his answer when the driver opened the door and dropped to the street, armed with an assault rifle. Double doors opened in back. Four men scuttled out with Steyr AUGs aimed at Brynstone.

"Drop your weapon," the driver growled with a faint accent. He was an intense-looking man with a wide forehead and thick eyebrows. "Then hands behind your head. Do it."

Okay, Brynstone thought, *let's explore my options here.*

He was outmanned, so gunfire wouldn't be a good move. Next idea? He could make an escape to the left. It seemed workable until a second car cut across the street from that direction, rolling onto the sidewalk. Three men jumped out, also training their weapons on him.

At that point, his options dropped into the toilet.

Brynstone lowered the PPS. He cupped his hands behind his head.

The passenger door opened.

A figure climbed down and strolled around the aging cargo truck, her body cutting through twin headlight beams. Her face came into view.

Nessa Griffin.

Disgusted, Brynstone shook his head. "How many people do you have working for you?"

"Three fewer after your car wreck. I'm not happy about losing Kane and the others to the Police Nationale."

"I liked you better when you were an archaeologist."

"You never liked me. And archaeology doesn't pay for shite."

"Yeah, but it doesn't land your ass in jail."

Griffin laughed. "Jaysus, you're adorable, John Brynstone. What a shame you're gonna die tonight."

Hearing footsteps from behind, Brynstone turned. He caught sight of a man with a handheld Taser. The current was fast and brilliant as the barbs stabbed his back and shoulder. It rocketed inside his muscles, sending him into involuntary contractions. His head reared back as he yelled and dropped to the sidewalk on his knees, still shaking.

He couldn't catch his breath. All his muscles were in revolt, focused on collapse.

Someone rolled him onto his side. They pulled the probes, leaving twin puncture wounds on his skin. In a sweaty haze, he saw Griffin standing over him, hands fixed on her hips.

"Load him in the truck," she called. "Let's get out of here."

PART II
The Keeper

The truth is a snare: You cannot have it, without being caught. You cannot have the truth in such a way that you catch it, but only in such a way that it catches you.

—Søren Kierkegaard

Chapter 16

Cori had never been happier to see her little brother. Opening the door to the Resnick apartment, she hugged him tightly, not wanting to pull away.

"What's wrong?" Jared Cassidy asked. "You haven't been like this since Mom died."

She closed the door. Walking down the oak-framed hallway, she ran her fingers through her short blonde hair and said, "I'm still trying to sort it out."

She hadn't seen Jared in three months, though they talked on the phone a couple times a week. The kid was successful. At twenty-five, he had quit a job as an investment banker to take work in-house with a client of his former banking firm. Dressed in a black pinstripe power suit, Jared wore a nondescript white dress shirt with a red patterned tie and sported a sleek professional hair-style. She remembered back in high school when his brown hair was disheveled and he owned one suit. Now he had a closet full of them.

Sliding off his suit coat, he looked around.

"Who lives here?"

"A friend."

Jared noticed Shay on the floor playing with ponies.

"Oh, wait a minute. That's the girl, isn't it?"

"Her name's Shayna Brynstone." Cori tugged on his arm, dragging her brother to the kitchen. "Listen to me first, okay? Jared, please?"

"That's the girl," he repeated, looking back. "The one you're obsessing over." He leaned against an island in the center of the brightly lit kitchen, placing both hands flat against the speckled granite countertop. "Her parents know she's with you?"

"No."

"So this is Shayna's home?"

"No. Look—"

"This is serious," he said, cutting her off. "The mom doesn't know her kid is here. You realize that's kidnapping?"

"Some men shot her mother today."

"*What?*"

"They tried to kidnap Shay outside her school. They shot Kaylyn Brynstone. We got out of there."

He pulled out a chair and dropped onto it. Loosening his tie, he said, "Cori, this is crazy."

"Tell me about it," she said in a hushed voice.

"Do you know who wanted to kidnap her?"

"I need to tell you something," Cori said, taking a seat. "Should have told you back when it happened."

He cocked his head, listening.

"This happened after Mom died of leukemia. You were on vacation during the Christmas holiday with Dad and his girlfriend."

"Yvette."

"Yeah, Yvette. Anyway, I met this man named Edgar Wurm, a mathematician and a cryptanalyst. He worked for the government. He was studying this thing called the Voynich manuscript."

"Where'd you meet him?"

"In, um, a psych hospital."

"You were working there?"

"Not exactly. It's a long story. Anyway, I met Wurm when he was a patient."

"If the guy was a mental patient, maybe he was telling a bunch of lies."

"Trust me, Jared. The guy was brilliant. Wurm knew about Mom's work. You know her last book, *The Perfect Medicine*? He'd read it."

"The one you helped her research."

She nodded. "He was studying the Radix. It was this root—"

"I read Mom's book," he answered. "I know about the Radix."

"Then maybe you know this," Cori said, adjusting an orange in a bowl of fruit. "The Radix could be used to create something called a chrism. It was a special mixture based on different ingredients. According to legend, the White Chrism could heal. The Black Chrism could kill."

"Sounds trippy."

"I'm serious, Jared. I admit, I didn't believe this stuff at first."

"But Mom did."

"Yeah, Mom did. And so did a man named John Brynstone."

"The little girl's dad?"

"Exactly." She leaned onto the table with crossed arms. "Actually, Brynstone didn't believe at first. That guy I mentioned earlier? Edgar Wurm? He and Brynstone worked together to find the Radix. Everything turned bad after that."

"What happened?"

"I was with Wurm. He was murdered."

"When?"

"Five years ago this coming Christmas," she said. "That's what I'm telling you. Wurm died." Cori glanced down, twirling hair around her finger. "Using the Radix, John Brynstone was able to create the White Chrism. He gave it to his daughter. The White Chrism saved her."

"Why not use it to save Wurm? He died, right?"

"He swallowed a sliver of the Radix, but he was never given the White Chrism. John gave the medicine to Shayna and it changed her."

"Changed her how?"

"Hard to explain." She pursed her lips, then cut off her words. Shayna walked into the kitchen.

"Cori, is everything okay?" she asked.

"Everything's terrific, sweetie." She tapped her brother's arm. "This is Jared."

"Your brother?"

"Sure is. Can you say hi?"

"Hi, Jared."

He gave her a smile.

"Why don't you play a little more?" Cori said to Shayna. "Can you do that?"

"I'm hungry. Can I have that banana?"

"Sure thing." Cori snatched it from the bowl. She peeled the skin halfway from the top and handed it to Shay. The girl turned and skipped back to the living room.

"Cute kid," Jared said. "She know about her mom?"

"Not sure."

"They shot her. Did she die?"

"I can't find out. I've called a couple hospitals."

"So, bad guys come in and open fire outside a school, start blowing people away. Any idea who they are?"

She shook her head. "I thought CIA at first."

"C-I-A? Are you serious?"

"Edgar Wurm claimed one time that the director of the CIA wanted the Radix."

He laughed. "Crazy guy told you about a government conspiracy, huh? Did he say anything about Roswell or the Bermuda Triangle? Maybe how Lee Harvey Oswald killed JFK 'cause he knew where to find the Radix?"

"Can you not be a dick right now?" she pleaded. "Do that one thing for me. Okay?"

His voice lowered. "Sorry, Cor. Tell me what you were saying."

"Might not sound like it to you, but Wurm wasn't crazy when I met him. Not much, anyway. You know that whole thing about a fine line between genius and insanity? That was him. Call me crazy, but I believed him about the CIA."

"So, the guys with guns at the school. You think they were CIA officers?"

"Not anymore I don't. I have no clue what to think right now."

"Did you call Dad? Ask him about this?"

"Right," she muttered. "How do you ask somebody for advice when he refuses to talk to you?"

"He's still angry about you leaving Johns Hopkins."

"He's angry about everything I do. I remind him of Mom."

"Come on. That's not fair."

"I don't want to get into it. I need to figure out what to do here."

"Tell me something." Jared leaned forward with a weight coming over his face. "What exactly are you mixed up in, Cori?"

Queens, New York
6:36 p.m.

"We're working on finding that girl, Mr. Director," Stephen Angelilli said into his cell, hustling through LaGuardia Airport. "For now, we have NYPD's cooperation as well as the hospital in withholding details about Kaylyn Brynstone. We'll determine how long we want to contain the story. We're in the process of initiating contact with Cori Cassidy, the woman we identified as assisting the child at the school."

"Let me get back to that," CIA Director Mark McKibbon said. "Jason Drakos was killed in his car. Did you say Ms. Cassidy retrieved his phone and tried to call in?"

"Yes, sir. She got a busy signal because we jammed the phone after the Drakos hit. We turned off the jamming device and back-traced the call. We've been able to track the phone."

The director interrupted, saying he needed to take another call. Angelilli agreed to hold.

Walking at a brisk pace, he looked around. LaGuardia wasn't bad today, thank God.

He navigated around a young couple, tanned and rested, as they strolled with vacation luggage. Black hair pulled back in a ponytail, the woman reminded him of a girl he'd dated in college. This one had mesmerizing green eyes. Passing them, he shared an interested glance with the woman, Angelilli giving a half smile. He allowed his mind a quick diversion, imagining her look in a black bikini. She was a good twenty years too young, but he never allowed reality to interfere with fantasy.

His reverie was interrupted when Patrick Langston joined him.

"We apprehended the suspect, sir," he said. "Follow us."

The tanned woman recognized the urgent tone in Langston's voice. She seemed impressed.

Angelilli followed Langston while another agent, Jack "Ripper" Rickerson, held a door open. It led down a long white corridor and curious travelers—including the green-eyed woman and her boyfriend—took a peek before the door closed.

Angelilli darted up a flight of stairs after the younger man. Director McKibbon came back on and said he had to take a meeting with Andrew Peterson, the director of the National Security Agency. A three-star general, he had replaced the late James Delgado as DIRNSA. Peterson was a former sniper and Angelilli could only imagine the stories the guy could tell. Not that he would. The NSA wasn't known for storytelling. McKibbon apologized for once, then asked for another update in an hour before ending the call.

Angelilli tucked away the phone and caught up to Langston.

The officer touched his earpiece. "Right this way, sir. Behind that door. LaGuardia security assisted in apprehending him."

"*Him?*"

Angelilli was expecting to see Cori Cassidy. He was under the impression she had the phone.

Langston opened the door for Angelilli. "He's waiting for you, sir."

Inside the room, a man in his early fifties was seated behind a table. He had a round face and slicked-back hair. Three CIA officers and two airport security personnel stood around him. The guy looked ashen. A cell phone rested on the table in front of him.

Angelilli glanced at airport personnel. "Thank you for your help, gentlemen. You may go."

"You sure?" the shorter of the two asked. "Because we—"

"Thank you, gentlemen," Angelilli said, stepping aside so they could leave the room.

Rickerson escorted them out into the hallway. Waiting for the door to close, Angelilli eased into a chair opposite the suspect.

"What's this guy's name?"

The man started to answer, but Langston blurted his name. "David Ronnestrand."

Angelilli stared at the man, letting the seconds roll into an unnerving silence. He waited until that first bead of sweat traced down the man's forehead and curled toward his chin.

"Mr. Ronnestrand, I have a question," he said in an even voice. "Any idea what I'm about to ask?"

The man looked at the phone on the table. In a strained voice, he said, "Something about the cell?"

"Something about the cell," Angelilli repeated. "Nice job. So, tell me. You got an answer?"

"Swear to God, I never saw the thing until that one agent—the Asian guy who was in here first—pulled it out of my messenger bag."

"Is that right? You have no idea how it came into your possession?"

"No, sir. None at all."

"I see." A pause. "See, that's a bit of a problem for us. That phone belonged to a murdered government official. Somehow it ended up in your possession, Mr. Ronnestrand."

The man's eyes widened. "Look, I'm a former broker at Sachs, Kidder, and Carnegie. I've had high-profile clients, but I've never worked with the government."

"*Former* broker."

He frowned. "I was fired last week. Anyway, I don't have connections to government people. I mean it when I say I've never seen this phone before. I can't explain it."

Angelilli motioned at Langston. He said, "Picture."

The officer stepped forward, reaching inside a folder for an eight-by-ten glossy. Langston held up the photograph for the man's inspection.

"Recognize this woman?"

"Don't know her." He squinted, adjusting his glasses. "Wait a minute."

"What?"

"I saw her in the city. I think it was her. Yeah. Perky little thing. Short blonde hair. Looks like a cheerleader or something. That's her."

"Where in the city?"

"Upper East Side. Outside my apartment building."

"Address?"

"Uh, 1111 Park."

Langston pulled out his phone.

"What was this woman doing?"

"Getting in my cab."

"You shared a cab with her?"

"Not exactly." He looked down. "I sorta took her cab. Cut her off before she could get in."

"You're such a gentleman. So, she never entered the vehicle at any time?"

He shook his head. "She stood there on the sidewalk while I loaded my stuff into the taxi."

Angelilli played scenarios in his head, imaging Cori Cassidy slipping Jason Drakos's phone in this guy's suitcase.

"Was anyone with this woman?"

"A kid."

"What kind? Boy or girl?"

"Girl."

"How old?"

"Don't know. Skinny kid. About this tall." He waved his hand about four feet above the floor. "Give or take a little."

Langston ended the call and returned to the table.

"Kid's hair color?" Angelilli asked.

"Beats me. The woman was a blonde. I know that."

Langston held up another photograph, this one of Shayna Brynstone.

Ronnestrand frowned. "It could be. Like I said, I didn't pay much attention to the kid."

"You saw them on the sidewalk outside your building. Where did they go?"

"Don't know. I was in a hurry to get to the airport." He glanced at his wristwatch. "I'm still in a hurry."

"Yeah, I sorta got that impression."

Langston came over. "Sir, can I talk to you?"

Angelilli moved away from the table. "What is it?"

"Interesting connection," the officer said in a low voice. "One of the women injured at the shooting today at the Brandonstein Center lives in the same building as this guy. She's a researcher at Shayna's school."

"Which one?"

"Tina Resnick. She's in intensive care right now."

"Ronnestrand saw Cori Cassidy in the vicinity," Angelilli said. "Maybe Cassidy was trying to contact Resnick, only she wasn't home."

"Might be worth checking Resnick's building."

He nodded. "Let's go."

"What about me?" Ronnestrand asked, standing up.

"We'll need to detain you, sir."

"I'm heading to a job interview in Chicago. A big meeting at Mesirow Financial. I have a flight to catch."

"Not anymore. I may need to question you again."

"I answered all your questions."

Angelilli shrugged and headed for the door. "Maybe I'll think up some new ones. I'm creative like that."

Chapter 17

London, England
11:36 p.m.

John Brynstone batted open his eyes, finding little to see in the darkened room. Rope bound him to a chair. His head was heavy and thundering. He recalled Nessa Griffin's men Tasing him back on the boulevard, but the haze inside his head felt drug-induced.

His arms burned. Both wrists were pulled behind his back in a handcuff knot.

Before Brynstone had been a Ranger, he'd overheard a grunt telling how he'd tied up a girlfriend with this kind of modified clove hitch, the man bragging about his skill with a "bitch hitch." The comment hadn't endeared the guy to the female soldiers in the room.

"Do you happen to be awake over there?" a voice asked in the darkness.

Eyes adjusting, he looked across the room, trying to see the shadowy figure. The phrasing revealed a distinct alveolar trill, marking the man as a speaker of Scottish English. Educated. Sounded like he was middle-aged or older.

"Who are you?" Brynstone called to the darkness.

"A fellow prisoner."

"Where are we?"

"I've not been outwith in some time, but I believe we are inside a factory. It must be near west Kilburn."

"Kilburn?" Brynstone shook his head, trying to make sense of it. He thought he was in Paris.

"We're in London?" he asked.

"We are, actually. You are unaware of the city you are in?"

He puzzled it over. Why did Griffin bring him to London?

"Did you see an Irish woman when they brought me here?" he asked.

"You mean Nessa Griffin?"

"You saw her?"

"A short time ago. Her men abducted me while I was on holiday with my sister."

After the accident back in Paris, Brynstone had taken the facemask from Kane. No doubt Griffin had the Roman artifact now. That didn't make him happy.

"I know you, Dr. Brynstone," the stranger called from the darkness.

"You know me?"

"Aye. And I can't say I care for you. Not at all. Perhaps, though, we should labor together if we are to escape this dreadful room."

"How do you know me?"

"Only through reputation. I knew Edgar Wurm for a time. What a detestable sort he was. I know of your association with Wurm. If he was your friend, then you are my enemy."

A Scotsman who hated Edgar Wurm? He searched his memory for a conversation from years back. He flashed back to a tapas bar in central Madrid. Wurm had been cursing a blue streak during sangria and fried chorizo, his wrath focused on the actions of a Scottish professor. What was the guy's name?

He had it.

"Math McHardy," Brynstone said. "You the guy I'm talking to?"

"What a perfect delight that you know me."

Brynstone had heard stories about the man. McHardy was a historian as well as a collector of antiquities. Independently wealthy, he had retired at age sixty from the School of Classics at the University of St. Andrews. Wurm claimed the man had retired too soon and was looking for some way to recapture academic glory.

McHardy said, "I knew you were an associate of Wurm's. For the longest time I thought your name was John Brimstone, as in fire and brimstone. Your name sounds a little like it, you know?"

"I've been told."

"Back to Edgar Wurm. I felt great cheer when I learned about his death."

Brynstone didn't deliver the news that Wurm was still around.

"Tell me," McHardy asked, "how do you know Nessa Griffin?"

"I knew her brother, Reece Griffin."

"Aye. My former student. That's another reason I loathe you."

"I don't get it," Brynstone said.

"You killed Reece years ago at his flat in Cork."

"Who said that?"

"His sister."

"Nessa Griffin told you that? She abducts you and you believe her about that?"

McHardy remained silent for a beat.

Finally, he said, "As you Americans say, Nessa has been dealing with some issues. Like Reece, she was my student. Never as brilliant as her brother, although a great deal tougher."

"Ever hear of a man named Torn Kane?"

"Can't say that I have."

"He's the man responsible. Kane killed Reece Griffin."

"How can you be certain?"

"I was there. Nessa Griffin lied to you. She hired Kane to kill her brother. I discovered Reece inside his flat in Cork and threw Kane out a window."

"Did you?"

"You wanna be angry at someone about Reece's homicide? Be angry at his sister."

"I see." He thought it over. "I remember Nessa saying you stole her brother's kitten."

"Yeah, well, that part is true."

Brynstone had adopted the orphaned cat. Banshee had saved his life that night.

"Well then," McHardy said, "if you took his kitten? I still loathe you."

———

New York City
6:37 p.m.

Viktor Nebola knew how to play it cool. It came naturally to him. Early on in his life, he had learned the art of making the other guy panic. Now he was behind his desk, staring at Markus Tanzer. Silently, Tanzer stared back at him. Guy was made of steel.

"Take a seat."

Tanzer shook his head. "No, thanks."

"Do it anyway."

Tanzer glanced around, then pulled back the chair. He looked crisp in his gray suit, with his head shaved to perfection. He glanced out the window, taking in the view, the ugliness of the city spread out to bake in summer swelter. Bored with the sight of traffic clogging the street, the slender African American man looked back into the room.

"Didn't realize the Shadow Chapter had a Manhattan office."

"It wasn't necessary for you to know." Nebola rose from behind his desk. "I'm troubled."

"I know."

Nebola straightened his tie. "I gave orders for the operation at the Brandonstein Center today. I made it clear I wanted Shayna Brynstone brought to me."

"You did."

He turned with a clenched fist. Growling, he said, "You assassinated a CIA officer. I'm fine with that. You shot Brynstone's wife. No problem. But you allowed a little girl to escape? That's unforgivable."

"We made a mistake. We know it."

"Stop the *we*. You were the team leader, Mr. Tanzer."

"Still am. That's why I need to get out of this office. We're going to find that kid for you." He rose from the chair. "Get me back on the street."

"You haven't asked about your father. Have you lost interest in the old man?"

"What have you done to him?"

"See for yourself."

He handed over a tablet computer. It streamed video from a California nursing home.

Tanzer looked up. "I don't get it. He's back in his room."

"We returned Martin Tanzer to San Bernardino, safe and sound."

The man bit his lip. "Thank you, sir. I appreciate your not hurting him." Tanzer handed back the computer, then held out his hand.

Nebola looked at it, but didn't budge. "Get out of here."

"Yes, sir." He pulled back his hand. "I'm not doing you any good in here. I'll find Shayna Brynstone for you."

Markus Tanzer headed for the door. As the man reached for the knob, Nebola pressed a button on his desk.

A crackle of electricity. A thousand volts rifled through Tanzer's body, rolling him off his feet in a violent twist. He gurgled before falling into a crumpled heap on the floor.

His charred hand twitched beside him.

Nebola stood over the dead man, taking in the stench of seared flesh.

"You were right when you said you're not doing me any good." He shook his head. "You thought Shayna Brynstone was just a child. That was a fatal mistake, Mr. Tanzer."

London
11:40 p.m.

Tied to the chair, Brynstone stared into the darkness. He couldn't see Math McHardy.

"Nessa Griffin abducted you. She still here?"

"How should I know?" McHardy snapped.

Brynstone had another question, but the door opened before he could ask it.

A swath of light cut across the darkened floor.

Véronique stepped inside, looking around. She ignored McHardy and walked to Brynstone. It was the first he'd seen her since the cavern beneath the Paris cemetery.

She knelt beside him, no apologies. She held up the Roman facemask.

"Why are you interested in this thing?"

Wrists bound in rope, Brynstone stared at the woman without saying a word.

"You study old bones. Mummies. Ancient diseases. You don't collect antiquities."

"And you're not the historian for Père Lachaise Cemetery. How long have you been working for Nessa Griffin?"

"Long enough to know she regards you as a worthy rival."

This brought a snort from McHardy. Her eyes darted in his direction, but she didn't turn her head. Véronique brought her gaze back to Brynstone.

"Annoying, isn't he?" Brynstone asked.

She smiled.

Then the unexpected happened.

There was a whirling sound. Véronique screamed and then seemed to shudder. She looked down. A round silver object with dagger-like edges was embedded in her hand. She dropped the Roman facemask, the scream trapped in her throat.

On instinct, Véronique ripped the throwing weapon from her bloodied hand and dropped it. The weapon landed at Brynstone's boot.

Breathing hard, she turned.

Dressed all in black, an Indian woman ran at her from the doorway.

Véronique prepared to defend herself, swinging out to strike the intruder. But before she could connect, the Indian woman dropped into a crouching surprise attack, her hand anchored on the floor as she twisted her body into a roundhouse kick. The woman's execution was flawless. Brynstone recognized it as a capoeira move, an Afro-Brazilian method blending disguised martial arts with dance. Compressing her body like a spring, the woman swung up with a payload kick. Her foot blasted into Véronique's stomach, probably rupturing internal organs while also snapping a rib or two. Flipping in the air, Véronique went down hard, the whole thing over before it started.

On the floor now with her head turned to the side, Véronique lay still—her eyelids fluttered, then closed.

Was she dead?

Doubtful, but not out of the question.

Unconcerned, the Indian woman glanced at Brynstone. She had piercing eyes and a stunning body. Keeping her cautious gaze trained on him, she knelt and took the Roman facemask.

He didn't say a word to her.

From across the room, McHardy spat, "Who in God's name are you?"

The woman reached down to an ankle holster. She stood and unfolded a knife, keeping her gaze fixed on Brynstone before turning away to see the professor.

As she stalked closer to him, still holding the weapon, McHardy closed his eyes.

Brynstone glanced at the stainless-steel disk on the floor where Véronique had dropped it. From the chair, he stretched his long leg and trapped it beneath his foot. He didn't want the woman to see him make a move for it. Keeping it quiet, he dragged the weapon toward him.

Holding the knife, the woman sliced ropes around McHardy's wrists. His hands snapped free.

"What do you want with me?" He tried to sound intimidating, but apprehension shadowed his voice.

She grabbed the man's rumpled dress shirt, then raised McHardy straight against the wall. They were the same height, maybe five nine.

"You're coming with me," the woman demanded, speaking for the first time. Her English was flawless.

"Under no circumstances," he announced with sudden defiance.

Brynstone drew the woman's throwing weapon toward him. Sensing movement, she glanced back.

Brynstone froze, making it look like he was watching Véronique. She hadn't moved since absorbing the devastating kick.

"Do you know who I am?" McHardy asked.

Turning back to the man, she directed her fist into his mouth. His head recoiled and struck the wall, silencing him.

Brynstone was starting to like this woman.

McHardy crumpled against her before she flipped him over her shoulder in a fireman's carry. She disappeared out the door, taking the professor with her.

Damn.

Brynstone had to move fast. The Indian woman had the Roman facemask.

He rose up in the chair and crashed it against the wall, the impact breaking the arms. Not as clean an escape as in the movies, but it gave him the freedom to wiggle free from the busted chair. Dropping to the floor, he slid his bound wrists beneath his butt and brought them out in front. Brynstone took the throwing weapon and worked on the handcuff knot. The stainless-steel teeth cut the rope, sawing it open.

Snapping the severed cords, he dropped them and moved to Véronique. He touched his fingers to her throat and discovered a faint pulse.

He found her cell. Back in the Paris cemetery, Nessa and her thugs had taken his phone. It was tempting to borrow this one, but he decided against it.

He dialed 999, the United Kingdom's emergency phone number, and growled into the phone, "Get an ambulance over here. I have a woman in her early thirties with possible internal bleeding."

Ignoring the operator, he placed the phone on the floor beside her, so they could trace the call.

The air outside the warehouse carried the fresh scent of rain. Looking down, he found two guards slumped on the wet ground.

Like Véronique, the men had faced the Indian woman and lost. He pulled a handgun from one guard but didn't check to see if they were alive. An ambulance would arrive soon.

He heard a car door.

Looking across the parking lot, he spied the woman with shoulder-length black hair shoving Math McHardy inside a black Alfa Romeo Spider.

Brynstone sprinted toward them.

It would be tough to catch her. She was already opening the driver-side door and he was still half the distance across the parking lot. That's when he noticed a red 1967 MGB roadster parked nearby.

Things were looking up.

Chapter 18

New York City
6:42 p.m.

"Cori," Jared Cassidy called from another room. "Better get in here fast."

Standing in the bathroom of the Resnick apartment, she had finished weaving Shay's hair into a waterfall twist braid. Cori hurried down the hallway as the girl stayed behind to line up small bottles of nail polish along the counter.

Turning the corner, Cori found her brother watching television. On the screen, a female reporter with a sweep of golden hair stood outside the Brandonstein Center for Gifted Children.

Jared turned up the volume.

"Bill, authorities are reporting that eight teachers and staff members were sent to a local hospital. We're told that one parent—a woman named Kaylyn Brynstone—was injured during the firefight. Sources tell our Eyewitness News team that her injuries are not serious and she should be released sometime tomorrow. Her daughter attends the school behind me. The little girl was picked up by her grandmother and is excited for her mother's release. The cause of the shooting is still unknown at this time."

The reporter signed off as the network cut to the coanchor.

Jared punched the Mute button. "Shayna's mom is okay."

"That's not right. Kaylyn was on the stairs behind me. They said her injuries weren't serious, but I swear she was hit near her heart."

"Maybe you didn't see it right."

"Jared, don't you believe me?"

"Look, everything happened fast. That's all I'm saying."

"I know everything happened fast. I was there. I saw the blood. Kaylyn was behind us." Her voice trembled. "They shot her. It was terrible. And what was that crap about the grandma? Shay's in the other room. They got that totally wrong."

He crossed his arms. "Yeah, that's weird. They talked to a cop before you came in. He confirmed what they were saying."

Cori rubbed her forehead and started walking away.

"Where're you going?" her brother called.

She didn't answer. She returned to the bathroom, kneeling beside Shayna.

"Sweetie, I have a question. Have you talked to your grandma today?"

She scrunched up her nose. "I have two grandmas. One lives with God now."

"Your other grandma. Where is she?"

"Grandma Brynstone? She's in that place."

"What place?"

"Um, I can't remember. It's super far away. She just went there on a jet plane." Shayna maneuvered a bottle of eggplant-colored polish, positioning it with others into an S shape.

"Know what state?"

She shook her head. "That other country across the ocean. It's hard to pronounce."

"But you haven't talked to her in a while?"

"Nope. I miss her, but I really miss my daddy."

<hr/>

London
11:43 p.m.

Driving the black Spider, Rashmi Raja glanced at the passenger slumped in the seat beside her. Watching Math McHardy rub his head, she decided he didn't have much fight in him.

As she drove on First Avenue, a London Ambulance Service vehicle blazed past her. Raja looked in the rearview mirror and saw red reflective chevrons on the ambulance's back doors. It was headed in the direction of the Kilburn warehouse.

She noticed headlights and saw a little red sports cloth-top trailing her.

Another glance at McHardy. His silver hair was disheveled. Midfifties, was her guess. He had a long bony nose and narrow suspicious eyes couched in darkened wrinkles. The man looked dazed. She checked the street ahead before stealing another look at the mirror. The MGB roadster stayed with her.

Interesting.

Hitting the accelerator, Raja turned onto Herries Street. The other driver seemed intent on tailing her around west London. She had taken out two male guards plus a woman back at the warehouse before abducting McHardy. Was a bodyguard chasing her? If so, he wasn't getting paid enough.

Raja took it faster, passing a primary school and a blur of shops. Earlier, she had seen a police station in Paddington Green. Thankfully, there hadn't been any sign of law enforcement so far.

The car behind closed in.

She swerved hard, cutting in front of the roadster. She smiled. On the rain-swept streets, the car slid as the driver overcorrected. Her smile vanished as the other driver managed to regain control. He was right back on her tail.

"What's going on?" McHardy called, his face all hard angles. He no longer slumped in the seat, but was braced upright.

"Put on your seat belt," Raja ordered. "People in the car behind us want to kill you," she lied, hoping to win his trust. "I'm trying to save you. Shut up and let me do my job."

She punched the accelerator again.

McHardy turned back to look at the roadster. He got the message and buckled his seat belt.

Raja tried a quick maneuver. She pulled the Alfa Romeo Spider onto a dirt strip behind a garage in Westbourne Grove. Bad move. The roadster caught up and collided with her car, pushing it against the wall of the metal garage. Her tires kicked dirt high into the air as she pulled away, but the other driver read her move. He cut in front, forcing her to swerve hard to avoid him. Beside her, McHardy scrunched back down in his seat, raging in a Scottish brogue. She didn't understand all the words, but they had the sound of profanity. It all turned ugly for her when a tire ruptured on the Spider. The disintegrating tread slowed the car as she headed for another street. The other driver took advantage, pulling in front again, this time to block her escape.

Enough games. It was time to kick some butt.

"This guy is after you," Raja shouted. "Wanna live? Stay in the car and stay low. I'll handle him."

She opened her door as McHardy crouched on the floor. She went into a stance and aimed her Beretta at the other car. She stared at the roadster, then blinked. There was no sign of the driver.

Where'd he go?

Made no sense. It was like a ghost had been driving the car. Maybe the guy had ducked beneath the dashboard. Outside the car, she stood on tiptoes, trying to see.

From behind, a gun barrel nuzzled Rashmi Raja's neck.

Chapter 19

New York City
6:43 p.m.

Jared Cassidy paced the kitchen.

"What's the name of the researcher who lives here?"

"Tina Resnick."

"Maybe she was injured in the shooting."

"Maybe so," Cori answered. "When she ran into the hallway back at the school, I heard gunfire."

"We can't stay here, Cor. We need to go."

"Where? The police covered up the truth about Kaylyn's shooting. I'm glad I waited before contacting them."

She dropped frozen pastries into the toaster's twin slots. Shay was eating the first batch in the other room. Never in her life had Cori owned a reliable toaster. She wasn't the only one. The Resnick toaster branded the pastry's hide with black stripes. She took a big bite, then recoiled as the pastry burned her mouth.

Her brother leaned against the counter. "Let's say Dr. Resnick was murdered. Now you're in her house? Doesn't look good, Cor. Plus, you got into that fight with Kaylyn Brynstone, then you take Shayna, and now you're hiding out. NYPD is gonna think you worked with the bad guys to get the kid."

"Thanks, Jared. I feel so much better now." She blew on the pastry.

"The woman on TV said there were no serious injuries. I know that's not true about the mom, but it might be true about Resnick. She might be on her way home."

Cori hadn't thought about that.

"Let's get Shay out of here. Then we'll decide where to go."

A few minutes later, they were in the stairwell. Jared was on the phone, making hotel reservations. Cori raised her tongue, exploring the inflamed ridges where the toaster pastry had burned the roof of her mouth. Good thing Shay hadn't bitten into that one.

"Is he calling about my mom?" Shay asked.

Cori frowned. "He's finding us a new place to go. We need to get you safe; then we'll find out about your mom."

"I wish Daddy was here."

"Me too, sweetie. Me too."

Outside, the August sunshine was still dazzling. Cori slipped on sunglasses, then noticed Shay squinting. She made a mental note to buy her a pair. By the time they'd stepped outside, Jared had made hotel reservations on Broadway at Forty-Seventh Street.

"We're all set."

"Why Times Square?"

"You told me one time locals stay away from that place."

"It's a tourist destination."

"Well, you live in the city. They wouldn't expect you to go there."

Right now, Cori had to admit that she didn't have a better idea.

Emerging from the subway, they walked by a vendor parked at curbside. Shayna looked up pleadingly at Jared. "Can I have some ice cream?"

She took his hand and led him to the vendor. He glanced back at his sister.

"Girl knows how to get what she wants."

Cori nodded. "I know."

Shayna chose a SpongeBob SquarePants popsicle, the frozen treat molded as a yellow wedge with a grinning red mouth and black gumball eyes. Cori grabbed a raspberry sorbet cone sculpted into two uniform mounds. Inspired by Shay's choice, Jared bought a Batman popsicle, the superhero's horned mask and lantern jaw impaled on a flat stick.

"Thanks, Jared," the child said, patting his arm. "Can my imaginary friends get some ice cream?"

"*Friends?*" he asked. "Most kids have one. You must be popular. How many do you have?"

"Twelve," Cori answered for her. "Only eleven are here."

"There're all here," Shayna corrected.

"The one you don't like is here, too?"

The girl nodded.

Jared made a puzzled look. Cori could tell what he was thinking. Why would you spend time with an imaginary friend you didn't like?

"Why don't you like him?" Jared asked.

"He's super mean. His name is Monkey Guns."

Jared laughed.

Shayna looked hurt. "I don't like to talk about him."

"Sorry, kid. Didn't mean to upset you."

A melting corner from SpongeBob's head dropped onto her shirt, leaving a yellowish stain. A tear welled in her eye.

"Is my shirt ruined?" she asked in a quivering voice.

"It'll be fine," Cori assured her, distractedly wiping the fabric with a napkin as she glanced down the street.

A man at the corner watched Shayna. The light changed. He remained on the sidewalk, not crossing with the others. Wearing a knit cap and a scraggly beard, he didn't look like an agent. At the last minute, he decided to move into the crosswalk.

He still managed a look over his shoulder at Shayna.

Cori whispered to her brother. "Shay's had a tough day. It's catching up to her." She looked in the direction of a tchotchke shop. "Let's get her a new shirt."

New York City
7:05 p.m.

Stephen Angelilli lingered in the kitchen of Tina Resnick's apartment. He knew her. Every six weeks, Angelilli consulted with Resnick at the Brandonstein Center. The school psychologist had worked one-on-one with Shayna Brynstone.

"No sign of them," Patrick Langston reported, coming into Resnick's kitchen.

"Maybe not, but they were here."

"Think so?"

Angelilli nodded. Everything in the kitchen was unplugged. The Vita-Mix blender. The coffee pot. The cell phone charger. Everything, that is, except the toaster.

He examined it.

Smelled like something had burned. Tina Resnick's husband was in Japan, and she was in the hospital. Their adult kids had all moved out. So, who was using the toaster?

He glanced across the apartment to Resnick's office, where he'd seen a computer. Had Cori Cassidy searched it for information relating to Wonderland?

Langston checked his phone. "Something interesting came in, sir. Cassidy's brother is in town. He called her earlier today."

"Track the signal," Angelilli ordered. "Maybe he can help us find his sister."

Chapter 20

Brynstone aimed the handgun at the Indian woman's head, the barrel pressing against her long black hair. With liquid speed, she spun around, kicking the gun from his hand. He'd let his guard down.

Stupid mistake—it wouldn't happen again.

Facing him now, she tried another capoeira move, this one a forward punch known as the *asfixiante*. He seized her wrist before she connected. Clutching her now, he sensed the vibrancy of muscles packed into her forearm. She was serious about the attack and he could tell the woman wanted to hurt him. She brought a swift palm strike. He snatched her left hand, holding both wrists now.

The woman seethed.

Brynstone sensed her foot raising, moving in for a thrusting kick from the front. He twisted her arms, spinning her away as if executing some violent tango, then wrapped his arms around her to draw her back close to his chest. Embracing her. Energy sizzled inside her taut body. She didn't like a man controlling her.

Brynstone unfurled his arms, flinging her toward the car. She caught herself before hitting it. She curled as she rebounded, then straightened and fixed her piercing gaze on him.

"You were at the warehouse," she said. "A prisoner. How did you escape?"

"With your help." He held up her throwing weapon.

She sneered and balled her hand into a fist.

"You tried that already," he said. "We both know hand-to-hand combat isn't working for you right now."

"At least I didn't draw a gun on a defenseless woman."

"You're not defenseless."

"Glad you noticed," she purred.

"Why do you want Math McHardy?"

"He's a brilliant thinker."

"You in the habit of kidnapping smart people?"

"If they have something I need."

"What do you need?"

She took a step forward. The woman reached up and clenched his chin, holding it with a firm grip. "What are you offering?"

He turned his head, pulling free from her hand. He glanced at the car. Still dazed from his abduction, McHardy was watching them as he held his head.

"He's not young," Brynstone said. "You were rough on him."

"He didn't come peacefully."

"Give me the Roman facemask."

"It's in the car."

"Get it."

"I have a feeling," she said, "we might be looking for the same thing. Maybe we want Math McHardy for the same reason." She flashed a sexy smile. "Wanna partner up for this job?"

Brynstone didn't answer. Muscles tightened around his jaw. Was this a game? He couldn't be certain.

All at once, he had the feeling he had cornered a black widow spider.

New York City
7:15 p.m.

Shay tried on sunglasses, looking heartbreakingly adorable the whole time. Her current pair were rimmed in Sleeping Beauty pink and adorned with sparkles. She cocked her head as she studied her look in the mirror, posing like a little movie star.

"What a cutie," a white-haired woman said. With red lipstick and an aggressive floral-print dress, she stood out among the tourists crowding the Times Square shop. "How old? Seven? Eight, maybe?"

"Almost six," Cori said, smiling.

"Tall for her age," the woman observed. "Long legs."

Jared walked up, holding a T-shirt. "Can I get it for her?"

He unfolded the white shirt. The front featured a playful cartoon figure—almost like a ghost—holding hands with a little girl. The word *BIFF* was centered in bold letters at the top of the shirt. At the bottom it read, "Best Imaginary Friends Forever."

"Buy it," the older woman ordered, then turned to find her husband.

Shay saw the shirt and tackled Jared with a hug.

Asking her brother to watch the girl so she could find clothes for herself, Cori grabbed the first T-shirt she could find along with a pair of gray sweatpants with the letters *NYPD* emblazoned across the butt. She also snatched a baseball cap before noticing another customer.

A guy with hair graying at the temples and puppy-dog blue eyes was watching her. The slender man wore a pinstriped Toledo Mud Hens jersey. The customer made her nervous until he turned away to examine a movie prop, a black statuette of the Maltese Falcon.

Shay came over as Cori paid at the counter. She held the *BIFF* shirt Jared had bought her. The child studied a row of snow globes, each encasing a miniature Empire State Building, before noticing an iconic photograph of John Lennon posing with the Statue of Liberty as a backdrop. He wore a dark coat, trademark round glasses, and a wry expression. His raised fingers formed a peace sign.

"That's the Smart One, isn't it?"

"In all his glory. He loved New York City."

Shay narrowed her eyes. "He looks sad."

"Maybe he was. He had Nixon and Elvis and everyone else after him."

After paying, Cori told her brother to wait. He nodded, but didn't look up from his phone as he laughed at a video of PewDiePie and his dog.

She led Shay to a small restroom at the back of the store. Locking the door, they changed their clothes. Cori popped open the swing lid on a trash can and ditched her dirtied tee and pink cap inside, then pulled on the new shirt, a powder-blue one that was a size too big. She then pulled out her ponytail before combing through it with her fingers. Beside her, Shay changed into the *BIFF* shirt and admired her look in the mirror.

Emerging from the restroom, Cori spied her brother on the opposite side of the store, near the entrance. Jared waved, then returned his attention to the PewDie video. Not far from him, two men dressed in suits walked into the shop. In unison, they removed sunglasses and looked around.

The men approached Jared.

Cori couldn't hear their conversation, but she saw Jared say something, then point to the storefront window where a bustle of people wandered Times Square. Following his direction, both men turned away to look outside. Taking advantage of the distraction, Jared glanced back at her and mouthed, "Go."

Cori pulled the baseball cap onto her head and tugged down the stiff brim. Turning around, she grabbed Shay's hand and guided her back toward the restroom, blocking the men's view of the child as they walked.

"Where we going?" Shay asked. "Is Jared coming?"

"He'll catch up later."

Passing the bathroom, they found an exit door. Cori didn't like leaving Jared back there. Still, she was confident her brother knew how to take care of himself.

———◆———

Stephen Angelilli hurried up a constricted stairwell leading to a second-floor comic book shop on West Fortieth. Taking a turn, he walked the hardwood floor, passing aisle after aisle of comics and trade paperbacks. The wall ahead featured a life-size replica of the Incredible Hulk busting in from Times Square. As he passed a counter filled with props and statues, a shaggy-headed fanboy wearing a faded Green Lantern shirt moved aside and looked over at the dark-suited CIA officer like he was an alien life-form.

Mason "Dixon" Eisermen saw him coming. An oversized Avengers poster hung on the wall behind the CIA officer. With his square jaw and grim expression, Eisermen almost looked like he belonged up there with the superheroes. He opened the door to the manager's office and Angelilli stepped inside.

Stacks of narrow white boxes filled the cramped room. A guy in his midtwenties hunched over a table, flipping through a comic book. Jack Rickerson and Patrick Langston stood behind Jared Cassidy, arms crossed, keeping him in their vigilant gaze.

Jared closed the Batman comic, smiling ironically at the agents. "So, the CIA makes its headquarters in a comic-book store. Tough times, huh?"

Angelilli kept his face expressionless. "Hey, kid, think this is a good time to be a smart-ass?"

"Probably not."

"One of my men has a brother who runs this place. And it's close." Angelilli wheeled around a chair, then eased into it. "Where is she?"

"Who?"

"Come on, Jared. Your sister's up to her eyeballs in trouble. We need her. And she needs us."

Jared glanced down, suddenly interested in his interlaced fingers. He thought it over.

"I have questions," Jared Cassidy said.

"You and everybody else. We're not in the business of answering questions."

"Why is the CIA interested in my sister? And the little girl?"

"Where's your sister?"

His gaze shifted to the Batman paperback. The cover had the word *Hush* in the title. Maybe it gave the kid ideas that he could shut up.

"You're not gonna find answers in a comic book."

"It's a graphic novel," he answered. "And I'd like to speak to my attorney."

"Yeah, well, your daddy's not here."

"Then someone at his firm."

"Let me impress this upon you, Jared. There are people out there who will do anything to get that little girl. Today, they killed one of my men. They shot the girl's mother. They will kill anyone who gets in their way." Angelilli sneered, "Right now, one person stands in their way. Your sister. Let me assure you, they will be more than happy to kill Cori."

"Who we talking about? Who are these people?"

Angelilli wasn't answering.

"The longer we sit here playing games, the closer those people get to finding your sister. Understand me, Jared?"

The kid raised his fist to his mouth, running the edge of his thumbnail along the bottom row of teeth.

Angelilli glanced at his watch.

Jared sighed. "We were in that shop. I don't know where they went. Even if I did, Cori wouldn't want me to tell you."

"I met your sister once, you know," Angelilli said. "We were on a flight from Europe a few years ago. Cori's a sweet kid." He rose from the chair and headed for the door. "After they recover the body, I'll be sure to send flowers to her funeral."

Midnight opened the door. Angelilli stepped into the hallway.

"Wait," Jared called.

Angelilli stopped, closing his eyes. A thin smile crossed his lips.

Chapter 21

Cori was grateful her brother had made hotel arrangements. The two-room suite was more upscale than she had expected. He'd paid over the phone, so all she had to do was check in. She hoped Jared would join them soon.

Propped on the bed, Shay curled up next to her, wearing the *BIFF* shirt that Jared had bought. Cori stroked the girl's blonde hair, noticing the color was a near match to her own. It was also about the same thickness, although Shay's hair was longer. With similar eyes and features, they could pass for sisters or maybe mother and daughter. She was certain the guy down in the Hilton lobby had thought so.

"I miss my daddy."

A deep sigh. "I know, sweetie. We'll find him. I know he wants to see you."

"Are you and my daddy best friends?"

"Um." Cori swallowed. "I like your daddy. He's smart, he's a really good guy, and he has clear blue eyes, like you."

"You have blue eyes."

"Yeah, but not like you and your daddy. Your eyes are light blue, almost like Cinderella's dress."

The child giggled.

Score a point. That line seemed to comfort her.

Cori remembered seeing something in the report from Shay's school. It was about a skill she had called the Hollow. She wanted to ask about it, but she didn't want to push the child. Was now the time?

"Shay, I have a question about the researchers at your school."

"Like Dr. Resnick?"

"Yeah."

The little girl looked up. "Hear that sound?"

Cori raised her head.

A card swiping in the door.

She moved off the bed.

"Where you going?" Shay asked.

"Jared's here." Her feet touched carpet as she pulled away from the little girl.

"Don't leave me," she pleaded.

"Honey, I'll be right back."

She hurried toward the door as it opened.

"Jared," she called.

It wasn't him. A man in a dark suit stepped into the hotel room, looking around. Three more came in behind him. The first guy saw her and raised an identification card.

Cori didn't make a sound. She pivoted on one foot, turning toward the bedroom. Running, she made it inside and reached for the door to shut it behind her. On the bed, Shayna's face was alight with fear. She could see the man. Eyes wide and her mouth open, she screamed. Cori slammed the door and wished the thing had a lock. Didn't matter because the man kicked it open, ripping the knob away from her hand.

Shayna was all that mattered. Cori had to get to the child.

As Cori reached the bed, the man wrapped his arms around her waist, lifting her feet from the floor. He swung her around to face the bedroom door. She twisted in his grip, elbowing him in the ear as she struggled to get free.

The child stood on the bed, her face scarlet as she screamed with outstretched arms. "Don't leave me, Cori!"

She remembered the little girl building a fortress of ponies around her. A little girl who needed to feel secure and who needed to protect the people in her life so they didn't go away.

Don't leave me, Cori.

———◆———

Stephen Angelilli watched as agents Jack "Ripper" Rickerson and Patrick "Midnight" Langston grappled with the woman. A wildcat in a T-shirt and sweatpants, Cori Cassidy was tiny, but a fighter. They dragged her into the next room. Back in the bedroom, Wonderland was holding her own, locked in Mason Eisermen's grip. He was now heading this way with the girl.

"Hold up, Dixon."

The man stopped at the door.

Angelilli studied Wonderland. For the past several years, he had been on special assignment, following orders to watch John Brynstone's daughter as part of Operation Red Opera. They had documented her every move, most of it mundane activity. CIA Director Mark McKibbon had handpicked Angelilli after he had had flown with Cori Cassidy from Europe to the United States. During the flight, Angelilli had riddled Cassidy with questions and listened to her unsatisfying answers. He had always sensed the woman was hiding something.

Over the years, he had watched Wonderland grow up. He witnessed virtually every public move she had made. Though he felt like he knew her almost as well as his own children, he'd never spoken to her before this moment.

"It's okay, Shayna," he said, softening his voice. "We'll help you."

"I . . . I want Cori," the child choked. "Cori."

"I need to talk to Cori for a minute," Angelilli said. "Be a good girl and go with this nice man. He'll get you candy." He shot a quick look at Dixon. "Get Wonderland inside the Suburban. Don't attract attention in the lobby."

As they went out the door, Angelilli turned back.

The Cassidy woman was still fighting, a whirlwind of rage as she hammered fists at Midnight and Ripper.

"Stop it, Cori," he said in a commanding voice. "Stop it right now."

As the tall officers held her arms, she finally stopped fighting. Ripper and Midnight backed off. Both seemed relieved.

"I know you," the woman said.

"Good memory."

"How do I know you?"

Angelilli slid onto a sofa. He motioned for her to sit.

"You got into trouble once upon a time. The police took you into custody; then I showed up and saved your ass."

"Paris." She eased into a chair, watching him. "You're the CIA agent who brought me back to the United States."

"You trusted me back then, Cori. You can trust me now."

Sniffing, she wiped her nose. "Where's Shayna?"

"Eating candy."

She made a face. "She's had a lot of sugar today."

"Why did you take her, Cori?"

No answer. The woman stared at the white tips of her manicured nails.

"We want to protect her," Angelilli said. "As you know, she's a special little girl. We're not the only ones who know that. Who were the people at the school today?"

"It was all so confusing," Cori muttered. "Tell me about Kaylyn Brynstone. Is she okay?"

"Dead."

Angelilli could have been less blunt, but he decided against sugarcoating the facts with this woman.

Cori sunk her face in her hands. She said something like, "Oh, God. Oh, God." At least, it sounded like it.

"Has Shayna asked about her mother?" he asked.

"Yeah," she said in a teary voice. "She knew that Kaylyn was shot. I talked with Shayna about her mom after we checked into this hotel room. She's a tough kid. Shayna wants to see her father. She keeps asking about him."

"John Brynstone."

"Have you talked to him?" she asked.

"Not so far. You?"

"We haven't talked in years."

"Sure about that?"

"I sent a couple e-mails, the last probably six months back, but he never answered." She looked at him. "I left two messages today. He isn't returning my calls. How did you find me?"

"Your brother."

"You have Jared?" Cori exhaled forcefully. "He didn't have anything to do with this."

Angelilli held up a hand, stopping her. "We talked to him."

"I want to see Jared."

"That's a distinct possibility," Angelilli said. "I can reunite you with your brother. Maybe Shayna, too. First, though, you have to talk to me. No bullshit. Deal, Cori?"

Chapter 22

Airborne over Germany
2:19 a.m.

There were three people flying on the private jet, none of whom liked each other. Who among the three, Rashmi Raja wondered, would be the first to stab the other two in the back? She didn't think it would be the professor.

That left Brynstone.

She had mixed feelings about the man. His dark and rugged American look fascinated her, and she marveled at his intelligence and his nomadic spirit. She sensed an instant and odd connection back in London.

Could she trust him? Probably not.

Did she want to trust him? Maybe.

That troubled her more than anything.

Back in her native India, her parents had hosted social gatherings for an elite circle of friends. Even as a child, Raja knew how to charm guests. Before long, she had learned to take command of any situation. At age eighteen, she had moved to the United States, where she had lined up her first jobs in adventure theft—something her family knew nothing about. Her career demanded a more solitary existence. Brynstone seemed to share that with her.

Tapping into the collective wisdom of Brynstone and McHardy would be an advantage—but could she do that without them knowing? And could they all work together?

McHardy looked relaxed in a leather club chair aboard his Bombardier aircraft. The midcabin interior was accented in cream hues and soffit lighting with polished rosewood doorways. The professor was filthy rich. Not as wealthy as her family, but enough to afford this jet.

"You hurt me, you know," McHardy grumbled. "Knocking me around like a punching bag."

"Be glad I went easy on you," she countered. "You should see what I can do to a punching bag."

The old man leaned forward. "I know we agreed to work together, Dr. Brynstone, but I do not want to work with that woman."

Raja made a hurt look, mocking him a little. She liked the way he talked. She'd always been a sucker for Scotsmen, even one as impossible as McHardy.

It shocked her when Brynstone answered, "I don't want to work with her, either."

The man was full of surprises.

"We don't have a choice, gentlemen," she said, tapping the arm of her chair.

They were seated around a small table attached to the midcabin wall. The polished black surface displayed the facemask she had taken from Nessa Griffin's people at the London warehouse. "We want the same thing," Raja continued. "And I have something you need."

"Show us," Brynstone said.

His voice was rich and deep. His eyes were icy blue, a striking contrast against his tanned skin. Her mother wouldn't approve, of course. Too American.

Raja dug in her backpack and brought out the Roman cheek guard. She placed it on the table beside the facemask.

"We cool now?" she asked.

Brynstone studied it. "Where'd you get that?"

"Bulgaria."

"Excellent." McHardy grabbed the cheek guard. He glanced up with a sly grin. "You paid a visit to Nikola Paskalev."

"Who's Paskalev?" Brynstone asked.

"His father was an Olympic athlete before joining the mafia. Some time ago, I tried to buy this piece from the old man. He was a monster."

"That's the difference," she said. "I didn't try to buy it."

"Nikola is even more cunning and intimidating than his father. He must be unhappy with you."

"Paskalev is not unhappy," she answered. "Paskalev is dead."

McHardy furrowed his brow. "What was his cause of death?"

She shrugged. "Bad karma."

Satisfied with her answer, the man slid the cheek guard into place beside the facemask. Its curving surface fit perfectly.

"I'm new to stealing Roman relics," she said. "Care to fill in the blanks about our mutual interest?"

Brynstone studied her. "You first."

"I like excitement," Raja admitted. "I take jobs that interest me. I'm a finder of lost things. In all honesty, I don't need the money; I just enjoy a good challenge."

His eyes narrowed. "It seems to be a challenge for you to give a straight answer."

A pretty smile flitted across her face. "We have that in common, don't we, Dr. Brynstone?"

"Someone hired you to collect this part of the helmet. Who is it?"

"I won't identify the collector."

"Do you have any more pieces of the helmet?"

"No," she lied. "Do you?"

"Just the facemask."

McHardy pointed to the mask on the table. "This is a central part of the puzzle. So is the cheek guard."

"You think it's a puzzle?" Raja asked.

"I know it's a puzzle." The man licked his lips. "You haven't noticed the engraved symbols inside the mask and cheek guard?"

"Some kind of code," she added. "Couldn't figure it out."

"I can figure out anything with time and resources," said McHardy. "The problem is that we don't have the complete helmet."

"How much is missing?"

"Four pieces, I'd estimate."

"You think the code stretches around the entire helmet?"

"That's my guess. From what I can decipher, it's a story or an interlocking series of stories. It's not just any code. Are you familiar with Linear A?"

They shook their heads. Brynstone looked at her. She liked his cool intensity. She sensed a competitive intelligence. And mystery—there was a great deal of mystery lurking inside the man.

McHardy cleared his throat.

"Linear A is an extinct and unsolved script that was discovered more than a century ago by a British archaeologist named Sir Arthur Evans. He located the legendary ancient city of Knossos on the island of Crete. In the palace of King Minos, Evans discovered thousands of clay tablets with two different linear scripts. Linear A was an undeciphered script that had been used to create the Minoan language. After decades of research, cryptanalysts were able to break Linear B."

"But Linear A remains a mystery," Raja guessed.

"Until recently. I'm not a cryptanalyst, but I corresponded years ago with one who taught me how to read the code."

"And the code on that helmet?" she asked. "Are those symbols Linear A?"

"They are," McHardy added. "As I said, Linear A is found on clay pottery from the Minoan culture. Later, sea traders brought their pottery to Asia Minor and parts of what today is known as England."

"How old is that helmet?"

"First century. A soldier in the Roman army would have worn it. At some point, a person identified as the Keeper began a journey recorded inside the helmet and mask. Now, if you'll provide silence, perhaps I can decipher it."

"Guess we better let the man work," Brynstone said, rising from his chair.

"Sure thing," Raja agreed. "Let's go be awesome somewhere else."

They walked the aisle to the galley near the front of the jet. Heading to the refrigerator, he glanced down at her shoes, low-top fashion sneakers with signature red and green stripes along each side.

"What kind of shoes you got there?"

"Gucci."

He arched an eyebrow. "What's wrong with Nike or Converse?"

"Not my image."

"How much you pay for those things?"

"Four hundred and thirty-five dollars."

Brynstone frowned but let it go, opening the fridge.

"Want something to drink?"

"I'm trying to imagine what Math McHardy keeps in his refrigerator."

"Mostly soft drinks."

"Does he have diet?"

He handed her an orange Irn-Bru can. She'd had the Scottish soda before and was happy with the choice. Brynstone opened a cabinet door and found whisky. He debated among the Speyside malts, then chose a Glenlivet bottle.

"You borrowed my phone to call someone," said Raja.

"My daughter."

He poured whisky into a tumbler emblazoned with the Scotland national football logo.

"Wanted to call before bedtime. My little princess. Tell her a quick story about Lucy and Lindsey."

"Who?"

"Two characters we made up. You ever read the *Prince and the Pauper*? It's like that. Girls who trade places. One lives in Brooklyn. One lives in Pinktopia."

She giggled. "You don't seem like a guy who tells bedtime stories about girls from Pinktopia."

He shrugged. "I put my twist on it. Lucy doesn't know it yet, but her dad used to be an intelligence agent. He's been missing for years. I had a good one planned for tonight. Lucy and Lindsey were supposed to discover a volcano on an island."

"You didn't talk to your daughter?"

"No one answered." He sipped, taking the whisky neat. "Maybe it's for the best. Because of my stories, Shayna told her teacher she didn't want to be a princess anymore."

"Yeah?"

"She said princesses are too helpless. They always get kidnapped." Brynstone grinned. "My daughter said she wants to be a ninja instead."

"A ninja?" Raja giggled again. "I totally like this kid."

"Glad you think it's funny." He looked down. "My ex didn't. She let me know it."

Raja had noticed he wasn't wearing a ring.

"When'd you guys divorce?"

"A while back." His face darkened and he took another swig of his drink. He clearly didn't want to discuss it, and she decided against pushing him. The silence became awkward, so she turned and raided a cabinet. Finding a box of Jaffa Cakes waiting inside, she pulled out the blue box and waved it with the zeal of a lottery winner.

"Look what I found."

"What is it?"

"Jaffa Cakes. Want one?"

"Never heard of them."

"Oh my God. These things are like crack. You Americans have no clue what you're missing."

"Thought you were an American."

"I am. Kind of. I don't know what I am." She took a bite and closed her eyes, flashing a look of ecstasy.

"That good, huh?"

She nodded and smiled and scrunched her nose.

"Why *cakes*? Things look like cookies to me."

"Well, that's a big debate," she said, studying the popular UK snack. "Right up there with the free will–determinism issue."

"No kidding? Cookie or cake. What side you fall on?"

"Dude, I don't care. I just eat the crackly chocolate coating, then I suck out the orange jelly stuff like a vampire. Then I munch on the spongy bottom." She held up the soft drink. "With this and the Jaffa Cakes? I'm headed for an orange-plosion in my mouth in a couple minutes."

"I'll stick to whisky."

"Why are we flying to Prague?" she asked.

"McHardy didn't tell you?"

"No."

He took another drink. "More than a decade ago, he visited a museum at the Institute for Classical Archaeology at Charles University. Most of the exhibits featured classical sculpture and architecture. The museum staff prefers Greek painted vessels over military armor."

"Mm-hmm."

"Anyway, McHardy saw a fragment of the Roman helmet. First time he'd seen it. Right side of the skull piece. It had a leather interior to protect the soldier's head. He could see encrypted characters beneath the leather cover. They let him inspect it, but only for a short time. He didn't get a chance to decipher the code."

"Why didn't he go back to examine it?" she asked before taking a drink, the soda's barley flavor playing on her tongue.

"Helmet fragment is no longer on public display."

"That sucks."

"It's not even available for scholars to examine."

"McHardy is a prima donna. Maybe the museum staff didn't want to deal with his personality."

"Could you blame them?"

"Not one bit."

"This collector who hired you," Brynstone said, shifting the conversation. "Tell me about him."

She shrugged. Brynstone was persistent, but she decided she didn't mind.

"He's a collector of antiquities. His private collection is extensive."

"What's his name?"

"Like I said, can't tell you."

"I told you about Nessa Griffin. I need to know I can trust you."

She bit her lip, pausing, then finally answered, "Nicholas Booth."

"You've found more than one piece of the helmet for Booth. Haven't you?"

The question surprised her. "I already told you—this is my first."

She was lying, of course, but she sustained eye contact. To her relief, McHardy walked into the galley, interrupting their conversation.

"Come here," he demanded. "The both of you. And stop drinking my liquor."

Brynstone followed them back to the midcabin. Hunkered over the table, McHardy fit together the pieces of the helmet, then traced his finger along the engraved surface.

"What's it say?" Brynstone asked.

"It is a rather meandering parable." McHardy rubbed his chin. "In part, it tells the story of Saint Lazarus."

"I'm a lapsed Hindu," Raja said, "but are you talking about the man Jesus brought back from the dead? That Lazarus?"

"Aye. There were two mentioned in the New Testament, but this refers to Lazarus of Bethany. Also known as Lazarus of the Four Days."

"Why that name?"

"He was resurrected four days after dying."

"Go ahead," Brynstone urged. "What does it say, McHardy?"

"As far as I know, the Gospel doesn't say a solitary word about Lazarus in his later years. According to some accounts, however, he traveled to Gaul—later known as France—where he became an archbishop. The helmet that we found? Well, it goes beyond what even the apocryphal statements tell us about Lazarus."

According to one Gnostic legend, McHardy explained, Jesus had used a special medicine known as the White Chrism to bring Lazarus back from the dead. Although a reliquary in France claimed to possess the bones of the saint, the helmet code asserted there was more to the story of Lazarus. It hinted that his fate took a dark turn near the end of his long life. Because additional information was inscribed on a missing helmet piece, the ending wasn't clear.

"At the end of the day, we don't have all the answers," McHardy said. "But, I've determined that the facemask contains a coded map."

"Leading to what?" Raja asked.

"Can't say." McHardy pinched the bridge of his nose. "But the person who wrote this code tells an interesting story. It concerns a man named Josephus of Massilia. I thought that the person who had engraved this helmet was the Keeper, but it appears I was wrong."

"Josephus was the Keeper?"

"Keeper of what?" Raja asked.

"The Radix."

Brynstone gave McHardy a sharp look. "Edgar Wurm told me that Joseph of Arimathea was the Keeper of the Radix."

"He was, for a time. Joseph of Arimathea was the father of Josephus," McHardy explained.

Known as one of Christ's secret followers, Joseph of Arimathea had been mentioned in all four Gospels. At the time, the man had been a wealthy Palestinian merchant from Jerusalem. He was also a member of the high-ruling council known as the Sanhedrin. According to one source, a physician named Luke had stopped him on his way to a council meeting. Taking him into confidence, Luke had given Joseph of Arimathea several possessions to safe-guard during dangerous times for the apostles who followed their controversial leader. Luke had believed that Joseph of Arimathea could be trusted with the Radix and the Scintilla.

According to a popular legend, Joseph of Arimathea had been given the cup used at the Last Supper, making him the first Grail Keeper. At the Crucifixion, he was said to have dipped the last known piece of the Radix in a cruet containing Christ's blood, preserving it. From that time on, he became the Keeper of the Radix.

After the Crucifixion, Joseph of Arimathea opened up his sepulcher and made arrangements to have the body of Jesus of Nazareth laid to rest there. It was suggested that he had worked with Luke and a man named Nicodemus to create a mixture including the Radix to preserve the body of the fallen Christ.

"Joseph of Arimathea was the first Keeper of the Radix," McHardy said. "After his death, he entrusted the Radix to his son, Josephus of Massilia."

Around 36 CE, according to one tradition, Joseph of Arimathea had sailed to Gaul, a region of Western Europe during the time of the Roman Empire. Together with his wife, Elyab, Joseph raised sons named Adam and Josephus. For several years, they lived in Marseilles, known as Massilia in the ancient world. Later, Joseph of Arimathea traveled to Britannia, where he was consecrated as the apostle of the British Isles. McHardy told how the travelers settled on a land once called Ineswitrin, later to be known as Glastonbury.

"The Radix was with them the whole time?" Raja asked. "They took it to England?"

"That's the popular legend. It was said that Joseph hid the Radix somewhere near Glastonbury. It remained buried for ten centuries, but never forgotten as generations of mystery cults kept alive the Radix romance."

Raja crossed her arms. "So this Josephus guy was the Keeper of the Radix after his dad, Joseph of Arimathea, died. You think the helmet fragments have something to do with the Radix?"

"I have an opinion. I'm not sharing it."

"Opinion or not, tell us, McHardy."

"Do you know about the fate of the White Chrism?"

Brynstone nodded. "Years ago, Edgar Wurm and a woman named Cori Cassidy discovered an ancient document called the Scintilla in which was written a formula to create the White Chrism and the Black Chrism." He frowned. "Only problem is that when they found the Scintilla, the bottom half had been torn away. The vellum contained the formula for the White Chrism. The half with the Black Chrism formula was missing. After Wurm's death, the Arts and Antiques Unit at Scotland Yard seized the vellum that Wurm and Cassidy had found. The formula was locked away."

"Until three years ago," McHardy grumbled, "when a team attacked a transport vehicle carrying the formula for the White Chrism as it was moved from New Scotland Yard to a storage facility."

"Who would do that?" Raja asked.

Brynstone knew.

"Wish I had an idea," McHardy sighed. "Many people have an interest in these matters. Centuries ago, the Knights Hospitaller possessed the Radix and the formulae for both chrisms."

The Hospitaller organization had survived to the present day as the Sovereign Military Order of Malta. Brynstone knew that the Knights of Malta were not involved in the hunt for the Radix, but one of their most powerful members did have an interest. Wurm had claimed that Mark McKibbon, the CIA director, wanted to find the Radix and the chrisms.

"If I understand the helmet code, it's possible the map leads to the formula for the Black Chrism," McHardy said. "Several clues seem to lead to specific places."

"Like what?"

"The code on the facemask mentions something about 'where the terrible sister soars above the serpent king.' I have no idea what it means."

"Can you can figure it out?"

He shrugged. "Not until I see additional pieces of the helmet. That's why we're headed to Prague."

Raja crossed her arms. "Brynstone said there's a helmet piece at Charles University. Sounds like it's locked away."

"That's why McHardy invited us on his jet," Brynstone added. "That's why he's sharing information. What part do you and I play? We're breaking into that museum to steal the helmet piece."

Chapter 23

Dusk closed in hard as Cori stared out the tinted window of the Chevy Suburban. She let her eyes go wide—seeing without seeing—as the vehicle passed a blurring landscape. She was sitting behind the driver, the CIA agent who had tackled her in the hotel room. A red line scored his forehead where she had scratched him. Once in a while, he'd turn his head and the rearview mirror would offer her a look at the slash mark.

She didn't feel bad about it.

Stephen Angelilli was seated beside her. During the drive, she overheard another agent refer to him as Scarecrow. He was peppering her with questions, but she had some of her own.

"Tell me about Anne Bliss Niess."

"Don't know her," Angelilli said.

"She's a marriage and family therapist in Manhattan who did some couples counseling with John and Kaylyn Brynstone. Dr. Niess encouraged the Brynstones to test Shayna."

"Any chance you were reading confidential files at the Resnick house, Ms. Cassidy?"

"Shayna's a bright kid, but she was the only one to get a full ride in years. I wondered why. Now that I see the CIA's interest, I think I have the answer. You're behind the scholarship, aren't you?

Your people worked a deal with the Brandonstein Center, so you could monitor research on Shayna."

"I knew your dad was an attorney. Now you sound like one."

"Where did you take Shayna? I need to know."

"She's safe." Angelilli studied her. "You witnessed Kaylyn Brynstone's murder. We can't afford to take chances with Shayna. We moved her to a secure location."

"Edgar Wurm told me something the night he died," Cori said. "He claimed the director of the Central Intelligence Agency wanted the Radix."

"Wurm was barking mad," he snorted. "Guy was in a mental hospital for almost two years."

"You know, everyone talks about him being crazy, but I study clinical psychology and I knew him. He was a genius. Now tell me, is it true what he said about Mark McKibbon?"

"Look, Wurm was convinced everyone was conspiring against him. I can assure you, Ms. Cassidy, the director has more important matters on his mind."

The SUV slowed.

Cori glanced up. "Something wrong?"

He didn't answer. The driver pulled behind a matching Suburban parked alongside the highway shoulder. He didn't turn off the engine.

Glancing over, Angelilli said, "Get out."

"But what if—"

"Get out, Cori. Now."

She didn't argue.

She scrambled from the vehicle. Angelilli followed.

It was a hot night, maybe high eighties. Her heart thundered in her chest. She squinted at the other vehicle as the front passenger door opened. She stopped. A man in a suit stepped onto the pavement. She recognized him as another CIA officer from the hotel room in Times Square. He opened the back passenger door. She didn't know what to expect.

Shayna Brynstone jumped out.

Cori blinked, then gave a teary giggle. Shay ran toward her, arms outspread. Cori dropped to her knees on the gravel beside the road and scooped up the girl, the sharp embrace bringing tears of astonished joy to Cori's eyes. Shay wrapped her slender arms around Cori's neck so tight it almost hurt. On her feet now, Cori swung her in a lazy circle, the child's hair matted against Cori's tearstained face.

"Thought I'd lost you."

"No, sweetie," Cori answered in a soft voice, wiping a tear with the back of her thumb. "I'll never let that happen."

"All right," Angelilli called. "Hate to break up the reunion, but we're on a tight schedule." He waved to the first SUV. "Let's go."

"Where are you taking us?"

"We'll discuss it later."

Cori wasn't totally comfortable with the CIA and disliked how they kept her in the dark. On the other hand, Kaylyn's killers were still out there hunting for Shay. Maybe going with the CIA was her best option.

"Ms. Cassidy, you ride in the middle row. Shayna, go in back."

Cori had to hand it to them. Like the Boy Scouts, the CIA came prepared. They had a booster seat waiting back there. There was even a bag of Goldfish crackers.

Buckled in, Shay was positioned right behind Cori. An agent with short brown hair took the next seat. Agent Ripper was seated beside the little girl.

"Think you could scoot over, mister?" Shay asked Ripper.

"What's the problem?"

Cori turned in her seat. "She wants you to move, so her imaginary friend can sit there."

The agent looked bewildered. "I'm sorry?"

"Princess Rosalina wants to sit there," Shay added.

"Oh, yeah? How about the princess sits on the other side?"

Standing outside the open door, Angelilli had been talking to the driver. He looked at the backseat now. "Let's see some cooperation, Ripper. Give up your seat to the princess."

Grumbling, the agent unbuckled and moved his big frame farther away from Shay.

"Can you buckle in Princess Rosalina?" the child asked, all sweetness and light.

The agent looked at Angelilli.

Without turning, he ordered, "Do it, Ripper."

Nodding, the man stretched out the seat belt as if wrapping it around an invisible lap, then fastened the buckle. He stared for a beat, then reached down to buckle himself.

Cori swiveled around and faced forward with a smile. The kid was amazing. Not quite six, she already had the CIA doing her bidding.

"Are you coming with us?" Cori asked.

"No, ma'am," Angelilli answered. "Need to take a meeting."

"I want to see my brother."

"I'll make it happen."

"When?"

"It's in the works. Thank you for your cooperation, Ms. Cassidy."

He closed the door. The Suburban swerved back onto the highway, leaving Angelilli behind.

For the next ten minutes, Cori chatted with Shay. It was strained, the conversation going back and forth with agents seated beside each of them.

"Have you talked to my daddy?"

"We're trying—"

Without warning, Shayna screamed and pointed out her window. Eyes bright with surprise, Cori turned to look.

An out-of-control vehicle was careening toward them. It raced across the lane and smashed into their vehicle. The jarring impact rocked the Suburban and it swerved, spinning out of control. Out of nowhere, another vehicle suddenly hit the front of their car. The Suburban flipped sideways. Buckled in, Cori was slammed face-first into the window as a side airbag burst at her head. Blood spurted across the glass. The vehicle rolled, then came to a hard stop on the road.

It was over as fast as it had started.

A sick buzzing sound filled her ears. Her head felt thick and slow. "Shay," she moaned.

The brown-haired agent slumped against her shoulder, eyes closed. The driver was propped against an airbag. Pain surged inside her arm, then moved into her neck and up into her forehead. In back, Ripper was sprawled across the seat. Spidery lines of blood crossed his face.

As if in a hazy dream, she saw the little girl move from her seat. Cori tried to speak, but no sound escaped her bloodied mouth. She saw a cut across Shay's smooth cheek. The girl kneeled beside Ripper almost like she was praying. *What is she doing?*

Her small hand reached out. She touched the forehead of the CIA agent.

Cori couldn't keep her eyes open. The image of Shayna Brynstone dissolved in a blurry swirl. Fighting to stay conscious, Cori tried to move, but the airbag pressed against her cheek. She blinked slowly, twice.

Tilting her head to the side, she saw Shay crawling toward her.

Cori's eyes closed as she slipped into a sickening blackness.

8:44 p.m.

"Open the doors," Viktor Nebola ordered as he marched toward the Suburban. In the moonlight, the CIA's vehicle rested on its side eight feet from the pavement.

Nebola's men hurried to the vehicle. In case the CIA came out firing, Wingo went into a fighting stance with his semiautomatic pistol. His eyes looked fierce, highlighted by the white streak in his black hair. With Wingo covering him, Richard Eden opened the door.

Nebola peered inside the SUV and found a jumble of bodies. Splashes of blood stained the windows. The passengers were fixed in their seat belts except for a small child with the most luminescent pale blue eyes. She was in the middle of it all, staring at Nebola, her mouth frozen in a scream. Her sunlit hair was in disarray, but there wasn't a cut or even a fresh bruise on her face or slender arms. The child's small hand was poised in midair, frozen above the still figure of a blonde woman who must be Cori Cassidy.

Nebola turned to Eden. "Take her."

The man reached over the body of a CIA officer and grabbed the child. She kicked and shrieked and generally made a nuisance of herself. Nebola detested children for a multitude of reasons. This one was no different.

Eden dragged the child from the Suburban. As he loaded the screaming child into Nebola's vehicle, a guy in a red Subaru pulled onto the shoulder. A Korean man climbed out and hurried toward them.

"We got it under control. Thanks," Nebola called with a sociable ring in his voice. "Get back in your car. You can take off now."

"What's the problem?" the man said, apparently without listening. His eyes sparkled with concern. "Did you see it happen? Anyone call 911?"

"Ambulance is on the way. Go back to your car. Seriously, just drive away."

"I know CPR," the Good Samaritan announced. "Hey, where's he taking that girl?"

"Oh, for God's sake," Nebola muttered. He turned to Wingo. "Would you please shoot this idiot?"

Wingo reached inside his coat and pulled out an H & K, the gunmetal flashing in the headlights.

"Don't shoot." The man nearly tripped as he stumbled back. "I'll get outta here. I'm going."

"Little late for that," Nebola sighed.

Wingo fired. It was a pristine shot that dropped the guy right where he stood.

"You bragged about knowing CPR," Nebola called to the fallen man. "Try performing it on yourself."

He turned. On his signal, the two SUVs that had slammed into the Chevy Suburban fired up their engines.

"One second, sir," Wingo said, stopping him. "Got a female civvy here along with a vehicle full of CIA officers. What you want me to do with them?"

Nebola patted his shoulder. "Kill them."

———◆———

Lynbrook, New York
9:07 p.m.

Stephen Angelilli wanted a cigarette the minute he saw two United States Secret Service agents walking toward him. He had received a message from Mark McKibbon, the CIA director, to discuss protocol for the next phase of Operation Red Opera. In all honesty, Angelilli was curious about the director's next move. Wonderland was now in their custody, but it was clear the hostiles would stop at nothing to get her.

He'd expected McKibbon, but not men from the Secret Service's protective detail.

"Come with us, sir," one of the special agents said.

He followed Secret Service to the back of the warehouse. Turning a corner, he could see Mark McKibbon talking to Vice President Isaac Starr. Both men were interested in Wonderland, but the vice president had taken a lower profile on Operation Red Opera—in part, Angelilli guessed, because President Alexander Armstrong was wrapping up his term and Starr was deep in his first bid to become president. With a big election only a few months away, the man was tearing up the campaign trail. He'd given a stump speech earlier in the day to a capacity crowd in Philly.

Starr extended his hand. "Sorry to hear about the loss of one of your men."

His grip was tight. Angelilli gave a grim nod. "Thank you, sir."

"Been a challenging week," the vice president continued. "Mr. McKibbon tells me you have good news. I could sure stand to hear it."

"Yes, sir. I'm pleased to report we were able to bring in Wonderland."

He beamed. "Outstanding."

Director McKibbon said, "Shayna Brynstone and her father are a long-standing interest for the vice president and myself."

"Yes, sir. I'm happy to assist in the operation."

The vice president started to speak when Angelilli got a priority call. Excusing himself, he stepped away and took the call from a staff operations officer named Lopez. She had to say it twice before it registered.

"Wonderland has been abducted. We no longer have her."

He couldn't believe what he was hearing. It got worse. Lopez briefed him that his men were dead. Shaken but trying to appear composed, he ended the call and walked back to the vice president and the director. Both men watched in silence.

Angelilli's hand trembled at his side. Every step seemed like he was trudging through waist-deep snow. He didn't want to say the words.

"Gentlemen, I'm afraid I have bad news about Wonderland."

Chapter 24

Prague, Czech Republic
4:31 a.m.

A thousand years after arising from the unspoiled Bohemian countryside, Prague had earned its reputation as a "symphony in stone." The haunting cityscape seemed alive with mysterious spires and medieval curiosities. Steeped in history, every sculpture and tower seemed to whisper the undying legends of the city. At night, it took Brynstone's breath away.

He parked the mini-SUV on a darkened side street. Raja climbed out with him, leaving McHardy inside the Škoda Yeti. She went one direction, Brynstone the other, taking it on foot to a cobblestone street called Celetná.

Located in the heart of the city, Charles University was one of Europe's oldest universities. Not far from the center campus, the Institute for Classical Archaeology stood on one of the city's busier streets, leading away from the Old Town Square toward Wenceslas Square.

Brynstone and Raja had studied schematics for the five-story building. They had outlined a strategy based on entrances, exits, and the location of the helmet piece on the third floor.

Unlike Prague's more renowned museums, the Institute for Classical Archaeology was a university-based operation with only two campus security guards. The collection was decent, but not one full of priceless antiquities insured for millions of dollars.

Brynstone had already placed four wireless micro-cameras at the site. Years ago, he had walked away from the Special Collections Service and quit government work to save his crumbling marriage. Turns out, that wasn't enough. Back then, he had specialized in the placement of information-gathering devices in high-risk operations and settings. This thing tonight was a cakewalk in comparison.

Brynstone rejoined Raja near a linden tree. She greeted him with a breathtaking smile. Seeing her face in moonlight, he held her gaze a little longer than expected. Her almond eyes dazzled with contradiction: warm but intense, captivating but elusive. He couldn't deny a spark of attraction.

She was all in black tonight including her Gucci sneakers. She'd added leather gloves that extended past her wrists and stopped just shy of her elbows. Raja caught his gaze.

"Cool gloves, huh?"

"Let me guess. Gucci?"

"Lanvin."

He didn't recognize the name. "Tell me they didn't cost as much as the shoes."

"More. Eight hundred and fifty dollars."

"You must be a damned good thief. Either that, or you come from money."

"Both, actually."

She tracked campus security on a smartphone, but they didn't have a clear visual of the room where the Roman helmet piece was stored. He stayed in contact with McHardy, who was positioned back inside the parked Škoda Yeti.

Brynstone told Raja, "I've seen you fight. If we encounter security, don't kill anyone."

"I save that for when I'm in a bad mood," she purred.

McHardy chuckled in Brynstone's earpiece. "I cannot wait until Supergirl here gets her first taste of Kryptonite."

"Girl comes off as more Catwoman than Supergirl."

"Who's Catwoman?"

"Forget it."

Staying focused, Raja glanced at her smartphone. Faint muscles wrinkled on her forehead. "Lost one guard." She studied the touch screen. "Near the east entrance."

Brynstone turned toward the building, raising night-vision goggles. He had a clear look. She was right. No sign of the guard.

"What does it matter?" McHardy called, sounding impatient. "You're the specialist in such matters, Brynstone. Roll into that building and grab the thing, then we'll be out of here."

"John, look," Raja called.

He pulled away the binoculars. Their arms nudging, she touched the upper-right quadrant in the four-camera surveillance grid on her screen. Zooming in, the camera revealed a body sprawled on the floor. The guard lay facedown in a darkened oval of blood.

"What happened?" McHardy demanded.

"Someone already took out the guard," Brynstone growled. He took another look through the binoculars.

"John, I'm tracking movement. One, possibly two men," Raja said. "Proceeding around the east corner."

He caught sight of the shadowy figures.

"Got a visual on the hostiles."

"This is bad news. When the other guard finds his buddy, it's going to bring police. Maybe we should get into the building as fast as possible to grab the relic."

"If that's who I think it is," Brynstone told her, dropping the binoculars, "they've already stolen the helmet piece."

Rashmi Raja took off at a full sprint across the grounds. Her French-braided ponytail danced between her shoulders as she ran. Up ahead, she saw a woman and a man making their escape.

"Take the woman," Brynstone said, keeping stride for stride with her.

"You think men scare me?"

"She's lethal," he called. "You won't be bored."

Between buildings now, the two strangers turned. Coming up on them, Brynstone tackled the man. Raja chased after the redheaded woman, who pivoted with a knife in her hand, the blade wet with the guard's blood. She sliced at the air as Raja ducked. Her fist drove into the redhead's stomach. The knife tore open Raja's glove and cut her arm.

In her other hand, the woman clutched the helmet fragment.

Raja relaxed her guard when she noticed it. The woman capitalized on the distraction, coming at Raja with the knife. Back on her game, Raja caught the woman's arm with both hands and slammed it into the building. The helmet piece dropped. So did the knife. But the redhead had plenty of fight left in her, and with her good hand, she punched Raja in the mouth.

Raja slurped blood between her lip and tooth. That made her angry. Someone hits you?

Hit back harder.

Concentrating all her strength in one motion, Raja slammed the woman's nose. The impact rocked her head. The redhead slumped to the ground, her upper body collapsed against the building.

Raja sensed movement behind her and braced for another attack as she spun around. Surprise jolted her to a stop when she saw Math McHardy.

"Brilliant work," he said, staring at the fallen woman. He bent down to pick up the helmet fragment.

She looked over at Brynstone. He was fighting the other stranger not far away. Deciding to check on him, Raja stepped over the woman's legs and brushed past the professor. Behind her, she overheard the redhead speak with an Irish accent.

"Do they know we're working together, Math?"

Shocked, Raja turned her attention from Brynstone. Did she hear that right? She looked back in time to see McHardy strike the woman in the face. Aggression didn't suit him, but he punched her with an animal rage.

The woman's eyes closed.

He looked at Raja as if the whole thing hadn't happened. He straightened his tie.

Police sirens squealed in the distance.

Brynstone finished with the man and came over. "Where's the helmet piece?"

"I have it," McHardy answered.

"Who's the woman?" Raja asked.

"Name's Nessa Griffin."

"Who is she?"

"An unfriendly competitor," Brynstone answered. "Let's get out of here."

Chapter 25

Wurm's Disease.

It was a running joke at the National Security Agency. Brynstone had heard about it back when Wurm was a cryptanalyst there. Nearly everyone in the intelligence community had a flicker of paranoia, but NSA analysts took it to new heights. In response, the agency retained the service of two full-time psychiatrists to treat analysts diagnosed with paranoid personality disorder. The good side was that PPD patients demonstrated intelligence and were exceptional observers. The bad side? They were guarded and overly sensitive with an extreme distrust and suspicion of others. Despite competition from colleagues, no one could touch Edgar Wurm when it came to the disorder. In tribute, his fellow code breakers had renamed PPD "Wurm's Disease."

Brynstone checked to see that he was alone. He was making a call from inside an isolated hangar at Václav Havel Airport, located at the northwest edge of Prague.

Wurm hated phone conversations because he worried someone would listen in. The call Brynstone was making now would make the man uncomfortable, but it had to be done.

Wurm answered after the third ring.

"You still in Europe?" Brynstone asked.

"Is this call necessary?"

"I think so."

"You've taken protective measures?"

"It's a secure line. Where are you?"

A sigh. "Barcelona. You?"

"Airport in Prague." Brynstone updated him on finding the facemask, the right cheek guard, and the right skull piece. He gave an account of his encounter with Nessa Griffin, but didn't offer specifics.

"You've been busy," Wurm said.

"I've had help."

There was a halting silence on the other end of the line. He could tell Wurm didn't like the sound of that.

"Let me guess. You brought in Cori Cassidy."

"Actually, no. We haven't talked in a long time."

"That surprises me."

For years, Brynstone didn't allow himself to think about Cori. She was tied to bitter memories from that night long ago. More and more, though, he found he couldn't get her out of his mind.

"I turned Cori's life upside down once. Won't put her through that again."

Wurm snorted. "I think she rather enjoyed having you in her life. I saw how she hugged you at the airport that morning when we parted ways. One time in Europe, she slapped my face when I disparaged you."

"You disparaged me?"

"I disparage everyone," Wurm answered. "So who else are you working with?"

"Woman named Rashmi Raja."

"Never heard of her."

"And Math McHardy."

"Oh, God. Are you quite serious, John?"

"He's not as bad as you said."

"He's worse. The man is insufferable. Not an idiot by any stretch of the imagination, but he's a disaster. I've never seen such a bloated sense of self-importance."

"He broke code on the helmet pieces. He knows how to decipher Linear A."

"Because I taught him," Wurm blurted. "Everything the damned fool knows about that code he learned from me."

"Thought you and McHardy didn't talk."

"At one time, we did. That helmet artifact you mentioned, the right skull piece? I showed it to him. We met during a Prague conference. I had seen the helmet on display at Charles University and realized it was critical in the search for the chrism formula. I told McHardy about it over drinks." Wurm coughed. "The next day we skipped out on conference presentations to see the helmet artifact. Unfortunately, we got into an animated brawl and museum security kicked us out, so we weren't allowed access after that. Anyway, I'm glad to hear you have it."

"McHardy's deciphering it now."

"Urge him to be quick about it. We're racing against the Shadow Chapter. They want it almost as badly as we do."

"Speaking of the Chapter, do you know if Nessa Griffin works for them?"

"Oh, there's no telling. Everything's a secret with the Chapter."

"What did you learn about their guy? The one with connections to Erich Metzger."

"His name is Viktor Nebola. He served fifteen years in prison for manslaughter. After his release, he met a colonel in the Russian army and they started up a private arms-trafficking operation. After their fourth successful sale, Nebola had an outside source assassinate the colonel."

Wurm explained that even though Nebola didn't kill the colonel, he masterminded the execution, and contract killers followed his orders to the letter. No evidence was discovered regarding the disappearance of the Russian army official. After hearing about the "clean kill," executives at the Shadow Chapter approached Nebola about joining their organization.

Brynstone trusted the information. For more than two decades, Wurm had been one of the best analysts at the National Security Agency. The men and women of the NSA worked in silence, but important people knew that Wurm's code breaking had saved lives. He had connections all over the world. He was owed and he knew how to collect on favors.

"Nebola is a leader within the Chapter. I'll send a picture." Wurm sounded grim. "They believe the Black Chrism can be engineered to create another pandemic on the order of the Black Death. Let me assure you, John, the Chapter has big plans for the missing half of the Scintilla."

⸺⬥⸺

Cori Cassidy awakened, eyes batting open, and stared up with a look of horror. The white ceiling seemed to curve in a dizzy elastic band. Stretching around her, it started to descend. Like a casket lid closing, the curved ceiling shut out light as it lowered, locking her inside a suffocating vacuum.

She wiped her eyes, taking another look. *A hallucination.* Her mind seemed thick and watery.

She sensed something cold climbing her skin. She rolled her aching head and found a thin translucent serpent coiling around her bare forearm. With a yelp, she slapped at it. With another look, she realized she had swatted an IV tube. It connected to a drip chamber suspended beside her stretcher.

Raising both hands to her forehead, she cradled her throbbing skull. Her vision cleared and she had a better look at her surroundings, a cramped place with the feel of a white and stifling cocoon. A small barrier of monitors and medical equipment surrounded her, recording her vitals in a blipping language that brought the comfort of knowing she was alive.

She remembered escaping with Shay to a hotel room Jared had reserved for them. She remembered waiting for him to return, but fearing he wouldn't. She remembered cuddling with Shay on a bed before CIA agents stormed into their hotel room. A man called Angelilli had taken her into a vehicle. She had a hazy memory about an accident. Shay was sitting . . .

Shay.

Where was Shayna Brynstone?

Cori slapped both hands against the mattress and looked around, as if expecting to find the child. She shuffled on the uncomfortable stretcher, attempting to rise. Every movement heightened the thunder inside her head, but she was determined to find Shay.

Swinging her legs over the edge, she stared down. The floor seemed to drop twenty feet beneath her toes. Not trusting her eyes, she braced against the stretcher, willing herself to leave it. As she lowered both feet onto the cold floor, both of her knees buckled and nausea crawled inside her gut. Her legs were wobbly and her face blazed with a sudden heat. Without warning, Cori found herself collapsing on the floor, the snakelike IV tube clinging to her arm.

Disoriented, she looked up. A man in a white coat rushed toward her. Behind him, a middle-aged nurse scuttled around to crouch beside Cori. The doc slid his arms around her back and waist. He had dark friendly eyes and a brush of black hair. The nurse clutched Cori's legs and they lifted her. She didn't have the energy to protest, the nausea still thick inside her, sapping her strength.

She was back on the stretcher now, propped against the pillow.

"Did you climb out or fall out?" the nurse asked.

"Shayna," Cori mumbled.

"What?" the doctor asked. He looked concerned.

"The little girl," she answered, her tongue feeling as thick as concrete.

The doctor and nurse glanced at each other. Neither answered.

"It's important you get your rest," the nurse assured her, brushing a strand of hair from Cori's forehead.

"Want to see Shayna."

"A driver found you inside your vehicle," the doctor said. "You sustained extensive injuries from the accident."

"Thank God they got to you in time," the nurse chirped. "You'll need more surgery, but you'll be fine."

"You need your rest, young lady," the doctor warned in a stern voice. "We just rolled you out of recovery."

He inserted a syringe into her IV.

"I want . . ." Her words trailed off.

"What's that, dear?"

Cori swallowed the longest swallow imaginable. Closing her eyes, she knew she wanted to finish the sentence, but found she couldn't remember what she wanted to say.

Chapter 26

Slipping out of the hangar at the Prague airport, Brynstone ended his private call with Wurm. He took steps, two at a time, up the ramp leading into Math McHardy's jet. The professor had serious resources. As an only child, McHardy had collected an inheritance from a family tree with rich branches, including a founder of Saffery Champness—a prestigious accounting firm—as well as a former president of the Royal Bank of Scotland.

Moving inside the Bombardier aircraft, Brynstone saw that Raja was napping on the divan near the galley. Her forearm had been sliced during her confrontation with Nessa Griffin, but Raja seemed more troubled about the jagged tear in her leather glove. Brynstone had stitched up her arm. He didn't worry about the glove.

Passing through the doorway into the midcabin, he glanced at the table with the assorted pieces of the Roman helmet spread across the surface. Right now, they had collected the facemask, a right cheek guard, and the right skull piece. Wurm had the neck guard, presumably from the same helmet. Brynstone hadn't mentioned it to McHardy—there was no need to foster more bad blood between them.

He found the professor enjoying a whisky in his private state-room at the rear of the jet. He seemed unusually quiet after their encounter with Griffin.

"John, come in. Close the door."

"Why?"

"We don't want our conversation to wake Sleeping Beauty," he purred, "now do we?"

Brynstone didn't buy the reason, but he closed the door anyway.

"I'm still working on the Prague helmet piece," McHardy reported as he rubbed his temples. "This thing frustrates the hell out of me."

"Any breakthroughs?"

"Remember when I mentioned Josephus?"

"The son of Joseph of Arimathea."

McHardy nodded. "Josephus made a mistake of some sort that angered his father. As the Keeper, Joseph of Arimathea took the vellum that contained the formulae to create the Black and the White Chrisms—"

"The Scintilla."

"And he ripped it in half two thousand years ago."

"Wonder what Josephus did. Must have been bad to make his father tear up the Scintilla."

"There's more, John." McHardy studied the whisky, then took a sip, swirling it around his mouth before swallowing. "According to this, the Black Chrism was administered to several people in ancient times."

"Like a drug?"

"The man who wrote the message on the helmet makes an interesting claim. He tells us that the Black Chrism caused them all to develop some 'terrible gift.'"

"Meaning what, exactly?"

"I have no idea." He sighed. "Plus, there's another thing. I feel confident in saying that Josephus was not the person who inscribed the code inside the helmet."

"Let me guess. Joseph of Arimathea?"

"I'm afraid not. The author came from Roman heritage, but lived in Britannia. He was about the same age as Josephus and knew him. The two met around 64 CE in Glastonbury."

"The Roman Empire occupied England at that time," Brynstone said. "Maybe the Roman you're talking about was a soldier."

McHardy's eyes twinkled. "You're suggesting a soldier inscribed stories in the Linear A code inside his own helmet?"

"It's a guess."

"I'll keep it in mind." He stretched. "One final thing. This is perhaps the most tantalizing discovery. The helmet code mentions a hiding place for one half of the chrism formula."

"The formula for the Black Chrism. Does it say where it's hidden?"

"Egypt." He smiled. "We need to find it, John. I think it might be in Cairo. Of course, I still need to figure out where. Once I do, though, the facemask will lead us to the hiding spot. Even if we don't know the precise location, we can search for it."

"I'll tell Rashmi," Brynstone said, opening the door.

"Fine. I'll instruct the pilot to prepare a flight plan to Cairo."

Brynstone checked the time on his phone as he passed through the midcabin. He headed toward the front of the private jet, but stopped in surprise when he reached the divan. She was gone.

"Rashmi?" he called.

No answer.

Brynstone looked around the galley and checked the lavatory. He headed back to the midcabin. McHardy was standing over the table. The professor looked over.

"I'm afraid we have a problem, John. The facemask you found beneath the Paris cemetery? It's missing."

He scowled. "So is Rashmi. You have the other helmet artifacts?"

"Everything except the facemask."

Brynstone grabbed his backpack. "If I'm not back before takeoff, I'll meet you in Cairo."

———◆———

Cori could hear the sound of her own breathing, deep and unhurried, as her eyes blinked open. Her vision was hazy at first as she realized she was flat on her back, staring at the ceiling. It felt as if someone had gently pulled a gossamer veil over the contours of her face. The ceiling wasn't curving anymore. She remembered talking to a doctor, but she was someplace different now. But where?

Before she had dozed off, a nurse had mentioned something about surgery and about rolling Cori out of recovery. So much had been a blank. What had they said about the car wreck? She recalled the doctor mentioning it briefly, but nothing about details.

Rising, she looked around. Her petite body was draped in a thin cotton hospital gown. She was in a different hospital bed now in a different room. She looked around, but there was no phone or TV. There wasn't even a window, so she couldn't tell if it was day or night.

She glanced at the hospital bracelet around her wrist. Dusky gaps in her memory made it difficult to remember the accident. Cori bristled with anxiety when she thought about losing Shay. Where was she? Who was taking care of her? She had to find the child.

Her headache wasn't as bad as before, although her head was still sore. Shifting her body to the edge of the mattress, she landed on steadier feet this time. Groaning, she shuffled toward the door and opened it.

Moving into the hallway, she saw two nurses behind a blue counter, talking to a doctor. Dizziness came at her now, a fast rush of blood inside her head. She reached for a nearby wheelchair, trying to steady her body.

"Ms. Cassidy," a nurse called, "we can't have you out here."

In contrast with her cheery floral-print scrubs, the woman had a cold look. Still, she took Cori's arm gently as she directed her back inside the room. The Mount Sinai Hospital badge on the nurse's beaded lanyard identified her as Susan Rubin.

"Wanna see Shayna. She's—"

"There's plenty of time for visitors later. You've had major surgery. It's not a good idea for you to be walking around. We need to get you back in bed."

"I was with a little girl. About six years old. Blonde hair."

"Your daughter?"

"A friend. Is she okay? Is she in the hospital?"

Rubin helped Cori ease onto the edge of the bed. "I can't report on other patients due to confidentiality laws. I'm sorry."

"Tell me about the car wreck."

"You don't remember?"

"Only bits and pieces. I was in an SUV with Shayna. Some men."

"Your vehicle was hit from the side by one car. A second car struck yours as well, I believe. You must know important people. Someone insisted you be transported back here to the city."

She thought of Angelilli, then sighed. "Don't remember any of it."

"That happens sometimes with closed head injuries. Anterograde amnesia. You blank on things. Dr. Spanos will give you a full report."

Easing onto her pillow, Cori said, "I need to make a call. I don't have a phone in my room."

"Someone requested private care with security." She frowned. "They don't want you making phone calls just yet. That's why they took your cell."

Cori sighed. The CIA brought her here, so it was no surprise they were cutting her contact from the world.

"Don't worry," the nurse said. "I've seen this before a time or two. It's a security precaution. They'll let you make a call soon. Now, get your rest, dear."

The sting of the concussing headache returned, but she grabbed the woman's arm. "This is important. Please tell me if Shayna Brynstone is in this hospital."

Susan Rubin looked down. "I shouldn't say this."

"I have to know," Cori begged. "Tell me. Please."

The nurse looked around. Her mouth tightened. "I was told that when paramedics arrived at the accident scene, you were the only survivor."

Chapter 27

Barcelona, Spain
6:14 a.m.

Too bad John Brynstone wasn't here. Edgar Wurm knew his old friend would be perfect for the job. On the other hand, Wurm had directed an operation like this one three years ago in London. It had been a success, winning him ownership, once again, of the Scintilla.

Wurm remembered his first trip to Barcelona. He had been twenty-three and traveling with a college buddy named Tony. They had stayed in a hotel off Las Ramblas, the "main drag," as his friend had called it. They discovered a city bustling with crowds and chaos, alive with tourists and pickpockets. Their first night in the city, they went to see FC Barcelona play at Camp Nou. The scale of the stadium and the enthusiasm of the crowd heightened the experience. Wurm and his friend had met two women at the game. In a legendary moment of Wurm's youth, they spent the next sun-drenched afternoon at Gaudí's Park Güell, perched on a hill above Barcelona, gazing at the pristine ocean in the distance.

The next morning, he had awakened to find his friend missing. By noon, authorities arrived at the hotel to question Wurm. That's when he learned that Tony had assassinated a politician outside the Sagrada Família church. Wurm had no idea that his college friend was a professional killer. Tony had slipped away without explanation. The two never saw each other again.

Tony had understood the value of mixing business with pleasure. Sadly, tonight was all business for Wurm.

He waited in a car not far from the Generalitat Palace. He watched on a monitor as his men infiltrated the Casa de la Ciutat, a fourteenth-century palace in the Gothic quarter in Sant Jaume Square. The place served as Barcelona's city hall. He had watched as Banan and Chavez navigated through the reception room. They were in the cabinet office now, casting shadows on aged murals covering the walls. Three security guards had offered little resistance. His men seemed home free as they kicked in a door.

Wurm was surprised that the mayor of Barcelona was not in his office. Raimon Escolà was a notorious workaholic. From the little he knew about Escolà, the guy was a decent politician. He also had a notable fascination with antiquities.

His office was airy with an eclectic sense of decoration. Not far from his desk, Escolà had placed the Catalan flag and a painting reflecting his interest in surrealism. It made an odd mix with a tall museum-like glass cube nearby in which was displayed the uniform of a first-century Roman cavalry sergeant, including a tunic and sword belt. Although the military dress and the half helmet originated from slightly different eras—certainly not worn by the same soldier—the mayor had placed them together on exhibit. Escolà had been a military man himself and his mother had been born in Rome, perhaps explaining his decision to exhibit the Roman uniform. Whatever the reason, Wurm knew one thing as he watched the monitor: he wanted the helmet.

"Smash the glass," he ordered into the two-way radio.

Dressed all in black, Banan swung a crowbar into the glass. A portion collapsed in brilliant fragments onto the floor. Not wasting time, the man reached inside for the helmet, then held it up for inspection on the small camera mounted on his eyeglasses.

"This what you wanted, sir?"

"Peel back the leather," Wurm ordered.

Reaching inside the half helmet's shell, Banan pulled back the leather covering. It revealed a constellation of tiny symbols on the inside. Wurm couldn't decipher them at this distance. He had to get his hands on this artifact.

"Someone's coming," Chavez called.

Wurm cursed.

The lights came up and a young security guard raised his gun. Dark-haired with a thin moustache, he shouted something in Castilian Spanish. He wanted Wurm's men to put down the helmet and raise their hands.

Even on the monitor, Wurm could see apprehension in the man's eyes. The guard had discovered his unconscious buddies on the floor. He wasn't used to this kind of action, and it showed in his trembling hand.

Before Wurm could give an order, Banan opened fire. Chavez joined in.

"What are you doing?" Wurm shouted.

His question went unanswered.

The guard managed a shot, but it missed wide, hitting near the fireplace. Banan and Chavez each fired with a suppressor. As their bullets found him, the guard jerked violently, his leg twisting in the air before he hit the floor.

"You didn't kill the other guards," Wurm said. "Why did you take out that guy?"

"Sorry, boss," Banan offered.

"Bring me the helmet. Now."

Wurm ripped off the headset and tossed it on the seat. He watched them sprint down the stairs leading out of the Casa de la Ciutat. He shook his head.

In its time centuries back, the Roman helmet had seen its share of bloodshed. Some things never changed.

—————————

Cori Cassidy was reeling. She curled her hospital pillow, stained with tears, and buried her head. A great cry poured out in a rush of desperation and sadness. The crushing grief ached more than she could imagine, almost more than she could bear. She hated it, the terrible balance of her survival leveraged against the death of a child. *Poor Shay.* It wasn't fair.

And John. Without Kaylyn and Shayna, he was alone now.

Did he even know? Where was John Brynstone during this tragedy?

She pulled up from the pillow when she heard the door open. She hoped to see her brother, but instead a man in a white lab coat rushed into her hospital room. A blink or two later, she recognized the guy as her doctor.

He studied her face. "What's the matter?"

She wiped a tear. "I lost Shayna."

He didn't seem interested in her loss. Instead, Dr. Spanos placed a brown paper sack on the floor beside her bed. Without speaking, he leaned in and removed her IV.

"I have something important to tell you, Cori."

"Is it about—"

"Be quiet and listen carefully," he whispered, looking back at the door. "This is urgent. You must do everything I say. Do not panic."

Cori paled as a haunting thought found her, one where her condition might be more serious than she had imagined. The nurse had mentioned a second surgery. Was it risky?

"Am I going to be okay?" she asked.

"Not unless we act quickly."

Dr. Spanos grabbed the paper sack. He balanced it on the bed and reached inside. Removing her gray sweatpants and a new T-shirt, he passed her the clothes.

"Your shirt was bloodied, so we threw it away. I found another. Get dressed."

Cori scrunched up her face. "You're discharging me?"

He didn't answer. He reached in the sack again and brought out green scrubs with her pink and gray running shoes. "Wear the scrubs over your clothes."

"I don't get it." She stared at the folded clothing on the bed. "Why should I wear scrubs?"

"Put them on." A steely coldness came over his eyes. "Now. Hurry."

He turned his back on her, the shoes dangling from his fingers.

She flipped away the covers and eased onto the floor, the cold tile biting her toes. She untied the hospital gown, revealing the curve of her hip above pink silk panties. Watching him from behind, Cori pulled on the sweatpants. She stripped away the thin cotton gown and tossed it on the bed. She covered a bare breast with her arm as she glanced at the surgical bandages embracing her shoulder.

"As soon as you dress, you must leave here," Spanos said, his back still turned. "Do you understand? Disguise yourself as a doctor and try to get to the street. Get away from this building."

Cori didn't speak until she'd pulled on her purple shirt. This whole conversation was bewildering.

"Wait. What? I was in a car wreck," she said. "Is it okay for me to leave? The nurse said I needed another surgery."

"She lied about the surgery. Everyone has lied to you." Spanos looked at the floor. "I agreed to this because of the money, but it's not ethical. I don't know why you are here, but I can't go on with this charade."

She tilted her head. "You're not a doctor?"

"I am a doctor."

She gave a blank look, rubbing her forehead. Was she drinking in another hallucination?

"I still feel groggy," she confessed. "Guess it's from the surgery."

"You didn't have surgery."

"But you—"

"We lied to you," he snapped. "You didn't have a torn rotator cuff or nerve damage or anything else they might have told you. Check your body later. You won't find sutures under your bandages. You're groggy because we medicated you with a powerful hypnotic drug."

"You drugged me?" she asked, pulling the green medical top over her T-shirt. "Why would you do that if I didn't have surgery?"

"Because we were ordered to do so." Spanos rubbed his temple. "I should have never agreed to it."

"Are you with the CIA?"

He turned. His face darkened with shock. "The CIA?"

She pulled baggy scrubs over her sweatpants. "CIA agents were with me in the accident."

He handed her the shoes. Her socks were rolled inside. Trancelike, she moved to the bed and pulled them on. Why had the doctor and the nurse lied about the surgery?

Spanos studied her. "The American intelligence officers. Do you know their names?"

"One. A guy named Stephen Angelilli. The other agents call him Scarecrow, but he called himself Angelilli when we met years ago."

"He was in the accident?"

She shook her head. "He wasn't with us."

"So, he is alive?"

"I think so."

As she tied her left shoe, the hospital door opened. Turning at the sound, Spanos whispered, "Hurry, Cori. Get in the bed."

She scurried onto the mattress. A nurse came into the hospital room. Susan Rubin. Spanos stepped forward, blocking her view of the bed.

Trying to be subtle, Cori eased the hospital sheets over her body to hide the scrubs and her shoes. She dragged the blanket to her chest, but didn't want to be too dramatic while covering her body.

"I'm sorry, doctor," the woman said. "What are you doing here?"

He looked back and forced a smile. "Checking on my patient. Ms. Cassidy was asking about her surgery."

Rubin peered around him. "Why is Ms. Cassidy wearing scrubs?"

The doctor swallowed, fumbling for an answer. "She was about to take a walk."

The nurse looked suspicious. "She's dressed up like a surgeon so she could go for a walk?"

"Her clothes were bloodied from the accident."

The woman noticed the hospital garment draped on the bed. "What's wrong with her gown?"

"She didn't—"

"Stay here," the nurse interrupted, her voice sounding icy. "I'm calling security."

"You shouldn't have told me that," Spanos said.

He tackled the woman from behind. He looped one arm around her neck, forcing her chin into the crook of his arm. At the same time, he shoved her head forward, thrusting her neck deeper into his flexed arm. Rubin's face turned a brilliant red. The nurse kicked and struggled, trying to break free from his grip.

What the hell is happening?

Cori jumped off the bed. The woman's eyes closed as she collapsed in the doctor's arms.

"Oh, God. Did you kill her?"

"Only a choke hold. We can't trust her."

Spanos carried the nurse to the bed. He rolled Susan Rubin onto the mattress, then reached into his white coat and brought out a syringe. He uncapped it and pulled up her sleeve, then injected the needle into her bare arm. Cori watched it all in bleary surprise and bewilderment. He turned Rubin on her side and raised the sheet over her head, leaving her mouth uncovered so she could breathe.

"We must hurry," Spanos said in an agitated voice. "Let's get you out of here."

Glancing back at the woman on the bed, Cori followed him out the door. It was all so baffling.

——◆◆——

Dressed in green scrubs, Cori walked down the hallway with Dr. Spanos. He glanced back once or twice as they approached an elevator. None of this made sense. They passed room after room in the corridor. She didn't dare peek inside. The doctor had ordered her to walk straight ahead without arousing suspicion.

She didn't want to risk someone overhearing. In a low voice, she asked, "Why can't we trust the nurse?"

"Can't tell you." He punched the Down button.

"Why am I here? Who told you to lie to me?"

"I don't know them or their plans. All I know is, they wanted to keep you drugged and for you to think you had surgery after the accident."

She turned at the sound of a soft ping as the elevator doors slid open. Spanos grabbed her hand and stepped inside, pulling her into the car. He released his grip and punched the button for the first floor. Cori looked up, seeing the number three illuminated inside a metal strip.

The doctor stepped outside the elevator, leaving her. He turned to watch her. She stiffened with panic and reached for the doors to prevent them from closing.

"Wait," she said. "You're not coming with me?"

"I must cover for you. The park is not far from here. Hide there if you can. I'll try to meet you."

She knew the Mount Sinai Hospital was located on the eastern border of Central Park. Still, she didn't want to leave him.

"Good luck, Cori."

He stripped her fingers from the door. She released it and watched him turn, his white coat flapping as he rushed down the hallway. The doors closed.

A sinking feeling churned inside her stomach. Cori huddled against the back wall. A hundred thoughts roared inside her mind. Could she trust the doctor? Why was this happening?

The elevator car shuddered. She glanced up at the metal strip above the door. The number two brightened above the door as the elevator rumbled to a halt. Spanos wanted her to get out at the first floor. She hadn't expected the elevator to stop here. Who was on the other side of that door?

Her throat tightened. She could feel the tension rising in her muscles, waiting to see what happened next. Cori watched helplessly as the elevator doors began to slide apart.

Chapter 28

New York City
4:01 a.m.

"We have progress to report," Stephen Angelilli said into the phone as he adjusted the knot in his tie. "Sorry for the early-morning call."

"It's what I requested," Vice President Starr answered.

Down the hall from his office, Angelilli was taking a conference call with Starr and Director McKibbon. The vice president had requested an update from the CIA's Directorate of Intelligence about the men who had abducted Shayna Brynstone.

"Here's what we know from our DI analysts," Angelilli said. "We're looking at an organization that began in the late 1990s, started by ten European crime lords from ten different countries. We call it the Shadow Chapter."

"Why that name?" Starr asked.

"INTERPOL gave the name to the organization after evidence was lacking and no leads came from a major drug-trafficking case. They were unable to link any connection to any one person or any other crime ring."

"That's correct, sir," Director McKibbon added. "This was the first time INTERPOL encountered anything of the sort, so they came up with the name the Shadow Chapter to describe the organization behind the criminal activity. Basically, more blanks were drawn from this case than ever before. It was a shadow chapter in INTERPOL's history, so to speak."

"From what I'm told, the organization has adopted the name, though I can't confirm that," Angelilli said. "What I can tell you is that currently, the Chapter boasts over a thousand members. As far as we can determine, it is broken into local groups assigned by the ten organizers. Only members who are known and deeply trusted by the ten are allowed to lead a group. Trust is a must."

"Tell me about their members," the vice president said.

"It's a diverse group. To stay ahead of their competition and the authorities, all members of the Chapter are required to be well educated. They hold degrees ranging from business management to accounting to sociology. We're talking about well-rounded individuals who know how to execute an operation. They also blend into different cultures, posing as legitimate citizens in regular clothes or business suits. They don't do or own anything or talk in any way that would set them apart from the average citizen in their respective country."

Angelilli continued, "If authorities apprehend a member, they must be willing to commit suicide and burn everything connecting them to the Chapter. INTERPOL has only caught them once, so they are a hard group to track."

He outlined their alleged activities from human trafficking to drug trafficking, mostly heroin, crack, MDMA, and designer synthetic drugs. In the early years, the Shadow Chapter had been involved in currency counterfeiting as well as prostitution of women from war-torn or politically unstable regions. Since that time, they had branched into more sophisticated operations.

"On occasion, they are also involved in assassinations," Angelilli said. "The ten crime lords know this is messy and can lead to a quick downfall for the organization when too many institutions get involved, so they play it safe in that arena."

"One question," Vice President Starr asked. "How do you play it safe with an assassination?"

"Well, sir," Angelilli answered, "you hire Erich Metzger."

———◆———

Cori Cassidy backed into the corner of the elevator car, trying to stay out of sight. Her gut felt like it was twisted into knots. She pressed her butt against the wall along with the palms of her hands. The metal surface against her hands turned her skin fish-cold as the elevator doors opened on the second floor.

Pull it together, she thought to herself. She couldn't look like some frightened escaped patient to whoever was getting on.

Her heart drummed inside her chest. She coached herself to play it cool, standing tall, trying to look like a doctor.

The doors glided open all the way.

No one was waiting. She sagged with a sense of relief. Someone had pressed the button before deciding against taking the elevator.

As the doors began to slide closed, she found the courage to move away from the wall and look down the second-floor corridor. She took a couple steps forward to peek out.

What she saw didn't make sense.

The area outside the elevator looked nothing like the third floor. In fact, it looked nothing like a hospital at all. Instead, it resembled an army compound. She saw soldiers dressed in black tactical clothing and combat gear. Armed with assault rifles, they stood in a circle listening to a hardened-looking man with dark brown hair who appeared to be their leader.

There was no sign of doctors or nurses or medical equipment.

The doors closed all the way. The elevator continued its journey down to the first floor.

Terror sunk in, deeper than before. What was happening on the second floor? Huddled against the elevator wall, she was bewildered as she hugged herself. She had been reluctant to contact NYPD before, but now she was determined to find a cop the minute she escaped this place.

The elevator reached the lobby and the doors opened. If the third floor seemed like a hospital ward and the second like a military base, then this floor resembled a Wall Street lobby, all metal accents and soaring windows. A handful of people milled around in business suits, attaché cases in hand.

More confused than ever, Cori spied an exit to her right. Fighting for composure in her walk, she headed for the door, then pushed it open and moved outside. Dazzling sunshine greeted her as she stepped onto the sidewalk. She took a quick glance at her surroundings.

She straightened up and rolled on her feet, jerking back in disbelief and apprehension. In stunned silence, Cori snapped her head around, looking in every direction. Nothing made sense. She raised her eyes, taking a peek at a street sign.

Her face became ashen. A ripple of unwelcome surprise overtook her.

She wasn't outside the Mount Sinai Hospital.

Hell, she wasn't even in Manhattan.

There were no skyscrapers or honking yellow cabs scattered in traffic or sidewalks jammed with bustling pedestrians. Nothing here looked familiar. Instead, blocks of aging flats and café bars crammed with tourist and craft shops lined the street. The hospital experience had been creepy, but this was a whole new level of weirdness. Lost in this *Twilight Zone* moment, she discovered her mouth was still gaping.

On instinct, she started walking, her feet moving almost without her knowing. The doctor had told her she had to hurry to a park, but she didn't even know where she was right now.

With no police in sight, she needed to get to a phone fast.

Cori saw her reflection in a store window. The place looked like a taverna with the sign spelled in a language that appeared to be Greek. The same was true with the next store. She knew that Astoria had a Greek neighborhood, but this didn't look anything like Queens. The doctor claimed she had been given hypnotic drugs. Was she hallucinating again?

Now that she was outside, Cori wished she could ditch the green scrubs. Keeping her head down as she walked, she didn't want to be noticed and she worried the clothes made her stand out. She glanced around but didn't dare stop. She passed two women, both tanned in summer dresses, but she didn't make eye contact.

She peeked at a row of compact, European-style vehicles parked curbside and stopped behind a green Renault. The license plate was imprinted with three letters and four digits, along with two additional white letters—*GR*—on a blue rectangle.

GR? It didn't make sense. She rubbed her eyes and looked again. None of the cars looked American, and they all had similar plates. Could that be right?

I'm in Greece?

Cori's mind was spinning. How could she be in Europe? She couldn't remember much about the accident, but she thought she'd been in New York City. At the very least, she'd thought she was in the United States.

Not Greece.

Something made sense now. She remembered waking a while back when she thought she was hallucinating. The ceiling seemed curved and too low for a typical ceiling. She had wondered at first if she had been in an ambulance, but she thought it had to be a room.

She realized now that she must have been inside a jet. Whoever had taken her had drugged her and flown her to Greece. Someone wanted her out of the country.

Who did this to her? And why was she here?

Cori looked back at where she had first stepped onto the sidewalk. Two men walked a half block behind her. They were dressed all in black like the soldiers she had seen on the second floor of the building. The sight of them back there swung her from paranoia to outright panic. As far as she could tell, they did not have combat gear or rifles, but she didn't hold her gaze for too long. She turned around and forced herself to keep walking, so the men behind her wouldn't become suspicious or catch up. Had they followed her out of the hospital or whatever the hell that place had been?

She walked a little farther, then decided to take a different street. Before turning the corner, Cori glanced back. Everything inside told her not to, but she was desperate to look again.

The two men had closed the gap. There was no doubt about it—they were definitely coming after her. A look of menace flashed across their faces.

Burning with adrenaline, Cori knew one thing. It was time to run.

—————

Shayna was asleep, cuddling a stuffed animal.

Nebola stood beside the bed, watching her. His men had gotten a couple of toys for her. It had been funny to see the bewildered expressions on the men's faces when Nebola had ordered them to buy stuffed animals. They had obliged and returned with several for Shayna to choose from as a traveling companion. She had picked a black kitten with green eyes. Personally, Nebola had liked the plush porcupine, its back an explosion of brown bristles. Maybe that said more about his childhood than he had realized.

Wingo came up to him. "Mr. Nebola, mind if I interrupt?"

He motioned Wingo to the door. He didn't want to wake the kid.

"What is it?" he said, stepping outside the room.

"Cori Cassidy escaped our facility."

"What? How'd that happen?"

"A doctor helped her escape. One we hired to staff the mock hospital."

"Sonuvabitch," Nebola growled.

"A nurse tried to stop them, but the doc took her out. Caught us with our guard down. Happened during a shift change."

"You tracking Cassidy?"

"She's a couple blocks from the facility. We have men in pursuit."

"You better," he snarled. "Apprehend her, fast."

"Yes, sir."

He cursed again. Nebola had learned that the Cassidy woman was good friends with John Brynstone, and that his daughter was close to the woman as well. The idea was that Cassidy might prove useful in winning Shayna Brynstone's trust. Which is why at the last minute, Nebola had spared Cassidy when he had ordered the hit on the CIA officers in the wrecked SUV. He had staged a hospital on the third floor of a Shadow Chapter building and had sequestered her there.

"Tell me about the doctor who helped Cassidy escape."

"Peter Spanos. He's on the run as well."

"With her?"

"Don't believe so. We have leads. We'll find him."

Nebola glanced at the sleeping child. "Let me know the minute you find that prick. He's gonna pay."

Chapter 29

Vienna, Austria
10:05 a.m.

Edgar Wurm gloated. He had settled into a room at Le Méridien Vienna, a luxury hotel located on the famous Ringstrasse, not far from the Vienna State Opera and the Imperial Hofburg Palace. Settling into a crisp blue armchair, he studied the left skull piece of the Roman helmet. He had learned a few tricks about getting around security measures after years of working at the National Security Agency. It had been a little risky smuggling this thing out of Barcelona, but it had been worth the effort.

This skull piece gave a detailed story about the origin of the helmet and the man who had engraved a code on it. It gave new insights. He understood now that the legend of the Holy Grail blended with the legend of the Radix, revealing Joseph of Arimathea as a central figure in both stories.

The left skull piece revealed the name of the Roman soldier who had engraved a code on his helmet. Quintus Messorius Gallienus had served with the Roman army in England somewhere around 64 CE. During that period, he had been sent to Glastonbury to break up a fight between Christians and pagans. The conflict in Britannia centered on Joseph of Arimathea and a pagan king named Crudel, originally of North Wales.

On a peacekeeping mission, Quintus had tried to stifle hostilities between the two camps. It did not go well. During the visit, Crudel had fatally stabbed Quintus. The pagan warlord insisted that Joseph of Arimathea take responsibility for the murder. Despite protests from his son, Josephus, Arimathea agreed to accept the blame on the condition that it would bring peace between the Christian and pagan camps.

The pagans had hauled away Joseph of Arimathea. Presenting him to Roman officials, they demanded that the Christian leader be placed on trial for the murder of Quintus. In a rush to save his father, Josephus had created the Black Chrism without fully understanding its power. The dead Roman soldier was still sprawled on the ground outside the Glastonbury camp. Josephus had poured the formula down the throat of the dead man. According to the helmet's code, the Black Chrism brought Quintus back to life. When Quintus arrived at the trial, revived and healthy, Joseph of Arimathea was granted his freedom.

The story was beginning to gel in Wurm's mind. He had spent considerable time researching everything he could find on Joseph of Arimathea and his son. After decoding what he had of the engraved helmet pieces, Wurm better understood the role that they along with the soldier Quintus played in the Radix legend.

Eighteen years after resurrecting Quintus, Josephus was hunting with his son, Nathan, in the woods of Glastonbury when they became separated. The legend took a critical turn at that point, almost two thousand years ago. As Wurm put together the story, he learned about a fateful day, one on which everything would change for Josephus of Massilia. A day on which he would emerge as the Keeper of the Radix.

—◆—

The Keeper's Tale

A terrible revelation came to Josephus as he staggered alone and half naked through the wilderness. John the Baptist, lost in the depths of wretched isolation and zealotry, could not have summoned greater insight from near madness. The revelation came to Josephus with an understanding of what it meant to lose everything. The old ways in this land—the pagan law—had survived for ages, resisting the seed of Christianity.

The old ways were winning.

Josephus and his people were losing.

Twenty years before, he had sailed to the Britannic Isles on a vessel with a ragged band of believers clinging to hope more than certainty. His father, alone, had a vision that escaped the others. Joseph of Arimathea had left his native home north of Jerusalem some fifty years before, with hope of spreading a message. In a trek from Judea to Gaul, they had finally arrived on this soil. As a gift, King Arviragus had granted parcels of land—without taxation—to Joseph and his brother, Bron of Arimathea. They had constructed an abbey that rivaled the Tabernacle in the Wilderness in scope if not in grandeur. They cultivated a simple hope. A destiny. A dream dedicated to the careworn and humble prophet known as Jesus of Nazareth.

The dream had all but died.

And now, at thirty-eight, Josephus was on the run.

Hunted.

He climbed a tree, moving from branch to branch. As he looked for those who hunted him, a terrible curiosity came into his mind. Within his clan, Josephus was the recognized hunter, more accomplished with spear and bow than with the Gospels. Perhaps that was why his new role—more prey than hunter—sickened him.

He peeked out from the shelter of his leafy fortress, searching the surrounding meadow. Daggers of late-morning sunlight cut through the glade. A silent breeze pulled branches beneath his feet, leading his body into a wide, yawning sway. In his desire to find his lost son, Nathan, he had wandered into a territory that had brought great danger. His boy had been missing for seven days now. Bron and his dozen sons had joined in the search for Nathan, but no sign had been uncovered. Josephus had not given up. Nothing would make him abandon hope for finding his son.

Climbing down, he crawled through the wooded area with his weapon poised, searching for movement. His stomach rumbled, reminding him that he had been without the comfort of food for days. He had hunted game in that time, but he offered it to his people to sustain their search for his son.

The silence of the birds filled him with an uneasy feeling.

Despite the hushed wilderness, he took a risk and climbed down from the tree, hunger teasing him with the notion that the clan had discovered Nathan. Even his father, now close to ninety years in age but still vital, had searched for his grandson. Others in their clan had given up hope. Joseph of Arimathea was a man unable to escape hope.

As Josephus hurried down a slick green hill and made his way deeper into the forest, he spied movement against an oak tree. He recognized Nathan.

The image sickened him.

The boy, no more than eleven, was pulled tight against the bark, his thin wrists strained against misshapen branches. His stance was no accident; it mimicked Jesus of Nazareth when the Romans fixed him to a cross some fifty years before. Josephus's heart seemed to stop inside his chest. Had his thoughts tricked him into seeing Nathan here? He couldn't imagine hunger devising such an elaborate illusion. The frightened brown eyes. A quivering lip. His son looked starved, his ribs pushing through the thin veneer of skin near his stomach.

Josephus scrambled across rocks and fallen trees. At last, he made it to the boy. Josephus sliced the leather cord binding his son's wrist. Tears filled Nathan's eyes when he saw his father.

The boy cried out, but Josephus didn't hear the words. Not at first. When he did, it was too late.

"Father, behind you."

Josephus turned.

They were everywhere.

The pagans had slathered their faces and bare chests with mud and reddish paint. They emerged from bushes and ferns and, as if with magic, they seemed to appear from the rocks themselves. He might convince himself that hunger or madness had conjured this army of the forest, save for one thing.

Nathan saw them first.

Josephus reached for his spear. Six men descended on him, whooping with the cries of night demons. Their eyes burned wide and white. He threw the spear. The blade found the chest of an advancing warrior. At the same time, Nathan used his free hand to untie the strap confining his other arm. Glancing back at the enemy, Josephus reached for his knife. The blade swept across air before slashing the neck of a pagan. As blood splashed Josephus's face, he had already stabbed a third.

But there were more. Many more. Twenty pagans, all dressed in demonic forest paint.

A weapon whistled past his ear. He turned. Was the spear meant for Josephus, only to miss its mark?

No.

The horror was unimaginable.

The weapon was buried in his son's chest, trapping him against the tree. Blood gurgled from Nathan's mouth. He cried like a dying animal. His vacant brown eyes sought out his father beseechingly.

Then he was lost forever.

Nathan!

Josephus sensed the pagan rank closing around him. Bright with rage, he vowed to kill them all. He fought with renewed fury, losing count of the pagans dropping around him. The faces blurred, but he recognized their tribe. They followed Crudel, the pagan chieftain who made a sworn enemy of Joseph of Arimathea and his clan. Crudel, the man who bolstered his numbers even as the people in Arimathea's clan had dwindled. Crudel, the man who tied a boy to a tree, then sent an army to kill him.

In the face of overwhelming numbers, his diminished strength betrayed him. They swarmed Josephus, one after another, rolling him on his back, the breath rattling inside his chest.

Eight pagans held Josephus to the ground. One stood over him. Was it Crudel in his terrible forest disguise? The man raised a long saber over his head. Josephus sensed this was the last thing he would see in this world—or perhaps any other—so he looked at his dead son, caught between tree and weapon, the serenity of his face serving to cast a final vision.

Without warning, the pagan standing over Josephus began choking. His knees buckled and he dropped his weapon as it cut into the earth. He choked again, then collapsed across Josephus's leg.

What happened?

Josephus saw an arrow lodged in the man's back, pointing toward the heavens. All around him, the pagans began to drop, one after another, each falling with the swift action of a bow.

Not a pagan was standing now.

Josephus crawled out from beneath the fallen pagan warrior. He staggered to his feet, still blinking at the collapsed bodies around him. Looking up, Josephus saw Roman centurions marching across the forest. All were dressed in cavalry gear, each adorned with gleaming helmets. The soldiers wore terrible bronze masks that looked human but held such cold expression that they gave the look of an assembly of phantoms.

The leader raised his mask. Josephus knew the man.

Quintus Messorius Gallienus.

Almost twenty years before, the pagan warlord Crudel had slain Quintus. He was the man that Josephus had brought back from the dead, so that Joseph of Arimathea would be spared a prison sentence.

Quintus. The dead soldier risen from the dead. The man with the Black Chrism living inside him.

———◆•◆———

Josephus had walked all afternoon. He had marched under the protection of the Roman army until they reached the edge of Glastonbury, late in the day. At Quintus's command, the centurions halted, then parted and allowed Josephus to pass. He staggered down the path, carrying his dead son in his arms.

His beloved wife was the first to catch sight of him. Ellice was washing clothes in the stream when her head arched up and she saw the Roman army. She then saw Josephus carrying their missing boy. She watched in disbelief as water swirled around her knees. Ellice let out no cry at first. She hurried from the stream and ran toward them, silent tears racing down her cheeks. She had prayed for the return of Nathan, but not like this.

Not like this.

Ellice's screams stirred the notice of the village.

She stood before her husband now, staring into his eyes for answers. Finding none, she looked at her only child, caressing his cheek as her tears consecrated his face. Josephus began walking again. He was almost home. He wanted to take Nathan to his bed, long cold since his disappearance.

He saw his mother, Elyab, hurry over, wiping her hands on her apron. Seeing that she could do nothing, she choked back tears, then reached for Ellice, hoping to comfort her.

Joseph of Arimathea held out his gnarled hands. Anguish seemed to swallow the whole of his face. Josephus had never seen his father look so weak or so small as at this moment. While the soldiers remained at their post, Quintus joined Josephus and his family, placing his hand on the fragile shoulder of Joseph of Arimathea.

They made their way to the center of the village. All came out to drop their heads in respect, some mumbling prayers as they passed. Their looks of grief and consolation did not move Josephus. Nothing could move him except his trembling legs.

Walking into his house and to his son's bed, Josephus folded to his knees and lowered the child to his cot.

Josephus's shirt was stained with the blood of his enemies and his son. His chest felt sticky and cold. Ellice ran her hand across his shoulder as they stared down at Nathan. He lingered with his wife and mother before realizing that his father was not among them.

Josephus pulled away from his grieving wife and moved outside.

At the edge of the village, he saw Quintus talking to Joseph of Arimathea. The soldier looked hardhearted as he made a gesture, slamming his fist into his open palm. As Josephus approached, they took notice and walked to meet him.

"You must do something for us," Joseph of Arimathea said.

Josephus was bewildered as he walked back to the village with them. His son had died. His first thought centered on his loss and not on any duty to his father.

"My son is dead. His blood drips from the hands of Crudel. The pagan king is responsible. He must die a death far greater than my son's."

Joseph of Arimathea frowned. "That is not our way."

"Perhaps it should be our way. Perhaps our way brings only failure."

"Listen to your father," Quintus urged. "This is not the moment to seek revenge on your enemy."

"You are a Roman warrior," Josephus answered, his voice rising. "Seeking revenge is all your empire does."

"I am not my empire." A faraway look came to his eyes. "I am more than my empire."

They stopped outside Josephus's home.

"Do something for us," his father repeated. "Go inside and bring out your boy. Gather Nathan in your arms and take him to Glastonbury Tor. Make certain no one follows. Not even your wife."

"Father, I must prepare his body for burial. I cannot take him to the Tor."

"You can," Quintus ordered, "and you will."

<hr />

Josephus suspected that his wife would never forgive him.

Holding his dead son, he staggered through the village of Glastonbury. His wife trailed him, begging to know where he was taking Nathan. He didn't answer. At the moment, he couldn't.

"We need to wash and anoint his body with oils and spices," she pleaded. "We need to wrap him in linen and take him to the tomb. Josephus, listen to me."

"Go back, Ellice. Leave me with my son."

"Where are you taking him? Tell me."

"I cannot tell you," he shouted. "Go back and stay with my mother until my return."

Her mouth trembled. The people of the village turned away as if they had not heard. His words had shamed her before their clan. She turned without argument, and he trudged down the muddied street, following the command of his father and Quintus.

The centurions remained camped outside the village. They watched in silence as he carried his boy to the great hill rising above the meadow. The Tor was serene in the twilight. After a long climb to the summit, he lowered Nathan onto a bed of tangled grass. He stared at the boy, whose body was lying flat on the natural altar. He thought of Abraham climbing Mount Moriah to sacrifice his son.

With the blessing of God Almighty, Abraham never had to sacrifice Isaac. Where, Josephus wondered, was God's blessing for him?

In his grief, he had not noticed Joseph of Arimathea and Quintus as they climbed the Tor to join him. He marveled at his father's vitality in making the journey. Josephus stood to face them.

His father embraced him. That had never been the old man's custom and his sudden compassion gave Josephus a shudder. Joseph of Arimathea handed his son a scroll. Josephus began to untie the lacing to unroll it, but his father stopped him.

"Read it after you return to the village." He ran his withered hand along Josephus's face. "Go now, good son."

"I must take Nathan back home."

"Leave him," Quintus demanded.

"I tell you, I cannot. I brought him up here as you asked, but I will not leave him."

The Roman soldier looked at the dark and endless plains beyond the Tor, then considered Joseph of Arimathea. "Do you want your son to remain here with us?"

"Do as the Roman said," Joseph of Arimathea answered. "Go, Josephus."

"Only to make amends with my wife, then I shall return for my son."

"As you wish it," Quintus said in a softer voice.

Josephus knelt once more to kiss his son's cold forehead. As he staggered down the knoll, tears burned his eyes. Almost without thinking, he found himself removing the seal around the scroll that his father had handed to him.

Far from reason, his gaze drifted over the words. Scrawled in his father's hand, the message explained that Joseph of Arimathea had met in secret with Bron. He had given his brother the twin cups that had been used to collect the blood and sweat of Jesus Christ at his Crucifixion. Bron was now the Keeper of the Grail.

He had entrusted Josephus with a much greater treasure.

Joseph of Arimathea gave instruction about where to find a hidden box that contained the Radix along with the method to create the chrisms. Josephus was now the Keeper of the Radix. He realized his father's message was a farewell.

A farewell?

Halfway down the Tor, Josephus clenched the scroll. He couldn't return to the village. He had to see his father.

Brisk evening air drew inside his nostrils as he turned and ran with all remaining strength back up Glastonbury Tor. Over the last days, his body had been pushed beyond all known limits, but somehow he found strength in his urgency to return to his father. Bewilderment scattered Josephus's thinking. His mind was blank about the old man's intentions.

Arriving near the summit, he saw Quintus standing above Nathan. In the misty torchlight, he looked like a priest presiding over an altar. Beside him, Joseph of Arimathea kneeled with hands raised in prayer.

Quintus reached down, then ripped open the robe that sheathed Nathan's chest. He placed his hand on the wound where a pagan spear had brought an end to the boy's life. The Roman soldier flattened the fingers of his left hand over black-crusted blood on the boy's skin.

What is he doing?

Quintus closed his eyes as Joseph of Arimathea concluded his prayer. The soldier reached down and wrapped his big hand around the older man's frail wrist. Joseph of Arimathea's eyes shot open. The old man glanced over, staring right at Josephus.

Joseph of Arimathea convulsed, gritting his teeth, but Quintus did not relinquish his iron grip. Joseph was shaking in such brutal fashion that his head rolled. Sweaty white hair blanketed his face. Running up the Tor, Josephus screamed, demanding that the soldier release his father. With one last violent jerk, his father's eyes closed. His body fell limp.

Quintus opened his fist.

Free from the soldier's grip, Joseph of Arimathea collapsed, rolling down the side of the grassy altar.

Coming up the hill, Josephus caught his father's body with his hands, stopping him. He placed his ear against the old man's chest.

There was no sign of life. His son had died. And now, so had his father.

He chastised himself for trusting the Roman. Enraged, Josephus came at the soldier with the same fury that had inspired him to kill the pagans earlier in the day. The Roman made no defensive gesture. Instead, he seemed drained of energy, unwilling to fight, even if he could. It made no matter. Josephus would slaughter him. After that, the other Roman soldiers could do to him as they wished in retaliation for the death of their leader.

Raising his fist to strike, Josephus saw Quintus cast his gaze down at the boy. Josephus did the same. He looked at his son.

The boy's eyes opened. His nostrils flared. His cheeks flushed with vigor.

Nathan of Glastonbury was alive.

Chapter 30

The Black Chrism. Edgar Wurm now understood its dangerous secret.

Eighteen years after Josephus had used the Black Chrism to bring a Roman soldier back from death, pagans had murdered Nathan of Glastonbury. Because he had been given the Black Chrism, Quintus had gained a terrible gift, the ability to heal as long as he also killed. Joseph of Arimathea knew his secrets. Back in the first century, the old man had willingly sacrificed his life, so that his grandson would live again.

More than ever, Wurm wanted to find the formula for creating the Black Chrism.

He had the neck guard as well as the left skull piece from Barcelona. Brynstone had seen the neckpiece back in late February when they had met in Central Park. Since that time, Wurm had learned something new. Thirty-three years after taking the life of Joseph of Arimathea, Quintus had returned to see Josephus and his son, Nathan. The soldier had chosen his helmet to document the story in code.

For thirty years, Quintus had spent a considerable fortune tracking the "Lost Ones," the men and women revived with the

White Chrism or the Black Chrism. All had been brought back from death. None had ever been the same.

On the neck guard, Quintus had mentioned three who were brought back with the White Chrism. He had spoken to them all. One woman had been twelve when she was raised from the dead. Her name was Amarissa, daughter of Jairus. She had lived in Galilee at the time. Seth of Nain was another. He had been eighteen and the son of a widow when he was brought back. The third, Lazarus of Bethany, had been a friend to Joseph of Arimathea. Without question, the once-dead Lazarus had been the most famous of the Lost Ones.

Wurm had no idea if the people brought back with the White Chrism had a gift, but he suspected that they did. He had told Brynstone that much, and it had inspired him to learn more, so that he could better understand his daughter's gift.

Quintus had also tracked down the Lost Ones who had been returned with the Black Chrism. People, like himself, who had the power to heal a wound or raise the dead, at the price of inflicting a wound or killing another. A woman named Tabitha had been brought back with the Black Chrism. So had Eutychus, who as a boy had fallen out of a three-story window and died. A man named Zarad had been stoned to death. Wurm thought that Rafal had the most terrible death of all. As a criminal, he had been bound with rope and sunk up to his neck in a pit of animal excrement. His mouth had been forced open while molten lead was poured down his throat.

Wurm had no idea why a criminal had been brought back from the dead.

The last member of the list was Quintus himself, slain at the age of twenty by a pagan warlord named Crudel and brought back by Josephus, also twenty years old at the time.

Wurm knew that the story of the Lost Ones contained mysteries. Eight men and women brought back for a second chance at life during the first century. Years after the chrism had granted the Lost Ones a second chance at life, seven of the eight had become victims of serial homicide.

Chapter 31

Crete, Greece
11:25 a.m.

Were they still following her?

Looking back, Cori Cassidy searched for the men who had trailed her outside the hospital—or whatever that place had been. There was no sign of them. It was true that she was a fast runner, and she was banking on the flimsy hope that she had lost them. Following the advice of Dr. Spanos, she slipped into a small park that bordered the street. In a panic, she stopped to catch her breath beneath the shade of a billowing plane tree.

Holding hands, a young dark-haired couple passed her. The woman spoke to Cori in Greek.

"I'm American," she told them. "I can't understand you."

Speaking English now, the man asked, "Are you lost?"

Before she could answer, a fighter aircraft blasted across the cloudless sky. Cori glanced up, seeing the muted tan and green belly as it passed over the city—it was heading in a direction she thought might be west. Her uncle had been in the air force and she recognized the twin-engine American military jet.

"That's an F-4 Phantom II jet," the man said. "It's flying with a combat group for the Hellenic Air Force. They buzz our city at all times, it seems."

"Where am I?" Cori asked in a dazed voice.

The couple shared a puzzled laugh. "You don't know where you are?"

"Athens? Where? Please tell me."

"Crete," the woman answered.

"A city called Heraklion." Looking at her scrubs, the man asked, "You are a doctor?"

"Yes, I am," she lied, her words coming out in a flurry. "I need some help. Where can I find the American embassy? Or local police? I need to talk to someone. It's really urgent."

The man pointed across the park.

"Thanks," she answered in a hushed voice.

The couple watched in wary curiosity as she hurried to the edge of the park. Running was a little painful now without her sports bra. She had awakened in the hospital without it. Looking back, it seemed really creepy to think about them taking off her clothes, but there was no time to dwell on that idea.

Spanos had said he'd try to meet her, but she was getting nervous staying here. Apparently, for good reason. Looking back, she saw the two men who had followed her on the street. She thought she had lost them, but they were here now in the park.

Cori made it to the street and ducked behind a car.

Waiting a beat, she peeked through the vehicle's windows. The two men in black were searching the park, though she didn't see any weapons on them. She glanced back to the street. There was no sign of a police station, only small tourist shops brimming with souvenirs and cards. It was only a matter of time until they found her.

She wanted to run, but where? Cori felt terror bubble up inside her. She was trapped, unsure about her next move.

——◆——

Angelilli ran an electric razor across his chin. Looking up from the small mirror balanced on his desk, he saw Joshua Klein rush through the door. That got his attention. Graying at the temples, Klein was a man of Zen-like composure whom Angelilli rarely saw excited.

"We have an international call from a Greek physician. Says his name is Peter Spanos. Better take his call, Steve."

Razor still in hand, Angelilli eyed him. "What's the situation?"

"He claims he's had contact with Cori Cassidy. They interacted a short time ago."

"Where?"

"Heraklion."

He lowered the razor and switched it off. "That's Crete, right? What the hell is she doing there?"

"She was in a facility that operated as a hospital. Or at least made to resemble one. Spanos said she was under his care."

Angelilli couldn't believe it. Cassidy and Wonderland had been missing from the vehicle. He had assumed both had been abducted and that Cassidy had been assassinated.

"How long was she under this doctor's care?" Angelilli asked, reaching for the phone.

"Didn't say," Klein answered. "Sounds like someone wanted Cassidy to believe she had been hospitalized in New York. From what I've learned, Spanos facilitated her escape."

"Thanks, Joshua." Angelilli snapped up the phone. "Dr. Spanos, thank you for calling."

Silence.

"Dr. Spanos? Can you hear me? Sir, are you there?"

On the other end of the line, the call disconnected. The dial tone buzzed in his ear.

"What happened?" Klein asked.

"He's gone," Angelilli said. "Track that call now and find the doctor."

<hr/>

Crete
11:31 a.m.

After slinking behind parked cars, Cori managed to elude the men following her in the park. But with no sign of the police station or the embassy, frustration settled in again. She ripped off the green scrubs and ditched them in a trash can.

Wearing sweatpants and a purple T-shirt now, she stopped an elderly woman and asked about the police. Waving her hands, it became clear she didn't speak English. As she fumbled a sorry-to-bother-you apology, Cori caught sight of a husky man wearing a tan suit. He was a new face, not one she had seen outside the hospital. He stood across the street, scanning the area with an earpiece curled beneath his crew cut.

Anxiety stirred inside her. She didn't get it. How were they finding her? Everywhere she turned, they drew closer, as if gathering an unseen net around her. Or was she super paranoid? This guy wasn't dressed like the other two men. Maybe he was someone else. Still, she didn't trust him.

She decided to head in a different direction. That worked until she spied a black car moving slowly down the opposite side of the street. *Okay, now what?* Crossing the street, she had her answer when she noticed an alley.

She headed that way and ducked down a narrow road of crumbling pavement. A twentysomething man on a bicycle headed her way. He didn't look like the others, but she decided to avoid eye contact anyway.

Looking down as he passed, she glanced at the laminated hospital bracelet on her wrist, shimmering in the sunlight. A realization hit her like a blow to the chest. She flipped the bracelet back against her skin, checking the underside. A tiny glowing circle was embedded inside its plastic surface. *A transmitter.* That's why she couldn't lose them; the men had been tracking her every move.

She had to ditch this thing.

She tried to tear it. No good. She pulled on the band. Too tight. She tried to stretch it over her hand. The band cut into her skin, but she eventually managed to drag the bracelet off her wrist.

She flung the bracelet into the air, throwing it so hard her arm sizzled with warmth. It landed on the far side of a tall chain-link fence. *Good.* That would throw them off her trail until she made an escape.

"Clever," a man called, "but a little too late, Ms. Cassidy."

The guy with the precision buzz cut and the tan suit walked toward her. Before she could think twice, the two men in black marched from the opposite end of the alley. She thought about outrunning them, but sensed she couldn't escape.

She looked again at the chain-link fence.

Cori raced to it. All three men sprinted after her. Although short, she got a good jump on it and attacked the fence like a chipmunk in a desperate scramble up a tree. The chains quavered as she dipped her upper body over, punching her stomach muscles against the top rail. From below, a hand wrapped around her ankle and one of them ripped her foot from its hold. Still halfway over, she clutched the fence, muscles blazing as she held on with all her strength. Another man arrived and grabbed her calf. Her chest scraped the top rail as he jerked her toward him. She struck the ground, landing on her hip. She didn't have a chance to breathe before the crew-cut guy grabbed her wrists.

"Let me go," she cried.

A man with curly brown hair reached around her waist, then raised her. Spinning in their arms, she managed to drop her body almost to the ground, but they caught her, lifting her up again. The men came at her with more aggressiveness than the CIA agents back at the hotel. They marched Cori down the alley—her feet scraping the broken concrete—with two men flanking her and the guy in the suit leading the way.

Chapter 32

Crete
11:40 a.m.

Rashmi Raja recognized the man the second she spotted him. She had never met Nicholas Booth in person, but the antiquities collector looked as sinister in person as he sounded on the phone. He checked his watch while standing outside a three-story office building, and she waited for him to notice her. It took a minute, then the squat, heavyset man looked across the street and started walking toward her.

She flashed a smile. He didn't notice.

Without making eye contact, he took her arm and directed her down the street. "Let's walk."

"You seem nervous," she observed. He didn't, but she thought the comment would catch him off guard.

"I'm never nervous," he muttered. "Brief me on your progress."

"You'll be pleased. I've collected several helmet pieces."

"You've had help."

"You know about that?"

Booth looked at her for the first time. "I know everything."

"Including things you didn't tell me."

"Like what?"

"Like the code inside the Roman helmet. You didn't tell me about a map leading to the missing treasure."

"I wouldn't call it treasure," he huffed.

They crossed the street and passed a shop selling Minoan pottery next door to a Starbucks storefront.

"If it's worth money, it's treasure in my book," she answered. "This job goes way beyond collecting an old chunk of metal."

"Let me guess. This conversation is about money."

Raja stopped. She brought out the facemask, holding it up for his inspection. The man glanced around, then took a closer look. He couldn't conceal the delight in his dark eyes.

"Where did you find this?"

"A cave beneath Paris."

"I don't say this often, but I'm impressed."

"Me too." She slid the mask inside a leather pouch.

"Wait," Booth said. "Give me that mask. I'm paying for the helmet pieces."

"Sorry. Can't hand it over right now."

"I don't regret hiring you," he said, "but I didn't hire John Brynstone."

"And I didn't plan on working with him, but it's worth it. Promise you, I'm controlling the situation. When the time's right, Mr. Booth, I'll ditch Brynstone and McHardy and take everything. They'll never see it coming."

————◆◆◆————

He should have seen it coming.

In a slow burn, Brynstone watched from a distance as Raja negotiated with her buyer. He had tracked her from Prague to Crete. He didn't have audio, only binoculars, but he saw her show the Roman facemask.

Nessa Griffin had taken his phone in Paris, but he'd picked up another one. On the new cell, Brynstone studied a photograph Wurm had sent after their last call. *Perfect match.* Short and overweight, the man displayed on the phone looked identical to Raja's buyer. The guy's name? Viktor Nebola.

Raja had said she was working for a man named Nicholas Booth. Did she know he was Nebola? Had she lied about the man's name?

Brynstone wanted to find Erich Metzger. Nebola offered the best chance at tracking down the assassin. In a way, Raja had done him a big favor. Thanks to her deceit, Brynstone was one step closer to finding Metzger.

Watching her walk with Nebola, Brynstone was ready to operate on instinct. That instinct told him to ram his Glock against Nebola's head and demand that he reveal where to find Metzger. But before he could move into action, he heard a woman scream.

Spinning on his heels, he looked over his shoulder. Three men were hustling a petite blonde woman toward an office building. One clamped a hand over her mouth, stifling her screams. He recognized the woman at once, but he couldn't believe it was her.

What was Cori Cassidy doing in Greece? And why were three guys wrestling her into that building? The whole scene was almost too surreal to take in.

He glanced back at Raja walking with Nebola, moving farther away. This was Brynstone's chance to apprehend the man and question him. Not to mention maybe the last chance to get the facemask from Raja.

Brynstone stole another look at the men carrying Cori into the building.

Nebola was getting away. If Brynstone helped Cori, his best lead on Metzger would disappear. If he took down Nebola, he couldn't be there to help Cori.

Save her or go after Nebola?

He growled. *Ugly choices.*

Chapter 33

Crete
11:44 a.m.

Nebola was sneaking a look at Raja. He had dated a Punjabi beauty years ago, until his wife discovered the indiscretion and things got messy. He had broken it off with reluctance, but the woman wouldn't go without a fight. Half his age, his mistress was spunky like Rashmi Raja. What was her name? He couldn't remember. He only knew it had been a shame to have her killed.

"So you want more money?" he asked.

"I'm worth it," Raja answered. "You know it."

She might be right about that. He glanced at her body as they walked. He wasn't paying to touch, but he was paying enough to take a look. He liked watching her strut in black midcut shorts. Riding below her bare midriff and curving up her outer thigh, they highlighted her tight little butt.

"You impressed me, Ms. Raja. If you continue to impress, you better believe I'll take care of you."

"That means what, exactly?"

He winked at her. "A nice bonus from me to you."

"How nice? And you better be talking about money."

"You bring me the whole helmet? Twenty thousand."

"Eighty."

He smirked. "You're psychotic. You know it? Hot but psychotic."

"Eighty."

"Twenty-five."

"Sixty."

"Did I mention I have a gun?"

"Did I mention I have helmet pieces? The ones leading to a treasure?"

"Thirty, but you're starting to piss me off. If they could still speak, lots of people could tell you how it's a bad idea to piss me off."

"Forty and I shut up."

"I got a feeling you'll never shut up. Not until the day you die." He studied her. "Bring me everything and we'll do forty."

She held out her hand.

He didn't move. "Forty with the understanding we put you on retainer for future assignments."

"You got it."

He shook her hand.

"Don't disappoint me."

"I won't, Mr. Booth."

"Here's what you're going to do," Nebola said. "You're going to work with Math McHardy. However, you cannot tell him about our partnership."

"What about John Brynstone?"

"Forget him," Nebola answered. "You can't trust Brynstone."

—◆—

From behind, a man in black shoved Cori Cassidy into a windowless room. The force sent her spiraling across the floor. Despite hitting hard on one knee, she tried unsuccessfully to make a graceful return to her feet, grabbing a metal chair and pulling herself onto it to catch her breath. She was still hurting after the drop from the fence.

Desperation set in. The men who had abducted her had dragged her back to the first floor of the building where she had been hospitalized. The door was open and they were talking out there, but her thoughts were focused on escape. She had no idea how to attempt it.

A clattering noise came from out in the hallway, and the men shouted profanities. Before she could react, the guy with the crew cut flew past the door. His body hurtled face-first into the wall, his tan suit coat curling over his head as he dropped. A second man, the guy who had ripped her from the fence, hit the floor out in the hallway and sprawled across the leg of the first guy. His face was a bloodied mess.

Cori darted up from the chair as the man with curly brown hair rolled across the corridor floor. She braced herself and stared at the open door. She had no idea what—or who—was coming next.

To her surprise, John Brynstone peeked in, both hands pressed against the doorframe.

"You okay?" he asked.

She couldn't speak.

After everything that had happened, he was here. Right here with her. Was it real?

Brynstone walked into the room and scooped her up in an embrace. Cori slid an arm beneath his backpack, holding tight, not wanting to let go. She broke down and cried tears of relief and joy. But so much more was more going on inside her. Lost in this moment of combustible attraction, she realized how many feelings she had denied herself since she had last seen him. Her chin tucked into Brynstone's chest, she felt safe at last. An explosion of emotion rocked her as she wiped her eyes. A dizzy lilt pulled her from elation to alarm as she stood on tiptoes and peered over his shoulder. Their reunion was brief.

"Someone's out there," she cried.

From the hallway, a man slammed the door closed. They heard a click as he locked them in the room.

Brynstone pulled away and rushed to the locked door. He didn't speak. Cori joined him as he ran his hands along the surface, his head craning as he studied the door. She bit her lip and curled her hands in frustration until her skin turned a pinkish-white tint.

———◆———

Rashmi Raja crossed her arms in protest. "You're wrong about trusting John Brynstone."

"Really?" Nicholas Booth gave her a cold stare. "Brynstone followed you here. You know that don't you?"

She looked around. "I wasn't followed."

"You're good, Rashmi, but you're not as good as you think."

He brought out a tablet computer and tapped the screen. He held it so she could see it. Video surveillance showed Brynstone entering a building from outside, moving down a corridor into a large open area, then turning a corner. He assaulted three men in quick succession, then hurried into a room. The camera was mounted outside and zoomed in to capture him hugging a cute blonde woman who looked a little like Tinker Bell. As they embraced, a man dressed in black cammies closed the door, locking them inside the room.

"Who's the woman?"

"A pain in the ass named Cori Cassidy. I thought I might need her help. Decided I don't. That footage you saw? It happened a few minutes ago, right over there." He pointed to the three-story building where she had first seen him.

"Brynstone followed you from Prague," he continued. "Big mistake on your part, Ms. Raja. Let's make sure it never happens again."

He grinned and tapped the tablet computer. She glanced at it, seeing a red rectangle on the screen.

"What are you doing?"

"Dr. Brynstone is a problem. Watch how I solve problems."

He tapped the screen again.

An explosion rocked the building.

Raja staggered, turning to see flames and smoke boil out the building's north side. Rolling back on her feet, she ran her fingers through her black hair. Her heart spiked with a rush of blood. A burst of anger welled inside and she turned to confront the man.

He pointed a gun at her.

"You've already made one serious mistake today, Ms. Raja—don't commit a second." He narrowed his eyes. "Connect with Math McHardy. Go finish your job. Bring me the complete helmet."

"Agreed," she said. "Conversation done."

A charcoal-gray SUV rolled around the corner and stopped at curbside. A man in a black suit popped out and opened the rear door.

"Don't disappoint me," Booth called. He lowered the gun and headed for the vehicle.

As he climbed inside the SUV, Raja caught sight of a blonde-haired child. As Booth took his seat beside her, the girl locked her gaze onto Raja. Her eyes were a crystalline blue, holding back secrets and mysteries.

Startled, she realized the child's eyes matched the color and character of John Brynstone's eyes exactly.

PART III
Mound of Shards

What is now proved was once only imagin'd.

—William Blake

Chapter 34

Crete
11:58 a.m.

Rashmi Raja sprinted toward the building.

The explosion had ripped open an exterior wall, where a ripe patch of flame and smoke was billowing into the sky. A handful of stunned people hurried out, coughing, with hands shielding their mouths.

She pushed past them and moved inside. A Greek man tried to stop her, but she shoved him hard and sprinted away through double doors. He didn't chase after her.

Turning a corner, she recognized a long corridor, now blackened with smoke. It looked like the one in the video. Covering her mouth, she found the room where Brynstone had hugged the woman. The door had been blown wide open and was embedded in the opposite wall. Flames curled out of the opening, warming her skin. She tried to see in the room, but it was impossible to make anything out in the blaze. She lost hope. No one could survive that blast.

＊＊＊

Smoke. Everywhere.

Brynstone curled forward, coughing and wheezing. A blanket of debris covered his body. Dazed, he rubbed his neck, his hand spotted gray with dust. His mind flashed to before the explosion. He and Cori had escaped from the locked room and scrambled out into the corridor. After the detonation, the room had disappeared in the blaze. It had blasted this wing of the building, rocketing them off their feet.

Cori. He had to find her.

Rising in a shower of shattered glass and plaster, he searched for her, finding nothing in his initial exploration of the wreckage. Then he spotted her motionless body sprawled on an altar of rubble. Her eyes were closed.

He dropped to his knees and pressed his fingers to her neck. He found a pulse. Running his hand along her forehead, he brushed back tangled bangs.

"Cori. Can you hear me?"

No answer.

He didn't want to move her. Her back was twisted in an awkward angle and dirt coated her face. He cleared away rubble from her leg.

Cori slowly batted open her eyes. He gave her a relieved smile. She rubbed her head, then curled on her side. Good thing. No spinal injury.

He reached down for her, and she wrapped her arms around his neck. Her head cradled against his shoulder. He hadn't forgotten the ever-present curiosity in her bright eyes or her sunshine-tinted hair, but this raw moment of survival heightened her charm. Even coming out of an explosion, she glowed. He enjoyed the lingering pleasure of her body pressed against his and mourned a little when she pulled back.

After a lengthy separation from Kaylyn, he had dated women, but he had never connected with them. It was different now with

Cori. He cared for her more than he had allowed himself to realize. Grabbing her hand, he directed her around chunks of masonry, then ducked under a bent girder beam. He knew the way out.

———————

Rashmi Raja didn't like it. Inside the destroyed building, she could hear the blare of fire engines and police sirens in the distance. She had to get out of here. Hurrying down the opposite end of the corridor, stepping over debris as she went, she followed a sign that must have spelled out *Exit* in the Greek language. She turned, making a right at the corner.

To her surprise, she saw John Brynstone and the blonde woman from the video surveillance. With filthy clothes and disheveled hair, they looked like they had survived a major earthquake.

Raja blinked. "Thought you died in the explosion."

He patted a dusty backpack. "Good thing I had a screwdriver and pliers. The door was locked, so I pulled out the pins on the hinges."

"He's fast," the blonde added. "Cut it close, but we made it out in time."

"Popping the hinges off the door, huh?" Raja marveled. "Gotta admit, I never would have thought of that."

"Let's get out of here," Brynstone said.

Raja followed them out of the building. Hellenic police and firefighters arrived at the same time. In all the chaos, the trio managed to slip into the crowd and escape without anyone asking questions.

Farther down the block, the woman introduced herself.

"I'm Cori," she said, walking on the opposite side of Brynstone. He didn't say a word, keeping a determined stride.

"Rashmi Raja," she answered, not hinting that she knew the woman's name after talking to Booth.

"Turn at this corner," he said, glancing back to see if anyone had followed.

They moved to the next street, taking them out of view from the exploded building.

"I have a question for you, Dr. Brynstone," Raja said. "Mind telling me why you followed me to Greece?"

Brynstone came around to face her. "I have a better question," he asked between gritted teeth. "Why are you working for Viktor Nebola?"

"Don't know him. Nebola? Told you, I work for Nicholas Booth."

"Guy you think is Booth is actually Nebola."

She didn't believe him at first.

Walking down the sidewalk, Brynstone told her a little about Nebola's involvement in an organization known as the Shadow Chapter. She had looked into Booth's background before working with him. It had checked out. Was it true about Nebola?

She didn't like that Brynstone had followed her here, but she didn't mention it. The man was angry. Let him cool down.

After that? Send Tinker Bell back to Neverland.

⬥

Cori couldn't stop looking at John Brynstone. It didn't seem real that he was here walking beside her. She thought about the best way to give him the news about Kaylyn and Shayna. There wouldn't be a good time to do it. And what about Rashmi Raja? How much should she say in front of her?

The other woman was a sultry beauty with long, lavish hair and gorgeous clothes. Cori sensed a connection between Raja and

Brynstone. She didn't know how to feel about that. She remembered meeting another colleague of his years ago, a woman named Jordan Rayne. Victim to an insatiable curiosity, Cori had wanted to know more about her, but Brynstone had made it clear back then not to ask questions about Jordan.

What had happened to her?

Now, Brynstone and Raja were talking about this Nebola guy, the conversation sounding intense. It wasn't a good time, but she had to interrupt. As they headed to his rental car parked outside a Greek restaurant, Cori touched his arm.

"John, I have terrible news."

"It can wait."

"No, it can't," she blurted. "It's about Kaylyn."

His eyes darkened. "What about her?"

"Sh-she was killed."

He looked down. The muscles in his jaw tightened as he swallowed hard. For a moment, his composure wavered, but he regained it. No doubt about it. John Brynstone was the Fort Knox of emotion.

"There's more." Her voice choked. "This guy chased after us back in New York. He shot Kaylyn."

"What guy?"

"Outside Shay's school."

"Did they fire at my daughter?"

"She wasn't hurt. I got her away from the gunmen. John, they came to kidnap Shayna and Kaylyn tried to stop them. That's when they killed her."

"Where's Shay?" he demanded.

"Don't know," she sobbed. "I'm sorry, John. I tried to protect her, but I lost her."

She became aware of the woman listening in on their conversation. Brynstone came at Cori with question after question. She recounted how she had fled with the child through Manhattan and how she had ended up in Crete. At least, she gave her best guess about ending up here.

Brynstone knew how to conceal his emotions, but a trace of pain colored his expression. A distant look came over his eyes. In a hushed voice, he said, "Gotta get back to the States. Need to find Shayna."

"You don't have to go to the United States," the Indian woman said. She stepped closer, cutting the distance between them. "I saw a little blonde girl, John. She was about six or seven. Maybe she was your daughter."

He grabbed her shoulder, intensity in his voice. "Where?"

"Hey, take it easy. I could be wrong."

He released her. "Why do think she was Shayna?"

"She looked like you. She has your eyes."

"When did you see her?"

"After the explosion."

"Where?"

"With Booth. Well, I guess you're calling him Viktor Nebola." She glanced at Cori. "He said he didn't need you anymore. Guess that's why he tried to blow you up."

"Nebola has Shayna?" Brynstone muttered.

"He climbed into an SUV. I saw the little girl with him, right before the door closed."

"Where did they go?"

"Don't know. I ran back to see if you were still alive."

"Can you get in touch with Nebola?"

"Only if he calls. He uses a different phone every time. Anyway, I should probably find Math McHardy."

"Why Math?"

"Nebola wants me to work with him. He'll be unhappy if he calls and I'm not consulting with Math on the helmet pieces."

"Does he know you worked with me?"

"Yeah," Raja confessed, "but now he thinks you're dead."

That gave Brynstone an idea. Cori saw it spelled all over his face.

He opened the car door. "Let's move. We have work to do."

Chapter 35

Airborne over the Mediterranean
4:32 p.m.

Briefcase in hand, Nebola strutted into a suite at the back of the luxury jet. Sitting cross-legged on the floor, Shayna Brynstone played with toys. She looked up as he entered.

Not a word from her.

He had to admit, the kid had a fierce stare.

"Nice jet, isn't it?" he asked. "You like flying?"

No answer, but she stared at the briefcase, curiosity in her eyes. She was a tough one to crack.

"Know what, kid? I like you."

He didn't, of course, but he was playing nice. If the Shadow Chapter was right about the girl, she could prove to be an important asset.

"Sorry, mister, but I don't like you," she answered. "You're a very bad man."

He smirked. "Sounds like you've been talking to my ex-wife and her attorney."

The child held her defiant gaze.

"What?" Nebola asked, chuckling. "Not a fan of divorce humor?"

He eased into a seat near her. The kid was missing two front teeth. It was a look that charmed on the face of a child, less so on a hockey player.

"I'm not a bad man, Shayna. I'm a good man."

The child furrowed her brow. "A good man wouldn't put me on a plane and take me away from my friend, Cori."

"Look, getting Cori Cassidy out of your life? I did you a huge favor. She is not your friend."

"Cori is so my friend."

"She's dangerous, my dear. A few years ago, Cori Cassidy escaped from a psychiatric hospital. Bet you didn't know that."

"I don't know what a psych-qwe-atric hospital is."

"Place where they keep crazy people. Baltimore police believed she killed two hospital workers before escaping. She was also suspected of attacking her roommate."

"I don't believe you," she answered with a hurt look.

"Better believe me." Nebola pulled a folder from the briefcase. It contained a forensic report on Cori Cassidy. "Want to see for yourself?"

The child dropped her head.

He placed the folder on a table. "I know something about you, Shayna. I know you are special."

"I'm not special," she said in a weak voice. "I'm just a girl."

"Perhaps that's what you hear. Perhaps that's what your parents and Cori tell you, but I know the truth. You have a gift."

When they had removed Cassidy from the accident back in New York State, she had a USB drive in her pocket. It confirmed what the Shadow Chapter had suspected about Shayna.

"I read the report from your school," he continued. "It said you have a name for your gift. What is it?"

She folded her small arms over her chest.

"What do you call your special ability, kid?"

"It's just a word. I don't know what it means."

He leaned forward. "What is it? Tell me the name."

"The Hollow."

"That's right. The Hollow. Strange word for a little girl."

"Told you, I don't know what it means."

"Where did you hear that word?"

She sighed. "My imaginary friend told me."

"Your imaginary friend has a peculiar vocabulary. Who told you about the Hollow? What's the name?"

"Monkey Guns. I don't talk about him."

"Why not?"

"'Cause. He's mean like you."

"I'm not mean."

"You're a bad killer."

A cold smile. "You're mistaken, my dear. I've never killed anyone in my life."

He wasn't counting Marcus Tanzer back in the Manhattan office. Electricity had killed him, not Nebola.

The child glared. "You get other people to kill for you."

Her words shocked him. How could she possibly know?

"You say all the right words to trick me," Shayna continued, "but your aura tells the truth."

"My aura?"

"A glow around your body. A tiny little fire that shoots out all around you. I can see it."

"Can you?" he asked. "That's how you knew I get people to kill for me?"

"If you were a killer, you'd have a black aura."

"What color's my aura?"

"Red, but the flames have little black tips."

"What?"

"Your aura is black on the ends," she said, concentrating like she could see something around his head. "Most of the time, you make people kill for you."

"You have quite the imagination, young lady."

"I'm not a young lady. I'm a big girl."

"A big girl who can see auras. Is that what you mean by a Hollow?"

"That's something else."

Nebola leaned forward. "Shayna, can you show me an example of the Hollow?"

The girl stared at him.

Chapter 36

A band of mocha-colored pollution crawled the skies over Cairo. Yawning, Cori turned her gaze from the airplane window. Still groggy from medication, she had slept most of the three-and-a-half-hour flight from Crete with a stopover in Athens. John Brynstone had done some fast-talking with contacts in the United States government and managed to get a quick flight for Cori, Raja, and himself.

Before takeoff, they had hit a cramped shop inside Heraklion International Airport where Brynstone had purchased a black T-shirt with a small silhouette of a Minotaur on the chest. Cori got one in blue with a labyrinth emblazoned above her breast. Another place sold herbal creams and oils as well as a few cosmetics. Raja went crazy and bought makeup for them both. Nice gesture, really, but Cori wasn't connecting with the woman. Was it an issue of trust? Brynstone seemed cool with Raja, but something about her made Cori uneasy. Maybe they just needed some serious warm-up time.

During the flight, Cori had slipped into the bathroom to clean up. Pulling off her ruined shirt, she had checked on the surgical bandages. Peeling them back, she saw that Dr. Spanos had told the truth—there was no sign of any incisions or sutures. Brynstone believed that Nebola was behind the hospital deception.

After a touchy landing in Cairo, they spilled out happily onto the tarmac. Situated northeast of the city, Cairo International was as congested as its skies, earning its reputation as Egypt's busiest airfield. Wandering inside the bright terminal, Cori saw curving ceilings, polished floors, and rows of potted palm trees.

Brynstone was back on the phone, talking to former colleagues in the intelligence community. He was trying to locate a retired professor named McHardy. She sensed he didn't want his conversation overheard. Cori got the message and wandered away.

Raja finished her call and strutted over to chat with Cori. They visited a little, playing nice. The woman was probing for clues about Brynstone.

"You and John seem close."

"We worked together once. It wasn't simple. Let's leave it at that." She bit her lip. "How do you know John?"

"I like your answer. It's not simple." Raja gave a sly grin. "Nothing about John Brynstone is simple."

"Can't argue with that one."

Raja pointed across the terminal. "I need to use the ladies' room. Be right back."

Cori nodded and watched her walk across the terminal. She had a graceful stride, almost like a dancer. She had mixed feelings about Rashmi Raja. There was too much she didn't know about the woman. How much did Brynstone know?

He had moved now, but was still talking on the phone. He was framed inside a window with an EgyptAir jet in the background. The rudder was emblazoned with a blue falcon symbolizing Horus, the Egyptian sky god.

The man was good at keeping his cool. Even when a little intensity showed, he seemed like he was holding back a million times more. As a psychology grad student, she prided herself on reading people, but Brynstone was opaque. Maybe that was part of his allure. His way of keeping her guessing gave him a natural mystique, and his blend of charm and mystery appealed to Cori.

It also worked magic on Rashmi Raja. That's the way it seemed anyway.

He came over, finishing a text as he walked. He looked at her with his legendary magnetism.

"You okay?" he asked.

"Yeah. You?"

"Will be once we find Shay." He took a step closer, speaking in that low voice. "I always knew we'd see each other again, Cori. Figured it would happen under better circumstances."

She smiled and found herself embracing him again, finding strength in his arms. His daughter had been kidnapped. His ex-wife had been murdered. She needed to give comfort, but here she was, taking it.

"Where's Rashmi?" he asked, pulling back to look around.

"Restroom."

"Which one?"

Cori pointed. "Over there."

"Do me a favor. Go check it," he said, his voice sounding urgent all of a sudden. "See if she's still in there."

Chapter 37

Chomping on a cigar, Nebola headed toward Shayna Brynstone. Despite the report from the school and the fantastic nonsense about auras, she seemed like a normal kid. Had they been wrong about her? If so, the CIA was wrong as well. Better not be the case.

The Shadow Chapter believed that the little girl had a remarkable ability, one that could produce profit for the organization. Erich Metzger had tipped them off about her. He had inside information that Taft-Ryder, an international pharmaceutical company, might have an interest in how the White Chrism had changed her. Metzger had never steered Nebola or the Chapter wrong before.

Shayna looked up, her gaze fixed on him. The kid reached for her stuffed kitty like it was a security blanket.

"Know what?" he said, making the question not seem like a question. "After we talked, I did some research on auras. Turns out you're not the only one who can see them."

The child cocked her head, studying him. "I'm not?"

"You said I had a red aura. I researched it. Tell me, Shayna, is there more red on the right side of my body or on the left?"

She considered him, then pointed to his right side.

"Ah, you see, that's not bad at all. According to the experts, red on the right side represents great passion. I have a fiery personality. That's what you're seeing."

"I don't know about experts," the child said. "I haven't known too many mean people, but the ones who are mean all had the red glow."

"Perhaps this time, Shayna, you were mistaken. Ever think about that?"

Nebola didn't like children. Detested them, in fact, their whispery-sweet voices and doe-eyed purity. Still, he found one redeeming trait. Free of world-weary cynicism and victims of elastic imagination, children were a dream to manipulate.

He feigned a look of benevolence like something he imagined a grandfather might give. But not his grandfather. Not the red-eyed old man who prowled the edges of Nebola's childhood memories, a man who could be dangerous if you got crosswise between him and his vodka.

Nebola could tell the Brynstone girl liked the grandfather look. He could see it in her eyes.

Children.

A dream to manipulate.

Vienna, Austria
5:11 p.m.

A century ago, Edgar Wurm's people had migrated from Austria. Before today, he'd visited the country exactly one time. Given his feelings about his mother and her family, it had made better sense to avoid the place.

Since June, Wurm had tried to coax an invitation to visit the Tersch Haus, which possessed a scroll that he believed could prove critical to his mission. The Viennese castle wasn't as celebrated as the country's royal palaces. Its sole moment of glory came in the late sixteenth century when the Tersch Haus served as a summer residence for Rudolf II during his reign over the Habsburg Empire. Like its more famous Viennese cousin, the Schönbrunn Palace with its colonnaded Gloriette, the Tersch Haus was known for a lush garden that stretched to a magnificent hill. Wurm had learned about it from a relative in the Austrian army—service was compulsory here—who had shared that soldiers trained by running the hills at the Tersch and Schönbrunn palaces.

Looking around, Wurm decided that the castle was suitably depressing. He took a stab at geniality while traipsing up a gloomy marble staircase with Gustav Trenker, an older gentleman who served as administrator. After considerable expense, Wurm had persuaded Trenker to permit him a visit.

He followed the smaller man to a wing of the castle framed with floor-to-ceiling bookshelves and an arched medieval window. Wurm's love affair with books began at age five when he had cracked open a Jules Verne novel. It had been a magical moment, exploring the mysteries of the seas with a complex and paranoid genius named Captain Nemo. As a child, Wurm dreamed about creating a vast library like the one Nemo kept deep inside the *Nautilus*. His school buddies didn't understand his passion, and they had teased him about it, time after time, calling him Book Wurm.

Simpletons.

Wurm took a seat at the end of a long oak table in preparation for seeing the scroll. He was not allowed to take notes or to photograph the document, and Trenker insisted that he wear gloves to prevent oils on his fingertips from desecrating the ancient scroll.

Fair enough. After debating the amount of time he could study the archives, the old man left him alone. *At last.* Relaxed now with an open thermos of coffee he had smuggled into the castle, Wurm inspected the aged document.

In May, he had discovered a journal in a French archive that had belonged to a fourteenth-century woman named Jeanneton. On one page, she had hinted that the Roman facemask had once been in the possession of a Greek named Kyros. If she had known anything more about him, she didn't share it. Wurm had spent considerable time tracking down the historical figure, scouring the past to find the right person. Facing one false end after another, he finally decided that Jeanneton had been referring to a scholar of Greek descent named Kyros of Cyrene. Born in Libya, he had lived in various parts of Egypt during the fifth century.

Several weeks after learning about Kyros, Wurm had discovered that the Tersch Haus held in its private archive a deathbed confession that the man had dictated fifteen centuries ago. Known informally as the Kyros Scroll, it recounted events that he had shared in the final hours of his life.

Before dying, Kyros was desperate to record events about a woman who had served as his teacher and mentor. During the early 400s, Hypatia of Alexandria was considered to be the greatest thinker of her age, a person of dazzling intellect and beauty. She was a mathematician and an astronomer, a philosopher and an alchemist. And, most troubling for the time, she did not fear men.

Her father, Theon of Alexandria, had rescued a relic in the final moments before a temple associated with the Great Library of Alexandria had collapsed in flames. He cherished the helmet that had once belonged to a Roman cavalry soldier because it contained a code that Theon could never decipher. For the next fourteen years, he kept it among his most cherished possessions, dying before he could solve its riddles.

After a decade of effort, Hypatia of Alexandria had managed to decode the secrets that Quintus had inscribed on the helmet. She had teamed up with a reluctant student, Kyros, to uncover the truth. On a March night in 415, they made what Kyros called a "discovery of grave importance," one that pointed to a "dangerous mystery."

Did his scroll reveal what they had found?

Hell, no. Not even the site where they had found it.

Wurm pounded his fist against the table. It was like Kyros was taunting him from his deathbed.

Kyros had dedicated the last section of his scroll to a gruesome event. In detail, he described how he had become an eyewitness to an assassination that remained shocking to the present day. Wurm sensed that it was tied to the helmet and its secrets.

At the dawn of the fifth century, Alexandria was a volatile world of shady dealings and bloodthirsty power plays. The city was a historical time bomb, ticking with conflict and tension. Triggering the explosion, Hypatia was ensnared in a dramatic power struggle between Orestes, the Roman governor of the province of Egypt, and Cyril, the bishop of Alexandria.

Although Hypatia was admired throughout much of the known world, her enemies began to outnumber her friends. Inside the shadows of Alexandria's temple, monks called her a witch and accused Hypatia of drinking the blood of infants to preserve her timeless beauty. Kyros dismissed the gossip as jealous nonsense, but the peril was real.

The fallout came the morning after making her discovery with Kyros. Hypatia was riding in her chariot through Alexandria, a ballsy thing to do back in the day because women did not dare to drive chariots. A small army of monks pulled Hypatia from the chariot and dragged her to a church. In the past, Bishop Cyril had hired the monks to offer personal protection. It was rumored they had even committed murder. *Killer monks?* Wurm thought, shuffling in his chair. So it seemed. He took a drink of black coffee, then continued reading the scroll.

The monks ripped at her clothes, slashing open the robe to reveal Hypatia's bare breasts. Even three decades later, wasting on his deathbed, Kyros couldn't believe they would commit such an atrocity inside a church. She was assaulted inside the sanctuary to hide their actions from the citizens of Alexandria.

Because formal weapons were not permitted in the church, they had carried roofing tiles shaped like oyster shells. Hypatia had screamed and fought, but they attacked from all sides. Like bloodthirsty animals, the men had cut open her bare flesh and scraped her down to the bone. After flaying her, the monks hauled Hypatia's dismembered body to a local courtyard and burned her on a pyre.

Four hundred years before Hypatia's assassination, a pagan mob had tied a rope around the neck of Saint Mark the Evangelist. He had been dragged to his death on the streets of Alexandria. Kyros had understood that history had repeated itself, but in an even more brutal fashion. The greatest thinker of his time was gone.

So were her secrets.

—◦—

After sixteen centuries, historians still hadn't decided if Bishop Cyril had ordered the assassination of Hypatia. From what Wurm could determine, Kyros believed the bishop was responsible, but he lacked evidence to support the accusation. Fearing for his life,

Kyros had given the Roman helmet to Orestes, the governor of Alexandria. What became of it after that?

Kyros claimed that Quintus's helmet had been cut into six pieces and scattered across the known world. The sections had vanished from the pages of recorded history until Jeanneton de Paris described seeing the bronze facemask in her journal almost nine centuries later. In an entry toward the end of her life, she had made a passing reference to "the Devil's Gauntlet," but said nothing more. Wurm assumed it was a glove that perhaps belonged to the same soldier who had worn the helmet. The thing had to be significant or Jeanneton would not have mentioned it. His curiosity was aroused and he had hoped to find mention of it in the Kyros Scroll. No luck there. Whatever it was, the Devil's Gauntlet was lost to history.

Wurm rolled the scroll and downed the last of his coffee. For the first time, he had a suspicion about where to find the missing Scintilla. He had to contact John Brynstone at once.

Chapter 38

Cairo
6:41 p.m.

Cairo in the summer was cruel. It was worse still if you were stuck in the back of a dust-coated taxi. Rashmi Raja checked the time. She was running late.

How long would he wait before leaving?

She glanced out the window. In the distance, feluccas drifted on the serene Nile, their sails glowing with vibrant color. It was a haunting sight. At night, green lights dotted a mosque tower among a backdrop of restaurants and hotels farther down the great river. It was a striking city if you could ignore the chaos.

Back at the Cairo airport, she had slipped away, leaving behind John Brynstone and Cori Cassidy. It wasn't her style to offer up explanations or excuses—she simply left when the time seemed right.

A good disappearance took artistry. She was a virtuosa.

Raja was wearing the blue diamond necklace she had taken as a souvenir from Paskalev's house. In the back of the cab, she spritzed herself with a Narciso Rodriguez perfume, then checked the time again.

Late. Late. Late.

Would her fiancé mind?

Probably, if he was like the last one.

Raja didn't know that for certain since she had never met Mani. Tonight would be their introduction.

Her mother had arranged the marriage. The wedding was scheduled for October, based on the moon's phase and other considerations. The day was coming up fast.

Honking horns serenaded the bustling traffic in the heart of Zamalek, a district of Cairo on Gezira Island. The taxi rolled to a stop. Raja climbed out and darted across the street to a trendy restaurant where a fusion of American hip-hop and Arabic music drummed over the crowd noise. She gave her name and a woman about her age led the way to the patio. The aroma of *sheesha* cut a sharp tang in the air. She spied a man waiting at a table.

Must be her fiancé.

Mani stood when he saw her. Taller than the last one, but still a good inch shorter than Raja, he had moody eyes and aggressive eyebrow hair. He dressed well, which made sense. Her fiancé came from crushing wealth.

Raja embraced him, then bristled when she touched his shoulder. Clumped under his shirt, a thatch of back hair crushed down beneath her hand. The creepy forest back there was probably thick enough to cast its own shadow. Raja had an ugly thought about spending her honeymoon night with the Wolfman. Shuddering, she put it out of her mind.

"Your photographs fail to do you justice, Rashmi. You are more beautiful than I was led to believe."

A voice inside her mind responded, *And you are more hairy than I was led to believe.*

He motioned for her to take a seat. Their table was located near a man dressed in a black suit and a woman wearing a matching veil. She watched them as she slid into her chair.

After getting the compliment out of his system, her fiancé made a show of checking his wristwatch, then glared at her.

"Are you aware of the time?"

"I had a little trouble getting away."

"Is that so? Will you at least apologize for the insult of arriving late to our dinner?"

She thought it over.

"See, that's a bit of a problem. I don't really do apologies."

"I must confess, Rashmi, this is not how I imagined our first meeting."

"I know."

His eyes grew more severe. "You ask a great deal of me. Do you know it? My job carries significant responsibility. I had to abandon my work and turn it over to a man whom I do not trust."

"If you don't trust an employee then why don't you fire him?"

"I cannot fire him," he snapped. "Please know something. I did not fly to Cairo to listen to you tell me how to run my business."

She looked away, distracted. A cat had slinked onto the patio. The animal curled along her smooth leg, then wandered over to greet guests at the next table. In Cairo, cats roamed everywhere.

"Did you bring it?" she asked, looking back at her fiancé.

"Such mystery in your request. Why do you ask this of me?"

She looked down.

"Rashmi," he continued, "I need you to explain your actions."

"I cannot do that, Mani."

"Come on. You called me at my office. You told me about a key hidden in your home. I drove there. I unlocked your safe. I removed the strange object."

"Then you brought it here to Cairo?"

"As you requested, yes."

He reached down and raised a bag, then returned it to the floor near his feet. She beamed, flashing white teeth.

"I do not understand, Rashmi. Why did you not ask this of your sisters or your brother?"

"They can't know what I'm doing here."

"I will be your husband in a few months. It is imperative that I know. I ask you again to explain yourself."

"There are aspects of my life you cannot know. Neither can my family."

A smile crossed his lips. "You know, you are a mysterious young woman."

She reached down under the table, snatching the bag. He lunged for it, but didn't get there in time. She pulled back and brought the bag to her chest. The couple at the next table took a sudden interest.

"Thank you for bringing this," she said.

He looked at her sharply. "This entire affair does not set a good precedent for our marriage."

"Probably right about that."

She scooted back her chair and stood, slinging the bag over her shoulder.

"And where do you think you are going?"

"Come, Mani." She stared down at him. "Let's talk."

He tossed money onto the table. Grumbling, he followed.

The temperature was burning out on the street. Without wind, the heat seemed intense, making it almost a labor to breathe.

"It is my hope that you have supervised the details of our wedding. Can you offer me a sense of your progress?"

"The wedding?" She shrugged. "Been too busy."

Apparently, she had found his breaking point. Mani's temper erupted.

"You are a foolish woman. Many have warned me about your ways. I was told you have spent too much time in the United States. I have heard that you are an 'Americanized' woman. I see now for myself the truth in their warnings."

His words didn't injure her. In truth, she didn't care about his opinion. He was probably right, after all. Her fierce independence didn't play well in her native India, but she was too Indian for her adopted country. She was damned, it seemed, in both cultures.

"Mani, I have bad news," she said in a hushed voice.

"Bad news," he repeated with a burnished look. "How could you have news worse than not planning our wedding? How could you have news worse than summoning me out here only to play mysterious games?"

"Let me give it a shot. The marriage is off."

He didn't hear. He was too busy ranting.

"You think I am so foolish? This is a complete waste of my time."

She placed her hand on his chest, feeling the crunch of hair beneath the shirt. "Be quiet, Mani. Listen to what I have to say. I will not marry you. I am breaking off our engagement."

This time, he heard it. Loud and clear.

"Impossible," he sputtered. "You have no option. You cannot break off the engagement. That is the sole privilege—"

"I changed the rules."

"Rashmi Raja, you are a wretched woman."

"Then count yourself lucky you're not marrying me."

"Tell me, are you insane?"

"I don't love you, Mani. Okay?"

"Love?" he asked, exasperated. "Love is fairy-tale nonsense the Americans have fed into your brain. What does love matter to a marriage?"

"Before I would have said nothing. Now? I'm not so sure."

"You are mistaken about our engagement, Rashmi. I will marry you. It is the will of our families and it is your duty. You will live in India with me, never to return to the United States. I will reform you to be an obedient wife. You will see."

She shook her head. "You'll never be my lord and master, no matter how much my family wishes it to be so."

"Your family," he mocked. "If you respected your family, you would not speak such nonsense."

"I told you before, I'm doing things my family could never understand. I don't expect you to understand, okay? What I need you to understand is that we are over. Finished."

"You must marry me." He gritted his teeth. "You are too tall for many Indian men. A husband must be taller than his wife."

"You're not."

He didn't listen. He was probably in denial about his height. Or lack of it.

"In addition, you are old, Rashmi. You are already twenty-four and still unmarried. That is unacceptable."

"For my family, maybe. Not for me."

"Worst of all? This is your fourth engagement. Your face and body are highly desirable, but your independence is ugly. That is why the other three refused to marry you."

"Yeah, well, I was counting on you to do the same."

"I am stronger than the others. I made a pledge to your family," Mani replied. "I vowed to them that I would not break off our engagement. I will marry you in October. Do you understand me now?"

She kissed his cheek. "Too bad it ended like this. Thanks for bringing the bag. Hope you have a good life."

She started to turn, but he grabbed her arm, wrenching her around to face him.

"You are an immature and willful child, but I will break you, Rashmi Raja. You are coming with me to India."

"No," she said in a flat voice. "You are flying home alone. I will do all I can to honor my family, but not with you as my husband."

She tightened her mouth. "I'm not who you think I am. You need to accept that and move on."

He tightened his grip. "You will learn to obey me."

"And you will learn to listen when a woman tells you no." She brought out her Beretta and nuzzled the barrel against his stomach. "I will not marry you. Get it now?"

Perspiration dotted his forehead. His eyes seemed to bulge as he looked down. All he could say was, "A gun? You have a gun?"

"Like to see me use it?"

He swallowed.

"Fly back to India," she said. "Alone. Tell my family that *you* ended our engagement. Do you understand what I will do if you don't obey me?"

He stared at her, not breathing.

Looking around, Raja grabbed his neck, bracing his head as she gouged the barrel deeper into his shirt. "Do you understand?"

"I think—"

"You think?" she repeated. She lowered the weapon, pushing the barrel against his crotch. "Think I won't pull this trigger?"

"I will do as you say," Mani choked.

"Promise?"

"Yes, I promise."

"Good," she said, holstering the gun. "I have a long memory. And a terrible temper when I am wronged."

He stared without speaking.

Raja patted his cheek. "Forget me, Mani. Stop being a sexist jerk and go have a good life." She folded her hands together in front of her chest and smiled. *"Namaste."*

John Brynstone lingered outside an open-air coffee house in Cairo. Two elderly men argued about sports as they played chess beside him, one smoking apple-scented tobacco from an ornate glass hookah. Checking his watch, Brynstone slipped around the corner. He had spied Rashmi Raja as she talked to an Indian man. Their conversation had turned intense, leaving the guy seemingly in numb disbelief.

Brynstone was in disbelief himself. He had not felt anything since hearing the news of Kaylyn's murder. He'd always figured he would die before her, given his insatiable hunger for risk and the danger of his former government career. Bitterness had bled into their relationship over the last few years, but he still loved his ex-wife.

More than anything, his heart ached for their lost child.

Shaking himself back into the moment, he glanced down the street. Raja turned away from the stranger. What was happening down there? Brynstone had seen the man hand her a leather bag back at the restaurant. She was cradling it now, protecting it.

What was in that bag?

Sensing movement, Brynstone turned. An Egyptian man was standing near him, the guy dressed in a rumpled white suit like he had awakened in it. A bulging stomach pushed out above his waistline. He wore a thin mustache and unruly black hair plastered beneath a hat.

"Hate to see messy relationships, my friend." The man's amused expression revealed crooked teeth. "You an American?"

"Who are you?"

"Name's Ahmad Salem." He handed over a business card with a bent corner. "Private detective. You look like you could use some assistance."

Brynstone handed back the card. "Not interested."

A chuckle. "That's what they all say. Been in the business twenty-four years. One thing I've learned is that everyone needs help. She your mistress?"

Brynstone looked down at him. "Who?"

"The Indian woman. She's fiery." He adjusted the glasses on his bulbous nose. "I saw you outside the *ahwa* watching. I noticed how you looked at her. A woman like that? She is trouble. Still, I am happy to offer my services."

"Outta my way. I'm busy."

He started to turn, but the man stepped in front of him.

"You don't understand women."

Brynstone arched an eyebrow. "And you do?"

"Listen, my friend, I know—"

"I don't have time for you," he growled. He brushed past the Egyptian, leaving the guy behind. Brynstone sprinted down the street. As he headed toward Raja, Wurm called on the cell.

"John, we need to talk. I've read an important document. It's called the Kyros Scroll. Let me tell you about it."

"Little busy right now, Edgar."

"Real quick. A man named Kyros was a student to a scholar named Hypatia who broke the helmet code back in the early fifth century. This was before it was split into six sections. The helmet led Hypatia to make a riveting discovery. John, imagine if she found our missing chrism formula."

"Led her where?"

"I can't be certain. At the time, Hypatia and Kyros lived in Alexandria. You need to search there."

"Got it. Better go now, Edgar."

Brynstone ended the call and tucked the phone in his pocket. He was on the move.

Rashmi Raja turned the corner. She looked up.

No way.

John Brynstone was waiting for her. Arms crossed. His ice-blue eyes were blazing.

"Nebola was right," she smirked. "Better be more careful when I try to slip away from you."

"Don't listen to Nebola. Man is a sociopath." He frowned. "What's in the bag?"

She debated options, but didn't take long on her decision. This wasn't the time to mess with Brynstone. As he watched, she opened the bag like a guilty kid caught shoplifting and brought out a cheek guard. It resembled the one she had taken from Paskalev's home in Bulgaria.

"Back in London, you said you had only one helmet piece." His eyes narrowed. "One piece."

"Yeah. I lied. I do that sometimes," she said, sliding the helmet piece back into the bag. "It's a character flaw."

"When'd you get it?"

"Months ago."

"From where?"

"Istanbul. I was waiting to hand it over to Nebola."

"That still your plan?"

"I have a feeling you won't mind. Especially if it gets your daughter back."

"The man who gave you the bag. Who is he?"

"My ex." She fixed her gaze on him. "Any luck finding Math?"

"He lied to us. Seems to be a lot of that going around."

Her eyes widened. "What did he lie about?"

"He agreed to meet me in Cairo, but that was just a way to distract us. He's not here. He hoped to figure everything out on his own. That's my private hypothesis."

She raised the bag. "Bet he can't find it without this."

"Better be right about that."

"Where is he?"

"Not sure I can say. Trust seems to be a big issue right now."

"Come on, John. You can trust me."

"Yeah?"

"You know you can. Games are over. I promise."

"Math lied about Cairo. He went to Alexandria instead."

"Okay, since we're unloading on the guy, I have another McHardy dick move to report." Raja sighed. "I should have said this back in Prague. That woman who stole the helmet relic from the museum? The one we left behind for the police?"

"Nessa Griffin."

"You said she studied with Math?"

"A little. Undergrad history courses. After that, she turned to archaeology. Her older brother, Reece, earned a doctoral degree under McHardy. Nessa had her brother murdered. McHardy didn't know until I told him."

"Was he surprised, John?"

"I sensed a distance between them."

"They work together?"

"Not after Reece died. Remember in London? Nessa kidnapped McHardy and tied him up. You saw that."

"Right, but check this out. Back in Prague? After I took her down, she whispered something to Math. She said, 'Do they know we're working together?' Math punched her in the face. He wanted to shut her up."

"You sure, Rashmi?"

"Just telling you what I saw."

Brynstone thought it over. "We need to stop McHardy."

Chapter 39

Alexandria, Egypt
9:37 p.m.

They wanted to touch her hair.

Everywhere Cori went in Egypt, people came over and put their hands on her blonde hair. Her clothes also presented a problem. Like Raja, she had attracted unwanted attention with tight-fitting shorts and tees that revealed too much skin. One creepy guy leered and whistled and called the women "pretty babies." Brynstone shot him a look and the guy backed off real fast.

Brynstone steered Cori and Raja into a clothing store and encouraged them to change. He bought a woven cotton headscarf to wrap Cori's hair. Out of respect for the local culture, she and Raja decided on long-sleeve and loose-fitting cotton blouses and black skirts that reached past their knees. Cori still hadn't found a bra, however.

They had considered taking the train to Alexandria, but decided instead to hail a service taxi. Traffic was a nightmare between the two cities, but the driver thrived on it, swerving around one car after another at reckless speeds. Brynstone didn't mind. Neither did Raja. Cori tried to laugh it off, but she found herself closing her eyes and practicing deep-breathing exercises with every break-neck maneuver. Once, years ago, her mom had taken her on a ride called Colossus in England's Thorpe Park. The roller coaster had given her a tour of vertigo hell with two gut-wrenching corkscrews, a vertical loop, and five heartline rolls. Even as a teen, it had been a terrifying experience for her. When the cab pulled to a stop, Cori decided she'd rather line up for Colossus again than take another ride in this guy's taxi.

Compared with Cairo, the pollution and crowds seemed more bearable in Alexandria. As they headed on foot through a local marketplace, a wind drifted in from the sea, tempering the sting of heat. Markets were scattered along every street, flavoring the air with the scent of raw fish. Shoppers and tourists flooded the square, fighting past shop-front vendors who offered merchandise while purring, "This is just for you."

Cori slipped on sunglasses to avoid eye contact. Still, she noticed a local wearing a Gap shirt and Levi's staring at her. It seemed like wealthier Egyptians favored American and European brands. He approached her, apparently to flirt, but caught sight of Brynstone and turned away. *Nice thing to be in the company of a badass.* She nudged closer to Brynstone as they navigated through the market square.

As they walked, Raja pulled out her phone. It jangled with a filmi ringtone, a song from some Bollywood movie.

She glanced up. "McHardy's calling."

"Put him on speaker."

She punched the button. Cori heard the man's voice, with his light rhythm of a Scottish accent.

"Rashmi, how are you keeping?"

"Where are you, Math?"

"Egypt, of course," he answered. "Listen, I've been looking over the helmet, trying to piece together our little mystery."

Raja hit the Mute button on her cell. She looked up. "He can't figure it out. That's why he called. He's desperate."

"He needs the missing pieces," Brynstone agreed. "Just watch. He'll try to cover his ass."

McHardy continued: "Listen, Rashmi, I determined something of critical importance. I believe our destination is not Cairo after all."

Raja tapped the Mute button. "Oh, yeah?"

"I believe it is Alexandria."

"No kidding."

Cori had heard about McHardy's game. It sounded like the professor had lied to Brynstone and Raja about going to Cairo. During an earlier flight, Brynstone had made friends with McHardy's pilot. Suspecting that McHardy wasn't straight with him, Brynstone had called the pilot to learn the jet's true destination—which had inspired the hellish taxi ride to Alexandria.

"Tell me something," McHardy said. "Have you, um, been in touch with Dr. Brynstone? Since Prague, I mean."

As they walked through the square, she answered, "Matter of fact, I have."

"Recently?"

"Not long ago."

She stopped abruptly. Cori looked around, trying to figure out why they had stopped. A crowd of people wandered around them, some loaded with groceries and supplies.

Over the phone, McHardy asked, "Well then, where is Brynstone?"

Raja grinned. "Right behind you, Math."

Cori looked up. A silver-haired man in front of them made a violent turn, twisting his neck to look back. Surprise played on his bony features. John Brynstone crossed his arms and stared down at him.

"John," he said, lowering the phone. "What, uh, are you doing here?"

"You told us Cairo instead of Alexandria so you could search for the Black Chrism formula alone. The whole time you knew we needed to come here."

"No, John. Listen, I tried to—"

"Come clean, McHardy." Brynstone stabbed the man's chest with a finger. "You're working with Nessa Griffin. Why did we break into the Prague museum if she was already doing it for you?"

"I—I didn't know," he stuttered, his face growing red. "Nessa knew about the Prague helmet piece, but I didn't know she was breaking into the Charles University museum. I was thrilled when you and Rashmi rescued the artifact from her."

Raja stepped in. "You didn't look thrilled when she mentioned how you work together. You punched her in the face to shut her up."

McHardy stiffened. He was a man of awkward expression. "Remember in London, John? When we three met? Raja assaulted Véronique, a woman who worked for me."

"Worked for you? Or worked for Nessa?"

"Both, actually," McHardy said. "To be perfectly honest, Nessa works for me."

Brynstone narrowed his eyes. "You said Nessa and her men kidnapped you while you were on vacation in London."

"I did say that, didn't I? In truth, I planned the entire thing. A short time before my men delivered you to the warehouse, I had Véronique and Nessa confine me to the wall. I wanted you to believe I had been abducted, much like yourself."

"Why?"

"Because I didn't care for you, Dr. Brynstone. As it happened, I needed your help. I resolved to feign the role of a victim, so that you would prove more cooperative."

"Another lie."

"I prefer to see it as an unhappy necessity," McHardy answered. "Of course, I didn't anticipate Rashmi Raja sweeping into the room to kidnap me. Then you insisted on pursuing us, John. You went and crashed my beloved MGB roadster into our vehicle."

"That was *your* car back in London?"

"Aye. You were reckless with my car." He looked at Rashmi. "And you were reckless with me."

"Yeah, I feel bad about that," she added. "Looking back, I should have taken the time to really kick your ass."

"Now that we've all brought our frustrations to light," McHardy said, "may I ask who stole the facemask?"

"That would be me," Raja admitted.

"Please say you still have it."

She patted the leather bag. "Safe and sound."

"We have forged an uneasy alliance," McHardy said. "None trusts the other. That is clear, but we do share a common objective."

As the man spoke, Cori detected the scope of his intelligence and conceit. In that respect, McHardy reminded her of Edgar Wurm. As if reading her thoughts, the professor turned to her.

"I see another has joined our party."

"Cori Cassidy. I work with Dr. Brynstone."

McHardy gave a cold grin. "Is that so?"

"Tell me something," Brynstone interrupted. "What do you know about Viktor Nebola?"

He gave him a blank look. "No acquaintance of mine."

"Tell it straight. You and Nessa Griffin don't work with him?"

"Not a chance." McHardy pursed his lips. "May I presume that he wants the helmet?"

"Yeah."

"This is where our problem lies," he said. "I have examined the helmet and I am baffled. Without the missing pieces, we can conclude nothing except that we are supposed to search in Alexandria."

Raja made a cute shrug. "Maybe I can help."

"How could you possibly do that?" McHardy asked.

She opened the bag. They peeked inside, seeing a facemask and another piece of the helmet, positioned side by side.

"The left cheek guard." McHardy's eyes widened, his expression now invigorated. "I don't believe it."

"Wasn't easy, but I snuck it out of Istanbul. Aren't you going to thank me?"

"No," McHardy answered.

She turned to Brynstone. "You?"

"Maybe later."

Cori could see one thing for sure. They were drawn together in a common quest, although she wasn't sure the three would speak to each other under different circumstances. Then again, maybe she was wrong about Brynstone and Raja.

A current of attraction crackled in their conversation. Cori hated to admit the thought and it unsettled her. She had been attracted to John Brynstone since the night she had met him. Over the years, she had tried to dismiss her crush. The guy was married after all. She'd only found out about the divorce a few months ago. It was premature to guess what direction his life would take after the loss of his ex-wife.

As the others talked, Brynstone gazed at Cori. The powerful moment offered a realization. Math McHardy and Rashmi Raja enjoyed the challenge of finding the helmet. It was a quest, as much as anything. Not so for Cori and John. For them, it went beyond a challenge. It was about survival. In that shared glance, she remembered the purpose of their search. They had to save Shayna Brynstone.

Alexandria
10:13 p.m.

Positioned on a hill overlooking the Mediterranean Sea, the El-Salamlek Palace hotel sparkled with the vision of a palace. That's because it was one, serving as a royal resort during the reign of Fouad I, the first king of modern Egypt. Rashmi Raja had talked the others into getting suites here. She desperately wanted a shower, and God knows Cori Cassidy and John Brynstone needed one after the explosion back in Crete.

Wrapped in a towel, Raja lingered in front of her window, taking in the sight of the Montazah Gardens at night. Perched on a rocky bluff, the manicured palace grounds were cast in the glow of spotlights, alive with palms and brilliant flowers.

Raja dressed in a sarong, wearing it midcalf in case she ran into Arabic men. Putting on a final touch of thick black eyeliner, she thought about the Cassidy woman. She was bright and curious with a fresh, innocent look. Brynstone liked her. They had some history going, but somehow they had lost contact until today. Was there tension between them? As she grabbed a small package, Raja made a mental note to find out.

Leaving her suite, she hurried down the hall and pounded on the door of Cori's room. She had this sick feeling John Brynstone might be in there.

Cori opened it. She was alone in the room.

Good.

Except also bad. The woman looked stunning.

Raja had expected her to look better after a shower and a little makeup, but not this devastating. Cori knew how to rock the whole girl-next-door look with a little mascara, pink blush, and a touch of lip gloss, but she had stepped it up tonight.

Didn't bother Raja. She thrived on competition.

Bring it, Tinker Bell.

She handed the box to the woman.

Cori flashed the whole "for me?" reaction with her eyes.

"Go ahead," Raja said. "Open it."

"Yeah?" she asked, pulling the ribbon. "You picked this up?"

"Had it delivered."

She pulled away the lid, then pushed back tissue paper. She stared down at a purple lace bra. Cori looked up with a cute smirk.

"You shouldn't have."

"Sure I should," Raja laughed. "We need to get work done. John and Math can't concentrate if you're bouncing around all over the place."

Cori looked down at her conservative loose-fitting clothes. "Can they even tell in this thing?"

"They're guys. You could blindfold them and they'll still know you're not wearing a bra. It's wired into their brain."

"Or maybe south of their brain." Cori brought the bra to her chest. "Looks about right."

"You're shorter, but we're close to the same size. Made a good guess."

"Where'd you find this in Egypt?"

"Connections. I know people. Put it on. Let's go find the boys."

She closed the door as Raja waited outside, checking e-mails on her phone. Nothing interesting except an awkward message from Mani.

Cori came out. They walked down the hallway together, both playing nice.

The two women joined Brynstone and McHardy out on a private terrace. It offered a heavenly view of Montazah Bay, the cityscape lights shimmering on the black water. Leaning forward in a red and white lounge chair, McHardy was huddled over a table. He was back in mad-scientist mode, playing with helmet pieces like some kid with a toy.

Brynstone stood up when he noticed them. He smiled, showing all his boyish charm.

"You both look amazing."

Raja did a little spin in her sarong.

"Thanks, John," Cori said, standing on her tiptoes to give him a quick kiss on his cheek.

McHardy looked over. "The new helmet pieces help complete the picture. Can be a wee bit tricky to understand, but it will clarify the picture I know."

The old man had barely noticed them. Fashion and appearance were lost on him.

McHardy went back to work, puzzling over the antiquated code. Brynstone took a seat across the table from the professor. Cori eased into a seat beside him. Raja remained standing. She adjusted her sarong, pulling it up to reveal more leg. An evening breeze tingled her bare skin.

"The left cheek guard from Istanbul contains interesting insights. I found a curious sentence near the edge along the curved side of the metal." McHardy ran his finger along the symbols.

"Looks different," Raja said. "Than the others, I mean."

"Precisely. The helmet symbols conform to a Linear A code, with the exception of this handful of words. The characters you see are engraved in Greek and appear slightly larger."

"Quintus the soldier engraved the helmet in Linear A," Brynstone said. "Maybe someone else added the Greek characters."

"My thought exactly."

"What does the stuff in Greek say?" Cori asked.

McHardy pointed to his notebook.

Closed
the Unknown
for the Cursed

"'Closed, the unknown, for the cursed'?" Raja repeated. "Anyone here have a clue what that means?"

McHardy shook his head.

Raja ran her hand across Brynstone's wide shoulder. She knew it troubled the Cassidy girl when she flirted with him.

"How about you, tough guy?" she asked. "Any idea what that message means?"

Brynstone didn't answer. She kept her hand on his shoulder anyway.

Cori cut into the conversation. "Too bad Edgar Wurm isn't here."

"Why would you possibly say that?" McHardy wondered aloud.

"He was a cryptanalyst who sparked my interest in ciphers and codes. Years ago, he and I deciphered clues in the work of the psychiatrist Carl Jung. Wurm was a genius."

"If you had even five minutes in his company, then you have my deepest sympathy."

"You didn't like Edgar?"

"No one liked Edgar except Edgar," he snapped.

Brynstone looked at Cori. "Math and Edgar were rivals."

"Wurm wasn't in my league. Even if he had been, only one of us is alive today," he chuckled. "And that's the important thing."

"I'm surprised you didn't like Edgar," Cori said. "You remind me of him."

He glared. "Perfect rubbish."

Raja smiled. She was starting to like Cori Cassidy.

A musical ringtone sounded from Raja's phone, obviously annoying McHardy. His burning look gave her immeasurable satisfaction. She glanced at the caller ID.

"I think it's Nebola."

"You certain?" Brynstone asked, standing to face her.

"Never can be certain. He hasn't checked in since Crete."

"Answer it. On speaker. Keep him talking. We can't trace the call, but the more he says, the better the chance he'll reveal his location."

Raja took the call.

In a cool voice, Nebola demanded an update. "Are you working with Professor McHardy?"

"Yep. We estimate that the helmet was divided into six pieces. If that's right, we retrieved all but two. Math is decoding them now."

"How long will it take?"

"No idea."

"You said the facemask was a map. Has McHardy figured out what it means?"

"From what we can tell, it's a floor plan. We're trying to figure out the location."

"Where are you?" Nebola asked.

She looked at Brynstone, debating her answer. He nodded.

"Alexandria. What about you?"

"Still in Crete."

She looked at Brynstone again. They didn't believe the guy.

"I have a question," Raja said, going off topic. "Back in Crete, I saw you get into an SUV. A little girl with blonde hair was with you."

A pause. "Forget you saw her."

"Who was she?"

"You want payment for your services? Stay focused on the task." He paused. "Brynstone's listening, isn't he?"

"I want my daughter back, Nebola," Brynstone said.

A pause. "I underestimated you, Dr. Brynstone. That was a mistake, but I am a businessman. I have something you want. You're going to find something I want. Find the bottom portion of the Scintilla, the part with the Black Chrism. Bring it to me and I'll make a trade for your daughter."

"Why do you want the Black Chrism?" Raja asked.

"Why do I want it? Look, no one knows for sure what the Black Chrism can do. If it can do what I think it can do, who wouldn't want it?"

"I'll find the Black Chrism formula," Brynstone said, a cool threat in his voice. "You make sure my daughter stays safe. Ask Erich Metzger how I am when I'm angry."

"He already gave me a report. You have twenty-four hours to get your daughter back safely. I'll be in touch."

Nebola ended the call.

Raja looked at Brynstone. "Sorry, John. I'll do everything I can to help."

His face looked haunted.

"Good news," McHardy called. "I think I have determined where to find the formula for the Black Chrism. It appears to be in a catacomb."

"Are you serious?"

McHardy had made detailed translations of the Linear A code on previous pages of his leather notebook. Leaning in, Raja noticed where he had jotted entries about each helmet piece, including the location where it had been found and notes about its significance for their quest.

Facemask (Paris)
* Recovered by John Brynstone from cave beneath Père Lachaise Cemetery.
* Includes some variety of map. Appears to be floor plan.
* May lead to location of formula used to create the Black Chrism.

Right cheek guard (Bulgaria)
* Recovered by Rashmi Raja from Paskalev residence.
* Mentions that Josephus, son of Joseph of Arimathea, is the Keeper of the Radix and the Scintilla at the time the helmet code was created.

Right skull piece (Prague)
* Recovered by John Brynstone and Rashmi Raja (via Nessa Griffin) from Charles University museum.
* Hints that the formula for Black Chrism has a hiding place.
* Hints that Black Chrism grants powers in those who receive it.

Left cheek guard (Istanbul)
* Recovered by Rashmi Raja.
* Mentions that Chrism formula is hidden in a catacomb.
* Contains message in Greek language. Does not match Linear A code engraved on helmet: `Closed, the unknown, for the cursed."

Reading it, Raja felt a swell of pride. Among the four helmet fragments in their possession, she had provided two. Actually three, counting the one she and Brynstone had recovered from the Prague museum. Now all they had to do was find the catacomb.

Chapter 40

Egypt was a landscape of gritty earth renowned for mysterious pyramids that soared toward the heavens. Unknown to many, this unforgiving desert world also concealed rich secrets birthed deep beneath windswept sands. Carved into the soft bedrock at the end of the first century, the catacombs at Alexandria served as a private tomb for a wealthy pagan family. A century or two later, it was opened up to house hundreds of Egyptian dead in a complex network of subterranean caverns. In the ancient world, the catacombs had been called Ra-Qedil. Located in the Karmouz district of Alexandria, the site was known in the twenty-first century as the Catacombs of Kom el Shoqafa.

Brynstone guessed the helmet had led Hypatia of Alexandria and Kyros to this catacomb back in the fifth century. If so, it could be the hiding place for the missing Scintilla. He hoped his team was on the right track.

The catacombs had better security than the Prague museum, but not by much. Security for Egyptian antiquities became a critical issue after the 2011 revolution that had deposed Hosni Mubarak as president. A tragic outcome of the uprising came when looters had ransacked the Egyptian Museum in Cairo as well as other archaeological sites. For a time, the Egyptian army had guarded Egypt's museums. After that, state museum workers engaged in a long-running power struggle with the Supreme Council of Antiquities. In the years that followed, security had fallen back to the lax standards prior to the revolution. All of this was bad news for antiquities—but good news for Brynstone.

During typical tourist hours at the catacombs, two guards were posted outside a humble black iron gate. The officers worked for Egypt's Tourism and Antiquities police. They were wearing black berets and white uniforms trimmed with black epaulettes. In the moonlight, the guards chatted next to an oversized stone sarcophagus outside the gate. Brynstone estimated that a shift change had taken place about twenty minutes ago.

Cori Cassidy and Math McHardy stayed at a distance as Brynstone and Raja moved toward the guards. The team, even McHardy, was dressed in black. The women had stripped away their conservative apparel for more comfortable clothes, both wearing fitted T-shirts and leggings.

Brynstone studied the guards, looking for behavioral patterns that would help judge their reaction to uninvited guests. Police carried Uzis around some Egyptian tourist sites, but not the guys here tonight. They packed sidearms, but it didn't mean they planned to use them. How quickly would they go for their weapons?

Time to find out.

Earlier, Brynstone had purchased a rubber ball from a boy on the street, overpaying for the thing. The kid had been a tough little negotiator. From the foliage around the catacombs, Brynstone signaled Raja to toss the ball.

Both guards heard it bounce across the walkway. They turned their heads, looking in silence. Neither reached for their holstered weapons.

Good sign.

Their instinct was to explore, but without using their firearms.

They came over to investigate. Moving from the shadows, Brynstone took out the closest man with a right shovel hook followed by a left hook to the chin. Raja lunged at his partner, whipping out another capoeira move, this one an efficient and devastating kick. Another solid hit and her guy dropped.

She stayed low in a fighting crouch, glancing at Brynstone. Raja was a powerful addition to the team. He nodded his approval and pulled keys from the guards.

Brynstone unlocked the gate leading to the catacombs. Cori and McHardy hurried to join them. Not bothering to wait, Raja scaled the small fence, then landed with grace on her feet. Brynstone smiled. *Once a cat burglar, always a cat burglar.*

They dragged the tourist police into an adjacent building and locked them inside a room. Brynstone injected them with a soporific drug, making certain they would slumber through the rest of their shift. He led the others inside. A sign announced that the catacombs were closed for the week for construction and repair.

This place was a treasure. If you believed the celebrated local legend that tour guides preached like gospel, a farmer had discovered Kom el Shoqafa in 1900. Actually, credit usually went to his donkey. While working the land, according to one telling, the animal was pulling a cart when it had staggered into a small hole. The earth collapsed beneath the donkey's weight, sending it down a darkened shaft, and the alarmed farmer contacted local scientists who confirmed the discovery of a massive subterranean vault. The catacombs proved to be a stunning find for archaeology. Too bad the donkey didn't survive the nosedive.

Tough price to pay to become a legend.

Ninety-five years later, the catacombs were opened for the first time to the public. It remained a popular tourist destination ever since.

Walking through the entrance, Brynstone thought about the entries in McHardy's notebook. He had listed four helmet pieces, including the facemask, the left and right cheek guards, and the right skull piece from the Prague museum. What McHardy didn't realize is that Edgar Wurm had collected the remaining two pieces.

In their last phone call, Wurm reported that he had acquired the left skull piece from Barcelona. It told how the Black Chrism had been used to resurrect Quintus and how the Roman soldier had killed Joseph of Arimathea to save the man's grandson, Nathan. There was more to the story.

Back in February, when Wurm had shown up in Central Park as Brynstone played with his daughter, it had been a shock to see him. Wurm explained later that the Linear A code on the neck guard mentioned a string of homicides dating back to the first century. Starting with Saint Lazarus, all of the people brought back with the Black or White Chrisms had later become murder victims. The killer had tracked each person, stalking them from as far as Jericho to the ancient Greek city of Pergamon.

Wurm had two pieces. Brynstone and his team had four. Would it be enough to find the formula to create the Black Chrism? He had signed on to this project to understand how the White Chrism had changed Shayna. Now he hoped it would bring her back to him.

Inside the dusky catacomb, they found the central shaft where the celebrated but ill-fated donkey had made history with a dive of over sixty feet before striking bottom. The shaft had been constructed as two concentric cylinders. The outer section contained a spiral staircase that coiled around the inner section, the two separated by a curving wall.

Window-like slits had been carved into the inner cylinder, giving a glimpse from the stairs at the shaft's depth. Not flat like typical windowsills, the bottom frames of the windows angled toward the stairs. This ingenious design had allowed sunlight to filter from the top of the shaft onto the steps, lighting the way down to the tombs.

The shaft was wide, measuring almost twenty feet in diameter. Two thousand years ago when Ra-Qedil was used for burials, corpses were tied to ropes and lowered down the central shaft. Brynstone imagined what it would be like to peek through a window as an Egyptian cadaver descended the shaft before burial.

Ninety-nine curving steps later, the staircase brought them to a vestibule, an entrance hall where shell-shaped niches flanked each side. Each niche had a bench carved into rock where mourners found rest after a journey down the spiral staircase. McHardy plopped onto a bench, examining the map engraved on the inside of the bronze facemask. Brynstone had stored the rest of the helmet in his backpack.

He led the way to a rotunda, a circular room with another shaft encircled by six pillars. Raja touched the wall and traced her fingers along veins in the sandstone that revealed different layers. Cori gazed up at the ceiling. In a concession to the modern era, electrical cords ran overhead to mounted lights, casting the stone in a soft glow.

Along with Stonehenge and the Great Wall of China, Kom el Shoqafa was praised as one of the Seven Wonders of the Medieval World. A host of archaeologists over the decades had scoured the once-lost necropolis, looking for its secrets. Yet a century after its rediscovery, portions of the catacomb still had not been explored, and Brynstone hoped that something could still be found here that no scientist or grave robber had uncovered. He worked on a game plan in case they couldn't find the missing chrism formula. No matter what happened, he needed to convince Nebola that they had found it.

Time was running short. Brynstone had to do whatever he could to negotiate an exchange for Shayna.

Chapter 41

As McHardy puzzled over the site map on the mask, Brynstone peered inside a rectangular hall adjacent to the rotunda. A couple thousand years ago, people would congregate in this room to memorialize and celebrate the life of the departed. Known as a *triclinium*, a word meaning *three couches*, the banquet hall featured three benches carved from stone in a U-shaped formation. Back in the day, the benches were draped in elegant cushions and the hall was embellished with flat pillars and a high ceiling, inviting an open-air atmosphere. The walls were painted with red lines that gave the appearance of slabs, making it look like the room had been built rather than carved from sandstone. Giuseppe Botti led an 1892 excavation that revealed how people had gathered here for big funeral dinners. Family and friends brought down tall twin-handled jars brimming with wine as well as grilled meat and fish in terra-cotta pots. The parties must have been epic, because archaeologists discovered hundreds of broken plates and potsherds littering the floor. The finding inspired a new name for the ancient catacombs: Kom el Shoqafa, or Mound of Shards.

He found Cori and Raja outside the triclinium. They were giggling, the two getting along better than ever.

"What's so funny?"

"Our names."

"What?"

"All the alliteration," Cori said. "I mean, it just hit us that our names start with matching consonants. You know, Cori Cassidy. Rashmi Raja. Math McHardy."

"If you wanna join the club," Raja added, "better change your name to Bradley Brynstone."

He allowed a faint smile to flit across his face. "Nah. Doesn't roll off the tongue."

"Okay," Cori said. "How about Bartholomew J. Brynstone?"

"Not the image I'm shooting for. Let's search this place."

He ran his hand along the wall as McHardy stayed focused on the site map. Taking a look around the room, they discovered a breach in the original wall of the rotunda that opened into darkness.

Raja was the first to enter. Brynstone and Cori followed.

Within the walls, they found a second network of tombs. Like almost everything else down here, this chamber was a mystery. Back at the hotel, they had researched the place and had learned that in 215 CE, a Roman emperor named Caracalla ordered the massacre of young Christians. In a strange twist, the men were buried along with their horses in a bricked underground chamber. Known as the Hall of Caracalla, the main room featured a stone altar with faded paintings of mythical scenes. That's where they were at now.

The place was interesting, but he guessed it wasn't their destination. If they were right about the map, the answer to finding the chrism formula wasn't in the Hall of Caracalla.

They returned to the rotunda. No longer resting on the bench, McHardy had wandered over near the wall, staring at the shadows.

"See something?" Cori asked in a hushed voice.

"Movement." He pointed toward the corner. "Over there."

"What was it?"

"Wee beasties. Two or three of them."

Brynstone nodded. "Beetles. Saw one on the stairs coming down here."

Raja shivered. "Insects give me the crawlies."

McHardy looked to his left. "Let's try this way, shall we?"

"Do you know what we are looking for?" Cori asked.

"The map tells us to search for a place 'where the terrible sister soars above the serpent king.' Your guess is as good as mine."

Brynstone usually worked alone, but he liked the energy in this group. Funny how their relationship had evolved from bitter competition into a budding mutual respect.

They followed McHardy down a grand staircase that split into two narrow flights of stairs, each leading to a second level. Historians and archaeologists believed the catacombs had originally housed the remains of a single wealthy family. Later, in the second century, its doors may have been opened to additional families. Like a modern cemetery, others in later years could entomb their dead in the catacombs for a fee.

Exploring the chamber, they came to the bottom of the divided staircase. The façade of the main burial chamber greeted them with characters and symbols from Egyptian and Greco-Roman mythology. On opposite sides of twin composite columns, the front wall featured a carving of Medusa's face, her gaze so fierce it could turn about anything to stone.

"I believe we found our terrible sister," McHardy said.

Brynstone agreed. Greek mythology recorded that Medusa was a hideous monster called a Gorgon. Her two sisters, Stheno and Euryale, shared her scary monster genes, except they held a huge advantage. Unlike Medusa, her sisters were immortal. That was her big downfall when a guy named Perseus showed up to slay her.

For centuries, artists had carved Medusa's face on pendants and coins as well as on the walls of temples and tombs. Known as a Gorgoneion, the symbol grew in popularity. It would have been a common sight if you had lived in parts of the ancient world. People at the time believed Medusa's terrible features and snakelike tangles of hair could ward off evil.

Beneath Medusa's face, two massive serpents were carved in relief on the wall. Coiling along the side of the columns, both snakes wore crowns. The serpents resembled a basilisk, a mythical creature renowned as the "king of the serpents." An ancient writer named Pliny had claimed that the basilisk sported a crown-like spot on its head, similar to a king cobra. Like Medusa, the creature could kill with a single withering look.

Brynstone and the others wandered into the main burial area. Kom el Shoqafa was a necropolis, literally a "city of the dead," and this room felt like it. McHardy called aloud the names of objects and carvings described in the helmet's code. Running around like kids on a scavenger hunt, they searched the chamber, exploring symbols embedded in the columns, walls, and ceiling.

Four pillars carried the load of the vaulted roof. Around those pillars, they found three recesses in the burial chamber, each containing a sarcophagus. Large blocks of stone were decorated with additional Gorgoneion as well as the image of Dionysus, the Greek god of wine. On the wall above the sarcophagi, an image portrayed a mummy posed on a funerary bed.

They returned to the room with Medusa and the serpents emblazoned on the walls. A third level was visible beneath this one, but it was flooded. Long before the public opening in 1995, subsoil water had been discovered here on the second level and had been pumped out along with dirt, mud, and other debris. A disturbing thought suddenly occurred to Brynstone. What if water had washed over the treasure they were searching for? If so, the chrism formula would be ruined.

He also knew there was a chance that grave robbers had stolen it centuries before Brynstone was even born.

The divided staircase branched off to doorways on the left and right. Slipping through one doorway, they found that the second level contained carved box-shaped niches called loculi that were designed for sarcophagus burials. McHardy insisted that they had to pass a number of loculi before taking a right turn.

Near one corner, carpenters had loaded a table with power tools. A crossed network of wooden planks ran the length of the floor in many areas. Brynstone wondered if the construction project involved replacing the plank system with a more reliable floor design.

"I'm not certain this looks promising," McHardy called, following Brynstone.

"What are we looking for on this level?" Cori called.

Balancing on a plank, the professor consulted the facemask map. "We need to search the loculi along this wall. Look for one at the end. In the corner, I think."

Two tiers of loculi lined the U-shaped corridor. In its day, the catacombs boasted more than three hundred bodies, each entombed in oversized cubbyholes. It was like a body storage facility in a morgue, only bigger and without drawers. In this section, the walls and ceiling were rough-hewn and featured fewer carvings and paintings.

"What are we searching for?" Raja asked.

"All it says is that the 'truth will be revealed,'" McHardy said.

Moving away from the others, Brynstone walked along a row of loculi. He had to see what was back here. He rounded a corner and found nothing more than a flat stone wall.

Dead end.

He headed back to join the others.

Several loculi were positioned along the north corner. As McHardy studied the facemask, Raja leaned into one, shining her flashlight along the side.

Crouching, Brynstone climbed inside another while Cori moved into a third loculus. He searched the cramped area, imagining a corpse resting in this space a couple thousand years ago. It was claustrophobic back here, walled in with stone all around.

———◆———

"John," Cori called. "Check this out."

He pulled himself out from the coffin-shaped cell, then moved over to peek inside her loculus. The bottoms of her shoes pointed at him. He could see the edge of her face where she had holed herself at the end. This cubby was deeper than the one he had explored.

"Come here," she said, beckoning to him.

Brynstone eased into the recess, dragging his backpack with him. He squeezed behind her, the fit tight with their bodies pressed together. As he crawled to her, Cori ran her hand along the right wall of the cell.

"Give me your hand."

He reached around her slender shoulder. She rested her head on his left arm, already pressed against the floor. She took his right wrist, her skin fair in contrast with his as she directed the palm of his hand along the rough surface. His fingers touched a thin seam in the rock wall.

"Feel it?" she asked. "I thought it was a simple crack in the wall. It's not."

She was right. The line was too uniform. Her hand drifted from his wrist. He traced his fingers along the seam, running from the back corner about two feet toward the opening. The seam was a couple inches above the bottom of the loculus. At the back corner, it made a ninety-degree turn and ran up another two feet.

"What are you guys doing in there?" Raja called from the opening at the far end.

"Cori discovered something," he said, her blonde hair touching his lip. "Crack in the side of the stone, but it's uniform and straight. Must be man-made."

He explored the stone again. It made a full square in the right side of the loculus wall. *Interesting.* The upper part of the seam was much wider. It made a perfect fit for a fingerhold. That gave him an idea.

"I want to try something. Can you squeeze out for a minute?"

"Sure thing," Cori answered. "Give me a second."

She curled around, her butt sliding along his leg as she scooted toward the opening. She stayed down there without crawling out.

He repositioned his weight. With eight fingers in the upper groove, he pulled. The stone gave a little. He pulled harder, the square stone coming loose as it tilted toward him, like a cabinet door opening from the top edge down. As it slid out, dirt swirled into the air, blasting dust into his face. He coughed twice, but the discovery was worth it. The inch-thick slab of stone had been cut to fit like a small hidden door.

Brynstone eased out the stone square, pulling it inside the loculus. Getting it out of the way, he perched on his elbows and peered through the opening. His flashlight beam cut into the dusty blackness, revealing a secret corridor that ran parallel to the right side of the main tomb.

"Nice job," Cori called, crawling back toward him.

"You get the credit. You discovered it."

"Can you squeeze in there?"

"Think so."

Brynstone hunkered over the square stone. He snaked into the opening headfirst, his hands outstretched as he reached to the floor. His fingers dipped down into mud as he pulled himself into the corridor. Standing now, he looked around, using the flashlight to splash light on the coarse walls.

Behind him, Cori's face appeared in the square opening.

"So, what's back here?"

"Narrow corridor. Hand me the backpack."

She fed it through the opening. She began wriggling through the hole.

"Muddy back here," he warned.

"Doesn't bother me." She held out her hand. He helped her land on her feet, touching down in the mud. Her expression twisted into revulsion as she glanced down at her splattered shoes.

"Warned you."

"It's okay," Cori assured him. "I'm cool getting a little muddy for this."

"Not sure Rashmi will agree."

Anyone who explored Kom el Shoqafa could tell you that you leave with sand in your hair. Back in the banquet hall, he had seen Raja shaking her head and trying to brush it out. Looked like it was driving her batshit crazy. If she hated the sand, would she be up for mud?

He stuck his head back inside the loculus. To his surprise, he found Raja tunneling toward him. She fixed her gaze on him as she crawled forward on her forearms. He backed away as she made it to the opening.

"Hate mud," she sighed, "but I'm not sitting around while you two grab all the glory."

Raja crawled out, her slinky body touching down. She forced a smile, a bad attempt at hiding her disgust about the mud.

"McHardy," he called down the loculus. "What are we looking for?"

"Can't be certain, John. Doesn't make perfect sense. It appears you have to slide something."

Brynstone and the women moved along the wall, their feet squishing with each step. Their flashlight beams spiraled in crossing paths along the corridor. The walls looked rough and uneven, almost as if workers had rushed without finishing the job. There were no paintings. No etchings. No carvings or statues of any kind. The walls curved like a tunnel. The ceiling dropped low to four feet in some spots before rising a few feet higher toward the end.

"What now?" Cori asked.

Brynstone didn't have an answer. Cori had discovered a secret panel, so it didn't make sense it would lead to nothing. Thinking about it, he handed her the flashlight.

"What are you doing?" Raja asked.

Closing his eyes, he traced his fingers along the wall at the end of the corridor. He glided his hands in a systematic side-to-side motion. He touched a straight seam. His eyes snapped open.

"Shine the light over here."

The seam ran vertically from floor to ceiling about two inches out from the corner. Between the seam and side wall of the corridor, the surface changed. The stone was smooth. Unlike the loculus panel, the seam here was far too narrow along its entire perimeter to slide in a finger. Moving his hands around the left corner onto the long wall, he found another smooth section. About four feet wide, this one spanned the entire height of the corridor.

McHardy had mentioned sliding something. That gave Brynstone an idea. He reached into the sticky mud. He had to go by feel rather than sight. After a minute, his fingers traced a recess at the foot of the smooth section of the wall. The floor recess was not level, but angled, so it ran lower on the end near the corner. Reaching into the recess, he discovered two tracks.

It made sense now. If Brynstone was right, they needed to slide the massive slab up the incline. It was too heavy to pull, even for several people, but he suspected a clever design at work here.

"What did you find?" Raja asked

"A Hero door," he said.

"A what?"

"Back in the first century, a man called Hero of Alexandria invented an early version of an automatic door." As Brynstone talked, he searched the floor, looking for a lever to trigger the door.

He explained that Hero of Alexandria had been a brilliant Greek mathematician and engineer, considered by some to be the greatest researcher in antiquity. Before his death near the end of the first century, he had invented the first-recorded steam engine, a wind wheel, military machines, a force pump, an early automatic door—and even the first vending machine.

Unfortunately, most of Hero's writings had been lost or destroyed over the centuries. One of his works that survived? A book, *On the Lifting of Heavy Objects*, that described a stone slab that could function as a secret entrance. The slab would look like a wall, but could be opened from another room based on counter-weight engineering. It was known as a Hero door, and only a brief surviving description hinted at its design. For the past twenty centuries, no one had discovered a Hero door.

Until now.

Chapter 42

The Hero door didn't resemble a door. Instead, it looked like a massive slab of rock. If it followed Hero's descriptions, most of the ancient mechanism was hidden beneath the floor. Brynstone figured that it reached down to the third level, making it impossible to see the full design. If he remembered the sketch, the stone slab was positioned on an inclined surface. The design used counterweights, tracks for a sledge, and levers to pull the heavy stone up the incline. A series of triangular stopping devices held the stone in the open position. Inside the open door, a pressure-plate mechanism was concealed in the floor. The pressure plate could trigger the stopping device to release the stone slab. Gravity would bring it rocketing down the incline and the door would slam closed, trapping tomb robbers inside.

Searching in the mud, Brynstone found a mechanism in the floor. It was a lever.

Grabbing the lever with mud-coated hands, he forced it with all his weight. He heard a loud slap from below, then a deep groaning sound. The stone slab began sliding to the left along the smooth wall, retracting into the corridor. Cori took a step back as it approached her. Brynstone felt adrenaline surge inside. He sensed something big. If it worked the way Hero had intended, the sliding mechanism had opened a door on the other side of the wall.

"Cool," Cori marveled.

"Yeah, but what now?" Raja wondered aloud.

"We need to get to the other side." Brynstone patted the end wall. He spun around and headed through the muddy path back to the opening in the loculus.

As the trio climbed through the cramped opening, McHardy greeted them. Brynstone and the others were excited to see what the Hero door had revealed.

He led the group past the main tomb to the east end of the U-shaped corridor where the loculi ended. Before finding the lever, Brynstone had seen a flat stone wall that marked a dead end.

Turned out it wasn't a dead end after all.

The Hero door had now moved to the left, recessing into the wall behind the muddy corridor. The four of them stood at the doorway. For the first time in centuries, the long-dormant Hero door revealed a forgotten chamber.

"I must confess," McHardy gushed, "this is an incredible discovery."

Everyone else was too awestruck to speak.

Looking past the door, Brynstone could make out a few steps at the bottom of a stone staircase. As McHardy started to move past the Hero door, Brynstone grabbed his elbow and yanked him back.

"Watch your step," he warned.

"What is it?" the old man protested.

Brynstone scanned inside the doorway. His flashlight beam highlighted a stone embedded in the floor. It looked slightly lighter in hue than the ones surrounding it.

"See that? It's a pressure plate. Put your foot on it and the stopping device will be released. Provided it still works after all this time."

"That a good thing?" Raja asked.

"Not unless you want the door to slam closed. If it does, we're trapped inside."

"Oh-kay."

Going first now, Brynstone stepped around the pressure plate, then made his way to the staircase. The air was dense and musty. An arched ceiling covered the staircase. The tunneled stairs reminded him of pictures he'd seen of the City Hall subway station in New York, an Edwardian-era depot that had closed shortly after World War II. This place had the same haunting and claustrophobic feel.

McHardy looked around. "It's as black as the Earl of Hell's waistcoat," he said in a hushed voice.

Brynstone walked up the stairs with Raja at his side. Cori and McHardy trailed a few steps behind. It was as long as the divided staircase, bringing them back up to the first level, but separated from the rest of the catacombs. He was convinced that this chamber had not been seen with human eyes for sixteen centuries, not since Hypatia and Kyros explored its mysteries. The tingle of excitement was electric.

Arriving at the top landing, they found an alcove with pillars on each side of the entry. Near the ceiling, a decorative niche was carved into the wall above each pillar. Brynstone reached in his backpack and brought out two halogen lamps. He flicked them on, flooding the small room with light.

"Much better," McHardy said.

Cast in the lamps' glow, the walls revealed paintings inspired by Egyptian and Greco-Roman mythology. An engraved image of a raven, wings flared, decorated one side. Across from it, a crescent moon hovered above an alligator. An oversized sculpture of a black jackal huddled beside the wall, poised like a silent guardian on a curving fish tail. The creature's slitted red eyes seemed to track their every move.

An image on the front wall depicted an eye with a black tear-drop shape beneath it. Known as the Eye of Ra, it symbolized the Egyptian god Horus and was painted to resemble a peregrine falcon's eye. Like the Gorgoneion, the symbol was believed to possess the power to ward off evil.

They found a door made of stone beneath the Eye of Horus. Not a real door, but a flat block of limestone that gave the appearance of one. Centuries back, it had been painted red with black spots to resemble granite. Three frames were carved to look like protruding doorjambs, and a series of engraved symbols ran along the outside frame.

Cori touched the smooth surface. "It's a single block of carved stone. There's no way to open it, no doorknob or handle."

"We're not to open it," McHardy said in a gravel-raw voice.

"Why not?"

"It's a false door," Brynstone answered. "Thing was never designed to be opened. At least, not by us. It's a doorway for the dead."

Chapter 43

The false door was a common theme in Egyptian funerary architecture. Brynstone explained that its significance was rooted in the religion of ancient Egypt. A legion of gods populated their spiritual world, including Osiris, Anubis, Isis, and Horus. A false door like this one served as a barrier between the world of the living and the land of the dead. Using it as a portal, Egyptian gods could journey back and forth from the afterlife into the human realm.

The false door down here featured an image of the goddess Isis clutching an ankh, the symbol of eternal life. In Egyptian mythology, she was the protector of the dead and also the goddess of rebirth and resurrection.

"All this for nothing," McHardy grumbled as he slapped the false door. "No discredit to you, John. False door or not, the map led us to this chamber and tells us nothing more."

The man was right. It was literally another dead end.

"Know what's strange?" Brynstone said. "False doors were a dying fad when this catacomb was built. You don't usually see one from the Common Era."

"Maybe the answer is on the door itself," Raja said, leaning in to study symbols engraved on a side panel.

"Could be," Cori added. "Maybe the chrism formula is engraved on this door."

"It's a possibility," McHardy admitted.

They explored the surface of the door, sometimes reciting aloud what they were finding. A few symbols were random, even chaotic. None were carved in Linear A code. A strip of Egyptian symbols spelled out a curse on anyone who tried to damage or steal from the dead. Another gave a blessing to visitors who offered drink or food in honor of the deceased. In what they could decipher, there was nothing about a chrism.

Brynstone had hoped to find symbols that matched the helmet. It would verify that the false door was the destination mentioned in the facemask map.

He thought about the Voynich manuscript, rich with mysterious symbols. It had driven Edgar Wurm to madness. Many people suspected that the Voynich document was nothing more than an elaborate hoax. Was the same true about the helmet and the false door?

Chapter 44

2:23 a.m.

The false door was a dead end.

Cori sensed it, trying to quiet a flood of frustration. Time was running out to find something Nebola would exchange for Shayna. Her heart was breaking for Brynstone. Still, you'd hardly know there was a problem. Despite the seemingly insurmountable hurdles he faced, she couldn't detect a hint of frustration. If anything, John Brynstone seemed in constant possession of a never-say-die attitude.

Math McHardy? Not so much.

"Right, that's me," the professor said, signaling that he was finished. "See you at the hotel."

"You're leaving?" Cori asked.

"Don't know what else to do," McHardy grumbled, consulting the facemask.

"We can't give up now. We've come too far."

"Must have taken a misstep somewhere," Raja thought aloud. "We need to retrace our steps."

"I'm willing to give it one more try," McHardy said. "Perhaps we will stumble over something we missed."

He marched down the stairs with Rashmi Raja following behind him.

Cori turned and joined them. She knew from experience that sometimes you can rub up too close to a problem. You had to step back once in a while and return with a fresh perspective.

An eerie stillness settled over the chamber as they passed the Hero door and trudged back up the divided staircase. *This place is bewildering*, she thought as she trailed behind them. Years before, she and Edgar Wurm had explored Bollingen Tower, a spiritual retreat Carl Jung had built near a Swiss lake. Inside the tower, they had discovered wall paintings that Jung had painted from his dreams. Some were beautiful; others were fantastic and haunting. The images from Jung's tower reminded her of the catacombs.

Scattered carvings and paintings inside Kom el Shoqafa showcased a curious blend of Egyptian, Greek, and Roman themes. A few images seemed mismatched, like an Egyptian god dressed in Roman clothing, but they had an arresting presence. Like Bollingen Tower, the effect seemed to originate from an unconscious realm, not a conscious one. The catacombs had not been open to the public during the Swiss psychiatrist's lifetime. There was no way he could have visited here. Still, she sensed that Jung shared a similar vision and spirit with the people who had created Kom el Shoqafa.

Her short hair was swept back in a sloppy bun, and she stopped to fix it. Finishing, Cori looked back. Brynstone was not walking with them. McHardy and Raja were busy trying to figure out some mistake in decoding the facemask.

Leaving them without a word, she made her way back to the Hero door. Centuries of dust coated the staircase inside, revealing ghostly footprints from their first trip up to find the false door. It felt a little creepy this time, going in by herself.

Is John still up here?

Halfway up the stairs, she saw halogen lights burning outside the hidden chamber. She stopped and glanced back, having this weird feeling that someone was down below, watching her. Rubbing goose bumps on her arms, she started walking upstairs again.

At the top landing, she found Brynstone standing in front of the false door. The outer doorjamb framed his broad shoulders and thick dark hair. She studied him from behind, her eye drawn to the outline of his body in the dusky light.

She came around to him. Absorbed in thought, his gaze was intent as he puzzled over some hidden meaning in the door's architecture and he was unaware of her presence beside him until she spoke.

"Anything making sense?"

Brynstone turned, finally noticing her. He seemed surprised she hadn't been there all along. He looked around.

"Where's Rashmi and McHardy?"

"Retracing our steps. Seeing if they can figure out where we went wrong."

"We didn't. The mask led us to this chamber. The answer has to be here."

A small note of desperation sparked in his voice.

In sympathy, Cori glanced at the false door. A dizzy array of symbols covered the outer doorframe and her gaze drifted over a set of them carved three feet from the bottom. She had seen similar letters the day before on stores and signs around Crete. She couldn't read the language, but she recognized Greek characters interspersed with other symbols on the doorframe.

All at once, a realization flashed in her mind.

"John," she said, her voice pitched high in excitement, "I have an idea."

———◆———

"You can read Greek, right?" Cori asked, lowering to her knees.

Brynstone nodded. As a paleopathologist, knowing ancient languages was a nice plus. He crouched beside her, following her gaze.

An incomplete stone border framed the false door. A six-inch portion along the side had been broken away, giving the frame an irregular concave shape.

She pointed to a line of symbols near the edge of the uneven border. "Translate this part."

He touched the engraved characters. He had read it before, three or four times. "Says something like, 'Open the . . . Discover . . . Pray.'"

"Make any sense?" she asked.

He shook his head.

"Me neither." She studied it again. "But I have an idea."

"Tell me."

"You know that one piece of the helmet? The part that goes over the soldier's jaw or covers his cheek or whatever? The one Raja found in Istanbul. Where is it?"

Brynstone reached in his pack and brought out the curved metal left cheek guard. She took it from him.

"The words engraved on the inside surface here. They're Greek, right?"

"A few. They don't make much sense."

"What do they say again?"

"It reads, 'Closed, the unknown, for the cursed.' Whatever that means."

She looked down at the cheek guard in her hands.

"Wait a minute." His eyes flared with realization. "You think it matches the doorframe?"

"One way to find out."

Cori flipped the metal piece, then pressed it flush against the broken curve in the false door. Like one jigsaw piece interlocking with another, the words on the doorframe aligned perfectly with the letters engraved on the cheek guard.

"Look at that," she said in a soft voice.

"Amazing," he answered.

He studied the three rows of symbols. Each began on the stone doorframe and continued onto the metal cheek piece. Cori balanced the helmet piece against the frame as he deciphered the characters and wrote them in his notebook.

Open the	Closed
Discover	the Unknown
Pray	for the Cursed

She read the message. "Know what it means?"

"It means the false door is not a false door," he answered. "We need to open the closed door. There's something behind it. That's my private hypothesis."

He traced his fingers along the frame. "This door is made of fine limestone, but compare it against the wall."

"Looks newer."

"Because it was added later."

Brynstone knew that the helmet code had led Hypatia of Alexandria to a deadly discovery. The characters were not inscribed in Linear A like on the helmet, so he guessed that Quintus had not made the inscription. Maybe after Hypatia's assassination, Kyros had carved matching Greek characters on the cheek guard and on the false door. There was a good chance the truth would remain a secret.

Brynstone marched toward the stairs.

"Where are you going?" Cori asked.

"The false door is coming down," he called from the staircase. "We have to see what's behind it."

Chapter 45

Brynstone headed to the construction area on the second level, where he remembered seeing an assortment of tools scattered on a workbench and around the workplace. Angle grinders. Drills. Stone- and handsaws. It was a decent collection.

Cori arrived in time to see him slide on leather work gloves. He picked up a drill, then studied a case of masonry drill and core bits. The flutes looked like new.

"What's that thing?" she asked.

"Hammer drill."

"Seriously?" She studied him. "You're going to drill into the false door?"

"Sometimes you have to ruin a treasure to find a greater one. I've learned that the hard way."

"Not sure this is a good idea, John."

"Will be if we find something behind that door. We have to open the closed to discover the unknown. That's what it means, Cori. I'm betting on it."

"Mm-hmm. Remember the rest of the message? 'Pray for the cursed'? You think that's us?"

Brynstone didn't answer. All he could think about was Shayna right now. And the false door.

He grabbed a sledgehammer. Carrying it and the hammer drill, he passed the Hero door and climbed the staircase as Cori followed. He placed the tools near the false door.

Legs braced, he stood in front of it and fired up the hammer drill. With a two-handed grip on the drill, he pressed the masonry bit's tip against the surface. He bored a hole into the stone, then another and another, forming a triangle dead center on the face of the false door.

He laid down the drill and picked up the sledgehammer.

"I gotta bring it up, John. Say you destroy the door and nothing's behind it. You stop to think about that?"

He looked at her. "Stand back, Cori."

She did, without further protest.

Brynstone went to work, smashing the sledgehammer against the spot where he had drilled the triangle formation. He came at it again, debris flying everywhere. A cracking sound cut into the suffocating chamber, louder than the first. He wielded the hammer again, this time crashing into the false door with greater force. The blow created a deep fissure.

Nothing was going to stop him from opening up this baby.

———

Raja always had mixed feelings about Math McHardy. But right now, prowling around this creepy old catacomb, unable to figure out why they had come down here? Annoyance and suspicion were getting the better of her. The ranting old Scotsman was driving her crazy.

"This is a bloody waste of time," he grumbled.

She frowned. "What if the whole thing's one big practical joke? Know what I mean? Maybe some guy two thousand years ago got bored and put all these symbols on a helmet and cut it apart just to troll people in the twenty-first century."

"You honestly believe that?"

"That's how you make it sound. We're losing focus with all your complaining."

"You're growing upset with me, woman. I can see it."

"Gee, you think?"

"Haw'd yer weeshed. Keep eh heid."

Okay, she had seen him do this before. Whenever McHardy became flustered or emotional, he slipped deeper into an indecipherable Scottish accent.

"What did you even say, Math? Most of the time I can understand that Scottish crap, but sometimes—"

"I told you to be quiet. Keep your head."

"*Keep your head?* I don't get it."

"Don't panic. If we—"

A distant drilling sound came from deep within the catacomb. They stopped and listened.

"That racket," McHardy said, his mouth gaping in disbelief. "What is it?"

"Must be John and Cori."

"What in God's name are they doing?"

Now she heard a pounding sound.

"Tearing the shit out of something," she suggested.

As McHardy headed down the hallway to investigate, Raja turned her head. She caught movement from the corner of her eye. It happened fast. Was it wee beasties like McHardy had talked about?

No.

Squinting, she tried to figure out what she had seen. She had spied something bigger. Maybe a figure sneaking along the wall?

Was her mind playing tricks on her or was someone down here with them?

Maybe she had seen a security guard. But Brynstone had injected them with a hard-core drug. They should still be unconscious.

She had a better guess. *Nessa Griffin*. The woman had followed them down here, maybe tipped off by McHardy. Raja was ready for a rematch.

"You coming?" McHardy called.

"No."

"Don't be a feartie-cat."

"I'm not a . . . whatever you said."

She didn't tell McHardy about their guest. She had an idea that he had brought Nessa down here. Raja had started to trust the guy. Big mistake.

Not wanting to arouse suspicion or tip off Nessa, Raja said, "I could use a bit of fresh air. It's suffocating down here."

McHardy shot her a look of annoyance. He waved her off, then headed in the direction of the noise, what sounded like someone pounding stone against stone, another loud crack echoing through the catacombs.

She was glad to see him go. If anything got ugly with Griffin, McHardy would only get in the way.

Trying to appear casual, Raja headed for the spiral staircase winding around the shaft. *Where'd you go, Nessa? Come out, come out, wherever you are.* She passed the wall where she had seen movement seconds before. Darted her eyes, but she saw nothing. This place really was creepy.

Still convinced she had seen someone, Raja quickly pivoted on her right foot. She looked at the opposite wall.

Shadows.

That was it. Nothing but shadows.

Where are you? Where'd you go, Nessa?

Moving past the entrance to the triclinium, she took a few more steps, still wanting to look like she was headed upstairs for fresh night air. Come to think of it, a visit outside sounded like a good idea—maybe her mind was playing tricks on her. The desert air would be hotter than down here, but it had to be more refreshing.

She stopped.

Something didn't look right.

The small room facing the spiral staircase, the one decorated with shell-shaped benches, was completely dark. Overhead lights ran throughout the catacombs except for the hidden chamber they had discovered tonight. She thought back to when they had first arrived. The lights had been turned on here and in the rotunda. So why was everything black in the small area leading to the staircase?

Maybe it was an electrical problem, she told herself. Or maybe Nessa Griffin had turned out the lights. Didn't make a difference. She could kick the woman's butt in the dark.

Raja circled the flashlight in a path across the walls, stopping to highlight one bench. She couldn't shake the weird feeling that Nessa might be sitting there.

Nope. Empty.

She crossed to her left, checking the second stone bench. No one there either. She splashed light across the first step of the spiral staircase. She stopped again, listening.

She heard the sound of breathing behind her.

Freaked her out.

She stopped all at once, wheeling around with a fist raised. She scanned the chamber with the flashlight, her heart skipping in her chest.

No one. No one there. No one.

So who was doing the breathing?

Her anxiety was jumping on overdrive. She hadn't been this scared in a long time.

She heard breathing again. Only now it was her own.

Keep it cool, girl, she coached herself. *Even though hundreds of dead people have rotted in this place for centuries, you don't believe in ghosts. Right? You don't believe in ghosts.*

She had to chant the words three more times before they sounded halfway convincing.

Her mind was playing tricks on her. Had to be. She was sleep deprived. Was it possible she was hallucinating? That whole idea about fresh air sounded better and better all the time. All she had to do now was to climb ninety-nine curving steps around a deep dark shaft.

Wonderful.

Maybe she should forget it and go back to join Brynstone and the others. She couldn't decide. *You need to calm down.* She couldn't let Brynstone see her like this. Not Cori either. Raja knew she intimidated her. She'd lose her edge if Cori saw her in this condition, all Jell-O for nerves like some frightened schoolgirl on Halloween.

Drawing in a ragged breath, she looked ahead. Stairs wrapped around the shaft. After a second or two, she worked up the nerve to climb them. That was the moment when she heard a voice speak close to her ear.

A man's voice.

"I'm down here," he said. "You just can't see me."

Oh shit oh shit oh shit.

She spun around, her heart leaping in her chest. Time to bring out the Beretta, because that thing she heard? That was definitely not a hallucination. Someone was down here.

And he was close.

She glanced around the darkened ambulatory, sidestepping in a circle as she made a low crouch, her eyes darting everywhere all at once.

"Who are you?" she asked.

No answer.

"Who *are* you?" she called, annoyance sizzling in her voice.

"Shouldn't you ask where I am?"

The voice came from a different direction. The man had moved. He was playing her. She turned again, sweeping the gun in front of her.

He was standing a few feet away. A man maybe five nine in height. Short brown hair was cropped close to his head; he had flat eyes and a smug expression. Powerfully built, he was more lean muscle than bulk.

"Congratulations. You found me. *Finally.*"

She detected an accent. German.

"Now that you found me," he said. "What do you plan to do with me?"

"For starters? How 'bout I shoot you?"

That brought a thin smile. "We've only met and you already want to shoot me? Must be a challenge for you to make new friends."

She smirked. "Funny line."

"I try."

"Try a little harder. Who are you?"

"Some call me a poet. Some call me a butcher."

"I can add more names to your list, starting with—"

He cut her off. "I like you. That can be dangerous."

"Yeah? Well, guess what. *I* can be dangerous."

"*Ja,*" he answered. "Your ex-fiancé would agree. That was a nice touch, nuzzling Mani's crotch with your handgun."

"What?" Her eyes widened. She was thinking about this guy, wondering who he was and how he knew about her confrontation with Mani. "How do you know about that?"

"I saw it, dear girl."

Blowing a strand of black hair from her face, she asked, "You were in Cairo?"

"I'm everywhere, Rashmi."

All of a sudden it made sense.

"I get it," she said. "Mani sent you. Didn't he?"

The man gave a hard chuckle. "I'm afraid the poor boy couldn't afford me."

"Afford you?" she asked. "Who are you?"

"The best assassin in the world."

He wasn't bluffing. For the first time, she noticed a tremble in her hand. She had to keep it tough. She made sure her words didn't betray her.

"That right?" she asked in her best badass voice. "Big-time assassin, huh? You here to kill me?"

Another cold grin cut across his face. "I'm here to play with you, Rashmi."

Chapter 46

Cori backed away, giving Brynstone room. He paused, wiping his face and taking a breath for a minute as he leaned with his hand cupped on the standing sledgehammer.

She was glad he had finished with the hammer drill. The sound of it had been earsplitting, although the sledgehammer wasn't exactly quiet.

The false door was now marked with a hole in the center like a cannonball had blasted through it. He had explained earlier about compression and tensile strength and something about the mass pressure of the stone, but she had no clue what he was talking about. She had been a psychology major. Physics wasn't her thing.

Neither was breaking down walls.

Watching him, she asked, "Is it killing you inside to destroy this door?"

"If this were a mummy, yes. But I'm a paleopathologist. Not an archaeologist."

Cori wasn't buying it. Under normal circumstances, Brynstone wouldn't destroy something of ancient significance. This time, however, circumstances were not normal. With his daughter's life on the line, he could deal with the historical collateral.

From behind, she heard footsteps on the staircase.

McHardy arrived at the top step, his eyebrows curled in a deep furrow. "What in heaven's name are you doing?"

Brynstone didn't look back. "Isn't it obvious?"

"Americans are not content unless they are destroying things," McHardy grumbled. "It's coded into your DNA. Few things seem to give your people greater pleasure."

"We want to see what's behind the false door," Cori explained, aware that she was stating the obvious.

"Don't you understand that is why they call it a false door? There's nothing behind it."

"This time, you're wrong," Brynstone said.

He swung the sledgehammer and blasted away at the fractured door. Dust spilled from the opening. The cavity was almost big enough to climb through.

Covering her mouth to keep out dust, Cori waited until he had lowered the sledgehammer. She came over as Brynstone shone a light into the crevice.

"It's hollow," he panted, looking in. "A chamber back there."

He reached into the dark hole, extending his arm until it disappeared up to his shoulder. The moment made her uncomfortable. She'd seen too many scary movies, her dark imagination unable to resist the idea of something terrible on the other side, jerking Brynstone's arm deeper into the hole.

A pounding sound came from the other side of the wall.

Cori jumped in surprise. Catching herself, she squeaked with nervous laughter.

Brynstone pounded on the door from the inside. It looked like he was running his hand along the backside, maybe wrenching chunks of stone fractured from his assault. His neck muscles strained as he pulled out a big portion, staggering backward as he tore it free.

Pebbles sprayed at her. Cori shielded her face, swatting them away.

"No going back now," McHardy said in a resigned voice.

Brushing debris from her hair, Cori saw Brynstone peek into the opening. The moment was rich and powerful. It reminded her of reading about how archaeologist Howard Carter had first peered into a wall breach to see King Tut's gilded treasures in Egypt's Valley of the Kings.

"What do you see?"

"Blackness. Stand back."

Brynstone came at it again, directing the sledgehammer into the crumbling remains of the false door. When the dust cleared, she saw a hole large enough to step through.

———◆◆———

Raja narrowed her eyes. "You may be a hot-shit assassin," she told the German stranger, "but I'm the one holding the gun."

"I think I see the problem," he answered with an icy stare. "You have a limited understanding of what an assassin can do. Do you think I need a gun to kill you?"

"When I'm the one holding the gun? Yeah, I do," she said, trying to sound more annoyed than frightened.

"You do know he was spying on you. Don't you, Rashmi?"

"What are you talking about?"

"John Brynstone. He was in Cairo. While you were busy breaking the heart of your poor fiancé, he watched the whole thing. He followed you."

"Wasn't the first time. Anyway, he told me, so I already know that. Here's the question. How do *you* know?"

"I know," the German answered, "because I talked to Brynstone."

"You did?"

"In Cairo, I disguised myself as an Egyptian private detective. Couldn't help myself. Brynstone and I go back a few years. It has been some time since our last conversation."

"He knows you?"

"Better than he realizes." The man frowned. "Here's what you need to know about Herr Doktor Brynstone. He doesn't trust you."

"How do you know?"

"Did I fail to mention it? I know the man."

"You know, for an assassin, you do a lot of talking. That your epic game plan? You go and talk your victims to death?"

She was trashing it up with her words again. Was it working? She couldn't gauge a reaction. She knew how to overpower men with her will. But Brynstone had seen through her tough act. Apparently, so did this guy.

Unfortunately.

"I'm not here to kill you, Rashmi. Although, if you like, I will happily accommodate your death wish. It might come as a blessing to your parents and your legion of ex-fiancés."

A noise scuffled from her right. She swept the gun around. Some small creature—a rat or something—scurried into the shadows.

Big mistake, getting distracted like that.

She brought her aim back to the man, moving her eyes in his direction. Too late. He lunged with an almost inhuman speed, the guy taking advantage of a distraction that lasted barely a second. Her finger was poised on the trigger, but he was already pouncing, his hand tight around her wrist, raising the gun in the air. *Doesn't matter*, she told herself. *This guy can't stop me, even though he sounds tough and acts tough.*

His fist crashed into the right side of her face, shaking her hard as she chomped down on her tongue. She thought she had pressed the trigger, but she didn't hear gunfire. The man somehow ripped the gun from her hand. She knew she had to fight now, bring out some moves on this guy, but his elbow jammed into her throat, trapping oxygen as perspiration jumped from her forehead. He swung her out hard, one hand on the back of her neck, shoving her down. His other hand jerked her arm behind her back. His knee was rising now and he directed her face into it, the force feeling like she was slamming her head against a rock. Vivid red spots scattered across her vision. *Gotta bring a move on him.* She couldn't pull one off as blood splashed from her mouth. She was an expert fighter, but this guy was coming at her too fast. Too relentless. Her fingers tingled. Her legs buckled. She struggled to stay on her feet, but he slammed her against the catacomb wall.

Next thing Rashmi Raja knew, she was facedown on the floor, but managing to stay conscious. She'd never fought anyone like him before. She was sure he'd never fought anyone like her. She reached for the war quoit in her side pocket, anxious to slice the man's neck with its razor-sharp teeth.

Chapter 47

2:53 a.m.

The moment hushed to an absolute silence. Cori watched as Brynstone swung his backpack over one shoulder. Still holding the sledgehammer and a halogen light, he ducked through the wall, carrying so much emotional weight on his shoulders. The frustration. The doubt. The hope that a dark and lost corner of an aging catacomb held an answer that might return his daughter to him. He'd faced a situation like this once before, but his triumph had come at a terrible cost.

She waited a beat, then dipped her foot inside the opening, crouching a little to slip inside. More goose bumps rose on her arms as she passed through the false door. Brynstone's stories about Egyptian gods crossing over from the land of the dead had found a place inside her mind, bringing the eerie feeling to life.

Inside, the gray scent of mildew filled her nostrils. Unlike Tut's final resting place, the room was not crammed with jewels and priceless antiquities. Instead, it was suffocating and barren except for a massive sarcophagus in the center of the room. McHardy followed, taking cautious steps. Brynstone leaned the sledgehammer against a wall.

Suddenly, Cori shook her head, as if awakening from sleep. She had been so engrossed in deciphering the message on the door and getting in here that she had forgotten about the other woman.

"Rashmi," she said to McHardy. "Where is she?"

"Outside. She needed fresh air."

"Is she okay?"

"Trust me," Brynstone assured, leaning over the sarcophagus. "She can take care of herself."

Cori stood opposite him with the stone coffin between them. McHardy moved beside her. An enormous stone lid covered the sarcophagus. Linear A symbols spilled across its surface.

"'Assembly of the damned,'" McHardy translated, tracing the words with his fingers.

"'Open the closed,'" Cori muttered. "'Discover the unknown. Pray for the cursed.'"

"What exactly does that mean?" McHardy asked.

"We saw it on the false door."

McHardy added, "Before you smashed the bugger to pieces."

Cori looked at Brynstone. He wasn't listening. Instead, he stared at the back of the false door, his expression frozen with unblinking eyes.

What was he looking at? Following his gaze, she turned and stared in that direction.

Taking stiff, measured steps, Rashmi Raja climbed through the false door opening.

Not pausing, the woman made her way into the small chamber with them. She didn't speak. Her eyes were wide with fear. Black hair snarled around her face. Dirt blemished her features. A smear of blood colored her nose and mouth.

Cori's gaze dropped. She held her breath.

Rashmi Raja's chest was draped with explosives.

Chapter 48

2:56 a.m.

Brynstone assessed the situation. It looked bad on all counts.

He raised his hand. "Rashmi, move away from the exit. Do it slowly."

She shook her head. Her eyes looked bloodshot and there was swelling around her right eye. He had never before seen a hint of fear in the woman. Right now? She looked downright terrified.

He studied the explosives threaded into the brown mesh vest. She was rigged with about five pounds of C-4 as the main explosive along with three pounds of ammonium nitrate as an oxidizing agent, designed to make the explosives burn faster and hotter. Two receiving devices with antennae were strapped above each hip. A small monitor was centered in the web of explosives. The screen was black.

Cori came closer, standing beside Brynstone. McHardy, on the other hand, moved against the back wall, staying as far away as possible.

"They activated motion sensors when I stepped in here," Raja said in a breathless voice. "If I move from the opening, they'll trigger the explosives. They're watching."

"Who's watching?"

"Them."

Without moving her head, her eyes darted to the side. A small camera—infrared and night-vision capable—was mounted on each shoulder. She wore a headband with a round micro-camera centered on her forehead.

The explosives were laced into a circuit mechanism centered on her stomach. Brynstone guessed there was a collapsing circuit, making it harder to deactivate unless he snipped the correct wires in the correct sequence.

The thing that made him sweat? If she was wired with a double-trigger mechanism, it would mean someone else would need to help make the same cuts at the same time on the collapsing circuit wires. He could try it himself, but it would be risky under a time crunch. A second set of eyes could study the double circuitry, confirming that the right color wires were cut at the right time. Otherwise, it would eat up too much time matching colors and then making sure the wire cutters had been placed correctly.

If they tried anything like that, of course, the cameras would see it all.

Raja could tell what he was thinking. Swallowing hard, she said, "If you try to disable the explosives, they'll trigger the detonator."

Brynstone snarled. "I can—"

"No, John," she interrupted. "They're watching."

"Who did this to you?"

"Some German guy. He attacked me."

He's here. Erich Metzger.

The name inspired rage, but Brynstone captured the emotion before it leaked into his facial expression. Too bad he couldn't stop the assassin from contaminating his thoughts. Was Metzger on the other side of the false door?

Brynstone tried to peer around her. "He still here?"

"I don't know."

The screen came to life. Viktor Nebola's round face appeared on the monitor, eyes twinkling. "You need to do a better job at dying, Dr. Brynstone. I thought we eliminated you back in Crete."

"Where's my daughter?"

"That's the least of your concerns."

Brynstone arched his neck. "Answer me, you son of a bitch."

"Tough talk for a man locked inside a small chamber with explosives. Enough explosives, in fact, to blast this catacomb and two city blocks of Alexandria high into the sky."

"That's not gonna happen," Brynstone said, calling his bluff. "You won't risk losing what we find down here."

"Open the lid on that sarcophagus. We'll see what I do."

"Want it opened?" Brynstone asked. "Come down here and do it yourself."

"Erich Metzger told me you would say something like that. He gets you. God, you two could be brothers."

Brynstone gritted his teeth.

"Open the lid," Nebola ordered. "Do it now."

Brynstone glanced down at the sarcophagus. He had seen other sarcophagi in the burial chamber on the second level. Down there, the corpse would have been slid through an opening on the side. This sarcophagus had a traditional stone cover. He started to budge it, but called to Cori and McHardy for help. The professor took his time coming over.

"Need to create a diversion," Brynstone said in a low voice.

"Tell me what to do," Cori whispered.

"If we could take out the lighting or the camera, that would help. It'll take time to defuse the explosives."

"Can you do that?"

"Done it before."

Brynstone wanted time to brainstorm a new plan, playing out various scenarios in his mind. He had the necessary supplies in his pack to defuse the explosives wired to Raja's vest, but he couldn't try without Nebola seeing. His plays were limited. He needed a way out of this mess. He was good at thinking three or four steps ahead of his opponent, but Nebola had cornered him. The positive contingencies were diminishing second by second.

Centuries ago, Brynstone knew, the last people to work in this small chamber had created a false door to conceal its secrets. As Raja watched, doing her best to remain still, they moved the massive lid from the sarcophagus.

A cloud of dust boiled into their faces as they pushed off the cover. He peered in, not certain what he would see in the sarcophagus. What he found took him by surprise. Seven mummified bodies were crammed inside the stone box, three stacked on top and four on the bottom.

McHardy made a comment.

Brynstone didn't listen.

A body can mummify under many different circumstances, but he hadn't expected it in here. The soft-tissue preservation was excellent, bringing to mind a mummified Italian friar he'd seen years before in the United States. He took a closer look at a body centered on top. The desiccated man stared with wide glazed eyes, his mouth gaping open and wisps of gray hair curling around his sunken neck. Beside him rested the charred remains of a Roman cavalry uniform. Had this armor belonged to Quintus, the Roman soldier who had inscribed the code on his helmet? A bound scroll rested on the chest plate. Was it the missing half of the Scintilla?

"Tell me what you see," Nebola ordered.

"Too hard to describe," Brynstone answered, looking up. "Turn off the motion sensors. Have Rashmi step forward. You need to see this for yourself."

Chapter 49

Viktor Nebola could see through Brynstone's plan. Watching from cameras positioned on Rashmi Raja's body, Nebola saw the shadowy chamber behind the false door. He saw the sarcophagus. And he saw Brynstone fighting to gain an advantage in an impossible situation.

A bank of monitors surrounded Nebola, networked to cameras that allowed him to see every movement in Kom el Shoqafa. He was stationed in a building adjacent to the catacombs, away from the blast zone of Metzger's explosives. Even though Nebola held the upper hand, he had to use care with Brynstone. A high-ranking official in the Shadow Chapter was listening in on this conversation and his superior wouldn't tolerate another mistake.

"Is my daddy okay?" Shayna Brynstone asked.

Nebola punched off the mic and turned to the child, who was seated farther down the table. She watched her father on a monitor.

"I'm trying to help him," Nebola answered, making his voice as sickeningly sweet as possible. "Remember what I said? You need to be quiet. We don't want Daddy to make a mistake."

She nodded, her face forming a mixed expression.

"Good girl."

To her credit, she hadn't made a fuss. The child seemed intent on watching the monitor. He imagined she was thrilled to see her father.

"You hear me?" Brynstone called to the camera. "Better get close and see this."

Nebola slitted his eyes and clenched his jaw. Brynstone was trying to maneuver Raja away from the hole in the false door. Wasn't going to happen.

"Ms. Raja is not budging," Nebola said into the mic. "Tell me what you have discovered, Dr. Brynstone. Describe it *now*."

———◆———

Brynstone wanted to keep this thing going. He negotiated with Nebola, the whole time planning to draw Raja farther away from the false door. For all of his brilliance, Math McHardy didn't pick up on Brynstone's plan. He did exactly as Nebola ordered. McHardy's professorial instincts kicked in and he described what he saw inside the sarcophagus. Brynstone had never seen the man so cooperative. Apparently, the threat of explosives brought out his helpful side.

"We have seven bodies here," McHardy began.

Oblivious to Brynstone's irritation, he described each mummy in detail, as well as the Roman soldier's armor.

"Tell me about the body inside the uniform," Nebola said.

"The armor is empty. It appears blackened as if subjected to fire." McHardy snatched the scroll and held it up. "Shall I translate this?"

"Do it," Nebola ordered. "Bring it to the camera."

"Don't do it," Brynstone said.

McHardy turned to him. "Look at the explosives, John. Do you think he will hesitate to use them?"

Brynstone thought back to how Nebola detonated explosives inside his own building in Crete. The man wouldn't hesitate.

Seeing the answer in Brynstone's eyes, McHardy moved to face the camera on Rashmi's forehead. Brynstone frowned as the man unrolled the scroll.

A distant look fell over Raja's eyes. Sweat beaded on her smooth forehead. She was tough, but this was a new challenge for her.

Brynstone glanced at the scroll. It was made from pieces of glued animal skin, and the words were written in Latin rather than Linear A symbols like on the helmet. Did it contain the Scintilla?

McHardy raised it for Nebola's inspection. He translated with Brynstone reading over his shoulder.

The scroll identified the author as Quintus Messorius Gallienus. As a child, it seemed, he had been raised in Crete. His Minoan ancestors had passed down the Linear A language to his family. Growing up, he had learned the code long before inscribing it inside his helmet.

Just as he had written on the helmet, he told again here of how Josephus had resurrected him after his slaying at the hands of a pagan king. After returning from the dead, Quintus discovered his ability to heal others.

It came as an accident.

During a long nighttime march, a fellow soldier had toppled from a cliff and had fallen to his death. Climbing down, Quintus and another soldier had spied the body prone on a lower outcropping. Quintus had reached for the dead soldier's wrist. At the same moment, he lost his footing. The soldier beside him had caught Quintus's hand to steady him. Quintus watched in disbelief as the dead man returned to life and the man who had lived fell dead. At that moment, Quintus realized that his healing gift came with a terrible curse. In later years, he had used it once again to restore

Nathan of Glastonbury to life while taking life from Joseph of Arimathea.

"Haunted over the death of Joseph at his hands," McHardy said after reading the first passage, "Quintus came to see his gift as more of a curse than a blessing."

There was more. A smaller second passage contained a brutal confession.

Back in the first century, Quintus described his journey to visit each of the Lost Ones, the people brought back from the dead using the Black and the White Chrisms. He had found them all, including Lazarus, going from village to village and region to region. He had stayed with them, dined with them, all the time learning how their lives had changed after returning from the dead. When he had learned all that he could from them, Quintus admitted, he had murdered them.

There was a silence. Even for Nebola, it took a minute to sink in.

"He killed them," Brynstone said, looking down at the bodies. "Quintus killed all the people in this sarcophagus."

"Aye. In his mind, the Lost Ones were an assembly of the damned, not fit to live a second time."

"Seven serial homicides," Brynstone said. "All committed nearly two thousand years ago. The Roman helmet we've been piecing together? It belonged to a serial killer."

"Quintus felt cursed because the Black Chrism gave him a terrible gift," Cori said. "But what about the people with the White Chrism, the ones like Lazarus? Why did he kill them, too?"

Brynstone wondered the same thing. After all, he had given Shay the White Chrism. How had it affected her? It was the question that had inspired him to search for the helmet pieces.

"It doesn't say why he killed those brought back with the White Chrism, but he believed they were an unnatural threat somehow."

McHardy shook his head. "And it doesn't say what happened to him. Quintus placed the bodies in this tomb. He laid down his armor. He wrote his confession on this scroll and then he vanished into history."

———◆◆———

Staring at the bank of monitors, Nebola realized he didn't trust Brynstone. Why should he? The man wanted nothing more than to get out and find his daughter and Metzger.

Nebola believed he could anticipate Brynstone's actions. Before taking this assignment, he had consulted a man who had known Brynstone since childhood, the same man who had supervised this operation. Nebola had worked in the Shadow Chapter longer than this guy, but that didn't matter—this man was a big-time player and he was now running the show. He had flown in to Alexandria to collect whatever Brynstone found in the catacomb. And he came to take the little girl.

Nebola heard the door close behind him. His supervisor from the Shadow Chapter was here.

Needing to talk to the guy, Nebola stared at the camera. "I'll give you a minute to catch up with your daughter, Brynstone. After that, find the chrism formula. If you don't, you won't see her again."

Leaning to the side, Nebola whispered to Shayna, who was seated in front of a monitor, "Your mic is live now." He handed her a headset with an attached microphone. He adjusted a camera in her direction. "Talk to your father."

The girl's face brightened. "Daddy?" she squeaked. "It's me. Can you hear me?"

Nebola eased out of his chair and walked away from the monitors toward the visitor, who was waiting for him at the door. Nebola had started working for the guy a few years ago, managing his operation to retrieve the helmet pieces and to abduct Shayna Brynstone. Despite a couple of blips, Nebola regarded it as a successful operation.

He saw on the guy's face that he disagreed. Nebola was confident the man from the Shadow Chapter would change his mind when he had a look at how things were playing out in the catacombs. Nebola put an extra swagger in his walk as he went over to greet his supervisor—Edgar Wurm.

Chapter 50

3:14 a.m.

Edgar Wurm scanned the small office. He took Nebola's out-stretched hand in a brisk shake as he glanced at the little girl seated at a table of monitors. She moved back and forth in a swivel chair, swinging her slender legs as she talked to her father. John Brynstone's rugged face appeared on one screen, looking relieved to see his daughter.

"You're letting her talk to Brynstone? I didn't authorize that."

"Just for a minute."

"Take away his daughter and it weakens Brynstone." Wurm frowned. "Let him see her, even for a moment, and you grant him strength."

"Not sure I agree," Nebola said.

"You better agree. As long as I'm overseeing your work in the Shadow Chapter, you better agree with every blasted word that comes out of my mouth."

"Yes, sir."

Wurm silenced Nebola with a wave of his hand. The man was an annoyance. Right now, Wurm was interested in the girl with the honey-blonde hair.

Wurm was a collector. He was used to getting what he wanted. Ever since he had learned about Shayna Brynstone's power, Wurm knew he wanted to collect her. She was the last of her kind, too valuable to leave out in the world. He had convinced the Chapter to support his mission. They understood his vision and had bank-rolled the entire project, lending considerable resources to the operation.

Wurm had requested Nebola from their ranks, in part because of his connection to Metzger. Nebola was brought in to acquire the child. In his own fumbling way, he had attained that goal. Of course, Brynstone would protest Wurm's desire to add Shayna to his collection.

For that reason—and that reason alone—John Brynstone had to die tonight.

The gravity of the moment brought tears to Cori's eyes, and she felt her face brighten with heat as she laughed with relief. Shayna was right there, her face filling the small screen at the base of Rashmi Raja's neck. Such a perfect vision of a child. Despite everything, she looked wonderful. Alive. Happy, even.

When she had appeared a moment ago, Brynstone had shoved aside McHardy to see.

"Shayna," he had said. "Are you okay?"

"Sort of scared, Daddy."

"Sweetie, the man who was here a minute ago," Brynstone had said with urgency. "Where is he now?"

"Back there," she said in a low voice. "Talking to someone."

"Can he see the screen you're looking at? Can he see us?"

"Nope."

Brynstone turned to Cori, grabbing her arm. "Talk to Shay. Keep her calm."

He dropped to his knees and unzipped the backpack. He started rifling through it. From the corner of her eye, Cori watched as Brynstone brought out what looked like a small pair of wire cutters.

Cori cleared her voice. "I missed you, Shay. It's so great to see you. That's a cute shirt."

"Thanks, Cori. Missed you, too."

Speaking quietly, Brynstone motioned to McHardy. "I need your help."

Both men kneeled in front of Raja.

"John, I don't like this idea."

"Trust me, Rashmi."

"No plan B?" she asked.

"Like what?"

"Don't know. Something that doesn't involve me getting blown to bits."

"Keep still, Rashmi. Remember they can detect it if you move too much."

The woman's eyes widened as she tried to remain still. Cori had to admire her—Raja was keeping her cool.

Brynstone handed a small pair of wire cutters to McHardy and whispered something about a primer, a reactor, and an ignition timer. She didn't know what he was talking about, but hearing the words made Cori nervous. She concentrated on talking to the little girl.

"Shay, honey, where are you?"

"I don't know."

"Are you inside a building? Tell me what you see."

Yawning softly, she looked around. "An office or something. I see desks. I'm at this table with a whole bunch of TVs. I can see you on one of the TVs. You look sort of muddy. Eww."

"You're right." Cori laughed nervously. "It's really muddy down here."

She glanced at McHardy. Color had drained from his face as he crouched at Raja's feet, holding the cutters. She caught herself listening to Brynstone.

"Slow down and breathe, Math. Stop panicking. Doesn't do us any good."

"What do you want me to do?"

"That wire right there. See it?" Brynstone whispered. "Start with the blue one. We need to cut the same wires at the same time. Blue and blue. Then we move to the next wires. Red and red. We can do it."

"Can't you cut both wires?"

"I need you on Rashmi's left side," Brynstone growled. "Lighting conditions are not optimal. Time's short. We need to work together. Same color wire. Same time. Or else *boom*. Got it?"

"Okay, John. Say when."

Brynstone mouthed the words "on three," then used his free hand to count it out.

Cori started thinking about what would happen if the two men made a mistake. *My God.* Her legs started to tremble. She glanced at Raja. The two women locked their gaze onto each other. They exchanged a scared look, each thinking the same thing.

We're gonna die.

In the hallway outside the office, Edgar Wurm stared down at Nebola. "Have they found the missing half of the Scintilla?"

"Not yet. Ball is in your court. What's the next move?"

"Contact your men. Notify the pilot. Get the helicopter here. After that, find out if the formula is with the bodies."

Leaving Nebola, Wurm headed to the opposite end of the hallway. A door opened not far away, and a shadow fell across the wall.

Stepping into the hallway, Erich Metzger wore a serene expression. He was an ideal competitor for John Brynstone—no one was better suited to go face-to-face with him than Metzger.

Brynstone had the sole distinction of being the only person to survive Metzger's assassination attempt. He was the man's only failure, although Metzger wouldn't see it that way. Wurm sensed the guy couldn't wait for another chance at Brynstone.

The feeling was mutual.

Wurm had never met the assassin. He had seen photographs in a Shadow Chapter dossier, no two looking the same. With an uncanny proficiency in matters of disguise, Metzger was a creature of many faces. He watched the man approach with a wary gaze. Was it Metzger's real look, Wurm wondered, or just part of another bloody masquerade?

Metzger stopped and clasped his hands in front of himself. His dark eyes were terrible and piercing.

"Herr Doktor Wurm."

"Guten Morgen, Herr Metzger," Wurm answered. "I wish to discuss a matter with you."

Cori did not take her gaze off Rashmi Raja, each woman holding her breath. Each feeling the ragged tug of panic in her stomach. The moments stretched into eons.

"I can't feel my toes," Raja whispered.

"Wiggle your toes a little," Cori said, "but keep your body still. Focus. You can do this. Just a little longer."

"You talking to me, Cori?" Shay asked on the monitor. "Wiggle my toes?"

"No, Shay. Not you."

"Who are you talking to?"

Cori drew in a breath. She didn't want to get into details. "I'm talking to my imaginary friend."

"You have one, too? What's your I-F's name?"

"Um, Rashmi."

Raja took a halting breath. "How are they doing?"

Cori glanced down. Brynstone and McHardy were working on disabling the explosives. How were they doing? It was a good question. Cori had no idea. She didn't want to say that.

"Good," she whispered, looking up at the taller woman. "Hang in there, Rashmi."

"Everything okay?" Shay asked. "Why's Daddy doing that?"

"You can see him?" Cori asked, shaking herself back into the conversation.

"The third TV. On there. Yeah, I see him."

Cori didn't want Nebola to walk in and see Brynstone and McHardy working on the wires. "Shay, listen to me. Do you see a button on the TV where you see your dad? A power button?"

She turned. "Mm-hmm. A green light."

"Good. Push the button. Turn it off."

"Turn off the TV?"

"Only the TV where you see your dad." Her voice quivered. "I know you want to watch your dad, sweetie, but we really need your help. Turn it off. Make the green light go away."

The child moved out of the frame.

Raja closed her eyes. She bit her bottom lip.

Shayna returned on the small screen.

"That TV is all black now."

"Good girl."

"I don't like these men," Shayna said. "Viktor is nice I guess, but I don't trust him."

"Shay," Cori said, trying to sound relaxed, "how many people are with you?"

"Um, bad men with guns came in here. They said some bad words, then they went somewhere."

Raja glanced down at Brynstone. In a faltering voice, she called, "John, are you close? Can you do it?"

Frowning, he didn't look up but muttered, "Doing my best."

Cori returned her attention to the monitor. Heart rattling in her chest, she coached herself to stay focused on the conversation with Shay. "That guy who was with you? Viktor. Is he still talking to someone?"

"Mm-hmm."

"Who is Viktor talking to?"

"I can't see them."

"Can you hear them?"

She turned her head, the camera picking up shiny blonde hair as she looked back. Her face appeared on the screen again. "They're in another room. It's like I can kind of hear their voices, I think."

Cori needed to figure out where to find the girl in case they made it out of this place.

"Should I take off the headphones? Want me to go listen to them?"

"No, don't do that. That's okay. Just keep talking, sweetie."

"Is my daddy still there?"

"Right here," Brynstone called. "You're such a brave girl. Daddy is so proud of you."

Sweat streamed down his face. He pointed to a green wire. McHardy frowned as he eased the wire cutter around it with shaking hands. That made Cori nervous.

"Daddy, are you gonna come see me?"

"Soon as I can, baby girl. Soon as I can. Be strong, Shay. I love you."

"Love you, too." On the monitor, the little girl turned to her left. "Cori?"

"Yeah, Shay?"

"Viktor and the other man?" the child said. "Well, um, I think Viktor is coming back."

"Okay, Shay," Cori called, her voice frantic. "Turn that other TV back on. *Fast.*"

Chapter 51

3:21 a.m.

Viktor is coming back.

Shayna's words seemed to blast through the small chamber like a shock wave. Brynstone cursed. Panicked, Math McHardy dropped the cutters and jumped to his feet, scrambling back into place beside Cori.

Brynstone winced.

So close. So damned close.

Only two wires stopped him from deactivating the explosives on Raja's vest. He shoved the cutters in his pants pocket and hurried back to the sarcophagus. He made it just as Shayna moved to a nearby seat and Nebola's face appeared on the monitor strapped to Raja's chest.

"Where's the chrism formula?" Nebola demanded, appearing on-screen. "Show me."

Brynstone decided to lie. "I looked for it while Shayna was on camera. All we have are bodies and the scroll that tells about Quintus murdering the Lost Ones."

"You can't find the chrism formula?"

Resting his hands on the edge of the sarcophagus, Brynstone peered into the camera. "It's not here."

"Then there's nothing to stop me from blowing the hell out of the catacombs along with you and your friends." To make his point,

Nebola held up the detonation switch, his thumb poised above it. "Check again, Dr. Brynstone. Pull out all the bodies."

Brynstone frowned. Leaning inside the sarcophagus, he reached for the mummy with the long hair. He searched along the body, the tattered clothes falling apart in his hand, but there was no sign of the chrism formula. He hated moving the specimen, given its delicate condition, but he didn't have a choice. Raising it in his arms, he lifted the dead man from the sarcophagus and placed it with care on the floor.

On-screen, Nebola said, "That mummy. Any chance he's Saint Lazarus?"

He thought about it. Nebola could be right.

It gave him a chill. Had he just touched the corpse of the most famous back-from-the-dead person in history?

Brynstone brought out the armor next. Placing it beside the Lazarus mummy, he searched the next body, a woman, looking to be late fifties at the time of death. Once again, Brynstone marveled at the soft-tissue preservation. McHardy and Cori stepped in to help, each removing body after body and lowering them to the floor. It was tragic, handling the ancient corpses without gloves. Both in here and with the Lazarus Cross, he had committed unforgivable scientific sins. All in all, they brought out four mummies, leaving three in the sarcophagus.

"There," McHardy said, pointing at a piece of vellum trapped beneath the leg of the mummy at the bottom.

It seemed like an odd place. Maybe it had once been on top, but had fallen over the centuries as the stack of corpses withered into their present desiccated state. Brynstone reached in and coaxed the small scrap of vellum from beneath one man's leg.

Years ago, Edgar Wurm and Cori Cassidy had found the top half of the Scintilla. That same night, Cori had sent Brynstone the formula to create the White Chrism. Using it to save his daughter's life, he had done it all without ever seeing the Scintilla. He had always wondered how it would look.

Cori moved beside him. "That matches the torn document Edgar and I found. That's the other half."

"Bring it here," Nebola ordered. "Hold the Scintilla to the camera."

"Forget it."

"Are you serious, Brynstone? You're doing this?"

"If I show you this half of the Scintilla, what's to stop you from detonating the explosives?"

Nebola's face darkened. "Someone here needs to speak with you." He moved out of sight from the monitor on Raja's chest.

Brynstone narrowed his eyes. He expected Metzger. He expected threats. That's not what happened.

Edgar Wurm slid into view on the monitor. With flowing gray hair, the man had the look of an Old Testament prophet.

Disbelief hit as Brynstone tried to make sense of what he was seeing. It was bad enough that Nebola had abducted Shayna, but now he had Wurm, too. Since his "death," Wurm had been successful at staying off the grid. How did Nebola find him?

Cori grabbed Brynstone's arm. "Edgar, you're alive?" She raised her hand to her mouth, making a hushed cry. "Is that really you?"

"Cori, I wondered if you and I would meet again. How unfortunate our reunion arrives under the present circumstances."

"I, uh, I saw you fall that night," she said, still bewildered. "I thought you were dead."

"Edgar Wurm, you're too damned stubborn to die," McHardy grumbled, coming over. "Even if you did, you're too rotten to stay in hell."

Brynstone reached over. "Shut up, Math. I need to help my daughter."

Ignoring his rival, Wurm said, "John, do this for me. Bring the chrism formula to the camera."

Brynstone couldn't read the man's expression. Wurm looked a little frightened.

Or not.

"Listen, John," he continued, "I need your cooperation. Please show us the missing half of the Scintilla." On camera, Wurm reached over, and the small monitor showed him pulling Shayna onto his knee. Wurm looked down at her. "Remember me? We met in Central Park some months back? You were playing in the snow with your black cat. I gave you a scarf for your snowman."

She glanced up at him and nodded.

"Don't be afraid, dear." Wurm turned his attention back to Brynstone. "John, bring the chrism formula to the camera. We need you to do it. Both of us."

Brynstone looked down, thinking it over. Cori placed her hand on his arm, running her fingers down to his elbow.

He walked around the sarcophagus, stopping in front of Raja. The woman looked frazzled. Awash in perspiration, her graceful appearance had vanished and she looked ready to collapse.

This wasn't easy.

Brynstone held the small piece of vellum to the camera strapped across her forehead. Looking down at the monitor, he could see Wurm reading the document. Rashmi was watching Brynstone. He gave her a quick look and whispered, "Be strong."

After a minute, Wurm smiled. "Thank you, John."

Brynstone lowered the vellum. "Doesn't Nebola want to see it?"

"He has no interest in the Scintilla."

"Sure sounded like it."

"I made him sound interested."

"What are you talking about, Edgar?" he demanded. "What are you doing there?"

"Controlling things."

Strange answer.

"What do you mean?"

"Think of me as the puppet master, John."

He glanced at Cori. She had a puzzled expression. He looked back at the monitor.

"Wait. You're working with Nebola?"

"Not at all," Wurm corrected. "Nebola is working *for* me."

"I knew it!" McHardy shouted. "I've always said the bastard couldn't be trusted."

Fighting off surprise, Brynstone put it all together.

"Last February in Central Park, you asked me to help find the helmet pieces."

"I wanted you because you're the best, John. Three years ago, Nebola sent a team to help me take out a Metropolitan Police vehicle. We recovered the other half of the chrism formula from Scotland Yard. After that, I worked with the same team to track down the helmet pieces. Time after time, it was a miserable failure."

Off camera, Nebola said, "Our team pulled off a successful operation in Barcelona."

"That was a straightforward job," Wurm answered. "A simple break-in at a mayor's office. Even at that, they garbled it with a security guard."

"I hire good men," Nebola said. "If they screw up, I get rid of them. Look at Markus Tanzer and that Dutch commando, Abder Visser."

"After the first team failed," Wurm continued, looking at the camera again, "the Shadow Chapter brought in a special operator. She fared only slightly better."

Brynstone looked down at Raja. She closed her eyes. Didn't say a thing. Under normal circumstances, the woman would protest that statement. Right now, with explosives strapped to her body, she remained silent.

"But some operations require the Brynstone touch. Your discovery under Père Lachaise Cemetery? That was a masterwork."

"Is Nessa Griffin part of your team?"

Wurm chuckled. "Oh, God, no. I would not give a red cent to Math McHardy or his minions."

McHardy adjusted his tie, trying to appear indifferent.

"I wanted your help, John, because you succeed where others fail. The Père Lachaise operation offered the added bonus of getting you out of New York while we abducted your daughter."

"You played me."

"With your cooperation, I might add." Wurm peered into the camera, his eyes dancing under a hedge of black eyebrow hair. "But there's more bad news. Like the false door, nothing is as it appears."

"What do you mean?"

A serious cast came over his face. "Now is the time, John."

"Time for what?"

"To tell you the truth. I'm afraid you've been misled. That document you hold in your hand? It is not the formula for the Black Chrism."

"Yes, it is," Cori called, coming over.

On-screen, Wurm raised a piece of vellum that matched the one from the sarcophagus. It was the top portion of the document that Joseph of Arimathea had torn in half centuries ago. In a dry tone, he said, "*This* is the Black Chrism."

Cori peered at the monitor. "You're mistaken, Edgar. That's the one you and I found."

"Yes, it is," Wurm said. "Since that time, only a handful of people have seen it. Fortunately, I got it back. It belongs to me now."

"Maybe," Cori said, "but you're holding the formula for the White Chrism. We found the Black Chrism down here." She pointed at the vellum in Brynstone's hand.

Wurm chuckled. "Cori, I'm afraid I have to say the three most difficult words in the English language: I was wrong."

"What do you mean?"

"If you remember, Cori, we discovered the torn Scintilla under challenging circumstances. We were stressed and sleep deprived. The descendants of Cesare Borgia were hunting us. On top of it all, it was dark when I finally had a chance to translate the formula. Conditions were far from ideal. I translated the Aramaic script, reading aloud the ingredients to make the chrism. You stood beside me, texting the information to Brynstone."

"I remember."

"Years later, after I recovered this document from Scotland Yard, I realized my error. I had read the words *White Chrism* on this document and translated them as you texted."

"Yeah?"

"What I saw was the heading for the bottom half of the Scintilla—the missing part. Much later, under better conditions, I realized that we had discovered the formula for the Black Chrism. That's what you texted—"

"No," Brynstone muttered.

"Afraid so, John. My suspicion was confirmed a moment ago when you held your half of the Scintilla to the camera. I'm holding the Black Chrism formula. You're holding the formula for the White Chrism."

⊷•⊶

John Brynstone was reeling. His mouth went dry as his chest coiled up. If Wurm was right, it meant that Brynstone had given Shayna the Black Chrism, not the White Chrism.

"Why would you do this, Edgar?" he demanded. "When we talked in Central Park, you knew back then that I gave the Black Chrism to my daughter."

"Yes, I did." Wurm raised the child from his knee, asking Nebola to take Shayna.

"You should have told me, Edgar."

"I promised myself I would tell you when the time was right. Now is that time. I have confessed everything. I want to understand what you did to your daughter. Like Quintus and the others, Shayna has a remarkable yet terrible gift. I want to study her."

"Leave her alone."

"Sorry, John. Shayna is more important than you understand. You want her because she brings a sense of normalcy to your life. Cori wants her because the girl makes her feel complete in a strange and complicated way. I want her because I need to understand her power. Believe me, I will do all I can to exploit it."

"Don't touch my daughter," Brynstone growled.

"She's part of a greater vision now, John. Shayna Brynstone is the living embodiment of the Black Chrism in the twenty-first century."

Cori shouted at the screen, "You're insane, Edgar!"

"Considering that we met in a psychiatric hospital, the same might be said of you. It's better that you die."

"You won't kill us," Brynstone said, waving the vellum. "You're a collector. You want it. You need the White Chrism."

"You keep it. I have the formula recorded on video."

"No, Edgar."

"Goodbye, John. Goodbye, Cori. Believe it or not, I respect you both."

Chapter 52

3:26 a.m.

Brynstone scrambled around Rashmi Raja. He had to move fast if he hoped to deactivate the explosives before Wurm pressed the switch. Ducking down, he brought the clippers from his pocket, drawing them out like a gunslinger going for his revolver.

Cori followed his lead and scooped up the cutters McHardy had dropped on the floor. "Show me, John. Which one?"

It was faster to move than to speak. Brynstone took her hand and slid her cutter around the wire.

Raja's legs trembled hard. She looked pale and more ready to collapse than before.

"Hold steady," Brynstone barked as he moved around to her right side. No time to breathe. No time to think. Taking his cutter, he positioned it around the wire.

<hr>

Edgar Wurm saw Brynstone dart out of view. He reached across the table and grabbed the detonation switch.

"What are you doing, mister?" Shayna Brynstone said, coming over.

"All that is necessary." Wurm shot a look of aggravation at Nebola. "Get her out of here."

Nebola hurried over and grabbed her arm. "Come with me."

"Where are you taking me?"

"Go with him, Shayna," Wurm soothed. "Be a good girl."

He glanced back at the monitor. Cori Cassidy was down on her knees. Her youthful face was creased with worry. Was she praying? Didn't matter.

Goodbye.

Wurm's thumb pressed the metal switch.

Click.

Click.

Nothing.

On the screen, Cori stared at the camera. Wurm glared back at her.

"Damn it," he snarled, tossing the detonation switch across the room. Knocking over his chair, Wurm jumped to his feet and moved to the door. Shoving aside Nebola and the child, he hurried into the hallway.

Running down the corridor, he turned the corner and found Erich Metzger leaning against the wall, talking to his assistant, Franka, on the phone.

"Go to the catacombs immediately," Wurm demanded. "Get down there and kill John Brynstone."

In a serene voice, Metzger said, "Wasn't that the purpose of the explosives?"

"Brynstone must have deactivated them."

"I warned that it is dangerous to underestimate me," Metzger said, closing the phone. "It's almost as dangerous to underestimate Brynstone. If given time, he can find his way out of any trap."

"I'll triple your price," Wurm promised, red-faced. "Now kill Brynstone."

"It will be my distinct pleasure." Without another word, Metzger turned and sprinted down the stairs.

Marching back down the hallway, Wurm returned to the office. Nebola was standing near the bank of monitors. Shayna was back in the swivel chair, knees curled to her chin, watching him.

"Get out of the way," Wurm said, shoving Nebola.

"Take it easy, Mr. Wurm."

"Can I see my daddy?" the girl asked.

"Hush," Wurm said, hunching over to consult the monitors.

On-screen, Brynstone darted around Rashmi Raja. He slipped through the false door. Safe now, the Indian woman ripped off the headpiece and pitched it to the floor, then stripped the cameras from her shoulders. The image went blurry, then all three monitors turned instantly black. The image from the head cam remained on one screen. It showed the ceiling above the false door, picking up a visual from where Raja had thrown it down.

He glanced at another monitor and saw Metzger running across the catacombs near the divided staircase.

Wurm was furious. "You failed, Viktor. You have failed me. You have failed the Shadow Chapter. I can no longer tolerate your incompetence."

"How can you call me incompetent?" Nebola shouted back. "I abducted the Brynstone child for you. I made sure helmet artifacts were discovered. I even got you a look at the White Chrism formula."

"Sorry, Viktor. The Shadow Chapter no longer has need for your services."

"You're going to kill me?"

"Think of it as closure, if that makes any sense to you."

Wurm glanced at the monitor. A blur of Cori Cassidy and Rashmi Raja came into view as they stepped over the camera and escaped through the false door.

Wurm heard a soft whirling sound and looked over at the swivel chair. It was spinning. An abandoned headset rested on the seat. Shayna Brynstone was gone.

He glanced at the door. There was no sign of her.

Wurm started to chase her. From behind, Nebola tackled him. Both men crashed into a table, and Nebola rolled into the hallway.

"Run, Shayna," Nebola called. "Run!"

Full of rage, Wurm made it to his feet and kicked Nebola in the ribs. He glared at the fallen man. "You've made colossal mistakes, Viktor, but letting Shayna go free is your biggest yet. Why did you do it, anyway? I didn't think you cared about that child."

"I don't give a shit about her," he groaned, holding his side. "But if you're going to kill me, I'm going to go down pissing you off."

"You're deplorable," Wurm said.

He hurried to check the monitors. On one screen, Shayna Brynstone scurried through the first level of the catacomb. Wurm glanced at another monitor. The screen showed Metzger emerging from the shadow of a pillar with a gun in his hand. He stood twenty feet from the little girl.

Metzger's head snapped around.

He heard her coming.

———◆———

"Daddy?"

John Brynstone was halfway down the stairs outside the false door when he heard his daughter cry out, her words echoing off the stone walls. What was she doing down here?

"Daddy? Where are you? I can't find you."

"I'm coming, Shayna." Hustling past the Hero door, Brynstone stopped and listened. Frantically looking around, he didn't see her.

He heard another cry, her words sounding hoarse and desperate and small. She seemed closer now, but still distant.

"Shayna, where are you?"

He couldn't hear her. He called her name again.

No answer. God, where was she?

"John," Cori called as she hurried to the Hero door. "Where's Shay?"

"Can't find her."

Raja joined them at the massive door. McHardy caught up.

A scream. *Monkey Guns.*

"That your daughter?" Raja asked.

"She's here somewhere. Can't locate her voice."

"What's a Monkey Guns?" McHardy asked.

"An imaginary friend," Cori answered. "Let's split up and search for her."

"The three of you go together," Brynstone ordered. "Search the first level. I'll check the main tomb."

He sprinted around the divided staircase, then darted through the façade bearing images of Medusa and the crowned serpents. There was no sign of her near the sarcophagi or huddled in the shadows of the corner.

He checked the U-shaped corridor that housed rows of loculi. Sprinting across planks near the west wall, he stopped when he heard her voice again. There was no mistaking it this time— Shayna was not far away, on this level. How had he missed her?

He sprinted back toward the divided staircase. He took two steps before stopping again. His daughter screamed, her voice tinged with such fright that she seemed to be alive inside a nightmare.

"Monkey Guns! Monkey Guns!"

Her words came out muffled, but he tracked her voice. She wasn't on the first level with the others. Her voice echoed from beyond the Hero door. Shayna was calling from the chamber up by the false door.

Heading in that direction, he made it to the Hero door and came to a halt as he looked up the stairs. He slid the backpack from his shoulders and tossed it behind him.

Erich Metzger stood at the top of the stairs, clutching Shayna's wrists in one hand. Her face was bright red as she cried.

Chapter 53

Rashmi Raja prided herself on keeping her cool. But this ordeal tonight pushed her too close to the edge. Remaining still while the others had cut wires and deactivated the explosives, she hadn't wanted to move an inch until the vest had been stripped off her body. She knew she was safe now, but the stress of facing the German man and the terror of wearing a bomber's vest left her feeling sick and numb. Still unsettled, she acted self-assured around Cori and McHardy.

Looking for Brynstone's daughter was a growing frustration. *Where is she?* Imagine a little girl in a place like this, frightened and lost in the shadows.

Raja and the others had not heard the child cry out for a couple minutes as they searched the first level. Sound was elusive in this place. You could pick up an echo in one part of the catacombs but move somewhere else and hear nothing.

Raja started up the spiral staircase, leaving McHardy and Cori to search near the vestibule. She peeked inside a slanted window, making certain that the little girl hadn't fallen down the deep shaft. It was a little morbid, but it seemed like a good idea to at least check. She waved the flashlight around the shaft, but there was no sign of anyone at the bottom. When she returned to the vestibule,

Cori looked at her with trepidation. She could tell the woman had the same thought about the Brynstone girl falling into the shaft.

"Not there," Rashmi whispered.

McHardy frowned. "Brynstone should blame himself for this mess."

"John didn't know Edgar would betray him," Cori shot back.

With smug assurance, he said, "The Wurm has turned. Did that surprise anyone?"

"Let's concentrate on finding Shayna," Rashmi advised.

Heading toward the triclinium, Cori said, "You two check outside. I'll see if John has had any luck."

John Brynstone took one measured step after another up the stone staircase. He didn't blink. Seeing Metzger with Shay turned his stomach, and he had to fight a swell of rage. He couldn't admit to the fear, but it was there, too, deep and raw inside him. Metzger was an expert with firearms and also a formidable fighter. He could kill with or without a weapon.

"Let go of her, Metzger," he said in a cool voice.

"Daaaaddy," she cried at the top of the stairs. "He's here. Monkey Guns caught me and he won't let go."

Metzger grinned. "Isn't she precious?"

"Daddy, help me." Shayna tried to drop to her feet, but Metzger held her wrists, stretching her arms above her head.

"Monkey Guns won't let go."

The assassin's dark eyes flickered. "Your daughter has a pet nickname for me. I must confess Monkey Guns makes no sense, but such are the ways of children. I'm flattered she remembers me."

"Damn it, Metzger," Brynstone growled. "Let her go or I'll—"

"Or you'll what, Herr Doktor Brynstone?"

"I'll kill you."

Another smile. "Promise you'll try? You mean it? Will you try your absolute best to kill me?"

Games. This twisted bastard loved his games.

"Our good friend, Herr Doktor Wurm, is watching," Metzger said.

That's when Brynstone spied the small camera on the stairs. Raja had worn it as a headband. The camera was propped near the assassin's foot, angled to pick up a shot of Brynstone.

Metzger squeezed Shayna's wrists.

"Wurm tells me you keep your promises," Metzger continued. "He'll be disappointed if you don't do your best to kill me."

"Makes two of us," Brynstone said, halfway up the stairs.

"Actually, it makes three. Four if you count the little girl." The assassin looked down at Shayna, still struggling in his iron grip. He purred, "Run, little girl. Run to Daddy. Let's see if he can kill me. We'll see if he keeps his promise."

Metzger opened his fingers, releasing Shayna. His daughter almost stumbled at first, but she regained her balance and hurried down the stairs toward her father. Brynstone didn't budge. He had to keep a safe distance. He wanted to run to his daughter and scoop her up, but he had to let her come to him. He couldn't afford a mistake. Not now.

Not with Metzger.

Two steps away, Shayna jumped and vaulted into Brynstone's arms, squeezing tight around his neck. He fought the instinct to close his eyes. Her tears ran wet against his neck and a swelling rose in his throat. He wanted to live in this embrace forever. He brushed her blonde hair, kissing her cheeks and forehead, never pulling his gaze from Metzger.

The assassin reached down and picked up the headband camera, holding it so that Wurm could get a good look. He dropped his foot to the step below, walking down.

Shayna sobbed in Brynstone's ear, then turned to see the man. She pointed a rigid finger at Metzger, her mouth curled in horror. Eyes wide, she began shrieking, "Daddy, get me out of here. Please, Daddy. Don't let Monkey Guns get me. Don't let him get me. Please, Daddy!"

Brynstone hugged his daughter tighter than before. She was jolting in his arms, her little body quivering with frenzy as the assassin took another step closer. He couldn't keep her still.

"Please, Daddy, get me out of here."

Metzger licked his lip. "Don't forget to keep your promise, Herr Doktor."

Brynstone wanted to turn and run. More than anything, he wanted to get his daughter to safety. He knew if he turned his back on the man, Metzger would lunge at them. Should he try to escape with Shayna or release her and let her run through the darkened catacomb, hoping she'd find Cori or Rashmi?

Ugly choices. So damn many ugly choices.

"Do you realize, Dr. Brynstone, that if your daughter had lived two thousand years ago, she would be one of the Lost Ones rotting up in that sarcophagus?" He took another step down. "Are you so certain that Shayna Brynstone should be saved?"

"Stay back, Metzger. This is between you and me. Leave my daughter out of it."

"Don't you realize everything revolves around your little girl? She is at the center of this entire ordeal. You are responsible for that fact."

"Because of you, I had to give her the White Chrism."

"You mean the Black Chrism," Metzger corrected. "You're still lying to yourself, aren't you?"

He moved closer.

"John," Cori Cassidy called from behind.

He took a breath. It was a relief to hear her voice. Still, he couldn't afford to turn around. He heard her footsteps close behind now.

"Cori," Shay called, reaching for her.

Brynstone whispered, "Sweetie, you have to trust me. Daddy has to stop Monkey Guns."

"No, Daddy, don't let go of me."

"Shay, I need you to go with Cori," he whispered in her ear.

"Something bad will happen to you," she moaned. "Something bad."

Coming along his side now, Cori reached for the child.

Metzger moved another step closer. "How lovely," he teased. "The babysitter has arrived."

Brynstone handed Shay over to Cori. He hated giving up his daughter, but he had to face Erich Metzger.

Then everything happened fast.

Metzger took the stairs at full speed, bursting into Brynstone, the clatter of body smashing body. Metzger grabbed him by the neck and punched him in the gut as they rolled down one unforgiving step after another. In a blur, he caught sight of Cori running ahead with Shayna in her arms. She was a fast runner, thankfully, and she made it to the bottom landing. He had to do everything he could to keep the assassin away from them. Metzger flipped him, sending Brynstone down the stone staircase. He crunched hard on one step, pain shooting through his arm. Shayna and Cori made it to the Hero door. He didn't want his daughter to see this.

"Get her out," he yelled at Cori.

"What are you afraid of, Herr Doktor?"

Metzger lunged again, the man executing his fighting style with command and confidence. Rising up, Brynstone turned to confront him. He was face-to-face with the assassin; now was his chance to take on this man who had wrecked his family.

Metzger pivoted into a standing kick, plunging his boot into Brynstone's stomach. The blow rocked him on his feet as Metzger wielded a fist into Brynstone's face, sending him rolling down the stairs, spiraling to the landing.

Moving at an unreal speed, Metzger caught up and blazed another direct strike into Brynstone's face. It was a precision shot. There was no waste of energy. Every jab efficient and elegant. The guy was a killer in every way imaginable.

Brynstone saw another attack coming, but ducked to avoid the man's fist, more on instinct than deliberate execution. Driving hard off his back foot, Brynstone came with a forearm smash that connected with Metzger's jaw, the shot sending the assassin in a helix move that whirled him away.

Blow after blow, he was holding his own, fighting back hard against the guy. Brynstone had waited years for this moment. He came back another time, but Metzger caught his arm after the strike. The assassin slammed him into the wall near the Hero door. The surface came at him like a bulldozer, and his legs buckled as he crumpled against the wall. The man squeezed Brynstone's neck, pain exploding in his head. He couldn't break free. Metzger had surprising strength.

"When we faced each other years ago, you shot me," Metzger spat. "You're the only person who can make that claim. You will suffer for that indignity."

Brynstone was wearing down. Barely hearing the words. Putting all his focus into his next move, he pushed off the wall and came at Metzger, driving their heads together, skull bashing skull as he managed to break the assassin's hold.

On his feet now, Brynstone headed for the stairs, running to the landing. He had no idea where Cori had taken Shay, but he wanted to draw Metzger as far from them as possible. He took the stairs three at a time, barely sensing his feet on each step. Lunging more than running now, he heard Metzger following right behind.

Brynstone made it to the false door. He ducked inside the small chamber, alone with the broken bodies of the Lost Ones. He staggered backward, crushing fragile mummies under his boot, fighting to catch his breath. He needed to think through his next move.

A shadow dashed across the opening to the false door as Metzger stepped inside the room. He grinned like a demon and Brynstone saw the reason. The assassin had found a deadly toy.

Erich Metzger raised the hammer drill.

He pumped the trigger, the torque driving the bit with a metal scream.

Chapter 54

"Is Daddy gonna be okay?" Shay called in a delicate worried voice.

With the child embracing her, Cori made it past the main tomb. She had only heard about Metzger, but had never met him before now. Getting a glimpse of him, the man had terrified her.

Back as a psych intern, she had worked with criminal patients diagnosed with antisocial personality disorder. That summer, she had dealt with serial predators who had committed unspeakable brutalities against their victims. None of the ASPD patients came close to matching Metzger in terms of cunning and ferocity. He was the closest thing she had seen to perfect evil.

Did Brynstone stand a chance? He had survived an attack from Metzger once. She prayed he could do it again.

"Daddy will be fine," Cori called in a thin voice, hoping it calmed the child.

"Good," Rashmi Raja called. "You found her."

Cori was thrilled to see the woman.

"Rashmi, you have to do something," she panted. "John is fighting Metzger. On the stairs inside the Hero door. Can you help him?"

Raja's eyes narrowed. "The German guy, right? The creep sandwich who dressed me up in explosives? Yeah, I'm there."

Metzger wielded the hammer drill.

Brynstone moved into a fighting stance.

These weren't good odds. Metzger didn't need the drill, but it was an amusement for him. A new way to kill.

"Do you know how long I've waited for this moment?" the assassin said, standing in front of the broken door. "Exhilarating, isn't it?"

"Didn't know you were so excited to die."

Metzger chuckled. In a sincere voice, he said, *"Ich danke Ihnen."*

"What was that? Are you thanking me?"

"I am," the man answered. "Because you make it all so meaningful."

He pressed the trigger and charged with the hammer drill. Brynstone pivoted and grabbed the German's arm, but he still managed to swipe the drill. It grazed Brynstone beneath his arm, shredding open a line in his shirt. He released Metzger's arm as the instinct of pain pulled him away. He darted around the sarcophagus, still feeling the sting of the hot masonry bit on his rib. In the darkened chamber, he nearly tripped over the sledgehammer.

Metzger was coming fast, ready to bore the drill through Brynstone's skull. *Not this time.* The guy had chased him into the chamber, but there was one thing he hadn't counted on. The beating had made Brynstone mad as hell. He wanted to punish the assassin.

He reached down and grabbed the sledgehammer.

Tonight, the blood feud ends.

One survivor.

No rules.

Metzger charged again, the drill bit churning. Swinging the sledgehammer like he was trying to knock one out of the park, Brynstone caught the edge of the drill. The tool flew across the room and smashed into the wall, cracking open as it hit the floor.

Rock defeats scissors. Scissors defeats paper. Sledgehammer defeats hammer drill.

Metzger pulled back with a look of genuine shock on his face. He hadn't seen the sledgehammer until it was too late.

Brynstone's arms sizzled with fatigue and pain, but he had enough power to get the twenty-pounder in the air again. He took another swing.

Metzger ducked this one, his brown hair rising as the sledgehammer swooshed over his head.

Before the assassin could make another move, Brynstone jabbed the hammer's handle, catching Metzger in the gut. Pushing him up against the stone sarcophagus, Brynstone slapped the handle up across Metzger's throat, crushing his windpipe, trapping air inside. Brynstone looked down into the man's eyes. They were eerily calm, like he was voluntarily holding his breath, like he didn't need or even want air at the moment.

That's when the knife came out.

Metzger had pulled it from his boot. The serrated blade swiped Brynstone's collarbone, slicing his shirt as it cut a ragged trail to his shoulder. His muscles raged, the searing line of pain bright beneath his neck. Blood splattered across his exposed skin.

Metzger wasn't finished. Raising the knife, he plunged the blade into Brynstone's chest.

Brynstone gasped hard, dizzy with pain, his entire body seeming to convulse with the weapon jammed in him. His heart screamed inside his damaged chest.

Metzger cackled.

Running on last reserves, Brynstone dropped the hammer and picked up the man, Metzger's feet coming off the floor. He slammed the assassin down inside the sarcophagus. The German landed on three ancient mummies, crushing them beneath his weight. Metzger's head hit the side of the stone box, the impact causing his eyes to close.

Wincing, Brynstone clutched his chest and stared down at the knife. He wrapped his fingers around the blood-spattered handle. Every instinct told him to pull it out, but he fought the urge. He knew that removing the weapon could make it worse, causing greater damage to the surrounding flesh. Pulling out the serrated blade would release a profusion of blood.

Brynstone wanted to close the stone lid on Metzger, but he didn't have the strength to drag and lift it into place over the sarcophagus. He stared down at the man. Blood streaked his face like war paint. Metzger was trying to move, bracing himself to sit up, fighting to climb out like some wretched zombie emerging from his grave.

Can't let him out.

Brynstone reached in to slam the man's head against the sarcophagus wall. Before he could, Metzger reached up and grabbed the handle, ripping the knife from Brynstone's chest. Blood sprayed out onto the stone floor.

Brynstone's agonized scream echoed inside the chamber.

Light-headed now, he staggered back toward the false door. His muscles seemed to clench all at once as pain streaked out from his chest to his arms and shot down to his legs. A deafening roar filled his ears. It wouldn't be much longer until he blacked out.

He had to get out of here. He had to see Shayna.

One last time.

He reached for the wall near the broken opening, leaving a bloody print as he slipped through the false door.

"Where are you going, Herr Doktor?" the assassin called. "You have not kept your promise."

Brynstone didn't look back. He was fading fast. It took all his concentration to get down the stairs without collapsing, watching one foot chase the other. Halfway down the staircase, he heard Metzger again. The man was pulling through the false door.

"You disappoint me," Metzger called. "I never thought you would run, Herr Doktor."

Pain exploded inside Brynstone's chest. A fever burned behind his eyes. His vision closed in tight as the stairs swirled in a confusing blur. He willed himself to make it down to the bottom landing.

Shayna.

Shayna.

One last time.

Please, God.

"You are a disgrace," Metzger called. "Look at you. A pitiful disgrace."

Brynstone heard him starting down the stairs.

Raja appeared outside the Hero door. Her eyes widened when she saw blood flooding down Brynstone's chest, his face drained and white. Her eyes darted. She saw Metzger coming down the stairs. She went into a stance and aimed her firearm, but Brynstone was blocking her shot on the narrow staircase.

Didn't matter.

Brynstone had one more play in him.

He had saved his strength for this next move, the final one of his life. Clutching his chest, he looked back. He wanted to see the assassin's face.

Metzger knew.

He had figured it out. He could see now what Brynstone was planning. Losing his calm demeanor, he burst into a full sprint down the stairs.

Got to do this.

Straining like hell, Brynstone charged to the door. In surprise, Raja lifted her gun back as he came at her. He jumped, then rolled past the Hero door.

His timing had to be perfect.

He pounded his elbow down on the pressure plate, activating it. Rolling on his side, he landed at her feet, coming to rest on his back. The Hero door roared to life, sliding fast down the incline. Raja crouched over him, keeping her gun low, aiming at the assassin as she covered Brynstone down on the floor.

Metzger made it to the landing, his eyes blazing with hatred. With bruising speed, he dove toward the opening, trying to clear it before the door slammed closed.

Brynstone held his breath. Could Metzger roll through the doorway?

He was close.

But not close enough.

Metzger's body hit the sliding stone door with a sickening thud, bouncing him away as it closed tight.

A deafening silence fell over the catacombs.

Brynstone stared at the Hero door. Imposing and majestic, designed almost two thousand years ago, it had helped him defeat his most bitter enemy. The great door had closed, sealing Erich Metzger inside a black hell for eternity.

Chapter 55

3:41 a.m.

Viktor Nebola watched the monitor. His ribs still ached, but he couldn't tear his gaze away as Brynstone activated the pressure plate in the chamber floor. The move was flawless and gutsy.

"You see that?" Nebola called. "He got him. Metzger's trapped."

Edgar Wurm stood near the door, talking on the phone. Reception was better over there. A few minutes before, they had been watching the Brynstone-Metzger fight on the monitor. At the time, Wurm had been holding the five-inch barrel of his Kimber 1911 Rimfire against Nebola's head. It was a relief when the call pulled Wurm away.

"Shallow heroics by Brynstone," Wurm said from across the room. "Is Metzger dead?"

"Not at all."

"Whatever happened to Metzger, he'll get free," he muttered. "But we're running out of time."

Back into the phone, Wurm repeated the news about Brynstone. Nebola didn't know the caller's identity, but it was someone from the Shadow Chapter.

Nebola watched monitor five. It was recording the live feed from the headband that had been strapped around Raja's head. It had fallen during the struggle, but it was still recording a look down the stairs. Pacing at the bottom, Metzger had the look of an enraged animal. Nebola had known him for a while, but he had never seen the assassin like this. There was no way in hell the guy was getting free and he knew it.

Metzger marched up the stairs. He had spied the camera. He leaned in and peered into it, his face filling the screen. His reptilian eyes narrowed. He knew he was being watched. His mouth curled into a sneer. In a rare moment of frustration, Metzger picked up the small camera and threw it.

The screen went black.

Metzger, this man known for his legendary cool under the most trying circumstances, understood the gravity of his fate. He realized, perhaps, that like Fortunato in Edgar Allan Poe's "The Cask of Amontillado," he was a man sealed forever inside a vault.

It was a brutal fate for a brutal man.

Wurm came over. No phone, but the gun was back and it was trained on Nebola.

"Brynstone's desperate move bought you a second chance, Viktor."

"What are you talking about?"

"I'm talking about redemption. Understand? If you want to redeem yourself with the Chapter, you will go down into the catacombs and you will get Shayna Brynstone for me."

Wurm pointed at monitor four. On-screen, Cori Cassidy huddled with the child near the triclinium. Cori jolted her head to the right, like she had heard a sound. She picked up Shayna and they hurried out of the camera's view, no doubt to join Brynstone and Raja.

"You asking me to go down there?"

"Not asking, Viktor. Ordering." He flashed the Kimber. "Don't think about leaving the catacombs. I have men posted on the roof outside. A man in the hallway will hand you a firearm."

"Have him get Shayna."

"She won't go to him. She knows you. Get the girl or die. Your call. What will it be?"

"The girl."

"Go. I have a chopper waiting."

Nebola hurried toward the door, then moved to the hallway outside the office.

Cori was carrying Shayna when she found John Brynstone sprawled on the floor outside the closed Hero door. Wet blood glistened on his torn shirt.

Raja was leaning over Brynstone, covering his chest wound with her hand.

"Cori, get over here!" she shouted.

Shayna jumped down to the floor. Cori hurried with the girl to Brynstone. His eyes were open, but they didn't look focused. Still, he reached over and slid his bloodied hand around his daughter's small round shoulder.

He didn't speak.

"Rashmi, call an ambulance," Cori choked. "Get someone here fast."

"Okay," she said, waving Cori to her side. "Keep pressure here. Take over for me."

Cori crouched beside the child and her father. She slipped her hand beneath Raja's hand, pressing down on the chest wound.

"Stay with him," the woman said as she jumped up and sprinted around the corner.

Brynstone's breathing became shallow. His head rested on the ground. He stared at the ceiling.

"John, can you hear me?"

"Be okay, Daddy," Shayna pleaded. "Be okay. Please?"

He blinked. A line of blood trickled from his mouth down to his ear. His eyes shifted to the side, finding his daughter. He swallowed hard. "Love you, Shay."

Her knee curled near his shoulder. She ran her small fingers across her father's forehead. Never a believer, Cori found herself on the edge of some desperate prayer.

"Cold," he mumbled.

He had lost so much blood. He was going into shock. His eyes drifted back inside his head.

"Rashmi went to get help," Cori said, tears streaming down her cheek. "Stay with us, John."

"Stay with us, Daddy."

His eyes closed.

"John? Can you hear me? Say something."

"Is he," Shay said, unable to ask the most terrible question she could ask.

"Sweetie," Cori choked. "Sweetie, I think you need, um—"

"Is he, Cori? Is he?"

Cori had been pressing down on the wound, but it was like something had changed somehow in his body. His chest seemed to loosen, somehow, and sag beneath her fingers.

She looked at Shayna. "I'm sorry. I'm so sorry."

The little girl placed her left hand on top of Cori's hand. She seemed so alone. Her mother had died. And now . . .

How could he die?

Shayna looked up at her with a pleading innocence as she tilted her head, strands of hair touching her shoulder. There was a distance in her fresh eyes.

"Cori," she said in a hushed voice. "Why didn't you get the ambulance?"

"What do you mean, honey?" she sobbed.

"You sent that woman to get it. I wish you had been the one to go get the ambulance."

Her right hand slipped beneath Cori's palm, the girl covering the chest wound now. The fingers of her left hand wrapped tightly around Cori's hand.

The child stared up. Something had changed in Shayna's eyes, an innocence clouded. A pained expression passed over the girl's soft features, one mixed with burden and maybe regret.

"What are you—"

"Sorry, Cori," Shayna said, her face moving into a frown. "I hate it, but it has to be."

No.

Shocked, Cori pulled her bloodied hand from Shayna's grip and turned from her crouching position. She tucked her hands away, hiding them inside crossed arms. Feeling more protected now, she faced the child.

"I need to ask you something, Cori. A favor."

"No, Shayna."

"Can I hold your hand?"

The serenity in Shayna's voice scared Cori. A bitter sensation churned inside her stomach. A sickening sweat chilled her brow. One reckless thought after another darted across Cori's mind, but she suspected why the little girl wanted her.

"Come here, Cori. I need you."

Oh, God, is this really happening?

"I miss my daddy. He's the most important thing in the world to me. I need to hurry. Please, Cori?"

"No," she muttered. "No."

"Ms. Cassidy," a voice barked from behind. "Bring the girl to me."

Shocked, Cori turned.

A heavyset man aimed his gun at her. She recognized his face from the monitor strapped on Raja's chest.

"Changed my mind," Nebola growled. "Move to the wall, Ms. Cassidy."

She hesitated.

"You think I'm playing here? Get away from the girl," Nebola ordered. "She's coming with me."

"Shayna's been through enough. Leave her alone. Leave us alone."

"Not how it works. Edgar Wurm wants this little girl. Get back against the wall."

Cori stood her ground, her hand clenched into a bloodied fist.

Nebola aimed the weapon at the child. He looked serious.

"I have orders to take the kid. Right now, I don't care if Wurm gets what he wants. Either I take her or I kill her. Now move to the wall."

Cori staggered backward, reaching behind until her fingers brushed the rough stone wall. She had to do something, but what? What could she possibly do?

Moving his aim back on Cori now, Nebola looked at Shayna.

"You know me, kid," he said, coming over. "We had lots of good talks, right? You know I'm not a bad guy. Metzger was the bad guy and your daddy locked him behind that door. Now it's time to leave. Let's go find that cute little stuffed kitty."

The child stared at him, not budging from the side of her fallen father.

He grunted. "Look, kid, I'm in a bad mood. You don't wanna see me in a worse mood. Get your scrawny butt up here and let's go. Uncle Edgar has a helicopter waiting."

Shayna didn't say a word. She was frozen in place like a statue.

"Ever been in a helicopter? Lots of fun. We need to go now."

Shayna glanced at her father.

Nebola's impatience came to an end. "I tried to ask nice, but you're pissing me off. We need to get outta here."

Going to the child, Nebola reached down to grab her shoulder. He didn't get a good hold, and she jerked away. Still training his gun on Cori with his right hand, Nebola reached again with his left.

Kneeling beside her father, Shay saw the man's hand coming toward her. She raised her small fingers and snatched the wrist of Viktor Nebola. At the same moment, she pressed harder on the wound in her father's chest.

The Hollow.

The Black Chrism.

Shayna Brynstone.

Cori saw it happen. The little girl's power, drawing the life force from one man before transferring it into another. She was an innocent child making a dark choice. A lost angel with a terrible gift.

Nebola went into a fury of convulsions. The gun dropped from his hand, hitting the floor. He came down hard on his knees. In the middle of the two men, Shayna's body began to shudder like she was standing at the epicenter of an earthquake. Her eyes darkened with fierce concentration. The muscles around her small mouth contorted, but no sound passed between her lips. Her head rolled in a lazy circle and then her eyes closed, her face flush with some terrible shock like she was grabbing a lightning bolt. The brutality of the moment—the raw exchange of death with life and life with death—seemed to charge the room with electricity.

All at once, John Brynstone's eyes snapped open. Drained of life, Nebola collapsed onto the floor beside him.

Brynstone stared ahead with a blank expression. It was as if he had awakened from a terrible nightmare and was trapped in that hazy moment between dreaming and waking.

Almost nothing surprised Cori. Not anymore.

But this . . .

Shayna slumped against her father, her eyes glassy and distant, as Cori rushed to them. Fate had left the child with no choice about her power. She was a hollow vessel—a conduit for taking life and giving it. The violence of her act had consumed Shayna, sapping her energy. What was going through her mind now? A sickening sense of emptiness? A cacophony of banshees howling at her? Or the quiet redemption of knowing that she had saved her father's life?

Chapter 56

Brynstone looked down, studying the blood on his shirt. He felt nauseous and bewildered and spent. His hands and face tingled.

He rubbed his eyes. *What happened?* He couldn't explain it. Didn't want to try.

He embraced his daughter, her love making him whole. Cori wrapped her arms around them from behind. He didn't know the extent of what Cori and Shay had been through together, but it was clear they shared a powerful bond. He kissed his daughter again, then looked at Cori, finding a swell of emotion that surprised him.

"You feel so good to hug," Shayna said.

Brynstone answered her, the words sounding thick as they played in his ear. "You feel so good to hug, too, Shay."

"I could hug you all day and all night, except I would be tired."

He made a weak smile.

Climbing to his feet, he looked down at Viktor Nebola's body. He remembered trapping Metzger behind the Hero door, but it seemed like it had happened months ago, not mere minutes. He glanced at the stone slab, needing the verification that it had all happened. It remained closed, sealing the demon in the tomb.

Brynstone was stronger now. Looking at Cori, he asked, "Where's Wurm?"

"Nebola said something about a helicopter."

"I was next door, Daddy. There's a building right across from here. I was there with Viktor. I saw the old man with long gray hair."

Brynstone reached down and grabbed Nebola's service pistol, a Springfield XD. Shayna scrambled into his arms. It was clear she didn't like him holding the weapon, but she didn't protest. With her skinny legs wrapped around his waist, he hurried up the divided staircase.

Cori followed as they made their way to the first level of the Kom el Shoqafa catacombs. He moved to the vestibule and darted toward the spiral staircase that wrapped around the massive shaft.

He hurried outside, hoping to see Wurm. Instead, he found Math McHardy.

The man was sprawled on the ground, clutching his side, with fresh blood glistening on his fingers. Without letting Shayna go, Brynstone hurried over and kneeled down to rip open McHardy's shirt. The old man's eyes were wide and flat. His chest was rising and falling. It was a gunshot wound. A serious one, but it looked like the bullet hadn't penetrated deep enough into the abdomen to reach major blood vessels.

McHardy forced his mouth to work. "Tried to get down," he wheezed, pointing a bloodied finger at a building near the catacombs. "Bastard shot me."

Shayna held still and tight in his arms. Brynstone looked up.

Edgar Wurm stood at the edge of the roof, staring down at them. He was aiming a pistol.

In one fluid motion, Brynstone scrambled to his feet with his daughter still in his arms.

Cori lingered at the catacomb entrance. She saw them coming at her and scooted backward on her feet. Moving inside with her, he swung his daughter around, handing her to Cori. He brought out Nebola's service pistol, going into an isosceles stance.

Wurm had disappeared from the roof's edge.

Brynstone ordered Cori and Shay to take cover farther inside the catacomb entrance. He turned and sprinted toward the office building.

Running around the corner, he headed for the entrance. The thundering rhythm of a helicopter came from the roof. He burst through the door and darted up the stairs, a collision of thoughts and emotions raging inside his head. Wurm had played him on this entire mission. He had to take down the man.

Coming around the corner, he saw a shadow and trained the Springfield on it. Coming into view, Rashmi Raja aimed her Beretta at him. Her eyes brightened when she recognized him.

"You're okay?" she said, blinking in surprise. "I thought you—"

"Wurm's getting away. Where are the stairs to the roof?"

"Just saw them. Follow me."

"McHardy's shot," he called. "Needs an ambulance."

"On the way."

Following Raja, Brynstone sprinted up a dim stairwell. He came to an abrupt halt at the top landing. After making sure the area was secure, he spied a white metal ladder on his side of the wall. It led outside to the roof.

Climbing, he took it two rungs at a time, finding the small hatch above him cracked open. He could hear the copter's turbine grinding up. The bird was taking off. The sound was thunderous as he pushed open the hatch door. He had to catch Wurm.

———◆———

Rashmi Raja was right behind Brynstone on the ladder. He burst out the access hatch. As they scrambled onto the roof, she saw a helicopter rising into the early-morning sky.

Brynstone sprinted toward the edge of the roof, his pistol out. Inside the bird, Edgar Wurm fixed his unblinking gaze down on Brynstone. Long gray hair swirled around his face.

Brynstone fired at the chopper.

It was too far away.

The helicopter buzzed across the city of Alexandria, cutting a path toward the Nile. It sickened Raja to see Wurm escape.

She didn't have long to think about it.

Glancing from the roof, she saw a dozen black vehicles burst onto the Kom el Shoqafa grounds. They blazed along the front of the building.

"Crap," Raja said. "You know these guys?"

"I'm thinking CIA. They don't look like Egyptian authorities."

The whole thing made her feel sick. She didn't like CIA here. After all the chaos back in the catacomb, she had thought about slipping away after calling an ambulance for Brynstone. It would have been so easy. No one would have noticed and she'd be free. Something had drawn her back. Something had made her follow Brynstone up here.

Maybe it wasn't too late to disappear.

Brynstone stood at the edge of the roof, turning his attention to Wurm's helicopter as it flew over the city.

Under her breath, she said, "Bye, John. Fun while it lasted."

He didn't hear or see Rashmi Raja slipping through the roof access hatch and climbing down the ladder.

Chapter 57

Commandos seemed to appear from everywhere. Cori was holding Shayna inside the catacombs when they ran up and surrounded her. Behind them, a stern-looking man came up and identified himself as a CIA officer. It was bewildering. Then she saw a familiar face. Stephen Angelilli.

Was she happy to see him? She couldn't decide.

Angelilli explained how Dr. Spanos had called from Crete. Though Angelilli hadn't talked to him before he had been murdered, the CIA had been able to trace his call. As Angelilli flew to Europe, CIA officers had searched the rubble of the Shadow Chapter compound. Cori overheard Angelilli say something to another agent about a National Intelligence Support Team uncovering intelligence that led them here.

Cori filled in Angelilli on several details, though she decided against any mention of Rashmi Raja, and she left out the part about Shayna using the Black Chrism's power on her father.

Brynstone emerged from the office building with several CIA officers. As they came over, Shayna ran and embraced her father. Cori gave them a moment until the girl beckoned with an outstretched arm and she joined them.

As they hugged, a young officer from Angelilli's team came over and reported to him. "Sir, Nebola has been confirmed dead. Appears he suffered a heart attack."

Cori looked at Shayna.

They left it at that.

Angelilli asked, "What about Erich Metzger?"

"Sir, we cannot verify any sign of him at this facility."

Angelilli gave Brynstone a hard look. "You sure Metzger was here? We're not even certain what the assassin looks like, so it would be understandable if you mistook him."

"Metzger was here," Brynstone said, handing over Nebola's service pistol. "I promise you."

"What happened? They say the guy is like a phantom, but he couldn't have disappeared."

"We've been through hell," Brynstone said. "Give us a couple minutes?"

The man thought it over. "Five minutes."

———◆———

A CIA officer handed Shayna a bottle of water, chatting to her. Watching them talk, Brynstone pulled Cori aside. "You okay?"

She nodded. "Any word on Math?"

"Critical condition in a nearby hospital."

"Will he be okay?"

"Could've been worse. He'll make it."

"What happened to Rashmi?"

He looked at the building. Last place he had seen her was on the roof. The woman knew how to pull off a vanishing act. This time, Raja got away without him catching her. He enjoyed the challenge of finding her. *Another time.*

His eyes drifted to his daughter. Cori picked up on it.

"John, I'd like to do what I can to help Shayna. I want to be there for her. After we get back to New York, would you let me spend time with her? Come over once in a while?"

"She deserves so much more than I've given her. Don't know what it's going to be like for her without her mom."

She touched his arm. "I want to help."

He liked the idea. Cori studied child psychology. Maybe she could make a difference.

"Shay would appreciate it." He paused. "Me too."

Shayna wandered over to them. He bent down and held her hand. Yawning widely, his daughter looked exhausted and totally drained.

"Can we go now, Daddy?"

"I have to answer a few more questions from the man in the suit. After that, I know a nice hotel where we can take a nap."

"Can Cori come?"

"Yeah. Cori can come. Can you hold on a bit longer?"

Shayna rubbed her eyes. "Okay."

Angelilli came over to Cori. He handed her a phone. "Your brother. Remember, you are not allowed to mention anything about what happened here. We're listening, and we'll cut you off if we hear something we don't like."

She nodded and turned to answer the call from Jared after quickly glancing back, smiling at the reunion of father and daughter.

Outside the catacombs, Brynstone carried Shayna over to a chair, one used by the tourist police. He eased into it, her long skinny legs dangling over the chair arm.

He was thinking everything over. So much had happened.

She looked up. "Did you go into your little world just now?"

He blinked. "What?"

"Yeah, Daddy. Sometimes, you go into a little world where you don't hear people outside your world."

He frowned. "I'm sorry."

"It's okay, Big Ol' Daddy Bear. Can you tell me a story about Lucy and Lindsey?"

"Now?"

"Please."

He cleared his throat. "Let's see."

"They were on the island, remember? Looking for Lucy's dad. The mermaids brought them there. And Lindsey wants to get back to her palace in Pinktopia. And they're hungry."

"I remember," Brynstone said, picking up the thread of the story. "Okay, it's nighttime."

"How dark?"

"Moon is out, so not real dark. Lucy and Lindsey are walking on the cool pink sand. All of a sudden, Lindsey hears her stomach growl. It reminds her of the gurgling sound of the pink fountain, the one where a face appeared in the water. Now, the girls have to make a choice. Should they go into the jungle where the ninjas might be, or should they walk around the edge and stay on the moonlit beach?"

Brynstone didn't tell typical little-girl stories. But one thing Shay liked was that he made it interactive for her. She had a say in the characters' decision making.

"Which one do you think the girls should do?"

"Hmmm?" Shayna asked in a sleepy voice.

"Should they search the jungle for Lucy's dad or stay on the beach? Tell me and I'll make sure the girls do what you say."

She didn't answer. She looked at him, then her eyes closed.

He smiled and pulled her close to him. She was already sleeping in his embrace, maybe dreaming about lost girls on an island and a jungle teeming with ninjas.

He looked down at her small face.

"My sweet beautiful girl, you've been through so much," he whispered. "I've put you through so much. And now you've lost your mother." His voice cracked. "Shay, I'm so sorry about Mommy."

Despite bitterness from the last few years, he knew some part of him would always love Kaylyn. Seemed like long ago, but they had shared good times.

He curled his daughter up close, a strand of her blonde hair catching on the bristle of his chin stubble. Brynstone looked at the ghostly desert sky, rich with hot silence. Two hours until sunrise. He saw the promise of a new day and found the question that refused to leave his mind.

What do I do about Metzger?

Brynstone had held back when he told Angelilli about the assassin. Raja knew he had sealed Metzger behind the Hero door, but she had vanished. Did Cori know? If so, she was too smart to mention it. Aside from them? No one else here knew the truth. One of the cameras had carried a live feed from inside the chamber. Brynstone had seen a bank of monitors in a room in the building adjacent to the catacombs, but they had been destroyed along with other equipment. Had Wurm's men done that before climbing inside the helicopter? Maybe. Whatever had happened, it robbed him of any chance to see Metzger inside the chamber.

He thought about the assassin dying alone in the tomb. How long would it take? Even underground, the blistering temperature in Alexandria could shorten his time of survival. Brynstone tried to calculate the time a man could last with a limited oxygen supply and no food or water. Under the best conditions, people could survive eight weeks without food, but only if they had water.

Can he survive six weeks? Seven?
Maybe.

He thought about Metzger down there, day after day, week after week, dealing with the effects of dehydration and advanced starvation. The muscle spasms and irregular heartbeat. Convulsions and confusion. Brynstone knew the hallucinations would be damning as Metzger grew mad with hunger. Would his cold mind finally punish him, showing all the faces of his scores of assassinated victims?

Brynstone had set up halogen lights after they had discovered the false door. Eventually, the batteries in the lamps would fail, leaving the man to face his demons in bitter darkness.

A comforting thought.

The guy was a brutal murderer. Didn't he deserve the most brutal death imaginable? A fresh idea came now. Would Metzger kill himself before he died of starvation? Imagine that. The world's most elite assassin committing suicide.

Brynstone *could* imagine it. Hell, he would pay to see it.

He had a choice here: Leave Metzger sealed behind that door, rotting with the mummies of the Lost Ones? Or get the man out of the catacombs and force him to face justice?

Depends on how you define justice.

Brynstone had always been able to divorce emotion from his decision making. This time, though, with Metzger, he was having a harder time pulling it off. Was there a right decision in this situation? He honestly didn't know. A debate raged inside his head, the answers changing from moment to moment.

Shayna stirred in his arms. He looked down at her round, soft face and he kissed her cheek. She puckered her mouth and made a soft breathing sound. Her eyelids fluttered open then closed, heavy with fatigue.

Half asleep, she mumbled, "Nothing can destroy our love."

Powerful words. They seemed to hang in the night air.

Brushing back her hair as she slept, he saw serenity and inno-cence. The hard emotions began to fade. Like always, his daughter made him a better man.

"Everything okay over here, Dr. Brynstone?" Stephen Angelilli asked as he came walking up.

"There's something I need to tell you," Brynstone answered, holding on to a breath. "It's about Erich Metzger."

Chapter 58

John Brynstone marched down the divided stairs leading to the second level of the Kom el Shoqafa catacombs. Behind him, Stephen Angelilli followed with six paramilitary operations officers. Dressed in black tactical gear, they belonged to the CIA's Special Operations Group within the Special Activities Division. In a concession to the Egyptian government, five General Intelligence Service agents joined them under CIA advisement. The Egyptians wore desert cammies and, like the CIA team, were armed with suppressed M-4s and G-36s.

Brynstone made a ragged leader. His shirt was torn and bloodied. Mud coated his hair. He looked as if he had traveled through hell itself. Considering the demon he had chased for the past several years, maybe he had.

Down on the second level, Brynstone strapped on a headset and advised two SOG operators. They needed to climb through the loculus to make their way through the secret corridor. Once there, they could activate the Hero door. Leaving them, he brought Angelilli and the other men around to face the door, which looked now like a flat stone wall.

What was Metzger doing right now on the other side?

"You sure this wall is supposed to move?" Angelilli asked. "Doesn't look like a door."

"Trust me," Brynstone answered. He explained about the pressure plate and warned the men to not trigger it.

"When we gain access," Angelilli said, "you stay back. My men go in first."

"Hold up. We made a deal. I go in first to face Metzger. *You* provide backup."

"Change of plans, Dr. Brynstone. You already had your shot at the man. Now it's our turn."

He gritted his teeth. "That's not what we agreed on."

"Please move behind us, sir," a young SOG officer told Brynstone.

He studied the kid. Bright eyes. Big chin. Reminded him of a guy he had known in the Rangers. Angelilli backed away and moved to the side. Brynstone fought the idea at first, but decided to join him.

"At least give me a weapon," Brynstone said. He had handed over the Springfield semiauto.

"You don't need one. Besides, you don't have authorization here to—"

"You're kidding me."

Angelilli called out, "Be prepared to tear it up in there, gentlemen, but you bring this unholy bastard out with a heartbeat. As much as I want to light him up, we need Metzger alive."

The man's words had Brynstone's blood pumping. Angelilli turned and gave the order to open the door.

A rumbling sound came from deep inside the wall. The floor stuttered a little where they were standing. The door opened, sliding on the incline. It was different seeing the stone move from this vantage point. It seemed more mysterious, like a great mouth yawning.

And then silence.

The Hero door had moved to the side, revealing the chamber. Dark in there. Metzger had turned off the halogen lights.

No sign of the assassin.

Moving in a buttonhook system, the lead operator made a turn around the inside of the Hero door, clearing the area as he entered. A tactical light was mounted on his Heckler-Koch assault rifle. The second operator moved in and cleared the hard corner.

Brynstone strained to see inside the darkened stairwell. Where was Metzger?

The SOG team stacked in a single file as they moved past the Hero door. It was killing Brynstone to watch them. It wasn't his style to hang back and wait like this.

The four-man team ascended the darkened stairwell. Brynstone wondered if they would use a flash grenade, but they didn't. The team leader updated them as he made it to the top landing and moved through the false door. Over the headset, he reported seeing the sarcophagus along with broken mummies scattered around the floor. Otherwise, the chamber was empty.

Then all hell broke loose.

From what Brynstone could tell, Metzger had dropped down from the decorative niche in the wall above the top landing. He hit them at the fatal funnel, the point where team members were most vulnerable. The assassin came down with the sledgehammer and slammed it into the head of the second operator. The man's body rolled down the stairs and collided into the third operator.

"He's trashing your men up there," Brynstone growled.

"Not for long," Angelilli answered. "Hang tight."

Up above, the third operator charged up the stairs. At the same time, the team leader climbed back through the opening in the false door. He came at Metzger on the top landing. It wasn't even a close fight. Metzger snapped the man's neck, then slashed the throat of the third guy with the knife he had used to stab Brynstone.

Gunfire.

Chaos.

Metzger had grabbed an assault rifle from a downed operator. He opened fire at the last man on the stairs. Brilliant light from the firefight cut through the darkness. Three Egyptian GIS agents sprinted past the Hero door.

Brynstone wasn't waiting any longer. He shoved aside Angelilli. Before he could make a move, the last two Egyptians blocked him.

"You will stay here," Angelilli yelled at him. He called into his headset for backup.

More gunfire.

Like a demon emerging from the darkness, Metzger started running down the stairs. He had taken out four operators and dropped three Egyptian GIS agents as they returned fire. Angelilli stepped out to bark an order, but his words were cut short. A mist of blood sprayed over his shoulder. Angelilli dropped. The remaining two GIS agents moved toward the stairs.

Brynstone heard more men coming up far behind. No way in the world he was waiting for them to arrive.

One GIS agent was already dead on the floor. Metzger emptied his weapon on the last Egyptian. He tossed it aside as he hit the bottom step. Brynstone didn't have a weapon and there was no time to grab one. Didn't matter. Nothing was stopping him now.

Metzger saw him coming. His eyes blazed. At the landing, the two men crashed into each other. They twisted hard in the air, coming down on the stone floor. They rolled across the landing. Metzger didn't have the knife, but he brought out the drill bit from the hammer drill.

"You can't live with me," he growled. "And you can't die without me."

He jabbed it, but missed Brynstone's eye as he ducked. Brynstone slammed Metzger's head into the wall. It was a hard hit and the assassin lost his hold on Brynstone's arm. Rolling away, he made it to his feet. Holding his head, Metzger staggered up, but a new wave of officers swarmed them, pulling the two men away from each other.

"Let me go," Brynstone growled. Four operators pulled him back, moving him outside the Hero door and restraining him. He was trying to jerk away from them, looking inside at the stairs.

Officers shoved the assassin to the ground, facedown, and ripped his hands behind his back to cuff him. Holding his legs together, they placed a belt around both ankles before they pulled up a strap, dressing him in leg-to-waist restraints.

A handful of emergency personnel rushed past Brynstone as they hurried up the stairs with equipment to treat the men Metzger had taken out. They were going to see a bloodbath near the false door. Brynstone doubted a survivor could be found.

He huffed, trying to cool down. It wasn't easy. He closed his eyes and thought of Shayna now. She was at the hotel with Cori. He dropped his head. Bit his lip. Opening his eyes and looking up, he found satisfaction in seeing Metzger in prisoner restraints.

Three more CIA and twenty additional Egyptian General Intelligence Service officers spilled around them. Angelilli staggered over and coughed blood into his hand. Brynstone didn't speak to him. His focus was trained on the assassin.

They raised Metzger to his full height. He made no attempt to resist as they surrounded him with weapons raised, barking orders at the assassin. He didn't blink, staring straight ahead. Except for a solitary second. Without turning his head, his eyes darted to the side. Metzger's cold gaze found Brynstone among the officers, the men still holding him back. They glared at each other.

Brynstone had waited for this moment.

Part of him had wanted the man to be imprisoned either in a penitentiary or in an ancient chamber deprived of oxygen. More than anything, though, he needed Metzger to know the truth.

Brynstone was alive.

For Metzger, failure was intolerable. The harshest punishment that could be devised for the assassin was to know that he had failed to kill Brynstone. Not once, but twice.

That's why he had decided to open the Hero door. He wanted Metzger to live with his own failure. Had he remained locked in the tomb, the man might have spent his final days living with a delusional sense of victory, thinking that his stab wound had killed Brynstone.

Not now. Metzger knew the truth.

The officers brought him toward Brynstone.

Metzger remained cool, but Brynstone sensed fury in the man's expression. Maybe it was just wishful thinking. Whatever it was, Brynstone knew he would replay Metzger's expression in his mind for years to come.

He held his steely gaze on the man.

"We will battle again," Metzger said. "You know the old expression, Herr Doktor Brynstone. The third time is a charm."

Brynstone didn't answer. Didn't need to. He didn't need to say a damned thing.

Angelilli, however, couldn't resist. As Metzger passed, the bloodied CIA officer called, "You're not gonna see Brynstone where you're headed. Hell takes no visitors."

The line brought muffled laughter from the men, the words relieving tension. A crowd of paramilitary operations officers escorted the assassin down the corridor.

Angelilli turned back and called out something.

Brynstone didn't really hear the words. If he did, he didn't pay attention.

Standing beside the Hero door, he watched them lead Metzger up the divided staircase before they marched out of sight.

Brynstone stayed a little longer, thinking.

Thinking about life without Kaylyn, something he had started doing years ago. Thinking about helping Shayna overcome all of this madness. Thinking about what he had done to his daughter when he had given her the Black Chrism.

After all that?

He'd start thinking about the best way to track down Edgar Wurm.

Author's Note

My first two novels gave me an opportunity to indulge a long-standing interest in history, science, and religion. Although most of the action in this book takes place nearly five years after the first one, a number of parallels played out between the story lines of my first two novels. The final scene in my debut novel, *The Radix,* inspired the opening scene in *The False Door.* And, because I'm just a little compulsive, the last two words in both books are identical (I'm pretty sure this isn't significant to anyone but me).

As the second book in the series, *The False Door* hints more at the broad scope that the Radix played in history. Let me warn you now that this author's note contains some major-league spoilers.

As described in this novel, Joseph of Arimathea straddles the legends surrounding the Holy Grail and the Radix. Since I was a kid, I have been fascinated with Arthurian legend. Robert de Boron, a French poet of the medieval era, claimed that Joseph brought the Grail to Britain. A later author named John of Glastonbury suggested around 1350 that King Arthur had descended from Joseph of Arimathea. Some even claimed that Joseph created a Grail Table that served as later inspiration for Arthur's Round Table.

In developing my stories about the Radix and the chrisms, I put a heavy emphasis on Josephus, the son of Joseph of Arimathea. Josephus plays an important role in the Arthurian legend, especially in the *Estoire del Saint Grail* (the history of the Holy Grail) section of the *Vulgate Cycle*, a French series from the 1200s that recounts legendary stories about the Knights of the Round Table and their quest for the Holy Grail. In some legends, Josephus was entrusted with the Grail, and I dovetailed that tradition by making him the Keeper of the Radix.

Although Josephus is sometimes described as a "holy man" and some regard him as the first bishop of England, I wanted to give the Keeper a warrior-like personality that meshed with later generations of Arthurian knights. In my book, his archrival is Crudel, a pagan king from North Wales who, according to the *Estoire del Saint Grail*, imprisoned Joseph of Arimathea and his followers. Finally, Glastonbury Tor is a real and impressive hill at Glastonbury, Somerset, England, that was likely occupied during Roman times and has several ties to Arthurian legend, with rumors swirling that the area served as the inspiration for Avalon as well as the final resting place for Arthur and Guinevere.

The Catacombs of Kom el Shoqafa (meaning *mound of shards* or *potsherds*) do exist as a necropolis carved beneath Alexandria, with the exception of a hidden chamber and corridor that live only in my imagination and this book. Known as Ra-Qedil in the ancient world, it was used as a burial chamber from the second century until sometime around the fourth century CE.

Kom el Shoqafa does not actually have a false door, but as Brynstone mentions, it was a common theme in Egyptian funerary architecture. The false door was often placed on the west wall of a funerary chamber. This was consistent with the idea that the land of the dead resided in the west. According to folklore, Egyptian gods like Osiris, Isis, and Horus used the false door as a passageway to travel from the afterlife into our world and back again.

Some ancient Egyptians believed that the moment of death happened when a person's spiritual essence, or *Ka*, departed his or her body. For that reason, a false door was sometimes known as a "*Ka* door." Family members brought offerings for the deceased or for a favored deity and placed the funerary gifts at the doorstep. In some cases, an engraved image of the deceased was carved into the central niche or panel.

There is no connection between Kom el Shoqafa and Hero of Alexandria (sometimes also called Heron of Alexandria). Hero was a mathematician and engineer who flourished during the first century, possibly living until 84 CE. Several scholars believe that he served as the director of the Museum of Alexandria, a sister institution to the Library of Alexandria. His most celebrated invention was the first steam turbine, made as a novelty toy and called the *aeolipile* (meaning *wind ball* in Greek). He has also been credited with inventing the fire engine, a mechanical bird that could sing when powered with water, and the first vending machine, an intriguing device that could dispense holy water when a worshiper placed a coin in a slot. As mentioned in my novel, Hero did, in fact, invent the first known automatic door, an ambitious design that was created for the purpose of opening temple doors. However, as far as we know, it was only a small model and came nowhere near the scale of the door described in my book. Hero's design did not include a pressure plate. The invention of the first foot-pressure-activated door did not come along until an inventor in China created one around the seventh century CE.

The character of Kyros in my book is fictional, but the brutal assassination of Hypatia of Alexandria at the Caesareum church in 415 is as true as it is tragic. She was a brilliant thinker during the Christianization of the Roman Empire and, perhaps unwittingly, she may have become ensnared in the power struggle between Orestes, the Roman governor of the province of Egypt, and Cyril, the bishop of Alexandria. As Edgar Wurm notes in the book, no one today can be certain if Bishop Cyril was involved in her execution, although many believe he played a role in the decision.

While down in the cavern with the Lazarus Cross, John Brynstone studies Lost John and mentions the link between porphyria, a group of rare genetic blood disorders, with vampire legends. For decades, several people have claimed that porphyria can account for a number of traits associated with the vampire canon, including fangs, light sensitivity, and an aversion to garlic. As Brynstone knows (but I didn't give him a chance to say), the vampire-porphyria hypothesis is a compelling idea, but it suffers from a lack of scientific evidence. Mostly, it has proven to be a way to stigmatize people with the disease.

The Radix and *The False Door* inspired me to write several works of shorter fiction. A short story called "The Brotherhood of Blood and Dust" revolves around the relationship between Josephus of Massilia—desperate to escape the shadow of his legendary father, Joseph of Arimathea—and the Roman soldier known as Quintus Gallienus. Spanning a period from 64 to 115 CE, the story takes us beyond their first fateful encounter and offers greater insight into Quintus's terrible gift. A novella, set three hundred years after "Brotherhood," explores the discovery that Hypatia of Alexandria makes with the help of her dedicated student, Kyros. Working together, and sometimes against each other, they become players in a historical drama that will change their lives forever. *The Lost Necropolis* will answer questions you might have about the elusive helmet, both its disappearance and its dismemberment.

The Devil's Gauntlet is a novella that unfolds during the autumn of the Middle Ages. Tyon Darc is a brash knight of the Order of Hospitallers and he faces one challenge after another as his quest becomes intertwined with the mysterious Jeanneton de Paris. It is her cryptic journal that drives Edgar Wurm to understand more about the Radix. The short novel answers a question that Wurm poses in *The False Door*—namely, what is the Devil's Gauntlet? He doesn't know, but you will if you read the story.

Thank you for reading *The False Door*. I hope you enjoyed the book. Please be sure to visit my website at authorbrettking. com and get in touch on Facebook or on Twitter. I'd love to hear from you!

Acknowledgments

It might sound cheesy to some—and I don't give a damn if it does—but I want to begin by acknowledging my amazing readers. Without each of you taking the time to read my books, this dream of mine would be without foundation. I have been overwhelmed by your generosity, enthusiasm, support, and dedication. My sincere thanks to you all.

As always, Cheri, my beloved wife (and former high school sweetheart), inspires me every day with her enthusiasm, intelligence, beauty, compassion, optimism, and editorial prowess. From the beginning of my journey as a writer and a psychologist, she has been a steadfast influence, never letting me lose focus or vision. My children, Brady, Devin, and Tylyn, bring the child alive inside me with their exuberance, imagination, humor, and love. If you know me at all, you know that my adorable little family means the world to me. As always, my parents, Don and Dee King, have been a wellspring of support and encouragement for as long as I can remember. Stick with me, you two, and someday we'll be on Easy Street.

My indefatigable agent, Pam Ahearn, continues to astonish with her wisdom, guidance, passion, and keen intuition. I've learned so much from you, Pam, and I appreciate your dedicated work on my behalf. I was thrilled to join the Thomas & Mercer family, and a big thanks goes out to everyone on their brilliant team for putting this book into the hands of my readers and working to promote it. In particular, I am indebted to Amara Holstein, my developmental editor, for her attention to detail and compelling insights as well as her diligence and professionalism. At every step, Amara's editorial skills proved to be an invaluable resource. My sincere thanks to Brent Fattore, who served as the acquisition editor and production manager for this book. Brent offered helpful guidance and proved to be a model of patience, especially when an unprecedented Colorado flood hit during a crucial September deadline. I am beyond grateful to Michael Trudeau, the best copyeditor in my experience as an author, for his refreshing expertise and painstaking labor on this novel. Last but far from least, my sincere thanks to Rebecca Friedman for her dedicated and meticulous help as a proofreader and to the wonderful Kristin Loke for her work as the author relations manager for Amazon Publishing.

Troy Barmore played an important role in several stages of this book, sharing wit and vivid insights during a memorable brainstorming session at a Boulder park. Brimming with creativity and charisma, Troy has been critical in helping to enlarge my imagination beginning with my first novel. Time after time, the great Zach Fedor offered helpful resources and countless ideas with charm and careful attention to detail, while answering more questions than I'm sure he had anticipated. I am also indebted to Tim Thompson and Robert Stegmueller for their expert counsel on a number of technical matters. Steg and Tim are both remarkable men who are as entertaining as they are intelligent. I owe a huge thanks to Deirdre Graham, Alexandra Maddi, Rachel Kimmel, Brenna Lyons, Kelsey Fisher, and Gary and Molly Vair. They are all terrific friends who shared their experiences and, in several cases, went out of their way to conduct research for me. Joshua Blackham of England's Metropolitan Police Service as well as Duane Morton, Caitlin Graham, and Marlea Kerr all shared insights that enhanced my book. I am very grateful to Meg Townsend, a brilliant person who was one of my first readers and who shared great wisdom that benefited my writing. Despite the guidance of everyone mentioned above, any errors in fact or detail found in this book rest with me alone (although I'll still probably blame Joe Berta).

While creating this book, I lost five longtime friends. I am a better person because I had the chance to know Noni Viney, Dr. Henry and Liz Cross, Mary Ann Tucker, and Kevin Crochetière, all fellow booklovers and cherished friends. I'll always treasure memories of the good times with you, Hank and Liz, Noni, Mary Ann, and Kev. I'm forever grateful for your impact on my life and I honor your memory.

For two books now, I have enjoyed the support of a band of faithful friends. My family is blessed to know Kyler and Candice Storm and I'm grateful for their never-ending inspiration. Kathryn Keller's enthusiasm and support of my work has been nothing short of astonishing. Ashlee Tripp and Jen Shaw have been so critical in helping me reach this dream long before it was a reality. Kyle Reader and Clarke Reader and Mike Martis and Shaina Martis have all been remarkable friends and insightful readers.

A huge thanks for the long-term love from Ryan Christie and Tamara Davies and Nathan and Amanda Clay. Thanks for the good times and for reading everything I've ever written (no one should have to do that). My family has been so supportive, especially Aaron and Gayla Clay, LuAnn Harrah, Penny Morton, Charlene Beach, Amanda and Steven Sparks, James Thomas, and Connie Strommenger.

I also want to thank the incomparable Dr. Joseph E. Berta (as the Joker to my Batman, Joe has been my arch-nemesis for more years than I can remember), Dr. Wayne Viney, Jim Winsness, the incredible Droste family, Gena and Rich Prinster, Ryan Prinster, Terri Thompson, Michael Savage, Dan Barbier, Kristen Brake, Lindsay Benshoof, John Ramsett, Landon Mock, Becky Shea, the

Lucy family and the Doughty family (lifelong friends and each a true inspiration to me), Courtney Hibbs, Kristen Walker, Kendra Andrew, Jenny Hughes, Lynn and Stan Loucks, Laura Loucks, Lisa Hail and her amazing family, Dr. Eileen Wade-Stein, Thomas Myers, Tanya VanWatermeulen, Jenn Elliott Blake, Laura Mangum-Childers and Kelby Childers, Katie Parks, Muriel Falvey, Amy Tronnier, Dr. Doug and Lisa Woody, and Catherine Shaw. I will always be grateful to Don D'Auria for taking a chance on me as a first-time author. And thanks to all of my old high school friends and my Facebook buddies. I'm grateful to all of you for spreading the word about my books!

Finally, I want to share special thanks to Miss Tylyn King, back when she was age six, for the kind loan of eleven of her imaginary friends for use in this novel. Every king needs a princess and I'm blessed that you are mine!

B. K.

About the Author

Brett King is a psychologist, a historian, and a writer of nail-biting thrillers. His first novel, *The Radix*, was an exhilarating quest for a legendary relic. In its sequel, *The False Door*, John Brynstone is searching for another lost treasure of enormous power, racing against adversaries as he also tries to save his daughter from a perilous fate. With a background in forensic psychology and scientific history, King is an award-winning professor at the University of Colorado at Boulder in the Department of Psychology and Neuroscience who has deep professional and personal interest in the centuries-old mysteries about which he writes. He lives in Colorado with his wife and three children.

Made in the USA
San Bernardino, CA
16 August 2016